*E... mouth to Hol... feather-soft d... fool his aunt. ...pected lips were bold. And hot. And they smashed against hers.*

Their insistence didn't let her pull away. Instead, she swirled inside. Got lost in the moment. Let it go on several beats too many.

Until she could finally separate herself from him.

Holly feared everyone at the table could hear her heart pounding outside of her chest.

Ethan looked as shocked as she felt. But, after a moment, he picked up his fork and resumed eating. Following his lead, she did the same.

Fortunately, neither Louise nor Fernando noticed anything strange. Holly and Ethan were engaged, after all. Why wouldn't they spontaneously kiss?

But he wasn't helping her any with a kiss like that. Let that be a warning to her.

# HER NEW YORK BILLIONAIRE

BY
ANDREA BOLTER

First Published in Great Britain 2017
By Mills & Boon, an imprint of HarperCollins*Publishers*
1 London Bridge Street, London, SE1 9GF

© 2017 Andrea Bolter

ISBN: 978-0-263-92329-2

23-0917

Our policy is to use papers that are natural, renewable and recyclable products and made from wood grown in sustainable forests. The logging and manufacturing processes conform to the legal environmental regulations of the country of origin.

Printed and bound in Spain
by CPI, Barcelona

**Andrea Bolter** has always been fascinated by matters of the heart. In fact, she's the one her girlfriends turn to for advice with their love lives. A city mouse, she lives in Los Angeles with her husband and daughter. She loves travel, rock 'n' roll, sitting at cafés and watching romantic comedies she's already seen a hundred times. Say hi at www.andreabolter.com.

*Her New York Billionaire* is Andrea Bolter's debut title for Mills & Boon Cherish.

# For Alex

# CHAPTER ONE

"WHY IS YOUR face blue?"

Holly froze in shock. She had just opened the door to the apartment she'd expected to find empty. But instead of flicking on the lights in a vacant living room she'd walked in on lamps already blazing. And a shirtless man sitting in the center of the sofa. Reading a newspaper. A gorgeous brown-haired shirtless man was reading a newspaper.

"Why is your face blue?" he repeated. Broad shoulders peeked out over the newspaper he was holding.

*Why is your face blue?* Holly heard the individual words but couldn't put them together to understand them as a question. She could hardly get over the fact that there was a man in the apartment, let alone make sense of the sounds coming from his mouth.

She checked the keys in her hand. Perhaps she was somehow in the wrong place.

And then she saw.

Her hands were blue. Cobalt Blue Two Eleven, to be exact. She'd know that color anywhere. It was one of her favorites.

It suddenly made sense. Just a few minutes ago she'd ducked out of the rain and under the front awning of the building to rifle through her duffel bag for the piece of paper that confirmed the address. The duffel held paint tubes and brushes, paperwork, clothes and heaven knew what else. The cap must have come off her Cobalt Two Eleven.

And she must have touched her face with paint-covered hands.

"What are you doing here?" Holly asked the shirtless man.

"This apartment belongs to my company."

He lowered his newspaper, folded it matter-of-factly and laid it beside him. Giving Holly a full view of his long, lean torso that led down to the plaid pajama bottoms covering the lower half of his body.

"What is it that *you* are doing here?"

The lump that had balled in Holly's throat delayed her response. She hadn't seen a half-naked man in a very long time. And she hadn't seen a man who looked like he did while he was busy being half-naked in...well, possibly ever.

"I'm staying here," she answered.

It had been a grueling journey, and the last thing she'd expected was to have to reckon with someone once she got here.

She blinked her eyes hard to pull herself together and tried not to panic. "I was told I could use this apartment."

"That must have been a mistake."

Mistake? What was this man talking about?

"I've just arrived from Florida. My brother, Vince, works in the Miami office of Benton Worldwide Properties. This is one of the apartments they keep for visitors to New York."

"That is correct."

"Vince arranged for me to stay here. He confirmed it last week. And he called again yesterday to Benton Boston headquarters."

"I am Ethan Benton, Vice President of Benton Worldwide. As you can see from my…" he gestured down his chest "…state of undress, *I* am staying here at the moment."

"Okay, well, I'm Holly Motta and I was counting on using this apartment. See?" She shook the blue-painted keys. "The Boston office left the keys in my name with the doorman downstairs."

"I apologize for the mistake. I have just arrived tonight myself. In the morning I will look into who is responsible for this egregious error and have their head lopped off."

The left corner of his mouth hitched up a bit.

Ethan Benton and his bare chest sat on a black leather sofa. Matching armchairs faced opposite, separated by a modern glass coffee table. The furnishings were spare. Two large framed photos were the only adornments on the wall. Both black and white, one was of a potted orchid and the other a maple tree.

Bland as a plain piece of toast. A typical corporate apartment, Holly guessed, having never been in one before. Elegant, yet all business. With no personal touches.

It was hardly the type of place where a beautiful shirtless man should be reading a newspaper. Not at all the kind of place where one brown curl of hair would fall in front of that man's forehead as if it were no big deal. As if that wasn't the most charming thing that a wet and exhausted young woman from Fort Pierce, Florida could imagine.

"Again, so sorry for the miscommunication," said the man that curl belonged to, "but you are going to have to leave. I will have the doorman hail you a taxi."

"Not so fast."

Holly snapped out of her fascination with his hair. She stomped over to one of the chairs opposite the sofa. Keeping her blue hands in the air, so as not to get paint anywhere, she lowered herself down.

"If your corporate office didn't have you scheduled to stay here, maybe it's *you* who should leave."

The corner of his mouth ticked up again—which was either cute or annoying. Holly wasn't sure yet.

"Obviously I am not going to leave my company's apartment."

Holly couldn't believe this was happening. This morning she had taken a bus from Fort Pierce to West Palm Beach airport. Then her flight to Newark, New Jersey had been delayed. When it had finally landed she'd taken another bus to the Port Authority terminal in Manhattan. It had been raining and dark by then, and there had hardly been a taxi to be had. She'd got drenched flagging one down. The cab brought her to this address on the Upper East Side.

And now—same as always, just when she was trying to do something for herself—someone else's need was somehow one-upping hers.

"What am I supposed to do?"

"I would suggest you go to a hotel."

Hotels in New York were expensive. Holly had been saving money for months to make a go of it when she got here. She couldn't use up any of her funds on a hotel stay.

"I can't afford it."

Ethan fixed a strangely searching stare on her.

While he assessed her Holly's eyes followed his long fingers as they casually traced the taut muscles of his chest down and then back up again. Down. And up. Down. And up.

After seemingly giving it some thought, he reasoned, "You must know people in New York that you can stay with?"

"No. I don't know anyone here. I came here to…"

Holly stopped herself. This man was a total stranger. She shouldn't be telling him anything about her life. He didn't need to know about her ex-husband, Ricky the Rat, her crazy mom, or any of it.

Maybe all that chaos was behind her now. Maybe the whole world was at her feet. Or maybe there were more hard times ahead.

Holly didn't know. But she was going to find out.

Hard rain continued to pelt against the window.

An unwelcome tear dropped its way out of her eye. When she instinctively reached up to brush it away before Ethan noticed she found Cobalt Two Eleven was smeared on the back of her hand as well.

"Are you *crying*?" Ethan asked, as if he were observing a revolutionary scientific function.

"I'm not crying," Holly denied. "It's been a long day."

"Perhaps you would like use the bathroom to wash up," Ethan offered. He pointed behind him. "It is the door on the right."

"Thank you." Holly hoisted herself up without touching anything, and made her way past Ethan and his curl of hair. "By the way—I'm not leaving."

Behind the sofa was a small dining table made of glass and steel like the coffee table. Four orange leather dining chairs provided a much-needed pop of color. Beyond that was a teeny kitchen.

Her brother had told her it was a very compact one-bedroom apartment. It would do quite fine. This was to be a temporary stepping stone for Holly. Either she was in New York to stay or it was merely a transition to somewhere else. Only time would tell.

She found her way into the marble-appointed bathroom and tapped the door closed with her boot. Made a mental commitment to also slam the door shut on her intense immediate attraction to Ethan Benton…astoundingly handsome, half-naked. Although it took her a stubborn minute to stop wondering what it might be like to lay her cheek against the firmness of one of those brawny shoulders.

*Oh, no!* She caught her reflection in the mirror above

the sink. It was so much worse than she could have envisioned. She had Cobalt Two Eleven streaked across her
face in horizontal stripes. Like a tribal warrior. Her black
bangs were plastered to her forehead in sweaty points.
She was a scary mess. What must this man think of her?

Not wanting to get anything dirty, she used her elbow to
start the faucet. With both hands under the running water,
she saw color begin swirling down the drain. She rubbed
her hands together until enough paint was removed that
she could adjust the tap to make the water hotter and pick
up the pristine bar of white soap.

Eventually her hands were scoured clean—save for a little residual blue around the cuticles and under the nails. As
usual. She reached for the fluffy towel hanging on the rack.

Next, Holly wanted to get her jacket off before she tack-
led washing her face. She unzipped the sleek and stylish
black leather jacket she had bought at the shopping mall
in Fort Pierce yesterday. With Florida's mild climate, there
hadn't been a lot of selection, but she'd needed something
warm for New York. When she'd seen it, she'd known it
was the one for her.

Ricky the Rat would have hated it. He'd have said it
was highfalutin'. Yeah, well, falute *this*! Decisions were
going to be made *by* her, *for* her from now on. Not based
on what other people wanted or thought.

After her face was scrubbed she towel-dried her bangs
and peeled off her ponytail band. Fluffed out the dark hair
that had grown far past her shoulders. With the longer hair,
she realized she already had a new look. New hair. New
jacket. New city. She was ready for a new life.

Giving a yank on her tee shirt and a tug on her jeans,
she was more than a little concerned about how she'd look
to Ethan when she went back into the living room. Which
was, of course, completely ridiculous because she didn't
even know him.

\* \* \*

My, my, but Holly Motta cleaned up well. Distracted by the blue paint on her face, Ethan hadn't noticed the other blue. The crystal color of her eyes. How they played against her lush jet-black hair.

As soon as she returned from the bathroom a rush of energy swept through the living room. He didn't know what kind of magic she held, but it wasn't like anything he had been in the same space with before.

All he could mutter was, "Better?"

It wasn't really a question.

He was glad he had nabbed a tee shirt from the bedroom, although he was still barefoot.

"Yes, thanks." She slid past him to her luggage, still at the front door.

He reached for his computer tablet and tapped the screen. Best to get Holly out of the apartment right now. For starters, he had no idea who she was. Ethan knew firsthand that there were all sorts of liars and scammers in this world, no matter how innocent they might look. He had his family's company to protect. The company that he was to run.

As soon as he could get his aunt Louise to retire.

As if a heart attack hadn't been enough, his beloved aunt was now losing her balance and mobility due to a rare neurological disorder that caused lack of feeling in her feet. Benton Worldwide's annual shareholders' gala was this Saturday. Ethan hoped Aunt Louise didn't have any bruises on her face from the fall he'd heard she'd taken last week.

Ethan owed everything to Aunt Louise and to Uncle Melvin, who had passed away five years ago. Without them he would just have been an abandoned child with no one to guide him toward a future.

His aunt had only one final request before she retired from the company that she, Uncle Mel and Ethan's late father had spent fifty years growing into an empire. She wanted to be sure that Ethan was settled in all areas of his life. Then she'd feel that everything was in its right place before she stepped down and let him take over. One last component to the family plan.

Ethan had lied to his aunt by claiming that he'd found what she wanted him to have. But he hadn't. So he had a lot to take care of in the next few days.

His temples pulsed as he thought about it all. Commotion was not an option. This exhilarating woman who had blown into the apartment needed to leave immediately. Not to mention the fact that there was something far too alluring about her that he had to get away from. Fast.

On top of it all he had a conference call in a few minutes that he still had to prepare for.

But with a few swipes across the tablet's screen he confirmed that all the Benton properties in New York were occupied.

Holly slung her jacket on the coat rack by the door and sat down on the floor. After pulling off one, then the other, she tossed her boots to the side. Ethan was mesmerized by her arms as they rummaged through her bag. She seemed to be made up only of elongated loose limbs that bent freely in every direction. Lanky. Gangly, even.

Downright adorable.

Nothing about Holly was at all like the rigid, hoity-toity blondes he usually kept company with. Women who were all wrong for him. Since he wasn't looking for someone right, that didn't matter. It kept his aunt happy to see him dating. But, of course, now he had told Aunt Louise that was all coming to an end. And he had a plan as to how to cover that lie.

Under her boots, Holly was wearing one red sock and one striped. She rolled those off and wiggled her toes. "That feels good…" She sighed, as if to herself.

Ethan's mouth quirked. "Miss Motta, please do not make yourself at home."

"I have nowhere else to go."

Holly death-stared him right in the face, putting on her best tough guy act. In reality she looked terrified that he was going to throw her out. She'd already been in tears before she washed up.

"Can't *you* be the one to leave?"

His stern expression melted a bit. What was he going to do? Toss her out into the cold rain?

She said she didn't know anyone in New York that she could stay with. Funny, but he didn't either. There were dozens—hundreds—of colleagues and workers in the city, connected with various Benton projects. Yet no one he'd call late on a rainy night to see if they had a sofa or guest room he could use.

Ridiculous. He'd sooner go back to the airport and sleep on his private jet.

He could pay for Holly's hotel room. Or he supposed he himself could go to a hotel. But—good heavens. He'd been in flight all day, had already unpacked and undressed here. Why on earth should he leave his own property?

"I do not suppose it will do for either of us to try to find other accommodation at this late hour."

"What's your plan, then?"

Ethan always had a plan. His life was structured around plans. He was about to embark on his biggest yet—moving Aunt Louise into retirement and taking the CEO seat.

"We will both spend the night here."

"Oh, no, I couldn't. I'm sure you're a very nice per—"

"I assure you, Miss Motta, I have no motive other than getting a peaceful night's rest. You will sleep in the bedroom and I will make do out here." He gestured toward the sofa.

"I need to think about that. That doesn't seem right.

Maybe I should call my brother. Let me just get my things straightened out." Holly returned to her task of sorting out her duffel bag, quarantining paint-stained items in a plastic bag.

She didn't look up at him until she lifted out a pair of white socks. They were splattered with the same blue that had been disguising her lovely face. "Occupational hazard."

"You are a painter, I take it?"

"Yup."

"And you have come to New York to pursue fame and fortune?"

"Ha! That would be nice. Who wouldn't want their work to hang in a museum or a gallery here…?"

"I sense there is a *but* at the end of that."

"I've been making money doing large pieces and collections for corporate properties."

"Office art, lobby art, art for furnished apartments?"

Ethan was well aware of that kind of work. He'd spent many hours with interior designers making decisions about the art at Benton developments all over the world.

"Indeed, the right pieces are vitally important to a unified decor. They announce a mood."

"A point of view," Holly chimed in.

"It sets the tone." He pointed at the two black and white nature photos on the wall. "Those, for example."

"Dull."

"Safe."

"Yawn."

They both laughed in agreement. A sizzle passed between them. It was so real Ethan was sure he saw smoke.

How alive Holly was. The type of person who said exactly what she thought. A bit like Aunt Louise. And nothing at all like most of the women he knew.

He flashed on a possibility.

Then quickly thought better of it.

"My aunt's new husband selected this apartment. He frequently comes down from Boston."

Ethan rolled his eyes. Fernando Layne was no favorite of his. Definitely no substitute for Uncle Mel. Fernando was a plaything for Aunt Louise. Ethan tolerated him.

"I will remodel this property while I am in New York. Perhaps you can advise me?"

What a stupid thing to say. He was never going see Holly again past this awkward evening interlude. An unfamiliar sense of disappointment came over him.

He generally steered clear of his feelings. When they did arrive they were usually of the painful variety and proved too confusing.

"Do you want to look at my website?" Holly gestured to the tablet he still had in his hand.

"I am sorry to be rude but I have a phone meeting in five minutes. I need to prepare."

"At this time of night?"

"I am expecting a call from Tokyo, if you must know." He also wasn't used to explaining himself to anyone. "I will take it in the bedroom," he declared.

Then he picked up a roll of architectural blueprints from the desk and marched down the hall, perturbed in twenty different ways.

Ten o'clock on a rainy New York night.

Holly had left Fort Pierce at eight that morning.

Hungry and tired, she absentmindedly ran her hand along the sofa where Ethan had been sitting when she came in. The leather still held his warmth.

She probably should have been afraid when she'd opened the door to find a total stranger in the apartment. Yet she hadn't felt the slightest inkling of fear. She'd felt ticked off, maybe. Or something else entirely.

It might have something to do with the fact that Ethan Benton looked less like a serial killer than he did the lord of a countryside manor. With his imposing height and lean muscles and that stunning wavy brown hair that had a touch of red flecked in it.

His tone was bossy, but she supposed it must have been quite a shock for him that a woman with a blue face, a tattered duffel bag and a squeaky-wheeled suitcase had just barged into the apartment he'd thought he had to himself.

Now she was trapped here with him unless she was willing to face the stormy night. The man—who may or may not have a British accent—definitely had the most soulful eyes she had ever seen. The man who was now in the next room, conducting business halfway around the world.

New York was getting off to a rollicking start.

Would he be angry with her if she checked to see if there was anything to eat? Should she care, given that this apartment was supposed to be *hers*?

A rumbling stomach propelled her to the kitchen. She'd picked at snacks all day, but had not had a proper meal. On the counter lay one basket of fruit, and another of breads and bagels. The refrigerator held beer, milk, eggs and cheese.

Had this food been purchased for her arrival as a hospitality custom? Or was it Ethan's? Or did it belong to his aunt's husband, who Ethan had said used this apartment frequently?

The sight of the food rendered Holly too hungry to care. Being hungry was a unique ache that she had experience with. Surely Ethan wouldn't mind if she took one shiny red apple.

She hoisted herself up to sit on the countertop. Let her legs and bare feet dangle. Smiled remembering the apple's symbolism here in New York. Like so many others, she was here to take her bite. With one satisfying chomp after the next, her mind wandered about what might be.

"Miss Motta!" Ethan looked startled to find her sitting on the kitchen counter after he finished his call. "Must you always make yourself so...so *comfortable*?"

Holly shrugged her shoulders and slid off the countertop. *Whatever.* If her sitting on the counter was a big deal to him, she wouldn't do it.

She jutted out her chin. "I bet you haven't eaten."

"Not since early this afternoon on the flight," he confessed. "Is there food?"

"Looks like there's eggs and some things for breakfast."

"We will have something delivered."

"Sounds good to me."

"What would you like?"

"You know what? I haven't been to New York in years. Want to get some famous New York pizza?"

"Pizza it is." He swiped on his tablet. "Yes, Giuseppe's. I ordered from there quite a bit when I was last in New York, working on a project. What type of pizza do you like?"

It was nice of him to let her choose. This man was a bundle of contradictions. Scolding one minute, courteous in the next.

"Everything," she answered, without having to think twice.

"Everything?"

"You know—pepperoni, sausage, salami, mushrooms, onions, peppers, olives. The whole shebang."

"Everything..." he repeated. "Why not?"

"I'll pay for my half."

His mouth twitched.

"Twenty minutes," he read out the online confirmation. She eyed the kitchen clock.

"I guess I'm staying tonight." She crunched on her big apple.

A bolt of lightning struck, flashing bright light through the window.

# CHAPTER TWO

ETHAN HAD A peculiar urge. The minute he'd said he'd sleep on the sofa tonight he'd wanted to lie down on the bed with Holly. Not to get under the covers. Just to lie on the bed with her. He wanted to relax. To hold her body against his. Caress her hair. Find out if those ebony locks were as silky as they looked.

*Huh.* A woman he had never met before, who had charged into his apartment and refused to leave. He had no idea who she really was or what she was doing here.

Yet he wanted to hold her.

The thought had interrupted his phone call several times.

He wasn't going mad. He'd just been working too hard. That was it. It had already been a long evening.

From the moment his flight had landed it had been one thing or another. He'd managed to sort out some of the details for the shareholders' gala. Many more remained. He'd heard there were construction delays on the low-income housing development in the Bronx that was so dear to his heart. He'd talked to a few people at the Boston headquarters to see how Aunt Louise was doing after the fall she'd taken. The news was not good. Then he'd worked on trying to resolve problems with a building permit in Detroit.

It had only been about an hour ago that Ethan had

changed into pajama bottoms and quieted down to read the newspaper. Before Holly had arrived, with the sparkling blue eyes and the creamy skin he now couldn't take his gaze off.

"While we're waiting for the pizza would it be okay if I took a shower?" she asked.

*It would be okay if I took it with you.*

Ethan surprised himself with the thought he didn't voice. He settled for, "Go right ahead."

Ethan did not like the way warmth resonated from Holly's body when she passed by him en route to the shower. Did not like it a bit because it stirred sensations low within him. Fierce sensations. *Urgent.*

The bathroom door shut with the quick smack that only happened when you closed it with a foot. Did she *always* shut doors with her feet?

His tongue flicked at his upper lip when he heard the sound of the shower. He couldn't help but imagine which article of clothing Holly was removing first. What each long limb might look like uncovered. Her torso was straight, rather than especially curvy, and he envisioned the smooth plain of her back. When he started to imagine what her... Well, he begged his brain to move to a different topic. No easy task.

Normally Ethan maintained a controlled world, without surprises. A world that allowed him to keep the upper hand. Maneuver as he saw fit. Because he was usually right.

Mushroom pizza, for heaven's sake.

A thirty-four-year-old man knew his own ways. Protected his orbit. Holly seemed to tip the universe off-kilter. Made the earth spin off its axis.

He preferred his pizza with only mushrooms on it!

She had to be stopped.

Yet he hadn't the heart to force her out on the street—

especially given the time of night. He didn't doubt that she was capable of fending for herself. But he didn't want her to.

That insane idea glimmered again. He needed to get it out of his head.

Ethan had too much to think about already. He was in a bind. Aunt Louise needed to retire. She'd had a distinguished career, and Ethan wanted her to go out on top. Concern was growing that she would sustain a fall in public. That word would spread. That people might remember her as a woman who had stayed on past her prime. That she was doddering, weak, bruised... All things that Louise Benton was most certainly not.

His aunt and his Uncle Melvin—his father's brother—had taken Ethan in as their own when he was nine years old. Now the time had come for the roles to be reversed. Ethan needed to make sure his decisions were in his aunt's best interests. His father would have told him to. Uncle Mel would have counted on him. It was the very least he could do.

But Aunt Louise had that one condition before she stepped down and moved from frigid Boston to the sunny compound in Barbados they'd had built for just that purpose. She wanted to know that Ethan would run their global business with a stable home life as a foundation.

Even though she and Uncle Mel hadn't been able to have children of their own, they'd experienced the joys and the heartaches of parenting through Ethan. In turn, his aunt wanted *him* to know the profound love of a parent for a child. And the united love and partnership that only came with decades of a shared life.

Aunt Louise would retire once Ethan was engaged to be married.

And because he'd become so alarmed about his aunt's

escalating health problems, and his responsibility to guard her reputation, Ethan had lied to her.

"You always say that deep down in your gut you know when something is right," Ethan had said, twisting his aunt's advice when he'd given her the news that he had met the soul mate he would wed.

Trouble was, Ethan had no such fiancée. Nor would he ever.

That was why he'd come to back to the States a few days ahead of the shareholders' gala. Tomorrow he was having lunch with the woman he planned to marry. In name only, of course.

He'd found a beautiful actress who'd be a suitable bride-to-be. This was New York, after all. There was hardly a better place to find a performer capable of pulling off this charade. He clicked on his tablet to the talent agency website where he'd located Penelope Perkins, an educated and sophisticated blonde with a stately neck.

It was a simple matter, really, in Ethan's mind. He'd chosen the actress and scheduled a meeting with her under the guise of hiring her for a promotional campaign for his company. If he found her to be acceptable and unencumbered he'd have her thoroughly investigated by Benton Worldwide's Head of Security, Chip Foley.

While Chip was completing a background check and every other kind of probe there was, Ethan and his stand-in fiancée would get to know each other and create a history for their relationship. Their engagement would be announced at the gala.

Penelope would also sign numerous non-disclosure and confidentiality agreements. She'd understand that if she were ever to reveal the arrangement she would be sued. Benton lawyers played hardball. They never lost their cases.

For her services, this performer would be paid generously.

It was a solid plan.

"Clean at last." Holly emerged from the bathroom while towel-drying her hair. A fresh tee shirt and sweatpants made her feel cozy after the day's journey. "Traveling makes you so grimy, you know?"

"Yes. I showered on the plane before arrival," Ethan agreed.

"You showered on the plane? How does someone shower on a plane?"

"I have a corporate jet. It does have a number of creature comforts."

Holly whistled. Highfalutin'. "I haven't flown that many times in my life. I'm still excited to get free soda and peanuts."

"Yes, well…perhaps you would enjoy all the amenities on private planes."

She tilted her head to one side and squeezed a little more moisture from the tips of her hair onto the plush towel. Sure, she'd like to be on a private plane, with a shower and enough room for her legs not to feel cramped into a ninety-degree position the entire flight. But that wasn't something that was ever going to happen, so she didn't see any point in discussing it.

"You have a little bit of an accent. And a kind of formal way of talking." Holly had a sometimes bad habit of blurting aloud everything that came into her mind. She called 'em as she saw 'em. "Are you American, or what?"

That left side of his mouth quivered up again in the start of a smile. "Boston-born. Oxford-educated. I would be the complete cliché of an entitled rich boy save for the fact that my father died when I was nine and I was raised by my aunt and uncle."

"What about your mother?"

The landline phone on the desk rang. Ethan turned to answer it. "Thank you. Please send him up." He headed toward the door. "Our pizza is here."

With his back to her, Holly was able to take in the full height of his slim, hard build. Probably about six foot three. Much taller than she was, and she always felt like a giant rag doll.

Ethan moved with effortless authority and confidence. Of course this was a man who showered on planes. This was a man who had been born to shower on planes.

Speaking of showers…it had been weird to shower in the apartment with him there. She knew there was no way he was an axe murderer who was going to hack her to bits. But she couldn't be a hundred percent sure that he was a gentleman who wasn't going to come into the bathroom while she was undressed.

A devilish thrill shot through her at the thought that he might have.

Attraction to a man during her first evening in New York was not on her itinerary. Especially not a man who had put all her plans in jeopardy.

She'd just have to make it through the night. In the morning her brother would help straighten things out about the apartment.

Staying here for a few weeks was meant to be the leg-up that she desperately needed. It would buy her time to find work and decide whether New York was where she should be. It had been two years since she'd kicked out Ricky the Rat. Two years was enough time to move on and move forward.

It was her brother, Vince, who had finally convinced her to take a chance. To take a risk. To take something for her own.

Maybe someday a man would fit into the picture. Not any time soon. She needed to concentrate on herself.

"Join me." Ethan gestured for her to come sit on the sofa after the delivery. He laid the pizza down on the coffee table, then dashed into the kitchen, returning with two plates, a stack of napkins and two bottles. "Will you have a beer?"

She took one from him and popped the cap with a satisfying twist.

As they sat down beside each other Holly winced involuntarily and moved away a bit. Being close to him felt scary. Strange. Strangely great...

He noticed her sudden stiffness. "I do not bite."

*Pity.* She held back a laugh. It wasn't fear that he'd bite that was bothering her. It might have been fear that he wouldn't.

Ethan flipped open the box and a meaty, cheesy, tomatoey aroma wafted up to their noses.

"I do not believe I have ever seen a pizza with this many ingredients on it."

As if performing a delicate procedure, he used two hands to lift one hefty slice onto a plate and handed it to Holly. Then he served himself.

"Ah..."

They groaned in unison as the first bites slid down their tongues. Unable even to speak, they each quickly devoured their slices.

Holly was the first to reach for a second. Then she sat back on the sofa and put her bare feet up on the coffee table.

"'Everything' is now officially my favorite pizza topping," Ethan confirmed, after taking another slice.

Observing Holly stretched out and seemingly comfortable, he did the same. His leaned back against the sofa.

Tentatively he extended one leg and then the other onto the coffee table, and crossed them just as Holly had hers.

And there they sat, both barefoot, eating pizza, as if they had known each other for eons rather than minutes.

She thought of something to ask. "Where did you fly in from?"

"Dubai. Before that I was in Stockholm. I have been out of the country for a month."

"Where do you live?"

"I keep a small apartment in Boston, near our headquarters. Although I travel most of the time."

"Your company has properties all over the world?"

He nodded and washed down his pizza with a sip of beer. "Yes. Some we build. Some we buy and refurbish. In the last couple of years I have been spending a lot of my time on affordable housing for low-income buyers."

"Vince told me about the development you built in Overtown. He said he was so proud to have been part of a project helping people in one of Miami's neediest areas."

That left side of Ethan's mouth rose up again, but this time it continued until the right side lifted to join it in one full-on heart-melting smile.

Holly almost choked on her pizza. She thought a person might enjoy looking at that smile for the rest of her life.

"After my aunt retires I plan to turn most of Benton's focus toward housing for homeless or low-income families."

"When will she retire?"

Ethan sized Holly up in a gaze that went from the tip of her head down to her toes. As if he were taking her all in. Measuring her for something.

When she couldn't stand the moment any longer she reached for another piece of pizza and pressed, "Does your aunt *want* to retire?"

Holly watched his concentration return to the conversation at hand.

"I think she must, whether she wants to or not. She has peripheral neuropathy. It is a rare inherited condition. She's starting to lose some of her faculties."

"I'm sorry."

"I am, too. She is a wonderful woman."

"She's lucky to have you looking out for her wellbeing." Holly didn't think anyone would ever care about *her* that much.

"I would like to see her relaxing in Barbados. Swimming in warm waters and enjoying her silly trophy husband."

"But she doesn't see it that way?"

"She has a stipulation that she is insistent on before she retires, the details of which have not been worked out yet." Ethan reached for his beer. "So, tell me, Miss Holly Motta, you have come to New York completely on your own?"

What did his aunt want? Was there a family secret?

Holly was dying to know. In fact she wanted to know about all of Ethan's joys and triumphs and struggles and defeats. Wanted to tell him all of hers. Though she couldn't fathom why.

Even if she had been open to meeting the right man—a man with whom she would share the deepest, darkest nooks and crannies of her life—it wouldn't be a man who showered on airplanes.

A man like Ethan Benton had no business with a girl who had grown up in a trailer park in Fort Pierce. *Never going to happen*. And she wasn't looking for someone, anyway. This was *her* time.

She chewed her pizza, suddenly agitated by the way Ethan continued to examine her, as if she was an object he was considering purchasing.

"I have to say I cannot remember the last time I was with a woman who ate half a pizza in one sitting."

"Of course not. You probably only keep company with women who eat one green bean and then tell you how full they are."

That crooked grin broke into a hearty belly laugh. "You are absolutely right. If they eat anything at all. You are definitely not like the women I tend to meet."

"Should I consider that a compliment?"

"Please tell me why you have come to New York alone."

"Who would I have come with if not alone? I haven't seen my mother in years. My brother, Vince, is doing well in Miami. I have no other ties."

She'd grown up strategizing and compensating for her unreliable mother. Looking out for Vince. Then working around Ricky's bad behavior. Juggling two or three jobs. Keeping the house clean. Making sure people were fed. Paying bills. Always being the responsible one. Day after day. Year after year.

"I'm through with being cautious." She couldn't believe she was blathering this out to a man she'd only just met. "Yes, I came to New York alone. No job. No permanent place to live. I don't even know if here's where I belong. That's why I was going to stay in this apartment for a while—to figure it out. I'm sure it all sounds insane to you."

"How it sounds is brave."

Ethan furrowed his brow. A minute ago Holly had confided that she wasn't in contact with her mother. No mention of a father. He sensed there was plenty more that she hadn't said. That she'd been through more than her share of trouble and strife. Although it might be a made-up story meant to evoke sympathy from him to let her stay in the apartment.

Every previous experience he'd had with women other than Aunt Louise had led him to believe that they were never what they seemed.

Starting with his own mother.

Do not trust *trust*. It was a lesson he'd learned decades ago.

That was why he'd devised this scheme to set up a fake relationship, so that Aunt Louise would think she had gotten her wish. She would retire with her mind at ease and her attention on her health.

An imitation fiancée would suit him perfectly. The women he'd known before had always wanted something from him. With this arrangement he'd dreamt up everyone would get what they were after. Clean and upfront, with clear expectations and no disappointment.

After he and Holly had finished eating she retrieved a pad and pencils from her luggage and sat herself in the window, with its second-floor view out onto the street. She turned sideways, somehow wedging her long legs into the windowsill, and propped her sketchpad on her knees.

"You are welcome to pull a chair over," Ethan tossed out, not in the habit of contorting himself to fit into small spaces.

"I'm fine, thanks."

Unsure what to do with himself, he picked up his tablet to check emails. If he'd been there alone, as planned, he would have gone to bed. It was going to be a busy week.

He could ask Holly to take her things into the bedroom. Then he could turn off the lights, try to get comfortable on the sofa and hope to fall asleep.

Yet it was so unusual for him to be in an apartment with someone he craved her company and wanted to prolong it. He wasn't ready for her to retreat to separate quarters.

*How crazy was the idea that kept popping into his mind?*

As Holly drew, he began telling her more about Aunt

Louise. About the cruel medical condition that was taking away pieces of her.

"How did your family's company get started?" she asked, while working on her drawing.

"With nothing. When my father and Uncle Mel were in their twenties they saved their money from doing carpentry work until they had enough to buy the South Boston apartment they grew up in. Then they bought the whole building. And then the one next to it."

"That takes focus and determination. Hmm..." She shook her head.

"Hmm—what?"

She kept her eyes on her pad. "It's just that nobody I've ever known has done anything like that."

"After my uncle married Louise, she helped them grow the business. My father died twenty-five years ago. Then Aunt Louise took over as CEO when Uncle Mel died five years ago."

Ethan had only vague memories of his father. But he so missed the uncle who had become a second father to him. Melvin Benton had been a smart leader. A just and fair man.

"Uncle Mel would have agreed that it is time for Aunt Louise to step down. Before industry gossip sullies her reputation as the competent successor to his legacy that she was."

"What is it that your aunt wants you to do before she'll agree to retire?"

Oh, so Holly had been paying close attention earlier, when he'd started to tell her about Aunt Louise's request and then stopped himself.

"She wants to see me established in my personal life. For me to have what she and Uncle Mel had. She is waiting for me to be engaged to be married."

"And now you are?"

"So to speak…"

"There's no 'so to speak.' You're either engaged or you're not."

"Not necessarily."

Why had he started this? He'd revealed more than he should have.

"Tell me," she persisted, without looking up.

"I would rather talk about you. You have come to New York with no work here at all? This city can be a very tough place."

"I know. But I do have some people to contact. You're probably thinking my coming to New York was a really reckless bet. But if I didn't do it now I never would have."

When Ethan glanced down to the inbox on his tablet his eyes opened wide at the latest email. It was the talent agency, apologizing for contacting him so late in the evening and asking for the duration of his booking for Penelope Perkins, his soon-to-be "fiancée." Because, the representative explained, Mrs. Perkins had just informed them of her pregnancy. She expected to be available for a few months but, after that her altered appearance might be an issue for any long-term acting assignment.

Good heavens. *Yes*, Mrs. Perkins's blossoming pregnancy was going to be an issue! That would be too much to disguise from Aunt Louise. First an engagement and then a pregnancy right away? Not to mention the fact that Penelope was apparently *Mrs.* Perkins. And a certain *Mr.* Perkins was be unlikely to be agreeable to such an arrangement.

The veins in Ethan's neck pulsed with frustration. As if he didn't have enough to do! Now the engagement plan he'd worked so hard to devise was in jeopardy. Could he choose someone else and get an appointment with her in time? He quickly tabbed through the photos of the other actresses on the website. They were all of a suitable age. Any one of them might do.

Then he glanced up to lovely Holly, sketching in the windowsill.

What if…?

He'd been exchanging pleasant conversation with Holly all evening. Why *not* her? It might work out quite nicely. Perhaps they could have an easy, friendly business partnership based on mutual need. He had a lot he could offer her.

Of course the fact that he found her so interesting was probably *not* a plus. It might add complication. But who was to say that he wouldn't have been attracted to Penelope Perkins, or some other actress he'd chosen?

A sense of chemistry would be palpable to Aunt Louise and anyone else they would encounter. It would make them believable as a couple. And he certainly wouldn't be acting on any impulses. It wasn't as if he was open to a genuine relationship.

A fake fiancée was all he was looking for. Holly was as good a bet as any.

He gazed at her unnoticed for a moment. She turned to a new page on her sketchpad. Then, when she asked him again about whether or not he was engaged, he finally told her the truth.

He picked up the beer he had been drinking with the pizza. Carefully peeling off the label that circled the neck of the bottle, he rolled it into a ring. And then stepped over to Holly in front of the window. Where anyone in New York could be walking by and might look up to see them.

"I was intending to hire an actress," he explained. "But I think Aunt Louise would like you. You remind me of her. There is something very…real about you."

He got down on one knee. Held up the beer label ring in the palm of his hand.

She gasped.

"Holly, I do not suppose you would… If you might consider… Would you, please? Can you pretend to marry me?"

# CHAPTER THREE

"HEAR ME OUT," Ethan said, still on one knee.

Holly had been so stunned by his proposal that moments stood still in time. It was as if she watched the scene from outside her body.

In an Upper East Side apartment in New York an elegant man with wavy brown hair waited on bended knee after proposing to his dark-haired intended. Would she say yes?

Holly couldn't remember if she had dreamt of a moment like this when she was a little girl. A dashing prince, the romantic gesture of kneeling, white horse at the ready. She'd probably had those fantasies at some point but she couldn't recall them. They were buried under everything else.

Most of Holly's memories were of hard times.

Growing up, it had been her alarm clock that had snapped her out of any dreams she might have had. The clock had made her spring her up quickly to check if her mother had woken up and was getting dressed for work. Or if she wasn't going to get out of bed. Or hadn't made it home at all during the night. Leaving Holly to scrounge together breakfast and a sack lunch for her and Vince.

No, Holly hadn't had much time for fairy-tale dreams. She'd been proposed to before. After all, she'd been married. But Ricky's offer had been about as heartfelt as their marriage had been. It had been on a sweaty, humid day in his beat-up old truck and it had gone something like, "I guess you want to get married…"

At the time, she'd thought that was about as good as it was going to get.

"It would be strictly business, of course." Ethan continued with his proposition. "An engagement in name only."

So Holly's second marriage proposal was to be just as unromantic as her first.

A twinge of despair pinged through her.

Ethan was suggesting a fake engagement to appease his aunt and get her to retire before poor health tarnished her standing. She understood why he was asking, but she didn't see what would be in it for her.

He anticipated her immediate trepidation and added, "We can negotiate a contract that is mutually beneficial."

"That certainly sounds cut and dried, Mr. Benton."

Even having this discussion was making her uncomfortable. Because it brought up notions like a little girl's dreams and happily-ever-afters. Thoughts she couldn't afford to linger on. Not then and not now.

She squinted at him. "Could you please get up?"

"I can."

He rose, yet still held out the beer bottle label. Looking down at it he assured her, "We would purchase a proper engagement ring."

"Let's put the paper ring down for a minute, okay?"

He laid it gently onto the coffee table as if it was a thing of great value. "I have a scenario…" He gestured toward the sofa.

She followed him, but this time didn't sit next to him as she had when they were eating pizza. She chose one of the black chairs opposite him. Best to keep her distance.

"May I be frank?"

"Oh…okay," Holly answered with apprehension.

"You are new to New York. You mentioned that you do

not yet have work. You mentioned that you could not afford to stay in a hotel. I am offering you very easy temporary employment. Pose as my fiancée. What I would pay you will help you establish yourself here. Shall we bring it to the bargaining table? Name your price."

"Name my *price*!" Such a ruthless businessman! Everything was a deal to him. "Are you used to getting everything you want simply by demanding it?"

"Oh, I always get what I want." His stare drilled into her.

*Wow, what a predator.* And why did that excite her rather than repel her?

Just for entertainment's sake, she took a minute to fantasize what being his pretend fiancée might be like. She'd probably be physically near him quite a bit. He'd have his arm around her shoulder. Sometimes around her waist. They'd hold hands. He'd probably even place a kiss on her cheek in front of other people, just to put on a convincing show.

Holly snuck a glance at his mouth. Ripe lips that looked to be endlessly kissable. No way would a plan that involved her standing close to his lips ever, *ever* be a good idea.

But it didn't matter, because she was just playing along hypothetically. "I'm not for hire by the hour!" She feigned indignation.

"There need not be anything sordid about it, Miss Motta." Ethan eyed the paper ring on the table. "I assure you I am only proposing a trade agreement."

She didn't doubt that. This was a man who'd already said he kept company with stunning, glamorous women who ate one green bean. He'd never be interested in her romantically. She'd have nothing to worry about there.

But she couldn't resist throwing in for fun, "My brother, Vince, is up for a promotion in your Miami office. Let's say this deal included helping him along in his career…"

"Done," Ethan answered quickly. "I would have to look at his human resources file and speak with the people who work with him. But if he is deserving, I would certainly look to promote my future brother-in-law."

He leaned forward. Even though there was the coffee table between them, she could feel him zeroing in on her. Coming in for the kill. Determined to make the sale.

"What else, Miss Motta?"

He was so maddeningly sure of himself. Holly hadn't met many people who were like that.

She sat dumbfounded, way out of her league.

Ethan raised a finger in the air with a thought. "Shall we consider it another way? You need somewhere to live. How about if I give you this apartment? I will put it in your name."

Holly tried to keep her eyes from bugging out. *How about if I give you this apartment?* Who even *said* that?

"As you can imagine, real estate is something I have as a bartering tool. Regardless of what happens, you will have a home in New York."

*A home in New York.* He really did know how to persuade a deal.

"What is it that might happen?" She had no intention of taking him up on his offer, but she was curious. "How is it that you see this working?"

He'd obviously thought this through well. Today was Monday. His aunt Louise and her boy-toy husband, Fernando, would be coming down from Boston this week in preparation for their Saturday shareholders' gala. He'd present Holly to them on Wednesday night.

"Dinner. Le Cirque. Or one of the new Asian-Spanish fusion restaurants in Tribeca. Something flashy that shows us as a hip New York couple on top of the trends."

"How about instead I throw a pot roast in the slow cooker?" Holly countered, batting him the idea.

His mouth tipped. "A home-cooked meal? Like she and Uncle Mel used to make on Sundays? Brilliant!"

Holly was no gourmet cook, but she knew how to work with the basics. She'd had to learn if she and her brother were ever going to eat. When they were kids she'd search through the pockets of pants left on the floor. Between the couch cushions. Under the seats in the car. Somehow she'd find enough money to buy a few groceries and put a meal together for her and Vince. Restaurant visits had been few and far between.

"Mashed potatoes. Roasted carrots. Apple pie…" She completed the menu.

"Perfect. I will try to be of assistance."

"Continue," she requested.

It was amusing to hear Ethan's outline for the masquerade that she wasn't actually going to be any part of.

Their next appearance would be at the shareholders' gala on Saturday, where Holly would be formally introduced as Ethan's fiancée.

"So I'd look amazing that night? Dress? Jewels? Hair and makeup? The whole nine yards?"

He sat silent for a minute, as if lost in his own memories. But then he snapped back with, "Of course. A couture gown would be chosen for you. My tuxedo tie will match your attire."

"It'd be a crime if it didn't."

Then there would be an engagement party in Boston. A month or so later would come the announcement that Aunt Louise was stepping down. A grand retirement luncheon would send her off in style.

"In between those dates," Ethan explained, "I would travel, so that you and I should not have to attend many events together. I will devise reasons that I have to spend prolonged periods in Florence or Sydney or the like."

Ethan went on. After those appearances Aunt Louise

and Fernando would move to Barbados as planned. Ethan and Holly—the happy couple—would fly to the island for long weekends three or four times during the first year. In between those visits Holly would be free to live the life she chose, as long as there was nothing criminal or anything that attracted attention.

Then they'd evaluate. They could continue to visit Aunt Louise and make excuses as to why they hadn't yet married. Or they could tell fibs about a lavish wedding that would take an entire year to plan.

"Or," he continued, "especially if you were to meet someone else and need to be free, we could call off the engagement. Aunt Louise would be settled into her island life of leisure. By that point there would not be any danger of her wanting to return to frigid Boston and the working grind."

"And what if *you* were the one to meet someone?" she clipped, pretending to advocate a deal for herself.

"Impossible!" he spat immediately. "I will never marry."

His harshness hit her like a slap in the face.

Or perhaps it was a warning.

"I see," she assured him, and knew she'd understood his underlying message.

"Therefore, when we split up, you will own this apartment outright—which you can either keep, lease or sell. And the engagement ring. And whatever clothing and jewels have been purchased. Your brother's position will be secure. We can also agree on a monetary settlement. In exchange for very little labor on your part, I can provide you with a lifetime of comfort and luxury."

Game over.

Enough was enough.

Even if it could be as simple as he made it sound she had come to New York to get her own life straightened out. Not to get tangled up in someone else's.

"Ethan, I appreciate the offer. And I think it's great that you've done so much planning on this. It shows how much you care about your aunt. But this is not for me."

He swallowed hard. His Adam's apple bobbed in his throat. His jaw tightened.

Was he upset?

Of course. This was a man who was used to getting everything he wanted. It wasn't personal. She was a mere obstacle for him to overcome in order to reach his goal.

Ethan tapped his tablet. "Holly Motta dot com—is that it?"

She nodded, yes. What was he up to?

He typed.

"Huh…" His thumb slid through what she assumed to be her website's gallery. "Huh…"

What was he thinking? She took great pride in her work. Suddenly it mattered to her what he thought of it. Which was silly, because his opinion was of no concern to her at all. Yet she sat on the edge of the chair, spine held stiff as she waited for a comment.

His thumb continued to swipe the tablet.

"Hmm…" His next sound was at a higher pitch than the one before. It sounded like approval.

"Why are you looking at my website?"

Ethan ignored the question and continued. His finger slid less frequently. He was spending more time on each piece of work.

Holly imagined what it might feel like to have that thumb slide across her cheek instead of the tablet screen. Or slowly down the center of her chest. That thumb and its nine partners on those two big hands looked as if they'd always know exactly what to do.

More fantasy. She hadn't been touched in a long, long time.

Finally Ethan looked from the screen to her. "These are extraordinary."

"Thank you," she breathed with gratification—and relief.

He raised a finger in the air again. "Perhaps we can negotiate a merger that would be satisfying to both of us."

She squished her eyebrows.

"In exchange for you posing as my fiancée, as I have outlined, you will be financially compensated and you will become legal owner of this apartment and any items such as clothes and jewels that have been purchased for this position. Your brother's career will not be impacted negatively should our work together come to an end. *And...*" He paused for emphasis.

Holly leaned forward in her chair, her back still board-straight.

"I have a five-building development under construction in Chelsea. There will be furnished apartments, office lofts and common space lobbies —all in need of artwork. I will commission you for the project."

Holly's lungs emptied. A commission for a big corporate project. That was exactly what she'd hoped she'd find in New York. A chance to have her work seen by thousands of people. The kind of exposure that could lead from one job to the next and to a sustained and successful career.

This was all too much. Fantastic, frightening, impossible... Obviously getting involved in any way with Ethan Benton was a terrible idea. She'd be beholden to him. Serving another person's agenda again. Just what she'd come to New York to get away from.

But this could be a once-in-a-lifetime opportunity. An apartment. A job. It sounded as if he was open to most any demand she could come up with. She really did owe it to herself to contemplate this opportunity.

Her brain was no longer operating normally. The clock on Ethan's desk reminded her that it was after midnight. She'd left Fort Pierce early that morning.

"That really is an incredible offer…" She exhaled. "But I'm too tired to think straight. I'm going to need to sleep on it."

"As you wish."

Holly moved to collect the luggage she'd arrived with. Ethan beat her to it and hoisted the duffel bag over his shoulder. He wrenched the handle of the suitcase. Its wheels tottered as fast as her mind whirled as she followed him to the bedroom.

"Good night, then." He placed the bags just inside the doorway and couldn't get out of the room fast enough.

Before closing the door she poked her head out and called, "Ethan Benton, you don't play fair."

Over his shoulder, he turned his face back toward her. "I told you. I always get what I want."

Holly shut the door with her bare foot and leaned back against it. She pursed her lips together to keep from screaming. Her heart thumped so loud she was sure Ethan would hear it in the other room. *Goodness gracious.*

Ethan Benton and his proposition were quite simply the most exciting things that had ever happened to her!

A rush went through her as she recalled that devilish grin creeping slowly up his mouth. Those deep brown eyes that had stayed glued on her, assuring her he was listening to her when she spoke.

Holly hadn't talked and listened as much as she had tonight in a long time. She hadn't dated anyone since leaving Ricky the Rat two years ago. With her in Fort Pierce and Vince a two-hour drive away in Miami, she usually saw her brother twice a month. There was a girls' night here and there with friends. That was about it.

She hadn't really thought about it, but now when she did she realized she led a fairly solitary existence. Hopefully New York would jostle that, along with everything else.

But the change *wasn't* going to come by stepping into Ethan Benton's life. Although it might be the most fun she'd ever have. A jet-set world she'd only read about in magazines… Who wouldn't want to dash off to Barbados for long weekends? To walk on pink sand with her toes in sparkling blue water. Attend glitzy parties…throw some of her own. Buy clothes without looking at the price tag. Never worry about where the rent or her next meal was coming from. Have the best of everything.

It would be amazing—even if it was only for a short time—to be completely taken care of. After all those years of putting other people ahead of her.

Which reminded her of how this deal could benefit her brother. Becoming part of the Benton family, even in name only, might help him further his career in a way he'd never have the chance to otherwise. He'd get to spend more time with Ethan and Louise. They'd see up close how capable and special he was.

*No.* This wasn't about Vince. He'd be fine on his own. He was a grown man and his career was underway.

It was time for *her* future to begin. Period. In the morning she would tell Ethan no.

Besides, once he heard that she had already been married and divorced he wouldn't think she was an appropriate choice for his game.

Right now, she needed to get some sleep.

She stopped short at the sight of the room's king-size bed. This was where Ethan Benton had been planning to lay that tall, sturdy frame of his tonight. A wiggle shot up her spine at the mental image of him stretched out on this bed. Perhaps only wearing the plaid pajama bottoms as when she'd first seen him on the sofa.

On the bed she counted one, two…eight plush pillows, overlapped in a tidy row against the brown leather headboard. She imagined Ethan's head against those pillows, with that curl of hair tousled on his forehead.

The luxury pillowcases alternated in color, tan then black. Which coordinated with the tightly fitted tan sheets. She ran a finger along the black duvet, tracing it down the right side of the bed. Then across the bottom. Then up the left. It was all too matchy-matchy for her tastes, but clearly made of expensive fabrics.

She eyed the wall-to-wall closet. If she took Ethan up on his proposal it would become filled with designer gowns for glamorous black tie dinners. Trendy separates for groundbreaking ceremonies. Classic sportswear for sailing jaunts and tennis tournaments. The finest shoes and purses and jewels.

None of that was her. She couldn't picture it. Not even for make-believe.

Back on earth, Holly didn't know whether she should unpack her suitcase full of jeans, comfortable skirts and tee shirts. She slid the blond wood closet door open to see if anything was inside.

Four men's suits hung neatly on wooden hangers, with breathing room in between each. Dark gray, light gray, navy pinstripe and a beautiful maroon. They looked to be Ethan's size. He'd probably look especially handsome in that maroon. It would go well with his brown eyes and that brown hair with its speckles of red.

There were freshly laundered shirts. Complementary ties. Polished shoes. A tuxedo and its accessories. Two pairs of pressed jeans. A pair of casual boots. She resisted the temptation to open any drawers. She had seen an overcoat and a leather jacket on the coat rack by the front door.

It wasn't a large wardrobe. Ethan had said he traveled a lot, but hadn't mentioned how long he was staying in New York.

She fingered the lapel of the maroon suit jacket. Ricky

the Rat had only owned one wrinkly black suit. She could count on one hand the times he'd worn it. He was the jeans and workboots type. There were times she'd thought he was sexy.

One of the times he hadn't been sexy was when she'd come home from work early one day and the workboots were all he'd had on. While he was in bed with their neighbor Kiki.

The rain was heavier outside now. Holly watched the bedroom window being pounded with sheets of the downpour. A rumble of thunder emphasized the storm's strength. *Good*. Let it wash away her past.

Deciding to leave her suitcase on the floor for the night, she pulled back the duvet on the bed and climbed into the king-size reminder of the man who was already making her feel as if she were spiraling away from her old life. Even though her encounter with him would come to an end in the morning, her transition to something new had begun.

The bed was divine. The mattress firm. The sheets crisp. She pulled the thick cover over her. Beyond comfortable, she nestled in the oasis, away from cares and plans. It was a peaceful heaven on earth after such a long day. Time to rest her body and mind. She was going to sleep like a log...

Two hours later Holly tossed and turned with exasperation. She hadn't kept her eyes shut for more than a minute before her brain had assaulted her with more and more opinions.

What Ethan was proposing could be her lucky break. A commission to do the artwork for his big development in Chelsea... A chance to really get started in New York...

She'd come to the city armed with work references, but the life of an artist could be tricky. Maybe nothing would pan out from the names and phone numbers she'd collected. Or she'd get small jobs here and there but they might not lead to anything else.

Ethan's proposition was a multi-phase project that would probably be six months of work at least. In that time she could really put down roots here.

She was determined to make her entire living as an artist. Not to have to work anymore as a maid or a nanny during the lean times. Her goals were clear. New York was the place where dreams were made or broken. If it didn't work out here, so be it—but she was certainly going to take her shot.

Imagine how much easier it would be without any astronomical rent to pay. New York apartment prices were notoriously high. Holly knew that she would probably have to live with a roommate. Maybe several of them. Some might have come to New York for the twenty-four-hour-a-day lifestyle, for the party that never ended. The household might be full of noise and people and activity at all hours of the day and night. It might prevent Holly from getting her work done or resting when she needed to.

Or she might end up with people who were slobs. Not able to tolerate a dirty mess, she would end up cleaning up after them. Cleaning up after people—how much of her life had she already spent doing that? She'd never minded taking care of her brother, but her ex-husband hadn't ever seemed even to know where the trash can or the washing machine were. Nor had her mother.

Maybe these roommate slobs wouldn't pay their share of their rent and she'd get evicted. She might end up having to move from place to place through no fault of her own. That would be maddening.

Ethan was offering work and a place to live. This tasteful apartment all to herself. It was one thing to be allowed to stay here while she looked for a place. It was quite another to have it *belong* to her. She could paint here. Reposition the furniture in the living room to make the most of the natural light.

*Wait a minute.*

Part of Ethan's bargain was that he would pay her. She would be able to afford to rent studio space. A New York artist with her own studio… If *that* wasn't a dream come true!

But on the other hand…

And she needed to consider…

She couldn't really…

And then what…?

When Holly opened her eyes, a drizzly morning sky crept in through the window. At some point she had finally dozed off, her mind twirling about the past and what the future could hold. Now, with morning's dawn in Ethan Benton's bedroom, certainty hit her like a ton of bricks.

If something seemed too good to be true, it was.

Not cut out to be anyone's pretend anything, Holly was only who she was. Ethan was kidding himself. It could only end in disaster. She would do him a favor by acknowledging the impossibility of his proposal, even though he wasn't able to see it for himself.

His judgment was clouded by his deep love for his aunt Louise. How touching was his concern for her welfare, for her reputation and her happiness. Blood ran thick. A good man took his family responsibilities seriously…

She had to call her brother. She wouldn't tell him about Ethan's offer. But she *did* need his help sorting out this confusion about her staying in the apartment. It would be good to hear his voice. In the end, he was the only one she really had in her corner.

He'd be working out in the garage of the little house he rented in Miami. Lifting weights. Bench pressing and hoisting dumbbells before showering and getting to work at Benton.

"Vinz." She pictured him, no doubt in a muscle shirt drenched in sweat. His close-cropped blond hair so unlike her black. The round blue eyes marking him as her kin.

"Holz! How's the Big Apple so far?"

She explained the mix-up with the apartment.

Vince promised to make some calls as soon as he got into the office. "I'll get it fixed," he assured her.

"I don't know if you can."

"Listen to me, big sis. We're going to sniff out opportunities for you and you're going take them. You'll grab everything that's thrown your way."

"Yeah."

"Remember—straight up or fall down!" He chanted their lifelong rally call—the desperate bravado of two kids with no one but each other to root for them.

After hanging up, Holly held the phone in her hand and stared absently out the window for a while. Thick clouds in the sky moved horizontally across her vision.

There had always been rainy days. No one knew how many more were ahead. It would be such a gift to have an umbrella.

Finally she tossed the phone onto the bed and opened the door.

Ethan was in the kitchen. She watched him start a pot of coffee before he noticed she was there. When he did, she leaned against the doorway. Her hair was probably a mess. Surely she had bags under her eyes from her fitful night. She lifted her hand and looked at her fingers with their perpetual paint around the cuticles and under the nails. She was who she was.

"Okay, Ethan. I'll marry you."

# CHAPTER FOUR

*SHE SAID YES!* Ethan wanted to shout it from the rooftops. *She said yes!*

His blood coursed. His muscles tingled.

*She said yes!*

And then he caught himself. *Good heavens.* There was no cause for fireworks to be launched from his heart. There was no reason to announce his undying devotion in front of the citizens of Manhattan. He was not a giddy groom filled with bliss and anticipation.

A woman he'd met yesterday had agreed to a jointly beneficial contract. He signed deals every day. This was just another one.

With a flick on the switch of the coffeepot he shook his head, trying to dislodge the obvious cobwebs in his skull.

He'd gotten a bit carried away.

Truthfully, he hadn't been alone with a woman in a long time—and certainly not in the close quarters of a small apartment. Perhaps that had stirred up a primal reaction in him. While the mating ritual wasn't part of his daily life, it *was* a natural phenomenon.

Although Ethan employed thousands of women in all aspects of his business, he shunned intimate social situations with them as much as possible. Keeping a clear and level head was what he did best. Women were distracting. Distractions were to be avoided. Problem—solution.

This was the first lesson he needed in order to carry off his plan. He was going to be spending a lot of time with an attractive woman. He'd need to guard and defend himself against her feminine charms. It wasn't personal. It didn't matter whether it was Holly, pregnant Penelope Perkins or another actress he'd picked from a photograph.

In three measured breaths, with his face toward the coffeepot, he set his focus. *Guard and defend.*

Then he turned to Holly, still standing in the doorway. Dark cascades of hair fell around her pretty face, which had a just-woken flush in her cheeks. Her tee shirt was definitely not concealing a bra.

Involuntarily, his body began to lean toward hers. A kiss pushed forward from his lips.

*Guard and defend!*

In the nick of time, he pulled himself back. Her allure was something he'd need to get accustomed to. His body's involuntary response to her worried him...told him that might be difficult.

But he would be triumphant. For the sake of Aunt Louise he could conquer anything.

Ethan directed himself to talk, since he couldn't kiss. "How did you sleep?"

"Great," she lied.

Her eyes looked tired. He hadn't got much sleep, either. He was far too tall to stretch out comfortably on that sofa. Plus, his mind had taunted him with replays of the evening.

"That coffee smells good," she said as she massaged the back of her neck.

"It does. How do you take it?"

"Lots of milk or cream. No sugar."

Ethan opened one of the cabinets to look for cups. It held only drinking glasses. He hadn't spent enough time in this apartment to know where everything was kept. His second try yielded large white mugs. Setting them on the black granite countertop, he poured the steaming coffee.

The kitchen was Manhattan Minimal. Pint-size efficiency. Cabinets, sink and dishwasher on one side. Stove and refrigerator on the other. A one-person kitchen. Too cramped for two people to work in.

Which was why when Holly stepped in to open the fridge he felt her hips brush past him. In turn, his hips reacted of their own volition—which, fortunately, she didn't notice.

"What are we eating for breakfast?" she asked as she peered into the refrigerator.

"What do we have?" He'd only had bottles of water when he'd got in yesterday, and beer last night with the pizza.

"Eggs, butter and cheese. And the bread and fruit." She pointed to the baskets on the counter. "We can work with this."

The way she said *we* made Ethan's ears prick up. He wasn't used to *we*. He'd worked very hard at avoiding *we*. This was no time to start. Although for the first time he was curious about *we*. He reasoned that this fake engagement was a perfect way of safely pretending to experience *we*, with both parties knowing fully well that the truth was *me* and *me* achieving individual goals.

*Right.* However, now it felt somewhat confusing.

Holly pulled the carton of milk out of the fridge and handed it to him. Ethan was keenly aware of their fingertips touching during the exchange.

She laid ingredients on the counter. "How does cheese omelets, toasted bagels and sliced fruit sound?"

"What do you generally eat for breakfast?"

Holly giggled. A bit of blush rose in her cheeks. *How adorable.* "Was that a get-to-know-each-other question?"

"It was. If we are going to be convincing as an engaged couple, we have to know those sorts of things about each other."

He handed her a mug. She took a slow sip and exhaled her satisfaction.

"You put the perfect amount of milk in my cup, so we must be off to a good start."

Ethan felt ridiculously proud that she liked her coffee.

"How do you take yours?" she went up.

"Also without sugar. But not as much milk."

"I'll eat anything…" She went back to his question. "If we hadn't polished off that pizza, that's great cold in the morning."

"Cold pizza? Noted."

"Do you know how to cook?"

"I could probably manage to broil a steak without ruining it."

"Eggs?"

"Not really," he confessed.

"Today you learn, then."

"Is that so?"

"I'll put on a show for your aunt Louise, but surely you don't think I'm going to be cooking and cleaning for you." Her face stilled in a moment of earnest uncertainty. "*Do* you?"

"Of course not, phony fiancée."

"It's just that I've done plenty of taking care of people in my life. I just want to take care of myself."

Holly had been through a lot. He'd been able to tell that about her from the start—had seen it right through her spunky attitude. She was no fresh-faced hopeful, arriving in New York full of delusions and fantasies. There was a past. A past that he suspected included hardship and pain.

Another one of those innate urges told him to wrap his arms around her and promise that he'd make up for all her hurts. That now she would be the one taken care of. That he'd quite like to make it his life's mission to take care of her in every possible way.

Once again he had to chastise himself sternly. He had merely hired her to perform a service. For which she would be paid very well. With that opportunity she would be able to find whatever she'd come to New York to get. She didn't need him.

The agony of that shocked him. A reminder to guard and defend.

Holly handed him the carton of eggs. She gave him a bowl. "Four."

Finding a cutting board and a knife, Holly sliced cheese while Ethan cracked eggs. They stood side by side at their tasks, each dependent on the other in order to get the job done. Ethan appreciated teamwork. That was what made Benton Worldwide, and every other successful venture work. It must be the same in a marriage.

Two bagels were halved and popped into the toaster.

"Frying pan?" she mused to herself, and quickly moved to his other side to find one.

His mind flipped back to the past. To Aunt Louise and Uncle Melvin. It had been almost ten years since they'd done the normal things that married couples did. Mel had died over five years ago. Before that recurrences of his cancer had often had him bedridden. But they'd had moments like these. Hundreds, even thousands of cozy day-to-day moments like preparing breakfast.

Those moments strung together added up to a life shared between two people.

In reality, with their success and privilege it was not as if Aunt Louise and Uncle Mel had often been in the kitchen frying up eggs. But they had always cooked Sunday supper together whenever they could. It had been one of their signatures.

Ethan had potent memories of the two of them together as a couple. The way they'd been with each other. Even if it they had just been at the front door on the way out, helping each other layer on coats, scarves and hats to brave the Boston winter. How they'd maneuvered around each other. With effortless choreography. Totally at ease with each other, aware of each other's moves, each other's needs, each other's comforts.

He understood why Aunt Louise so wanted that same security for him. Why she was concerned with the way he jetted around the globe, working all the time, never stopping, never settling. The wisdom of age had shown her what might happen to a man who didn't balance power and labor with the other things that made life worth living. Family. Love.

But his aunt should accept that after all Ethan had been through love wasn't an option for him. He would never open his heart. Her destiny wasn't his. Yet he couldn't blame her for wishing things were different. That his past hadn't defined his future.

In reflection, Aunt Louise had valued her relationship with Uncle Mel above everything else in her life. She'd had a love so true it had never let her down.

Unlike him.

This ruse was the best solution. If the knowledge that Ethan was engaged to be married made Aunt Louise happy, and put her mind at ease, then he'd have taken good care of her. Ethan was in charge of all decisions now, and he wanted them to be in his aunt's best interests.

He and Holly sat down at the table with their breakfast. Just as she had with the pizza last night, she dug in like a hungry animal. She took big bites and didn't try to disguise her obvious pleasure.

Ethan asked if maybe she had gone hungry as a child.

"My mother was…unpredictable."

Something he himself knew more than a little about. Anger burned his throat.

A bittersweet smile crossed her mouth as she cut circular slices of an orange and handed one to him. "Vince and I used to call these rings of sunshine. There were always oranges in Florida."

He wanted to know how she'd been wronged. But he wasn't going to walk on that common ground.

"Aunt Louise and Fernando are coming for dinner on Wednesday." He cut to the matter at hand. "We need to prepare. Our first order of business is making this apartment look like we truly live here. We will start with…"

"The artwork!" they chimed in unison.

"We will visit my favorite galleries in Soho. You can make the final selection."

Outside, stormy skies had given way to more hard rain. "Dress accordingly."

He plucked his phone from his pocket and began tapping.

Half an hour later, a stocky man in a suit and chauffeur's cap held a car door open for Holly.

"This is my driver, Leonard," Ethan introduced.

"Ma'am."

Holly darted into the black car without getting too wet from the downpour. Sliding across the tan leather backseat, she made room for Ethan beside her. Leonard shut the passenger door and hurried around to the driver's seat.

As they pulled away from the apartment building, Ethan activated the privacy glass that separated the front seat from the back.

Holly didn't know what she'd gotten herself into. Fear and excitement rattled her at the same time.

Soho galleries and shareholders' galas… She didn't really know how she was going to fake her way through a life so different from hers. Being ferried around New York in a town car with a privacy glass.

Ethan had clearly noticed her discomfort at his shielding his driver from any conversation they were going to have. "Obviously we need complete discretion to pull off our little enterprise, do we not?"

"Yup."

"Off we go, then. Yes?"

As crazy as it was, she'd already said yes to this wild ride with him. "Yes."

She watched New York though the car window. The city was gorgeous in the rain. Buildings seemed even taller and grander beneath the turbulent skies. People in dark clothes with umbrellas hurried along the sidewalks. To her eyes, they looked as if they were from a bygone era. Her mind snapped mental pictures. She wanted to paint all of it.

While Ethan checked messages on his phone Holly was aware of every breath he took. Her lungs couldn't help synchronizing each of his inhales and exhales with her own. They were so near each other on the seat her leg rested along his. She detected a faint smell of his woodsy shampoo.

*You'll get used to him*, she told herself. *Soon enough, he won't be so enchanting.*

Ethan touched his phone and brought the device to his ear.

"Nathan. Did you receive my text? Have you made all of the appointments for today?"

He nodded once as he listened.

"Diane—got it. Jeremy—got it. Thank you. Set me up for meetings next week with Con East and the Jersey City contractors."

He looked toward Holly and licked his top lip, although she was sure he didn't realize he had.

"I will be in New York for a while this time. As a matter of fact I have quite the announcement to make at the sharcholders' gala."

A squiggle shot up Holly's back. No one had ever looked at her the way he did.

Ethan sent a sincere laugh into the phone. "All right, Nathan. I suppose I can spare you your beheading. *This* time."

He clicked off the call. "That explains the mystery about the apartment. Nathan had me booked in for the same dates but next month. You were right—it was meant to be yours. But now, to everyone concerned, the apartment is *ours*."

Holly pulled up the collar on her leather jacket as Leonard shuttled them downtown.

Curbside at the first gallery, Leonard helped them out of the car. And then back in as they made their way to the second. And then to the third.

Naturally the staff at each were overjoyed to see Ethan. They reminisced about art openings and museum dedications. Holly felt completely out of place, with nothing to add to the conversations. But she held her own, making intelligent comments about the art on display.

Ethan didn't mention anything about their upcoming nuptials. That announcement was for the gala. Instead he introduced Holly as a friend and painter from Florida whom he had been lucky enough to enlist for an upcoming commission.

Back in the town car again, they munched on the fancy sandwiches Ethan had had Leonard pick up from a gourmet shop. They discussed the paintings they had seen. Holly wanted two, and explained why she'd chosen them.

"If we had more time I'd have my brother send up some canvases that he's storing for me," she said. "If it was really our apartment I'd like to have my own work on the walls."

"I would like that, too," Ethan agreed, with such unexpected warmth it stretched at her heart.

He was masterful at throwing her off-kilter. When

they'd been making breakfast that morning she'd had the feeling several times that he was going to kiss her. At one moment she had desperately hoped he would, while in the next she'd known she must turn away.

Ethan Benton was a bundle of inconsistencies.

Such a precise way he used a paper napkin to brush away imagined crumbs from the corners of his mouth. He was so definite about everything he did. Hobnobbing with gallery people or eating take-out lunch in the car—he did everything with finesse.

It wasn't as if any crumb would dare stick to those glorious lips. Men who showered on planes didn't get food on their faces.

Yet Holly knew there was something damaged underneath all Ethan's confidence and class…

"Can I paint you?"

He contemplated the question as he slowly popped the seal on his bottle of artisan soda.

"You know those drab black and whites of the tree and the flower on the wall?" she went on.

Last night when they'd been critiquing those photographs, flickers had flown between them.

"Flat, corporate…"

"Impersonal," she finished. "That's where I'd hang a painting of you. It would bring personality to the whole room and really make it ours."

"Yes…" he concurred with reluctance. "I suppose it would."

In a flash, Holly understood his hesitation. People were often uncomfortable at the prospect of her painting them. It involved trust. They had to be reassured that she wasn't going to accentuate their pointy nose or, worse still, the loneliness in their eyes.

A good portrait exposed someone's secrets. What was it that Ethan was worried she would reveal to the world?

"Can I?"

"I doubt we could get a painting done in two days' time."

"Let me show you."

Once people had seen Holly's work, she was able to put them at ease. She pulled out her phone and thumbed to her website. "I don't know if you saw these when you were on my site last night. But look. I don't do a typical portrait."

She showed him the screen. "I call them painted sketches. See how they're a bit abstract? And not all that detailed? I would just catch the essence of you."

He whipped his head sideways to face her. "What makes you think you know the essence of me?" he challenged.

Holly's throat jammed at the confrontation. He was right. She *didn't* know him. They'd met yesterday.

But she knew she could get something. Those big and expressive eyes. And, yes, there was some kind of longing behind them.

She might not know him, but she wanted to. This morning at breakfast he had been visibly shaken when she'd hinted at the hardships she'd endured. She had sensed some kind of connection there—a fierce similarity.

She hadn't explicitly told him about the mother who had never consistently provided food for her children. She hadn't mentioned the father who'd come around every couple of years with promises he'd never kept. How Holly had often had to fend for her younger brother and herself.

Yet the damage that dwelled behind Ethan's eyes had made her want to lay her pain bare to him. And for him to lay all his beside hers. As if in that rawness their wounds could be healed.

But none of that was ever to be. They were business partners. Nothing more. Besides, she wasn't going to make herself vulnerable to anyone ever again.

"Never mind." She called his bluff. "I guess we won't

ever find out how much of the real you I could get on a canvas."

One side of his mouth hiked. "I did not say no."

"So you'll let me paint you?"

"I will have you know right now that I have very little patience for sitting still."

"You probably had to sit for family portraits with Aunt Louise and Uncle Mel, right? Dressed up in uncomfortable Christmas clothes by the fireplace? The dutiful family dog by your side? It was torture. You had to sit without moving for what seemed like an eternity."

"I absolutely hated having to hold one position while a greasy bald man who smelled like pipe tobacco painted us."

Flirty words tumbled out of her mouth before she could sensor them. "I promise I'll smell a lot better than the bald man did."

"No doubt."

"And it won't take long."

"I think it might."

Were they still talking about painting?

He lowered the glass separating them from the driver. "Leonard, we are going to change our next stop to Wooster and Broome."

Leonard let them out in front of a painting supplies store the likes of which Holly had never been in before.

She ordered a lot of her materials online, because there were no shops in Fort Pierce that carried fine products like these. When she was low on money she'd make do with what was available at the local brand-name craft store, that also sold knitting yarn and foam balls for school projects.

She cowered at another memory of her ex-husband. As usual, Ricky hadn't wanted to go shopping with her because he thought painting was silly and that she should spend more time going to motorcycle races with him.

Yelling at her to hurry up while she picked out some tubes of paint, Ricky had lost his patience. With a flick of his hand he'd knocked down a display of Valentine's Day supplies. Heart-shaped cardboard boxes, Cupid cutouts and red and pink pompoms had crashed to the floor as Ricky stormed out of the store.

Humiliated, Holly had been left to make apologies and pay for his outburst.

It had been a few months later that she'd caught Ricky in bed with their neighbor. But she'd known that day in the craft store that she couldn't stay married to him.

Now here she was, a million miles away in Soho, the mecca of the American art world, with another man who would never be right for her. Although in completely opposite ways.

Life had a sense of humor.

She chose an easel, stretched canvases in several sizes, new paint and brushes, and palettes and sketchpads, pastels and charcoals. All top-notch. This was the Holly equivalent of a kid in a candy shop.

At the checkout, Ethan opened up an account for her. "That way you can pick up whatever tools and materials you need for Benton projects."

"My goodness…" Her eyes bugged out. "Thank you."

"Of course, my dearest." He winked. "And the next item on the agenda is buying my pretty fiancée some proper clothes."

# CHAPTER FIVE

"WHAT'S WRONG WITH my clothes?" Holly demanded as Leonard helped them out of the car in front of a Fifth Avenue shopping mecca.

"Not a thing. You do the artist with paint on her hands bit quite well. All you need is a French cigarette in your mouth and a beret on your head," Ethan answered.

"Very funny."

He laid his hand on the center of her back to guide her through the store's revolving entrance door. Holly's shoulders perked up at his touch.

"However," he continued as they bustled through the busy sales floor, "there is the shareholders' gala, and then there'll be charity dinners and social occasions we will be attending. As we discussed, this arrangement necessitates an appropriate wardrobe."

When they reached the Personal Styling department, an older blonde woman in a sleeveless black dress and pearls was awaiting their arrival.

"Are you Diane?" Ethan extended his right hand. "My assistant, Nathan, spoke with you earlier."

"It's a pleasure to meet you, Mr. Benton." Diane took his outstretched hand with both of hers.

"This is my friend Holly Motta."

"Oh…" Diane gave her a limp handshake, taking notice of the paint under Holly's fingernails.

"Hi!" Holly chirped.

She was going to have to get used to the surprise in people's voices when they met her. Everyone probably knew Ethan as a wealthy playboy who dated fashion models and princesses of small countries. He'd have no reason to be with a mere mortal like her.

Ethan raised his eyebrows at Holly, which made her giggle and feel more at ease.

He peered straight into Holly's eyes while he spoke to the other woman. "Diane, my friend will be accompanying me to numerous events. She is an artist, with little need for formal clothes. Can you help us outfit her in a way that stays true to her creative and unique self?"

Holly's mouth dropped open. Could anyone have said anything more perfect? He wanted to buy her clothes but he didn't want to change her.

Diane was stunned as well. "Cer…certainly," she stuttered. "Can I offer you a glass of champagne?"

And thus began her trip to Fantasyland. While Ethan sipped bubbly on a purple velvet settee, Diane showed Holly into a private dressing room that was larger than all the fitting rooms in the discount shops she usually went to put together.

Six full-length mirrors were positioned to allow for a three-hundred-and-sixty-degree view. The carpet was cream-colored, as was the furniture—no doubt chosen so as not to compete with the clothes. A vanity table with padded chair was ready for any primping needs. Hats, gloves, scarves and purses had been pre-selected and lay waiting in a glass display case. A collection of shoes stood neatly on a shoe rack. Jackets and coats hung from pegs.

Diane ducked away behind one of the mirrors.

Holly whistled out loud as she took it all in. And then

laughed at her predicament. She'd overheard Ethan talking on the phone in the car about a Diane. And a Jeremy. He had prearranged the gallery visits and now this, too. And Holly had thought *herself* to be the taking-care-of-business type! She could take a lesson from him.

"We'll start with daywear," Diane announced as she wheeled in a rack of clothes.

Besides the fact that there hadn't been any money when she was growing up, Holly had never been especially interested in clothes. She dressed functionally and comfortably, and ended up staining most everything with paint anyway. But if she had ever dreamt of wearing stylish garments made of luxurious materials these would be them.

The first ensemble Holly tried on was a white pantsuit. The slim line of the trousers made her legs look eight feet long. And the coordinating blazer with its thin satin lapels was both distinguished and chic. Worn with a navy silk shirt unbuttoned one notch past prim, the outfit delivered "sexy" as well.

Diane moved in quickly to pin the jacket's waist for a trimmer fit.

She suggested Holly try a brown slingback shoe, then plucked the proper size from a stack of boxes waiting at the ready. Diane might be a bit snobby, but she sure as heck knew what she was doing.

"Perhaps you'd like to add a touch of lipstick?" Diane inquired—a polite way of reminding Holly that she'd need to attend to her makeup and hair.

Diane opened a drawer in the vanity table that contained a palette of options. Holly dabbed on some lip gloss, undid her ponytail and brushed her hair. Surveying herself in the mirror, she knew this was without question the best she had ever looked.

"Shall we show Mr. Benton?" Diane suggested.

When Holly stepped into the waiting lounge that

seemed destined for wealthy boyfriends and mothers of brides, Ethan was busy typing into his phone.

He leaned comfortably back on the settee with one leg crossed over the other knee. Effortless elegance. Although the wavy reddish-brown hair that always had a bit of a tousle to it made sure hints of his untamed side came through.

Ethan glanced up. His eyes went through her and then right back down to his phone.

Holly was delighted as recognition gradually took hold. His jaw slackened. Eyebrows bunched. Nostrils flared.

Only then did his eyes rise up again for the double-take.

And take her in he did, indeed. Ever so slowly. From the tip of her head to the pointy toes of her designer shoes. His gaze was wicked. As if she was standing in front of him naked rather than dressed in this finery. The feeling thrilled and aroused her down to her core.

That smile made its way millimeter by millimeter across Ethan's face. "My, my…"

"So you approve?" she flirted.

"To say the least."

"Do you want to see more?"

Focused on the opening of her shirt, where perhaps that questionable button should have been closed but wasn't, he sighed. "I would most *definitely* like to see more."

She pivoted, and when her face was out of view from him let a satisfied grin explode. This was so much fun. She was long overdue for some harmless fun. *Harmless*, right?

Diane helped her into the next outfit and pinned it for alterations. Another silk blouse—this one black, with a square neckline and a gold zipper down the back—tucked into a tan pencil skirt. The look was dressy, but edgy.

Ethan's reaction was all she could have hoped for as he lingered over the snug fit of the skirt across her hips.

Next, dark wash jeans tucked into boots and a flowing

white blouse were complemented by Holly's own black leather jacket.

"More," Ethan demanded.

A crisp red dress with a pleated skirt, short sleeves and matching belt provided a timeless silhouette.

A silver satin cocktail dress draped her curves without being tight. At the sight of her in that one, Ethan shifted in his seat.

As a kid, Holly had sprouted up early and had always been the tallest girl in her class. She remembered feeling big and awkward. It had taken her years to train herself out of slouching her shoulders forward. Slim, but with hips wider than was proportionate to her small bustline, she'd never thought she wore clothes well.

Until today.

With Diane's wizardry to pinch here and fold there, these clothes looked as if they'd been custom-made to flatter her perfectly.

In all, ten outfits were put together, ranging from casual to semi-formal. Extra pieces would be added to mix and match.

Ethan had promised that no matter what happened with their phony engagement the clothes would be hers to keep. That had meant nothing to Holly when he'd said it, but now she understood how important an offer that was.

In these outfits she was *distinctive*. They made a statement. The woman who wore them was someone to take seriously. These were clothes that were the epitome of good taste, that she could—and would—care for and wear for years to come.

But the *pièce de résistance* came when Diane brought out an evening gown for the black-tie shareholders' gala. Tears unexpectedly sprang in Holly's eyes at the artistry of it. She couldn't fathom *ever* needing a dress so fancy.

It was a pearly sky-blue completely covered in hand-sewn crystals. Holly was surprised at how much the gown weighed. Sleeveless with a deep-scooped neck, it skimmed the floor until Diane had her step into coordinating high-heeled sandals.

Whether the dress complemented Holly's icy blue eyes or her eyes enhanced the dress, it didn't matter. There couldn't be a more perfect gown.

She hoped Ethan liked it.

As she stepped into the lounge to model it for him, she wanted to be sure that she was wearing the gown rather than the gown wearing *her*. Standing up straight, with her shoulders back, Holly reminded herself of what she had learned from the posture correction videos that had helped her rid herself of her slump. Stand tall. Ribs over hips. Hips over heels.

She smiled demurely at Ethan as she approached.

He hiccupped as he almost choked on his sip of champagne.

Holly giggled. She high-fived herself in her mind. *Mission accomplished.*

She cooed, high on a unique rush of power she'd never known she had, "Do you still want to marry me?"

Ethan set his champagne flute down on the side table and cleared his throat. "You have no idea…"

"One more stop and then we will go to dinner," Ethan said as he ushered Holly back into the car.

Leonard shut the passenger door, then went around to slide into his place behind the wheel. He deftly maneuvered them away from the curb to join the Fifth Avenue traffic.

Ethan was thinking ahead. "What else do you need for the gala? I assume you would like to have your hair and makeup done?"

"Please."

"I will have Nathan book that."

Holly held her hands up in front of her. There was often a rainbow of colors staining her fingers and nails, but today it was just the Cobalt Two Eleven leftover from last night's spill. "And I think I need a manicure, don't you agree?"

"The way you look in that gown, I doubt anyone would notice."

No fair for him to say things like that. Things that made her want to lean over and cover his luscious lips with an hour-long kiss. Not fair at all for him to speak words that made her contemplate what it would be like to be with someone who made her feel good about herself. Who was on her side.

Not just for business purposes.

Gridlocked traffic was only allowing them to inch forward. The rain had ceased for the moment but the sky was a thick grey. Throngs of pedestrians rushed to and fro. Some darted across the streets, jaywalking quickly in between cars. Horns honked. Drivers yelled at each other. Music blared from taxicab radios. A siren screamed.

Together, it sounded like a riotous symphony. New York was alive and kicking.

One minute she had been crammed into an economy seat on a packed airplane, headed for the Big Apple and who knew what. And then a minute later she was modeling a jewel-encrusted evening gown for a young billionaire.

A smokin' hot young billionaire who had ogled her as if he not only wanted to see those clothes on her, but also wanted to see them in a heap on the floor beside his bed.

By the end of her fashion show Holly had been imagining it as well. How it might feel to have Ethan's big and no doubt able hands unzipping the zippers and unbuttoning the buttons of those finely crafted garments.

How far would it be safe to go with this charade they had embarked on? Surely not as far as clothes being strewn at the bedside.

Holly was going to have to learn to regally accept a peck on the cheek in front of other people without melting into a puddle of desire. She might have to place a reciprocal smooch on Ethan's face at some point. If push came to shove she might even have to receive a kiss on the lips at, say, the shareholders' gala when their engagement was announced.

She had no idea how she'd handle that, but she would cross that bridge when she came to it. However, under no circumstances would her make-believe fiancé's tuxedo —or anything else of his—end up crumpled at the foot of her bed.

No one would ever see them behind closed doors. And she'd do well to remember that to a man like Ethan Benton this was all just a deal. A game. A con. He'd only go as far as was absolutely necessary to do what he deemed right for his aunt Louise's future.

Holly would keep her eye on the prize. A great place to live, steady work, a leg-up for Vince. That was more than she could have ever hoped for. Let alone on her first day here. That was enough. That was astounding.

"Out." Ethan opened the car door in the middle of the street. "This traffic is unbearable. We will go on foot."

"What?"

He firmly grasped Holly's hand and slid them out of the backseat. "Leonard, meet us in front," he instructed, before thumping the door shut. He tugged Holly. "Come on."

"Where are we going?" she asked as he ushered her to the sidewalk.

"I told you. One more stop."

They joined the masses of legs charging north on Fifth Avenue. New Yorkers during rush hour. Always in a hurry. Always somewhere to go. The air was cold. The pace was exhilarating.

Maybe this would become home. Maybe this enthralling city itself would fill up the emptiness she'd always had inside.

Two blocks later she stopped dead in her tracks. They had arrived at their destination. She looked up to take in the majesty of the Art Deco architecture. The bronze sculpture of Atlas holding up the building's clock. The elaborate window displays.

People were moving in and out of the store's entry doors. Many of those leaving held the light blue shopping bags that were known the world over.

"I do not suppose it would do for my fiancée to wear an engagement ring made from a beer bottle wrapper," he said, and winked.

So he hadn't brought her to a jewelry store to get a ring. He'd brought her to *THE* jewelry store.

Ricky had never given her an engagement ring. They'd waited for a sale at the jewelry store in their local mall and bought the two cheapest gold bands there. It had only been last month that she'd gotten around to selling hers for bulk weight to help pay for her plane ticket to New York.

Now she was standing in front of the most well-known jewelry store in the world! Little blue bags!

Inside, Ethan gave his name and they were immediately escorted to the private salon. A man in a pinstriped suit introduced himself as Jeremy Markham.

Again Holly remembered hearing Ethan on the phone that morning with his assistant, Nathan, mentioning a Diane and a Jeremy. Diane was clothes…obviously Jeremy was jewels. Ethan had everything figured out.

"Jeremy, we will need some help with a wardrobe of jewelry in the weeks to come, but today we would like to choose a diamond ring."

"Of course, sir. May I present a selection?"

Ethan nodded.

A private appointment to pick out an engagement ring? Ho-hum, just an ordinary day.

"Please, sit down." Jeremy, chin up high, held a chair out for Holly after giving her a once-over. Like Diane with the clothes, had this salesman who clearly only dealt with VIPs already figured out that Holly was just one big fake? Another opportunist going after a rich man's money.

Using a key extracted from his jacket pocket, Jeremy let himself into a back room.

Ethan pulled a chair next to Holly's.

"Check these out!" she exclaimed at the glass case to the left of them.

A heritage collection of gemstone jewelry was on display. Elaborate necklaces and bracelets made from pounds of gold and carat upon carat of colorful stones. The pieces were too ornate for her taste, but she was attracted to the hues.

What had really caught her eye was a simple ring of blue topaz. The stone was a large oval cut, bordered on each side by two small diamonds.

"Look at how stunning that ring is. That blue is so brilliant it's blinding. Light is bouncing off it in twenty different directions."

Holly's eyes were light blue, like the stone. It had always been her favorite color from as far back as she could remember. Maybe that was why she'd instantly fallen in love with the sky-blue evening gown Ethan had bought for her.

While it had always been pink for girls and blue for boys Holly, as usual, had swum against the stream. It wasn't as if the trailer she'd lived in with her mom and brother had had any décor to it. The walls had been covered in flowery peeling wallpaper. Sheets and blankets had always been chosen by what was on clearance sale, which had usually translated to scratchy fabrics with dark prints. But Holly could remember a few occasions when her father had been in town for a day or so with some money and bought her new clothes. She'd always chosen items in shades of blue.

"It's just dazzling," she continued, pointing to the ring. "I've never seen anything like it."

Ethan glanced over to it and shrugged his shoulders, indifferent.

Jeremy returned with two velvet trays that held a wide variety of ring styles, all with humongous diamonds.

Ethan whispered to Holly, "We ought to be able to find something perfect amongst these."

She shot one final glance at the astounding blue topaz. "Whatever you say. You're the boss…"

"Feng, we will start with hot and sour soup. Follow that with the chef's special duck, beef with broccoli, shrimp chow mein. And oolong tea."

"Thank you, Mr. Ethan." The waiter bowed and hurried away.

After the jewelry store, Ethan had instructed Leonard to drive them to Chinatown. Now he and Holly were comfortably ensconced in a booth at a casual restaurant his family often frequented when they were in New York.

"I am famished," Ethan proclaimed. "Shopping is exhausting."

With a suitably enormous diamond engagement ring now on Holly's finger, the day's checklist was complete. They had been downtown, midtown, and now back downtown, but he was craving familiar food.

"Do you do a lot of shopping?" Holly questioned.

"I suppose I do my fair share, but it is not an activity I have a feeling for one way or another," he lied.

Watching Holly model one comely outfit after another would rank pretty darn high on his list of pleasurable pastimes. Although a lot of his other work had been accomplished today as well, thanks to the convenience of technology. Securing a fiancée had been at the top of his to-do list.

"Do you…" Holly twirled a lock of her raven hair "…shop for women on a regular basis?"

Hmm…fishing, was she?

"Women have dragged me to find gold in China, the finest silks in India, the best leather in Buenos Aires, if that is what you are asking."

She brushed her bangs out of her eyes and sat up straight. "Oh."

The previous women in his life were a sore point with him. In fact Ethan and women had never been a good combination, period. Going all the way back to his mother. Other than Aunt Louise, every woman Ethan had encountered seemed to him to be one hundred percent selfish. Only out for what they could get. Gifts, money, travel, status—you name it.

Which was why he was resolute that he'd never fall in love. To love you had to trust. And that was something he was never going to be tricked into again.

So it was a logical step for him to dream up this scheme that would allow Aunt Louise to think Ethan had found lifelong love as she had with Uncle Mel. Ethan would never have to marry a woman whose motivation he'd question. Intention, compensation and expectation were all upfront with this plan. It might be the brainiest partnership deal he'd ever conceived.

"Hot and sour soup." Feng placed the steaming bowl on the table. While he ladled out two servings he questioned, "May I ask if Mrs. Louise is feeling better?"

His aunt Louise had been in New York several times in the past few months. Feng had probably seen her more recently than Ethan had.

"Was she unwell when she was last here?"

The waiter pursed his lips and bowed his head, which said more than any words could.

Ethan's heart sank. This validated the fact that he was on the right track. Doing whatever it took to get Aunt Louise to retire and relax in Barbados before worse things than stumbles and bruises stole her dignity.

It was all going to work out.

As long as Ethan continued to stare past but not into Holly Motta's face. Because when he did steal a glance she didn't look like a business proposition. Or a gold-digger out to get what she deemed hers. With that slouch she kept correcting, and that milky skin, and the hint of ache in her eyes…

No, she was a living, breathing, kindred spirit who could shred his master plan into a million slices if he wasn't careful.

"Why are you looking at me like that?" she asked with her spoon in the air.

"Like what?" Ethan threw back his head with an exaggerated nonchalance.

She gave him a mock frown.

"Eat your soup," he told her.

One very ungenteel slurp later… *"Yummo!"*

"We should learn more about each other if we are to be convincing as a couple. You clearly like food."

He mocked her slurp until they were both laughing.

"My turn," she said. "You're an only child."

"You have one brother."

"You studied at Oxford."

"What is your favorite movie?"

Holly dismissed him with a wave of her hand. "Are you kidding me? If we're going to get to know each other we have to get real. What is the one thing that has hurt you the most in your life?"

*His mother.* Of course it was his mother. Nothing could

devastate a nine-year-old boy more than being left behind by his mother. It was horrible enough that his father had died instantly when a drunk driver had plowed into his car at racing speed, killing him instantly. But then shortly after that to lose his mother in the way he had… It was unthinkable.

"Beef with snow peas. Shrimp chow mein. Chef's special duck," Feng announced as he and another waiter positioned the platters in the center of the table. "Please enjoy."

Saved by the duck.

Ethan wasn't going to expose his darkness and despair to someone he'd met only yesterday. As a matter of fact he wasn't in the habit of talking about his feelings with *anyone*. It was better that way.

He scooped a portion of each dish onto his and Holly's plates.

But wasn't it rather amazing that this woman was so genuine she didn't want to discuss trivial matters?

As she lifted her chopsticks to grab at her chow mein he admired the diamond ring he had put on her finger. It was staggering in its size and clarity, and he knew any woman would be filled with pride to wear something so timeless and flawless.

Yet he could kick himself because he hadn't bought her the blue topaz ring she had admired at the store!

Quick thinking had told him to buy the type of ring that was expected of him. Anything other than a traditional diamond engagement ring would invite inquiry. Such as where and why and what sentiments had inspired him to buy such an unusual ring. Those were extra questions they didn't need. It would just add to the risk of them flubbing up as a believable couple.

But now he thought blue ring, purple ring, green ring— what would it matter if that was what she wanted?

Pulsing and vibrant, Holly Motta had careened into his apartment with blue paint on her face and, he feared, had changed his life forever. Forcing him to think about women differently than he ever had. Making him for the first time vaguely envision a role in which he cared if someone was happy. Edging him into speculation about what it would be like if someone cared about his happiness, too.

And now she was making it hard to concentrate on anything other than leaping across the table and planting a kiss on that sweet mouth that was busy with noodles.

After a bite of food to steady himself, Ethan resumed their interview. "Tell me something about yourself that I would not have guessed."

"I used to be—" she blurted, and then abruptly stopped herself. She put her chopsticks down and took a slow sip of her tea. Trying to recover, she finished with, "A pretty good softball player."

*Aha*, so it wasn't as easy for her to be as open and candid as she wanted him to believe it was. What had she been about to say that had proved too difficult to reveal? And what had she avoided telling him at breakfast that morning about the mother she'd characterized as *unpredictable*?

He'd gone along with her easy sincerity, but Ethan really didn't know the first thing about her. He'd garnered that she'd had a difficult childhood, but it wasn't like him to take anyone at face value. Not after what he'd seen of life.

*Guard and defend.*

He had his family's empire to protect.

"Excuse me," he said as he put his chopsticks down and pulled out his phone. "I have just remembered one more bit of business for the day."

He texted Chip Foley, Benton Worldwide's Head of Security. Just as he'd intended to do if he'd hired an actress for the fiancée job.

Chip, please run everything you can on a Holly Motta from Fort Pierce, Florida. Claims her occupation is artist. I would place her age at about thirty. Tall, slim, blue eyes, black hair. She says her brother Vince works for us in Miami. I do not know if it is the same last name. Do an across-the-board check on her for me.

After hitting the "send" button, his eyes returned to Holly.

She pointed her chopsticks at him and taunted, "Hey, you never told me what it was in your life that hurt you the most."

# CHAPTER SIX

IT WAS THE dead of night, but Holly could still hear New York outside the bedroom window. Cars drove by. A dog barked. People laughed boisterously on the street.

The city that never slept.

Lying in Ethan's bed, with her head sinking into his soft pillows, she could hardly make sense of the day. Visiting Soho galleries, buying all those art supplies, a new wardrobe, a diamond ring… Then that dinner in Chinatown.

She'd lived a lifetime in the last twenty-four hours.

Ethan was just beyond the door in the living room. Was he sleeping? Was he working? Or was he lying awake thinking about her as she was of him?

Of course not, Holly reminded herself. Ethan Benton had more important things on his mind then his wife for hire. She'd better remember that.

But when they'd watched each other's faces at the restaurant it had seemed as if maybe she would, in fact, linger in his thoughts and keep him up at night. He'd looked at her as if there was nowhere else he'd rather be. The restaurant might have been crowded and clamoring, but he'd never taken his eyes off her.

Through most of the evening they would have convinced anyone they were an engaged couple. Finishing each other's sentences... Digging their chopsticks into each other's plates...

And then there had been those awkward moments when they'd asked each other questions neither was ready to answer.

Holly hadn't been able to bring herself to tell Ethan that she had been married. She feared he would think of her as a used product and not want to go through with their agreement. He didn't need to know about her mistake in marrying someone who hadn't loved her for who she was. Who hadn't supported the person she wanted to become. Ricky Dowd wasn't a name that *ever* needed to come up in conversation.

They would go through with their pretend engagement so that Ethan could protect his aunt as her health declined. And, as he'd said, either they would continue to meet for official occasions or eventually call off their deal. Whatever happened, Ethan would never have to know about Holly's wasted time on wrong decisions that tonight seemed like a million years ago.

Just as she might not find out what he was hiding because he didn't want to tell her what had caused him the most hurt in his life. It had to be something terrible, because both times when he'd avoided the topic his eyes had turned to coal.

But the rest of the evening was a dream she never wanted to wake from. When they had got to unimportant questions, like favorite movies and television shows, they'd laughed themselves dizzy remembering jokes from silly comedies. Laughed some more about bad childhood haircuts and mean teachers they'd hated in school.

They had stayed long after the restaurant had emptied, until the staff had been ready to leave. Feng had walked them out to the street and waved them goodbye as they'd tucked themselves into the car so Leonard could deposit them home.

Holly drifted off to sleep, replaying over and over again how Ethan had gently kissed the back of her hand and thanked her for an unforgettable day before he closed the bedroom door.

In the morning, Ethan scrutinized his unshaven face in the bathroom mirror. He hadn't laughed as much as he had last night in a long time. Truth be told, he couldn't remember ever laughing that much. Everything was full power with Holly. Near her, he felt alive with a liquid fire.

That might burn down his life as he knew it.

After showering and dressing, he charted a direct route into the kitchen toward the coffeepot.

"Morning," she greeted him.

"Yes."

He was careful not to touch her as he crossed behind her in the tiny kitchen to pour a cup. It took stupendous will not to reach for her, to put his arms around her waist and find out what her hair might smell like if his face was buried in it.

Instead, more guarding and defending.

He gained distance by busying himself with checking the morning's urgencies on his tablet. His approval was needed on important architectural specifications for the Jersey City project. An email chain between several of the interested parties provided updates. Thank heavens for work. He needed the interruption from his growing and wholly off-track desires for more than what he'd signed up for with Holly.

Despite his efforts, his eyes of their own volition kept darting upward from the screen as he watched her lay out a light breakfast of toast and juice.

"Right, then, we have an important day," he directed

as soon as they'd sat down with their food. "Aunt Louise and Fernando will arrive at six o'clock. She does not like to stay out late in the evening. We should have dinner on the table by seven."

"I made a shopping list," Holly reported. "I'll go to the store, then get the pot roast into the slow cooker."

"I have several meetings today. Can you manage the shopping on your own?"

She snickered. "I've been doing the grocery shopping since I was seven years old. I think I can handle a New York City supermarket."

"I am the one who would have trouble."

"But after that I'll need you for the painting. I have the canvas size I want. And I'll use acrylic so it will dry quickly. We'll hang it later this afternoon, and no one will be any the wiser that I only painted it today."

With a busy day ahead, he'd selectively forgotten that he had agreed to her doing a painting of him. He had no time for posing. Although a painting by her would be a very eye-catching and convincing symbol that they were really a couple.

Plus, it would put him in proximity with her from midday. Which he had to admit he'd be looking forward to.

He mentally reprimanded himself for that thought.

In front of the building, Ethan watched Holly walk down the block while Leonard held the car door open for him. Her glossy hair swung to and fro. It was another gloomy day, but dry at the moment. Her jeans and that black leather jacket she seemed to favor would be sufficient for her shopping trip. Why he was concerned with how she was dressed for the weather was baffling. And disturbing.

But what would a Florida girl know about winter? She might catch cold...

Leonard ferried him from one appointment to the next. The low-income housing project in the Bronx was behind schedule and over budget. He pored over blueprints with the architect until they found a way to enlarge the kitchens for the exterior-facing units. The architect was feuding with the contractor over the selection of materials, but that always seemed to be the case. Ethan was able to smooth some ruffled feathers.

He stopped at the hotel where the shareholders' gala would be held on Saturday. Gave his authorization for the layout of the ballroom. Visualizing the room full of formally dressed people, he could picture them raising their champagne glasses as Aunt Louise offered a toast to him and Holly. His bride-to-be would charm the crowd with her engaging smile and shimmering gown…

In the silence of the empty ballroom, Ethan's heart pleaded for something he couldn't fully grasp. A dull ache thudded in the center of his chest.

Swiftly shoving those confusing feelings aside, he hurried out through the hotel doors to Leonard's car and his next meeting.

The multi-use development in Chelsea had come a long way since he'd last seen it. As he strode through he offered dozens of hellos to the many workers laboring on the project's five buildings. It was for this large venture that he'd offered Holly the commission to do the artwork. The opportunity that had sealed the negotiations for her to agree to pose as his fiancée.

Ethan's interior designer had been intrigued to hear about the up-and-coming artist from Florida he had brought onto the job. He had provided Stella with Holly's website address.

Midday, he returned to the apartment. Holly must not have had any trouble with the slow cooker, because the aroma of cooking meat practically had him salivating.

"My, my…" he said as he removed his coat and hung it on the rack.

The open area by the living room window had been turned into a temporary artist's studio.

"I've been working."

"I can see."

The easel they had bought yesterday was unpacked and in use. A side table with a tarp thrown over it for protection had become a paint station. Another tarp covered the area's floor.

"What have you done with my apartment?"

"Hey, I thought it was *my* apartment."

"Tonight it will be *our* apartment."

"Don't worry. I'll clean it all up after I do the painting of you."

"What do we have here?"

Three pastel drawings on paper lay on the floor. Moving vehicles was their theme. One was a bright yellow taxi done in abstracted horizontal lines that made it look as if it was in motion. Ditto for a blue city bus motoring along. And likewise for a silver train car that appeared to be whizzing by.

"I was working out some ideas. Will there be a valet and transportation station at the Chelsea development?"

Of course. He nodded with immediate understanding. Paintings like this would be stylish and hip, and convey the movement of the city. They'd be perfect. Even if their marriage arrangement proved to be the wrong move, Ethan was at least sure he'd hired an artist who would produce what he needed for the multi-million-dollar project.

"Excellent."

"We'd better not waste any time. When can you be ready to sit for me?"

A grin tried to crack at his mouth. "Let me just wash up. Dinner smells delicious."

Minutes later, he stepped onto the tarp of her studio area.

"I am ready for you," he said bravely, with arms outstretched.

In reality, he didn't know what to expect. Was not at all comfortable with how Holly might portray him. He reminded himself that this was ultimately for the good of Aunt Louise. He could put up with a little uneasiness for the sake of her wellbeing.

"I'll have you sitting on the stool." Holly, all business, gestured for him to take his place.

She studied him intently. Backed away to get one perspective. Inched to the side for another. Then came in close. So close he could feel the heat of her body, which made him want to do anything *but* sit still.

"What are you deciding on?"

"The perspective. I think I'll do it at an angle that's a partial profile."

"Will it be only my face?"

She ran a finger across his upper chest from shoulder to shoulder to illustrate the cut-off point. Blood pumped double-time to every inch of him she touched. He instinctively leaned away.

"Don't worry. I won't bite."

His voice came out a jagged growl. "It was not you I was worried about."

She smiled quizzically for several beats. His chest muscles continued to vibrate from her touch.

It occurred to him that for all the questions they'd asked each other about favorite things and childhood memories, they hadn't talked about past relationships.

Had a man broken her heart? Had she broken someone's? Was she looking for love?

Did she wonder about him?

Love wasn't on the bargaining table in their business deal. He'd never loved. Didn't love. Wouldn't love. That was a contract signed a long time ago.

Holly programmed some upbeat music into her phone and began. She wanted to do a preliminary pencil drawing on paper, and when she was satisfied with that move on to paint and canvas.

With a last adjustment to his angle, she requested, "Try not to move."

"Do I need to be silent?"

"I'll let you know when I'm sketching your mouth. Just keep your head still when you talk."

With his face turned toward the window, it was odd to feel her eyes on him when he couldn't see her face. Odd, but spine-tingling. And erotic. He wished he could rip off his clothes and have her paint him in the nude.

Holly made him want to let go of the well-bred and well-mannered businessman he was. With her, he wanted to howl naked under the moonlight. And to ravage her with the savage passion he kept tightly caged inside him.

"Can you soften your facial expression?" she asked, making him realize that he was not masking his arousal.

He neutralized his jaw.

"Tell me about your morning," she coaxed.

He appreciated her trying to help him relax. "There are ongoing issues with my housing development in the Bronx. I want to build the maximum number of comfortable units on the property to give as many families as possible a home of their own."

"What are the problems?"

"Materials are costly. I have shareholders to answer to. And Aunt Louise. I promised this as a break-even project—not one on which the company would lose a lot of money. I may have to move it into the category of charitable endeavor. I will have to present it accordingly. Tricky."

"Here, take a look." Holly unclipped from the easel the large piece of paper she'd been using for her sketch and held it up in front of her for him to see.

After preparing himself to hate it, he saw that it wasn't bad at all. She'd used those same short lines she had on the transportation drawings. Together, the strokes formed the likeness of a pensive man looking into the distance.

Holly's face was flushed. She was nervously waiting for his reaction.

With a voice tight and caught, she squeaked, "What do you think?"

"Is this how I look?"

"Well, obviously you're handsome. I hoped I could convey your seriousness, too."

She'd said "handsome" as matter-of-factly as it would have been to say he was wearing a white shirt. He liked it that she thought he was handsome.

"I suppose I am serious."

"That feels like your core. You're formal. You're measured."

"Whereas *you* just say or do anything that comes into your mind."

"And you don't seem like someone who ever loses control."

Oh, if she only knew the thoughts he was having about grabbing her and showing her exactly how out of control he could be.

She was uncovering wild ideas in him. Holly, with her mesmerizing black hair and sinewy limbs. He'd stripped open more of his true self to her in the last two days than he had with anyone in his life. Not all his secrets, but he'd revealed a lot.

And he must rein that in right now. She only needed to know what was relevant to their phony engagement. Nothing more.

He stood up from his stool to stretch and take a break. Checked messages on his phone. Fired off a couple of texts.

Using a sketchpad, Holly quickly drew more versions

of his mouth until she was satisfied. Then showed him the one that she liked.

"Interesting… It looks as if it is easy enough for you to make a small correction here and there and come out with a quite different result."

She shrugged her shoulders. "I guess so. Trial and error."

"I would not have a clue how to do that."

"I'll show you sometime."

"I would like that."

How absurd this was—letting someone sketch his mouth. In the middle of a workday. When he had a thousand other things on his mind.

But he didn't care. Inexplicably, he wanted to be near Holly. She'd definitely cast a spell on him.

She lifted a large canvas onto her easel and adjusted the height. Then picked out her first brush.

"I'm ready to paint. Let's begin."

"Holly Motta, this is my aunt, Louise Benton." Ethan made the introduction as soon as he'd ushered in the visitors.

With a welcoming smile Holly shook the older lady's hand. "I'm happy to finally meet you. I've heard so much about you."

"And I so little about you…" Louise assessed her. "How pretty you are, dear."

"I'd say the same about you. Let Ethan take your coat."

Holly reminded herself to stay focused in spite of her nerves. At this moment her end of the contract had come due. Louise had to be convinced beyond a shadow of a doubt that not only was she Ethan's true love, but that he had made the right choice in her.

As Ethan helped his aunt to remove her coat Louise almost lost her balance. A telltale sign of her medical condition. How difficult living with a chronic problem like that must be. Still, Louise had style despite her petite and frail frame. A sheet of thin white hair curled under at her shoulders…her simple dark green dress was the picture of good taste.

She was the type of accomplished woman Holly looked up to. Holly was glad she had chosen to wear the black trousers and gray blouse from the new clothes Ethan had bought her. Even though it was dinner at home, these were not people who dined in jeans.

"Such an unusual silver necklace…" Holly initiated conversation.

Louise looked to Ethan. "Yes, my dear nephew brought it back from…remind me where it was from?"

"Turkey."

"Yes, Istanbul. Ethan always brings me unique trinkets from his travels."

With Louise's head turned toward Ethan, Holly noticed the large bruise across her cheekbone. That must have been from the fall Ethan had said she'd taken last week. Holly understood his wish to shield his aunt from the public eye, with her decline so visible.

"Huh…low…oh…" Louise's husband, Fernando, finally insisted on being acknowledged. Ethan hadn't yet taken his coat, and nor had an introduction been made.

"Yes, Fernando Layne—meet my fiancée, Holly Motta."

"Charmed," Fernando replied, without extending his hand.

"Nice to meet you." Holly rocked back on her heels, unsure how to move on if they weren't going to shake hands.

"Are we having cocktails?" Fernando flung his coat to Ethan.

"Let me mix you something," Ethan offered.

"I know where the drinks are." Fernando rebuffed him and headed to the liquor cabinet.

Ethan had told Holly it was Fernando who had bought

this apartment. On behalf of Benton Worldwide and with the company's money, of course. And that he made frequent shopping trips to New York.

Forty-five years old trying to look twenty-five, judging from his slicked-back hair and skinny pants. No doubt Fernando preferred chic New York to less flashy Boston, although Holly couldn't say for sure having never been there. But in an instant she knew that she wouldn't trust Fernando if her life depended on it.

"Louise." Fernando presented his wife with a glass of brown liquor.

She refused. "You know I'm not drinking with the new medications," she said.

"A sparkling water, then." He took the glass and drank it in one tip, then scurried back to the bar to pour Louise some water. Not asking if Holly and Ethan wanted anything.

Fernando's eye caught the painting of Ethan, now on the wall where those impersonal black and white photos had been. "You two have certainly settled in."

Holly bit her lip. *If he only knew.* About her barging in on Ethan just two days ago… That this apartment Fernando thought was his had become part of Ethan and Holly's agreement… How no one in this room knew that her feelings for Ethan were becoming closer to real rather than the masquerade they were meant to be…

"Did you do this, my dear?" Louise moved toward the painting to take a closer look.

It had turned out well, especially for only an afternoon's work. It was all done in blue—a tribute to the paint color she'd had on her face and hands when she had first rushed into this apartment, expecting it to be empty.

She'd probably had more fun than she should have painting Ethan. What an impressive subject he was. With his upright posture. Finely chiseled jaw. The deep, deep eyes with just a hint of crinkle at the outer corners. And his mouth! That mouth! No wonder it had taken her a few sketches until she got it right. Lips not so full as to be feminine. Lips she longed to explore with her own, not with her paintbrush...

"The first of many to come, I hope." Holly slipped her arm through Ethan's in a way she thought a fiancée in love might. His muscles jumped, but at least he didn't bristle and pull away. "Ethan's not keen on sitting for me."

"He never was," Louise agreed. "Didn't we have to bribe you with sweets in order to get you to stay still for those Christmas portraits every year?"

"I told Holly about that crotchety old painter who smelled of pipe tobacco. She is lucky I was not scarred for life."

Conversational banter. *Check*. This couldn't be going better.

"I see you captured that distinctive curl of hair over Ethan's forehead," Louise noted.

That curl had captured Holly—not the other way around. The magnificent way his wavy hair spilled over in front. Just a little bit. Just enough...

It was the one thing that wasn't completely tamed and restrained about Ethan. Somehow that curl hinted at the fiery, emotional man she knew lay beneath the custom-made suits and the multi-million-dollar deals.

"I certainly never learned how to paint or draw," Ethan said, with a convincingly proud smile of approval at his fiancée's handiwork.

While they chatted about the painting Fernando moseyed over to Ethan's desk. Out of the corner of her eye, Holly saw him snooping at the papers on top of it.

Fernando was making himself a bit too much at home. Funny that Holly felt territorial after only two days. She knew that Fernando used this apartment frequently. But he didn't keep any of his personal possessions here because other employees and associates of Benton Worldwide also used it when they were in New York.

Still, she didn't think Fernando had the right to be looking at anything Ethan might have put down on the desk. But it wasn't her place to say anything.

"Louise, would you like to sit down at the table?" Holly suggested.

She took Louise's elbow and guided her toward the dining area. Ethan and Fernando followed suit behind them.

Holly overheard Fernando hiss to Ethan, "I know what you're up to. You've found a wife so that Louise will retire and you can take over. If you think I'm going to spend the rest of her life getting sunburned on a boring island, you've got another think coming."

# CHAPTER SEVEN

"So far so good," Holly said as she placed four plates on the kitchen counter so that she and Ethan could begin to serve dinner.

"Except that I had forgotten how much I detest that little Fernando," he retorted.

Holly was only playing the role of soon-to-be member of this unusual family. She shouldn't be privy to the disagreements and resentments that might lie beneath the surface. So it wouldn't be proper for her to ask Ethan what Fernando had meant about not wanting to move to Barbados when Louise retired. Obviously the comment had made Ethan mad.

She removed the lid of the slow cooker. "Where did they meet?"

Speaking in a hushed voice, because Aunt Louise and her man-toy weren't far away at the dining table, Ethan explained. "Our office manager at Headquarters hired him. His title is 'Client Relations Coordinator,' or some such nonsense. He does scarcely more than order fancy coffees for meetings and come here to New York or go to Europe to spend the company's money. Of course I cannot fire him." Ethan gritted his teeth. "As much as I would like to."

With serving utensils, Holly lifted hearty chunks of the pot roast onto each plate. Ethan reached in with a fork to assist her. They worked seamlessly as a team, anticipating each other's moves. Now pros at navigating the square footage of the small kitchen.

"What does she see in him?"

"Companionship. I suppose he makes her feel younger. She was devastated after Uncle Mel died."

"She must miss Mel horribly."

"They were a partnership in more ways than I can count. Not being able to have children brought them even closer. Taking me in was another thing they did together."

With Ethan having witnessed such a solid marriage between his aunt and uncle, Holly wondered why he was so adamant that he himself would never marry for love. What had happened to close him off to the possibility?

Ethan ladled mashed potatoes while Holly spooned gravy on top. "So Fernando has been able to fill the hole left by your uncle's death?"

"Hardly. He could *never* step into my uncle's shoes. But I will grant that he provides a diversion. Within a year of Uncle Mel's death Aunt Louise began having symptoms of this hereditary neuropathy that she remembers her mother suffering from."

"Losing your husband and developing an illness, one after the other. That's awful."

"She could have sunk into a depression. Fernando at least gives her something to do. He keeps her busy with Boston society dinners and parties on Cape Cod. He will do the same in Barbados. I will remind him that *I* am the boss as often as I need to. We know a lot of people there. He can develop a social calendar for her."

"Give her things to look forward to?"

"Yes. Without children, there are no grandchildren on the horizon. Although I suppose she assumes you and I will have…" He trailed off.

Children. With Ethan.

The mere thought halted Holly in place. A home of her own. Filled with noise and food and laughter and love. Beautiful toddlers running around with reddish-brown tufts of hair falling onto their foreheads. Tall Ethan reaching down to hold little hands.

Did he ever think about having children?

He'd frozen too, holding a spoon in his hand, also lost in contemplation. Was he picturing the same thing?

He'd be a good father. The way he put so much care and thought into his aunt and what was best for her was like the devotion and concern she had for Vince, having practically raised her brother single-handedly because her mother had proved incapable. She had more of that kind of love to give.

Someday.

It wasn't going to be now.

That was much further far down the line. If ever.

No, this current arrangement was ideal. A new life for herself in New York. Not being pulled down by other people. Putting herself first. Free at last.

Everything was upfront with Ethan. There was zero chance of her being hurt. Zero love. Zero disappointment. So he was intelligent and intense? And gorgeous? That was ultimately irrelevant to the duties at hand. They were two professionals, doing their jobs.

Holly used tongs to crown each dinner plate with roasted carrots. Forging ahead. Although she wished her fingernails weren't spotted with paint.

"We did it. Dinner is served."

As she carried two plates to the dining table, she saw Fernando's hand atop of Louise's. The older woman's face did seem to have a livelier blush with his attention on her. Even if Fernando's intentions were less than honorable, Holly could understand the purpose he filled. Life was all about compromises.

Ethan brought the other two plates. While he poured water she ducked back into the kitchen for rolls and butter before sitting to eat.

"Holly, this is delicious," Louise proclaimed.

"I'm glad you like it. You sound surprised?"

"Indeed. I don't know that Ethan has ever dated a woman before who would know how to make an old-fashioned pot roast."

Ethan leaned to pat Holly's arm. She smiled at the unspoken compliment, as a fiancée should. "Aunt Louise, I have never dated a woman who has likely ever eaten pot roast, let alone prepared it."

"Where did you learn to cook like this?"

"I took a course in cooking classic American comfort food," Holly fibbed, without missing a beat. Louise didn't need to know that if she hadn't taught herself to cook she and Vince wouldn't have eaten. "I'll have to make cheeseburgers for you next time."

"Now, Ethan, dear," Louise said, "you have been keeping your delightful lady a secret. You must tell us everything about where and how you met," she insisted.

Fernando buttered a roll and gobbled it down.

Holly and Ethan, the happy couple, gazed lovingly at each other as if to signal that they were off and running. They'd been rehearsing. Now they'd be put to the test.

"Aunt Louise, I wanted to be absolutely sure of myself before I said anything to you," Ethan began. "Holly's brother is Vince Motta. He works for us in the Miami office."

Aunt Louise listened attentively as she continued eating. Fernando chomped on chunks of meat that he yanked off his fork with his lower teeth.

"It was at the groundbreaking ceremony for the Coconut Grove project," Holly continued. For accuracy, Ethan had filled her in on the details of that luncheon. "We were both reaching for the same shrimp on the buffet table. Our hands touched."

"And it was magic."

Ethan fluttered his eyelashes, which made Holly giggle.

She'd visualized this fairy tale over and over—to the point that now she would have sworn it had actually happened. The elegant outdoor celebration… Her in a pink dress, talking to her brother, Vince, and a couple of his coworkers… After excusing herself she left them to explore the lavish seafood table. And just as she reached for the plumpest, juiciest-looking shrimp on the tray a hand from the opposite direction nabbed the same one.

She tugged on her end of the shrimp, the other hand on the other end, until their fingers intertwined.

They turned to look at each other.

He surrendered the crustacean.

The skies parted.

The angels cascaded down from heaven playing trumpets.

"It was love at first shrimp…" They sighed in unison.

"How romantic." Louise was sufficiently charmed.

"We talked for hours that afternoon." Ethan laid it on thick. "But then I had to board a plane for Bangkok."

"We didn't see each other again for months."

Caught up in their "reminiscing," they moved their faces toward each other. Involuntarily. As if pulled together by a magnet.

Ethan bent in and brought his mouth to Holly's. Only it wasn't a feather-soft fake dinner kiss, meant to convince his aunt. No, his unexpected lips were bold. And hot. And they smashed against hers.

Their insistence didn't let her pull away. She swirled inside. Got lost in the moment. Let it go on several beats too many.

Until she could finally separate herself from him.

Holly feared that everyone at the table could hear her heart pounding outside her chest.

Ethan looked as shocked as she felt. But after a moment he picked up his fork and resumed eating. Following his lead, she did the same.

Fortunately neither Louise nor Fernando had noticed anything strange. Holly and Ethan were engaged, after all. Why *wouldn't* they spontaneously kiss?

But he wasn't helping her any with a kiss like that. Let that be a warning to her.

Louise inquired, "Are your people from Miami, dear?"

Holly barely had a moment to catch her breath—nowhere near enough time to recover from that inebriating kiss before there came the next flaming hoop she had to jump through. She didn't have "people." And the people she did have she needed to keep a secret. Her people were not Benton kind of people.

"No. Fort Pierce."

"Fort *Pierce?*" Fernando tossed back.

Certainly not the kind of stylish metropolis full of chic hotels, South Beach beauties and all-night parties that would interest him.

"We met again last year here in New York, when Holly was exhibiting paintings at a Soho gallery," Ethan fibbed to move their story forward.

"Then wasn't the next time when you came down and we visited Key West?"

He leaned over to brush the side of her cheek with the back of his hand. "It was then that I knew for sure."

His tender touch across Holly's face made it a struggle to keep her eyes open. Especially after that not so gentle kiss had rocked her to the bone.

Ethan sensed he had made her uncomfortable. "More water, anyone?" he said quickly, refilling glasses without waiting for an answer.

Thankfully giving her a moment to regroup.

After a couple of quiet sips Holly ventured, "I'm so happy we're finally together in New York. I haven't been here in five years."

Ethan, Louise and Fernando all looked at her.

*Oh, no! Oh! No!*

Fernando's eyes narrowed. "I thought you said you had a painting exhibition here last year?"

*Gulp.* Ethan's soft stroke to her face had thrown her off course. Let her talk before she thought.

Dead silence. Which was finally broken by the sound of a fax coming in on Ethan's desk.

"I meant that I haven't explored the city in years." Holly took a shot. "That was a work trip. I hardly left the gallery."

"Shall we have dessert?" Ethan did his best to defuse the moment.

"Let me help you, dear." Louise slowly rose and followed Ethan into the kitchen.

Fernando kept his glare on Holly one uncomfortable moment longer before he shot up to strut to the liquor cabinet.

Left at the table, Holly stood and began clearing the dishes. Not knowing how badly she had messed things up. Whether Ethan would be furious with her or sympathetic over her flub. Unsure if anyone had bought her quick cover-up.

Louise, even with her reduced ability, had offered to help Ethan with dessert in the kitchen. She must want to say something to him that she didn't want Holly to hear.

Careful not to interrupt Ethan and his aunt's private conversation, she stacked the dirty plates and brushed crumbs off the table. The dessert dishes and silverware were on a side shelf, so she set those out.

The evening had been going so nicely. Louise seemed

to like her. Hopefully Holly hadn't unraveled everything with one slip of the tongue.

With each passing minute Holly had come to like the idea of being Ethan's pretend fiancée more and more. She wanted to make this work. To have the art commission and a place to live. It was a peculiar arrangement, for sure, but a better starting point for a new life than she could ever have imagined. At almost thirty, it was time for her to rewind and reboot. Put the bad choices—Ricky—and the bad luck—her mother—behind her.

When Ethan had sweetened the deal by agreeing to use his influence to help her brother, Vince, get a promotion, Holly had had to roll the dice and give it a try. Ethan had said he couldn't make any promises, but Holly knew Vince was a hard and devoted worker who could easily manage additional responsibilities. She'd never forgive herself if her mistake tonight had done anything to endanger his chances of success.

And, *wow*, she was going to have to lay down some ground rules about her physical interactions with Ethan. She was shocked at how she was drawn to him almost hypnotically, easily touching his arm and lightly laying a hand on the small of his back as if it was no big deal. Like a fiancée would.

But that kiss had shown her how quickly things could go too far. His mouth on hers had dizzied her, made her lose track of her thoughts, forget the company she was in. Ethan's lips were dangerous weapons. They could completely daze her, leave her woozy and unable to do the job he had hired her for.

What she needed was to figure out a system whereby his touch had no effect on her. She'd work that out. This *was* playacting, after all.

The dessert and coffee dishes set, an odd sight greeted Holly when she turned around from the table. Fernando was again in front of Ethan's desk. This time he was peering at the fax they had just heard come through. His eyes widened and he snatched the piece of paper from the machine, folded it and slid it into his pocket. Not noticing that Holly was watching.

Because Fernando supposedly spent a lot of time in this apartment, the fax might be something he was expecting. But it irked her that he was again hovering around the paperwork and personal items that Ethan had spread out on the desk. However, she didn't know all the facts. He was Louise's husband. She couldn't question him even though she wanted to. She was a hired hand who didn't know what went on in this family.

She had already screwed up. Her job right now was to keep her nose down. And do her best to salvage the rest of the evening.

Ethan's arm around Holly's shoulder, they said goodbye to Louise and Fernando as the elevator door closed.

Back in the apartment, Ethan clenched his fist in victory. "Success!"

"Do you think everything went all right? I was so worried. And then I bungled up about not having spent time in New York."

"You recovered. Aunt Louise adored you instantly."

"She did?"

"In the kitchen she told me she could tell right away that you had good character and were not out for our money or the family name."

"If she only knew…"

Ethan mused on that truth.

Together they cleared the remains of the apple crisp and cinnamon-flavored coffee. The kitchen looked as if they had just fed a hundred people. Dirty pots and pans were

strewn on every available surface. The sink was stacked
with plates. Spills puddled on the countertops.

"I will pay the housekeeper triple to clean this tomorrow!" Ethan said.

"Do you want to go out?" Holly asked.

"Out? Right now?"

"Yes. It's not that late. And I'm full of nervous energy."

Ethan contemplated the idea. Aunt Louise had started
to tire so easily the dinner had been over even earlier than
expected. "Where would you like to go?"

"Show me some of the Benton buildings in New York."

He whipped out his phone.

Ten minutes later they were curbside as Leonard pulled
up in the town car. It was a dry but very cold evening.
Holly wore that favorite black leather jacket, and looked
utterly lovable with a red beanie, scarf and gloves. Ethan
didn't bring a hat, but dressed warmly with his own brown
leather jacket and wool scarf.

Once they'd pulled away from the building Ethan recited to Leonard a quick list of addresses and the tour com-
menced. As usual, his driver maneuvered the car deftly
through the always-present Manhattan traffic.

Holly had had the right idea. The crisp night was in-
vigorating.

Or maybe *she* was the cause of the vigor he felt.

She had played her part to a tee at dinner, and he was
sure Aunt Louise suspected nothing of his ruse. How fragile his dearly loved aunt had looked tonight. With those
bruises on her face from the tumble she'd taken—in front
of employees, no less—at Benton headquarters.

He plugged a reminder into his phone to hire an expert
makeup artist for the gala.

But a nagging complication had plagued him throughout dinner. Nothing about the evening had felt fake. Everything had come naturally. From their comfortable banter

to the way he and Holly had served the food together and the electrifying kiss they'd shared while telling the story of how they met.

Moment after moment had passed when he had almost forgotten this was a charade. Worse still, the feeling had filled him with a jarring elation and contentment.

This was new territory and it petrified him. He'd never given serious thought to a real-life real wife, and now was not the time to start. Concentrating on moving Aunt Louise into retirement and moving the company into a more charitable direction was plenty for the foreseeable future. Plus, he had vowed long ago never to be swayed into forgetting one critical fact.

Women were not to be trusted.

Aunt Louise was the only exception in his life. Didn't he know that well enough?

All—and that meant *all*—the women he had ever dated had betrayed him. Society girls, daughters of noblemen and businesswomen alike. They might have approached him as a colleague. Or cozied up to him as the wholesome girl-next-door. Others had come on stronger and seduced him with sexual wiles.

Not that he hadn't gone along with them.

He'd satisfied his urges. Indulged in temptations.

Several of them quite memorable.

Yes, maybe a few of them had made him imagine going past three dates or three weeks. But in the end they had always showed their true colors. They hadn't been who they'd said they were. Even some of their body parts hadn't been real. They had all been something other than what they had seemed. Out for something. A piece of *him*.

And his mother—his own mother—had been the worst offender of them all. That a woman could turn her back on her own son for personal gain was a hurt he'd do well to remember for the rest of his life. Apparently women were capable of the unthinkable.

So, even though his aunt sensed that Holly's intentions were good, he mustn't forget that they were performing in a play. All he could really know was that Holly was a competent actress. Instinct told him that this enchanting woman had a kind heart and honorable aims. But he'd only known her for a couple of days. She might prove herself to be just like the others. And there was plenty she could be hiding. Ethan hadn't received the background probe from his security chief yet.

"This is the Seventy-Fourth Street development we did about a decade ago." He pointed out the window when they reached their first destination. "Leonard, can you pull over to the curb?"

Lit from within, the gleaming glass tower shot upward into the night sky. Ethan leaned close to Holly, beside him in the backseat, to show off some details.

"We did the first story with a wider base, and then the remaining twenty-nine floors in a slender tower coming up in the middle. The larger platform of the first level allows for greenery to encircle building."

"Is the first-story garden accessible?" Holly asked, wide-eyed.

"Yes. It was designed so that employees in the offices can go outside into green space whenever they want."

Their next destination was Forty-First Street.

"This one is over twenty-five years old. It was the last project my father worked on before he died. Here they had the issue of erecting new construction in between two buildings from the nineteen-thirties," he explained.

"New York is amazing like that, isn't it?" Holly seemed to understand him.

"You can see that we did not build right up against the buildings on either side. We created those cement walkways and benches." He pointed. "We built our structure thinner than we might have, so that occupants in the buildings on either side could still see out of their windows."

Ethan was enjoying this tremendously. He was so proud of what his father, Uncle Mel and Aunt Louise had produced. He loved to visit the Benton properties that his father had helped construct. They were all he had left of his dad. Steel, glass and concrete. But they were monuments that would endure for years to come.

They rode downtown to look at a low-rise housing development near the East River. Holly asked a million questions about why a door was placed where it was and what materials had been used for what.

Next was a refurbishment in Greenwich Village from the eighteen-nineties. "We spent a fortune on those windows!"

"They look original." Holly nodded in appreciation.

"That was the idea."

Then Ethan had Leonard park curbside in front of the massive Chelsea construction zone. The steel skeleton columns were up for all five buildings. Architectural renderings of what the finished project would look like were hung on fences and announced it to be "Benton Chelsea Plaza."

"This is all one property?" Holly was surprised by the size of the site.

"Five buildings of living, working and retail space. And I have commissioned a talented and, I might add, beautiful painter to do the artwork for the public spaces."

"The Chelsea project! This is it!"

Despite the cold, she lowered the car window and jutted out half of her torso to get a better view. Ethan bent forward to get an arm in front of her and pointed out some features.

Although he'd make sure Aunt Louise received the accolades, this venture was really all his. He'd made the difficult decisions and agonized over the setbacks. He knew this endeavor would have made Uncle Mel and his father proud if they had been alive to see it. And it would allow Aunt Louise to go into retirement on a high note.

His chest pressed into Holly's back as he pointed through the window. Impulse ordered him to move her scarf aside, so that he could kiss the back of her neck. Sheer will kept him from doing so. But it was being sorely tested in this close proximity.

It wasn't difficult to envision losing power over himself in an instant and laying her down on the car seat, climbing on top of her and delving into her softness. A softness he might not ever be able to return from.

Which was not at all part of their deal.

In fact, that kiss at dinner had been much too much. He himself had been startled by the force of it. He could sense it had unbalanced Holly as well.

He'd only meant to enhance their charade with some harmless and sanctioned affection. Prior to that his "guard and defend" strategy had helped him withstand her casual pats on his arm and his back all evening. Yet his own lips had barely touched hers when they'd begun to demand more, and he hadn't restrained himself in time. That kiss had been out of the scope of what was necessary in both intensity and duration.

His actions had overpowered him—a phenomenon he wasn't accustomed to. Lesson learned.

He forced himself back to describing the project. "For Building One we have leases for three fine dining restaurants and a food court of six casual establishments."

"So all that open space will be outdoor seating?"

"Exactly. And we will have a retractable awning with heating units for the colder months."

"I can imagine it."

He continued telling her about the plaza's features. As

with everything Benton Worldwide built, Ethan hoped to live up to architecture's fundamental principle of providing a building with both form and function for its users.

"I just thought of one other building I would like to take you to see. It is not a Benton property, but I think you will agree it has merit."

"You've brought me to the Empire State Building?" As she and Ethan got out of the car Holly craned her neck up at the monolith.

"As long as we were looking at New York architecture," he said, nodding, "I thought we ought to give this grand dame her due."

Taking her hand, Ethan led her into the Art Deco lobby, with its twenty-four-karat gold ceiling murals and marble walls. "Whew!" she whistled.

"Do you want to go up to the top?" he asked.

"Heck, *yes.*"

But as they rode the escalator up one floor to the ticketing level memory slapped Holly hard.

She didn't mention to Ethan that she had been here once before. With Ricky. They'd come to New York for a long summer weekend. Stayed in a cheap hotel room in New Jersey.

The Empire State Building had been one of the sights Holly had most wanted to see on their trip. The weather had been hot and humid and the ticket lines crowded with tourists. Unlike tonight—late on a winter Wednesday.

Ricky had got impatient. He'd wanted a beer. He'd tugged her back down to street level, found a bar and that had been the last Holly had seen of the Empire State Building.

"Are you nervous about the elevator ride up?" Ethan asked, reacting to what must be showing on her face.

"No! I was just…um…let's go!"

Rocketing into the sky, Holly felt excitement pump through her veins. She was happy to leave old memories as far behind as she was leaving the asphalt of Thirty-Fourth Street and Fifth Avenue.

When they reached the top Ethan guided her quickly through the indoor viewpoints and exhibits to the outside observation deck.

And there it was.

Three hundred and sixty degrees of New York in the dazzling clear night.

It was utterly freezing. Two sorts of chills ran through her—one from the cold and the other sheer awe.

"Oh. My. Gosh." That was all she could say.

The city was so glorious, with the grid of its streets, the grandeur of its buildings and the galaxies of its lights.

They passed a few other visitors as they circled the deck. Holly gawked at Times Square. At Central Park. The Chrysler Building. The Statue of Liberty. The Hudson River.

She begged for a second lap around. "Let's take selfies!" She grinned as she pulled out her phone.

"You look very beautiful," Ethan said in a husky voice. "Your cheeks are pink from the cold."

She sensed him watching her more than he was looking at the views. He'd seen the sight of Manhattan before. It was probably all ho-hum to a global traveler like him. He had seen all the wonders of the world. And was probably amused at Holly's enthusiasm.

But he gamely put his arm around her and they posed to get photos with the skyline behind them, the Brooklyn Bridge in the distance. Holly surrendered the phone to him, to lift it higher than she could. He clicked several shots.

As he handed the phone back to her he kissed her on the cheek.

"I am *so* sorry." He backed away. "I did not mean to do that. I have no idea why I did."

"Maybe because a million romantic movie scenes have taken place right here?"

"Yes, that must be it. My apologies. It will not happen again."

She braved it and said what she wanted to say. "Actually, I'm glad you did. At dinner in front of your aunt and Fernando I got so flustered when you kissed me. I think I'll need to practice physical contact with you until it feels more expected."

She wasn't sure if she had really said that out loud or merely thought it. Rehearse kissing Ethan? That was insane.

"You might be right."

He moved in front of her so they were face to face. With her back to the observation deck's railing. The glistening city behind her.

Her breath sputtered. "In order to be convincing..."

Ethan arched down and brushed his mouth ever so slightly against hers. A wisp of his breath warmed her lips when he asked, "So, for example, you need to practice doing that?"

"Uh-huh," she squeaked out.

Why did he have to be so attractive? This would be much easier if she had become the fake fiancée of an unappealing man who didn't ignite her inside.

Clearly practice was all that was needed. Practice would make perfect. Eventually she'd become numb to him. Kissing would be a choreographed action they'd perform like trained seals.

She was sure of it.

"What about this?" he taunted, and more strength applied a firmer kiss to her lips.

A jolt shot up her back. Her hips rocked forward uncontrollably.

"I… I…" She struggled to take in a complete breath. "I think I need to work on that one."

She tilted her head back for mercy.

Giving her none, he took both sides of her face in his two hands and drew her to him. He kissed her yet again. Harder. Longer.

"Do we need to rehearse this?"

Now he'd opened his mouth. And he didn't stop there. The tip of his tongue parted her lips. Forced her tongue to meet his. Drove her to take. Give. Insist on more.

A dark moan rumbled from low in his gut.

A group of tourists strode past, ignoring them and pointing out landmarks in spirited voices. Holly couldn't see them. Ethan was all she could see.

His hands slid from the sides of her face slowly down her arms to the tips of her fingers. His lips traced across her jaw and then he murmured into her neck, "Do you think an engaged couple might need to kiss like that on occasion?"

"I do," she whispered.

He took hold of her hips and crushed himself into her. Pinned her back against the railing. She stretched her arms up around his neck, going pliant and yielding against the steel of his body.

With New York as her witness, he kissed her again and again and again. Until they had only one heartbeat. Until there could be no doubt in anyone's mind that this was a couple who were deeply in love.

# CHAPTER EIGHT

FLOATING ON A CLOUD. Ethan had heard that saying before but this was the first time he'd experienced what it meant. Yes, his physical body lay on the uncomfortable leather sofa that was too small to stretch out on. But his heart and soul wafted above him in a silken, curvy vision he never wanted to wake from.

Of course, real sleep eluded him. It seemed an utter waste of time when Holly Motta was in the world. Sleep would just be hours and minutes spent away from thinking about her. What if, during sleep, his subconscious drifted away from the cocoon of her embrace? No, sleep was not time well spent. Not when instead he could linger in this half-daze, filled with the memory of her velvety lips on his and her long arms wrapped around him.

Though reality nagged at him.

After that mind-bending interlude of kissing at the Empire State Building they both knew that something unintentional, inappropriate and very dangerous had passed between them. Something they were going to need to backtrack from. To run from. And to return themselves to the "strictly business" contract they had made.

During the car ride afterward they'd chit-chatted about the architecture of a couple of noteworthy buildings along the way. Once they'd got home Holly hadn't been able to get away from him fast enough. She'd emerged from the bathroom in a tee shirt and pajama shorts, poured herself a glass of water, voiced a quick good-night and then rapped the bedroom door closed with her foot.

Ethan hoped that she was in his bed, resting in peaceful sleep. At least one of them ought to be. If he was being honest, he also hoped that she was having sweet dreams about him. Just as he was drifting in his trance about her.

As the endless night wore on Ethan's elation turned to irritation. This was not what he'd signed up for. Lying awake thinking about a woman? *No deal!*

He couldn't afford to have that kind of preoccupation in his life. None of his plans included a woman.

Sure, he could enjoy the company of the exotic and enticing females that his travels put him in contact with. That was a game he could play indefinitely. He wanted something from them that they'd readily give in exchange for a taste of his affluence and the limelight. Then they would want more and he would move on. He knew the routine well.

For all his aunt's prodding, Ethan hadn't ever truly acknowledged the possibility of really devoting himself to someone and building an inner circle with them. A private life together. Not after what he'd seen of the world. Not after his mother.

Blasted Holly! She'd exploded into his life and detonated every stronghold he held.

Worse still, to all intents and purposes he had reached the point of no return with her. He'd already introduced her to Aunt Louise. The gala was in three days. It would be a huge setback to back out now.

There was no choice but to see this through. However, once his aunt had stepped down and was securely ensconced in the warm Barbados sand, Ethan might have to cut the Holly engagement short. He couldn't take much more of this.

Uncle Mel had taught him that admitting and analyzing his mistakes was the crucial first step toward moving forward. Ethan had made a grave error in misjudging his own ability to keep this a purely business transaction.

Or perhaps it was just Holly. He'd chosen the wrong person for the job.

Holly was testimony that his aunt and uncle might be right—that an authentic love might be out there in the world for him. A love that was worth bowing to and sacrificing for. That defined his future and ordered everything else to work around it.

Which was not at all where Ethan was headed.

*Argh!* The road not taken… If only he had stuck to his original plan to hire an actress. She'd have been a consummate professional who knew exactly how to separate reality from performance. Her expertise would have shown him the way.

Just for torture, he flicked on a lamp and snatched his tablet from the coffee table. He clicked onto the website of the talent agency where he had located his original choice. The—unfortunately for him—pregnant Penelope Perkins. The website featured headshot photos of the talent they represented. Tap on the photo and a short bio appeared.

Ethan leaned back on the couch and studied Sienna Freeman. A willowy redhead with a daisy in her hair. An inquiring click told him that she had performed at regional theatres throughout the country, portraying the ingénue in famous American musicals. She looked as if she could have easily been groomed to play the fiancée in Ethan's little domestic drama. A sweet-faced young woman.

Trouble was, she wasn't Holly.

Gabrielle Rivera was a temptress with dark hair and crimson lips. A substantial list of her appearances in television comedies and commercials proved she was capable of working in a wide range of situations. Gabrielle would probably handle herself beautifully at important occasions. A fine choice.

Her fatal flaw? She wasn't Holly.

Glamazon Zara Reed was picture-perfect for a socialite wife. With her blond tresses swept into an up-do, Zara looked born to hang on a wealthy man's arm. Add in her master's degree in psychology and small roles in quirky films, and you had one convincing package. A jaw-dropper.

But—poor Zara. She simply wasn't Holly.

*Enough!* Ethan put the tablet down, turned off the light and attempted his now customary bent position on the sofa. Every molecule in his body screamed Holly's name.

He tossed until dawn, exhausted and annoyed.

Ethan came into the kitchen after he'd showered. Holly was picking at the apple crisp from the baking dish they had managed to stick in the refrigerator last night after Aunt Louise and Fernando had left.

Before they'd gone out looking at buildings. And at each other.

He joined her in scavenging through the mess of the kitchen for breakfast. "Is there coffee?"

She nodded. Once again, the cramped space was making her uneasy. Holly winced at every accidental slide against Ethan's starched white shirt or suit pants as she prepared two cups of java.

There had been quite enough touching him last night. She needed a break.

With him carrying the coffee, she followed him to the table with the apple crisp. She licked bits off her fingers as she folded herself into a chair.

"We could use forks," he suggested, "like evolved humans."

"Sorry if I'm not civilized enough for you."

"I did not say that."

He imitated her by gnawing his own fingerful of the leftover desert. Trying to make her laugh. Unsuccessfully.

Not that he didn't look cute doing it.

"I think it's obvious," she sneered.

Truth was, she was more than a little ticked off at what had happened last night at the Empire State Building. Even though she had asked for it. But how *dare* he kiss her like that if it didn't mean anything to him? That went way beyond the call of duty in this assignment she'd consented to.

Of course she'd had her part in it. She certainly hadn't pushed him away. The opposite, in fact. His kisses had fed a vital nutrient into her body that she had been starved of for so long she hadn't even known she was ravenous for it.

Nonetheless, she was still furious at him for stoking that hunger.

"What I think is obvious…" he paused for a sip of coffee "…is that you are angry at me and I do not know why."

"Welcome to marriage."

"No surprise I have steered clear of it."

She undid and redid her ponytail, buying a moment to regroup. Deciding to be honest.

"We went too far last night."

"I agree completely," he replied quickly.

"You do?"

His kisses hadn't offered any apology. They had been the kisses of a man entitled to his desires, who confidently took them with no cause for second guesses.

"Clearly we need to define the parameters of our physical contact," he stated, as if he was discussing an architectural floor plan. "It is important that we keep any sentiment out of the framework."

Was he admitting that he had felt as much as she had in that transcendental swirl of urgent kisses and intimate embraces? Or was he scolding her for crossing boundaries?

"It's my fault," she said, strategizing. "I asked you for some practice kissing because I don't want us to appear awkward in front of other people."

He took a minute to measure her words, carefully contemplating them before he responded.

"We simply got carried away," he concluded. "We will not do it again."

Inexplicably, her heart crashed to the floor. Which made no sense—because not passionately kissing Ethan Benton again was exactly what *did* need to happen.

"Right…" she granted. Yet sadness ricocheted between her ears.

As a diffuser, she munched on another chunk of the apple dessert.

Clearly no longer interested in the leftovers, Ethan reached for his phone. He ignored her to swipe, read and type.

She looked at her painting of him on the wall. She had never painted Ricky, nor the other couple of men she had dated. None of them had gotten under her skin like Ethan had. Filling her not only with the inclination but with the outright necessity to bring her brush to his likeness.

Ethan was like the multi-faceted diamond she wore on her finger. Every way she turned she saw something new. Something more. Something unexpected. Something unfathomable. She could paint him a hundred times and still not be done.

Eventually he glanced up and observed her, as if maybe he had forgotten she was in the room.

"So. Shall we establish some ground rules?"

"O-okay," she stumbled, unsure where he was going with this.

"I believe we *will* need to kiss on occasion. We will certainly want a convincing display of affection at the shareholders' gala, when our engagement is announced."

Holly braced herself, suddenly unsure if she was really going to be able to go through with this charade. She felt ill-suited to the task. It was too much.

"I think it will be beneficial for us to define what type of kissing is necessary," he continued.

"Absolutely," she bluffed, shifting in her seat.

"For example, I see no need for our tongues to touch, as they did last night."

Well, that was for sure. Her head and heart couldn't afford any more kisses like last night's. The kind that made a girl forget that she was only an employee of the most compelling and sexy man she had ever met. A man who had made it clear that he had hired her to help him protect his aunt, the only woman he'd ever love.

A fact she'd be wise to keep in the forefront of her mind.

Which his kisses completely clouded.

"Got it—no tongues." She nodded once and reached her hand across the table to shake his in a gentlemen's agreement.

Ethan's mouth hooked up as he shook her hand. He was amused by her gesture of sportsmanship.

Except he didn't let go of her hand after the shake. In fact he fought to keep it like a possession he'd battle to the ground for. He turned it over and caressed the tops of her fingers with the pad of his thumb.

"I'd prefer it if you didn't press your body into mine." Holly yanked her hand free and continued. She sparked at the memory of last night's six feet and three inches of solid manpower searing into her.

"How far away shall I stand?" he asked, holding his thumb and forefinger apart as a measurement. "This far?"

"Further than that."

Widening the gap between his fingers, he tilted his head. "This far?"

"At least."

"And would that be all of my body? Or just certain parts?"

Oh, Lordy, he was mocking her.

"Probably all parts." She kept going. "Of course we should have friendly hugs, but nothing prolonged."

"Shall I program a timer?" He smirked.

She lifted her palms in surrender. "Look, it was your idea to lay down some guidelines."

"You are right. I did not realize how ludicrous it would sound stated aloud." He abruptly stood and gathered his phone, tablet, keys and wallet. "For the moment we need not be concerned about our proximity to each other. My schedule today is filled with appointments."

With that, he turned toward the front door. Holly shifted her eyes to spy him putting on his suit jacket followed by his overcoat. He picked up a roll of architectural blueprints that had been propped up beside the door, and out he went.

Holly wasn't exactly sure why a sharp tear stung her cheek.

The left side needed more of the muddy purple she had mixed. Holly dipped thin bristles into the unusual color and applied them to her canvas. When they'd been at the art supply store Ethan had insisted on buying her a full range of brushes—a luxury she wasn't used to. She flicked tiny lines with a brush that was ideal for the task of depicting the rain outside.

Music blared from her phone—a pop singer belting on about how it was time to move on from a man who had done her wrong.

A wild sprawl of buildings and weather… Holly couldn't

decide whether or not she liked this painting. It didn't matter, though. The important thing was the *doing*.

Painting had always been Holly's best friend. It had kept her alive during a tumultuous childhood with an unstable mother and a man she'd called her father whom she had seen so few times she could count them on her fingers. Painting had got her through a disaster of a marriage to a selfish man-child. And then through an ugly divorce.

Painting was her escape. Her entertainment. Her coping mechanism. Her voice. Her salvation.

Early on, her brother, Vince, had found sports. And she'd discovered canvas and color. It was unimaginable where they'd be without those outlets.

In the past few years she had been fortunate enough to have been able to make some money creating artwork for paying clients. But in times of trouble she still picked up her brush purely for emotional release. For safety. For comfort.

Which was what was required now. Because she was disturbed and confused. Art gave her a little bit of a sanctuary in an unpredictable world.

So she had re-created her little studio area after packing it up for Louise and Fernando's visit last night. And she'd got back to work.

As often happened when she was painting, her problems became evident.

She had developed strong feelings for Ethan. And if that wasn't bad enough, she sensed the same might be happening for him.

How he managed to be so volatile while remaining so formal she'd never understand. He was in control of himself, yet there was a barely masked vulnerability there. Manners and restraint mixed with something brutal and pounding.

Those kisses atop the Empire State Building had come

from somewhere organic inside him. Beyond rational intent. That kind of intensity couldn't have been plotted.

In spite of that he would never care for her as anything more than an employee. Plain and simple. Even if he did, he would clamp his emotions down and lock them away as soon as he acknowledged them. He was too strong and too true ever to be swayed once he'd made a decision.

A means to an end. That was all she was to him.

And he to her.

Her phone buzzed.

"Ethan, here."

"Hi."

"I wanted to apologize for making light of your concerns about what physical interaction between us would be appropriate."

"I just don't want to mess up at the gala. I'm worried I'm going to get flustered, like I did at dinner last night. I want everything to go right for you and your plan for Aunt Louise."

"I agree that we could use more training sessions where we are surrounded by other people. I have a charity event to attend tonight. You and I will go together. As colleagues."

That was a terrific idea. She wanted to fulfill her end of the contract and make this arrangement work with Ethan. He was offering her the door into a New York that she could never open on her own. How hard could it be? He'd contracted her for a job that she was capable of doing. She just needed to keep the right mindset, purpose and goals.

An evening as colleagues. *Perfect.*

A couple of hours later the building's doorman knocked and handed Holly a delivery. She thanked him and carried the large white box to the table. Untying the gold ribbon that gave the box the appearance of a gift, she lifted the lid. A notecard was tucked on top of the gold tissue paper concealing the contents.

*Tiny dress. Warm coat.*
*See you at the dock.*
*Ethan.*

She unfolded the tissue to discover a black sequined party dress. It was sinfully short, with thin straps and a scooped back. Holly sucked in an audible whoosh of air. She couldn't believe that Ethan had sent her this sexy slip of a dress. Was this what his *colleagues* wore?

Tingles exploded all over her body.

For all the clothes he had already purchased for her, he must have thought none of them were just right for the charity event he was taking her to tonight.

Anticipation rocketed through her.

The warm coat—cream-colored, in a heavy wool—he had already bought her. The reference to a dock must mean they were going to be on or near a boat. The mystery of it felt hopelessly romantic, even though with Ethan she knew it wasn't. Nonetheless, she could hardly wait until nightfall.

Leonard picked her up at the scheduled time and transported her to the Battery Park dock where Ethan was waiting to open the car door. He extended his hand to help her out of the car. It was chilly, but there was no rain, and she wore her coat open over the new dress. Admittedly to show it off.

"Thank you, Leonard," Ethan called to his driver and closed the passenger door. To Holly he said, after a leisurely once-over, "I knew you would look stunning in that."

Their eyes met. She smiled. The left side of his mouth curved up.

"Shall we?" He offered his bent arm and she slipped hers through. But then he glanced down and stopped with caution. "Oh. Right." He lightly touched her engagement ring. "I generally do not bring a date to events like this.

Because our arrangement—rather, our engagement—will not be announced until the gala, would you mind terribly…?" His voice trailed out.

"No, of course not," she responded, hoping he didn't see the rush of disappointment sweep across her.

She slithered the diamond off her finger. She also hoped that, in the moonlight, he hadn't noticed that she'd been unable to remove every fleck of paint from her cuticles. She'd scrubbed her hands raw, but this was the best she could do. With any luck the stylists he'd hired to spruce her up for the gala would have some magic tricks up their sleeves.

"Shall I keep it?" he asked, and he took the ring from her and secured it in his pocket before she'd had a chance to answer. "I will introduce you as a coworker. We can have the evening to practice being comfortable with each other's company in public and nothing more."

"Exactly."

He presented his bent arm to her again. "All aboard."

As they ascended the gangway, Ethan waved politely to a few people, this way and that.

"Who was that?" Holly asked. "Where are we going?"

"Tonight is a fund-raiser for a private organization I belong to that supports maintenance of the Statue of Liberty as state funding is not sufficient. We will cruise to Liberty Island. The vantage point is spectacular. I think you will enjoy it."

The yacht set off into the New York Harbor, away from lower Manhattan. Champagne was passed on trays. Ethan and Holly mingled with a few guests onboard, sharing mainly superficial banter.

He introduced her as part of his interior design team and she shook a few hands. When they were out of anyone's earshot he instructed, "You can discuss the Chelsea Plaza project. Tell people you are currently analyzing the requirements. That you are handling the art, and much will depend on what materials the furnishings are made of."

During their next chat, around a standing cocktail table, the project came up. Holly interjected with, "We are assessing how people will move through the public spaces."

Ethan subtly nodded his approval. Holly was grateful for the positive reinforcement. She had never interacted with these mega-rich type of people before. Many of them were older than her—men in dark suits and women in their finest jewels. Wall Street leaders, heads of corporations, prominent doctors and lawyers. All of whom, apparently, with their charity dollars, were helping to keep the Statue of Liberty standing proud.

There would probably be many more people like this at the shareholders' gala on Saturday. Ethan had been smart to bring Holly here, so she could get a taste of this world she knew nothing about.

As they ferried closer to Liberty, Ethan led Holly to the yacht's railing to gain the best view.

"She is amazing."

Holly could only gawk up at the massive copper statue, famously green with its patina of age. From the spikes of Liberty's crown—which Ethan had told her represented rays of light—to the broken chain at her feet symbolizing freedom, she was a towering monument to emancipation. And her torch was a beacon of enlightenment.

Lady Liberty seemed to speak directly to Holly tonight. Holly looked into her eyes and pleaded for her wisdom and guidance.

"'Give me your tired, your poor...' Isn't that poem about this statue?" she asked Ethan.

"*The New Colossus* by Emma Lazarus."

"'Your huddled masses yearning to breathe free.'" Holly

had been suffocating in Florida. All her ghosts were there. "Maybe in New York *I* can breathe."

"What has constricted you?"

Making up for her mother's failings, with no father in the picture. Protecting her brother. Appeasing her explosive ex-husband.

"Where I come from nobody thinks big. Everyone is just trying to survive one more day."

Ethan moved a bit closer to Holly. They stood side by side while the yacht circled Liberty, allowing them to observe her from every angle.

"Fate has such irony. I know so many people who have everything," he said, "and yet it means nothing to them."

"Gratitude is its own gift."

He smiled wryly and nodded.

"As I mentioned, after Aunt Louise retires I plan to move Benton Worldwide's new construction solely into housing ventures for disadvantaged people. I like giving houses rather than just money. Because I can supply the knowledge and the labor to build them properly."

Colored lights began to flash on the deck and a band started playing in the dining room. Guests progressed to make their way inside the boat.

Ethan didn't move, and Holly stayed beside him as the boat turned and the tall buildings of Manhattan returned to their view.

"I have seen so much poverty in the world," Ethan continued musingly. "People living in shacks. In tents. In cardboard boxes. If I can help some of them have a safe and permanent home I will have accomplished something."

"You can only imagine what a house might mean to someone who doesn't have one." Holly knew about that first-hand, having moved from place to place so many times as a child.

"In any case…" Ethan shrugged "…for all my supposed

wealth and success, giving is the only thing that is truly satisfying."

Once all the other guests had filed inside, Ethan gestured for Holly to follow him in. At the dining tables they sat with some older couples who were discussing a landscaping project for the grounds around the statue.

When the band began a tamer version of a funky song that Holly loved, she stood and reached her hand down for Ethan's. "May I have this dance, sir?"

Ethan's signature smile made its slow journey from the left to the right side of his mouth. He stood and followed her onto the dance floor, where they joined some other couples.

She faced him and began to swing her hips back and forth to the music. When her hips jutted left, her head tipped right. Then she flung her head left and he hips responded to the right. Like ocean waves, her body became one undulating flow. Back and forth. Back and forth.

The dress was slinky against her skin. She loved how it swung a little with every move she made. From what she could surmise in Ethan's watchful eyes, he liked the movement of the dress, too.

At first he just rotated one shoulder forward and then the other, in a tentative sashay. But after a bit any self-consciousness dissolved and he let his body gyrate freely to the beat of the music.

He had a natural rhythm—just as Holly had known he would. It was part of that primitive side of him—the part he kept hidden away. The part she wished she could access.

Their eyes locked and their movements synchronized until they were undeniably dancing together.

There was no doubt of their attraction to each other. But they were doing a very good job of keeping the evening friendly and nothing more, just as planned.

As a matter of fact, when he had been talking on the

deck earlier, about the good feeling of giving, it had been as if Holly was an old pal he could confide in. Pals were good.

Which was why when the band switched to a slow song Holly turned to leave the dance floor. Slow dances weren't for buddies.

But a strong arm circled her waist.

"This doesn't fit in with our no touching policy this evening." Holly shook her head in resistance.

Ethan pulled her toward him and into a firm clinch. He secured her against him with a wide palm on her back.

Her breath hiccupped. Tonight was supposed to be time off from physical contact with him. After their intimacy at the Empire State Building last night had gone far outside the realm of their contract. Tonight, the last thing Holly needed was to have her face pressed against his neck, with the smell of his skin and his laundered shirt intoxicating her into a dangerous swoon.

"We may as well have a run-through, future Mrs. Benton," he murmured into her ear. "We will be expected to dance together at the gala."

He lifted one of her arms and placed her hand on his broad shoulder. He clasped her other hand in his.

"I don't know if I can do it," Holly protested.

"Surely I am not *that* irresistible."

She laughed, although that was only half funny. "What I meant was, I don't know how to partner-dance."

"Well, young lady, you are in luck. I happen to be three-time champion of the Oxford Ballroom Dance Society."

"Really?"

"No. Of course not."

He began moving and she followed in line.

"But it is not that difficult. Can you feel my thigh leading yours…?"

* * *

When they got home, before they retreated to their separate sleeping quarters, Ethan retrieved the engagement ring from his jacket pocket.

As he replaced it on her finger, he asked, "Holly, would you marry me…again?"

# CHAPTER NINE

"WHO ON EARTH would notice the difference between a napkin color called Eggshell and another called Champagne?" Ethan bellowed to Holly as she made her way across the vast hotel ballroom. "And good morning."

"There's actually a big distinction." Holly jumped right in and snatched the two samples from him. She held one up in each hand to catch some of the room's light. "See—the Champagne is iridescent. The Eggshell is matte. It's a very different effect."

"Thank you for being here."

About an hour ago Ethan had called Holly and asked her to meet him here to finalize the details for tomorrow's gala. Aunt Louise was not feeling well.

"I would call in my assistant, Nathan, but I have him on a dozen other tasks right now."

Ethan's brow furrowed as he remembered yet more specifications he needed to take care of.

"What's wrong with Louise?" Holly inquired.

"She said she felt a bit weak and lightheaded."

"Will she be okay by tomorrow?"

"I hope so. She will stay upstairs today, resting in one of the suites we booked for the week. Fernando is with her. Not that *he* is of any help."

"What do you think triggered it?"

"Rainy weather is especially difficult for her. And, even though she likes to be involved in planning these galas, I think the strain is too much."

He'd feel immense relief once his aunt had retired and no longer bore the weight of continuing as CEO of their billion-dollar company. With any luck she'd be flying in from Barbados for next year's gala, with no cares other than what dress she should wear.

"I'm here to help, Ethan. What can I do?"

Holly's concern softened his tension. He gestured to the table in front of him—the only one in the bare ballroom with a tablecloth on it. Several place settings were laid out for approval, each complete with different options for china, napkins, silver and stemware. There were modern styles, and those that were more ornate. Some in classic shapes, others unusual.

"Can you make these decorative decisions? You are the artist," he said, and added with a whisper, "and the fiancée."

There was no one directly in earshot, but hotel employees bustled about doing their work. With camera phones and social media these days, Ethan wanted to be sure details of his engagement weren't released to the world any earlier than he wanted them to be.

"Oh. Good grief."

"What?"

He pointed to her hand. "The ring again. I am so sorry."

She gamely glided it off her finger, handed it to him and filled her cheeks with air to make a funny face.

"It is ludicrous. I apologize again. Now, Aunt Louise had started to select a certain color palette. She picked out this tablecloth…"

Holly lifted a corner of the linen draping the table and found an identifying label underneath. "This color is called Stone. I like its earthiness. Instead of choosing a lighter napkin, how about a darker one? Can we see samples that might be called something like Pewter or Slate?"

"Sweetheart, you can see anything you want as long as you get this taken care of."

He immediately regretted the endearment. It had fallen from his mouth spontaneously. He supposed that was what he'd need to be doing once they were announced as an engaged couple, so he might as well get used to it. Still, he wasn't in the habit of referring to women by pet names. Holly's widened eyes told him she was surprised by it as well.

Thankfully, one of the hotel's event managers was passing by. Ethan flagged down Priya to come talk to Holly. And to get him out of the moment.

As the two women conferred he stepped away to return a couple of missed phone calls. Which was a bit difficult because the napkins weren't the only things that reflected light from the ballroom's massive chandeliers.

Holly's lustrous hair, flowing freely long past her shoulders, framed her face with a glowing halo. Her sincere smile came easily during her conversation. Sidetracking him from his call to the point when he had to ask his site supervisor on the Bronx project to repeat what he had just said. Which was both embarrassing and unacceptable.

How many reminders did Ethan need that a woman had no place in his life?

She bounded over to him after her consultation with the event manager.

"I hope you don't mind, but I've had a vision. I did go with a pewter napkin. And a minimalist kind of china and flatware..." She rattled off details at a mile a minute. "With a silver napkin ring to give it a sort of elemental look. Earth and metal, kind of thing."

He mashed his lips to suppress a smile, although he was charmed at her zeal.

"And, if it's okay," she persisted, "I thought we could do a sleek centerpiece with white flowers in clear glass vases, to bring in a water element as well. I think it'll all tie together with the lighting." She pointed up to the modern chandeliers with their narrow pieces of glass. "Do you think your aunt would like that?"

"She will appreciate your creativity," he said after Holly's debriefing. "Miss Motta, it sounds like you have a knack for this sort of thing."

She shrugged. "I guess it's just a painter's eye. And at my own wed—"

Ethan's phone rang. He lifted one finger to signal to Holly to hold that thought while he took the call. "Yes, Nathan?"

Holly's cheeks turned pink. She bit her lip.

Something he wouldn't mind doing.

*Sweetheart.* He'd accidentally called her *sweetheart.*

"Schedule me for a late lunch with him next Tuesday at that restaurant he likes on Jane Street. Thank you." He turned his attention back to Holly, "Sorry—what were you saying?"

"Oh. Um… Just that Priya says the tech crew are here if you're ready to go to the podium."

"Come with me."

He took her hand. After taking the few stairs from the ballroom floor up to the stage, Ethan and Holly turned to face the empty event space. Tomorrow night Benton Worldwide Properties would once again fête many of their shareholders with an evening of appreciation. Close to a thousand people—some from nearby, others who had traveled far—would fill this grand room for the annual event.

Holly whistled. "What a breathtaking location for a dinner." She pointed to the large gold wall sculptures that circled the back of the room. "Those give the idea of waves in an ocean, don't they?"

Ethan surveyed the familiar surroundings. "The burgundy carpeting is new this year. It used to be a lighter color. That is about the only change I have noticed."

"You hold the dinner here every year?"

"We have been using this room for as long as I can remember. These galas are as ingrained into my family as birthdays and Christmas are to others."

This year's event wouldn't be a run-of-the-mill evening, though, when his and Holly's engagement was to be announced.

Holly gestured with her head toward the podium on the stage. "Will you be giving a speech?"

"The baton will pass to me next year," he said. Uncle Mel had always given the speech and, after he died Aunt Louise had taken over the duty. "Only a few of us know that this is the last time Aunt Louise will deliver the CEO's report."

Louise's retirement wouldn't be revealed at the gala. Ethan and his aunt had decided that the first step in her exit strategy would be to introduce his fiancée. That would cause enough pandemonium for one evening.

Shareholders could be tricky. They didn't like too many changes all at once. Benton Worldwide had already made them a lot of money by sticking to the original principles Uncle Melvin and Ethan's father had established when they'd started the company with one small apartment building in roughneck South Boston.

So only the engagement announcement would come at the gala. In a month, they'd inform the shareholders in writing that Louise Benton was retiring after a distinguished career. A month after that they'd throw a splashy retirement party.

Tomorrow night would belong to him and Holly Motta. In addition to their proclamation to the shareholders, a press release would notify the world that Ethan Benton had finally chosen a bride. Photos of them would appear in the business sections of newspapers and websites across the planet.

Ethan peered at Holly by his side on the stage. Sudden terror gripped him. What if this masquerade was too risky? This pretty young woman appeared to be genuine and of good will. But what if she wasn't? What if she was like every other woman he'd ever met? Deceptive. Manipulative. Out for herself.

He'd only met her a few days ago, for heaven's sake. It wasn't long enough to put her intentions to the test. And he still didn't know much about her other than what she'd chosen to disclose. Hopefully his head of security, Chip Foley, would get back to him soon with any information he had found. If there was something he didn't want exposed he'd need to figure out how to bury it so that the press didn't have a field-day.

Doubt coursed through him. What if Holly simply wasn't as capable a performer as he'd hired her to be? Maybe she'd crack under the spotlight and the attention. Confess that this was all a set-up, causing Benton Worldwide embarrassment and loss of credibility.

His mind whirled. What had he been thinking? In his haste to plan Aunt Louise's departure from public life before her medical condition diminished her position of respect, Ethan had made an uncharacteristically rash decision. If it was the wrong one his family would pay dearly for it for the rest of their lives.

However, there was no choice now but to take a leap of faith.

"Are you ready for this?" He took Holly's hand, as he would tomorrow. Her fingers were supple and comforting, and immediately slowed his breath.

"I may faint afterward, but I promise to put on a show," she answered amiably, lacing her fingers in his.

"Imagine every table filled with people in tuxedos and evening gowns. Staring at you."

Her shoulders lifted in a chuckle. "Gee, no pressure there!"

Her humor reassured him that she could pull this off. She wouldn't have agreed to it if she didn't know in her heart that she could handle it. And she'd done fine on the yacht last night.

Aunt Louise wanted this one thing for Ethan before she stepped away and let him officially run the company. He was determined to give it to her.

An astute woman, his aunt knew that Ethan's constant travel was to avoid settling down. He didn't have any sustained commitments outside of work. Hardly had a base other than his rarely visited corporate flat near their headquarters in Boston. He dated women—and then he didn't. He spent months alone on a boat. Socialized, then disappeared into a foreign country. He was free. There was nothing to tie him down. He could do whatever he wanted, go wherever he pleased. And he did.

His aunt believed that a fulfilled life took place on terra firma. She wanted him to find a home. A home that would shelter him from the topsy-turvy world of highs and lows, change and disappointment.

Home wasn't a place.

Home was love.

An all-encompassing love that he could count on. That could count on him. That made life worth living day after day. Year after year.

Because of Holly, Ethan had now had a glimpse into what it might be like to coexist with someone. Like he had last night on the Liberty cruise, easily sharing his thoughts and plans and hopes.

But he would stay firm in his resolve to go it alone.

And that was that.

That was his fate.

That was his destiny.

So he'd give Holly to his aunt as a retirement gift. Deliver her on a silver platter. Let the one woman who had ever been good to him hold the belief she most wanted.

But Ethan would not forget the truth.

"Mr. Benton?" A voice boomed from a dark corner of the ballroom. "We'd like to do a sound-check from the podium, if you wouldn't mind."

"Of course," Ethan said to the unseen technician.

Still clutching Holly's hand, he led her to the side of the stage before they parted. His fingers were reluctant to let go. Yet he dutifully took his place at the lectern and adjusted the microphone. Substituting for Aunt Louise, who would be introduced tomorrow to deliver her speech.

"Thank you for joining us this evening at Benton Worldwide Properties' annual shareholders' gala. We are so delighted you are here... Test, test. Test. Testing..."

Ethan dummied through as the technician made adjustments to the sound system.

"Without our shareholders we would not have experienced the global development... Hello, hello. You give us the inspiration... Thank you, thank you. Testing one, two, three."

He turned to wink at Holly. She grinned in response.

"Thank you, Mr. Benton," the technician called out. "Now we'd like to run the video, if you'd like to watch and okay?"

"Will do."

Ethan escorted Holly back down the steps to one of the tables. They took their seats as a screen was lowered from above the stage.

"Hey, do we get to sample the food?" Holly asked. "Quality control?"

"No, that is one department Fernando *is* actually handling. He was here earlier, approving everything with the chefs, before he went to attend to Aunt Louise."

"Rats!" She snapped her fingers, cute as could be.

Which made him want to kiss her.

Which was more irrational thinking he'd need to get a handle on.

Kissing was only for show, when people were watching. No more recreational kissing. The Empire State Building kissing shouldn't have happened. Where he'd thought he might have been able to keep kissing Holly until the end of the world.

His body quirked even now, remembering.

He locked his attention on the screen as the presentation began with a graphic of the company logo and some sprightly music. A slick narrator's voice explained a montage of all the Benton Worldwide projects that had been started or completed during the past year.

In another montage employees were shown holding babies, celebrating their children's college graduations, tossing a football at company picnics.

A historical section flashed older photos—one of Uncle Mel and Ethan's father, Joseph, holding shovels at a groundbreaking ceremony.

"That is my dad." Ethan pointed. His heart pinged as the image quickly gave way to the next photo. Joseph had died when he was nine. Twenty-five years ago. "I do not remember much about him anymore," he admitted.

Holly put a hand on his shoulder. He prickled, but didn't pull away despite his automatic itch to do so.

"Tell me one thing you do remember about him."

"That photo shows him in a suit. I can only think of him in a casual work shirt. Uncle Mel was the businessman. My father was always at the construction sites."

One glimpse of memory Ethan did have of his father was of when he'd come home from work at night. He'd greet Ethan and then head straight to the shower to wash off his honest day's work.

His mother was not a part of that picture. She would sequester herself in her private bedroom before Ethan came home from school, and there she'd stay throughout the evening. It had been a nanny who'd tended to Ethan in the afternoon.

Another older photo had clients at a job site, with Joseph in a hard hat on one side of them and Uncle Mel and Aunt Louise on the other side.

"Do you have any pictures that include your mother?"

"Oh, she was in that shot. We had her edited out. We cut her out of every photo."

Holly tilted her head, not understanding. "Why?"

Now he shook Holly's hand off his shoulder. He couldn't take her touch.

"Because we did not want her in any way associated with Benton Worldwide."

"But *why*?"

"My father and Uncle Mel worked hard for every dollar they made. They earned it. They deserved it. And they were loyal to the people who were loyal to them. Values my mother cared nothing for."

Ethan's blood pressure rose, notifying him to end this conversation. When Holly started to ask another question, his glare shut her down.

Another photo documented him and Aunt Louise in front of a gleaming high-rise building. "Ah, the Peachwood Center in Atlanta. One of my favorites."

The last photo had Aunt Louise surrounded by ten or so Benton executives in front of their headquarters. Even though in reality Ethan had been running the company since Aunt Louise's health had begun to fail, he still made sure that she got all the credit and glory.

"Is everything correct on the video, Mr. Benton?" the technician called from the back of the ballroom.

"Yes—thank you."

"May I trouble you for one more thing, sir? Can I get an okay for sound and lighting on the dance floor?"

Ethan stood and made his way to the polished wooden floor in the center of the ballroom. Fully surrounded by the burgundy carpet and the tables defining the perimeter, the dance floor was its own little world, and it was lit as such with a yellow tint and spotlights beaming down from the ceiling.

"Mr. Benton, we'd like to check the lighting with some movement. Would you be able to find someone to do a quick waltz around the dance floor for me?"

Naturally Ethan gestured to Holly. Stretching out his arm, he beckoned. "So, we dance again."

Holly stood and navigated between the tables in the empty ballroom to reach Ethan on the dance floor. She envisioned what he had described—how tomorrow night the room would be filled with well-dressed shareholders gaping at her. Not giving in to panic, she reminded herself that she was here to do a job. To supply what she'd offered.

A love ballad suitable for ballroom dancing began from the sound system. Ethan started to dance and Holly's body fell in line with his.

He'd taught her well last night, and although she didn't think she could pull off any fancy ballroom dance moves she didn't trip all over his feet.

The lights were so bright on the dance floor that she could hardly see out to the tables. Which didn't matter that much because she really only wanted to close her eyes and enjoy the moment. The croon of the singer... Ethan's sure steps... His rock-sturdy chest...

Dancing with him, she thought they really were a couple—an entity that was larger than the sum of two individuals.

*Ah...* Her head fit so well underneath his chin as they danced. Being tall, she'd always had a sense of herself as being gawky around Ricky and the other men she had dated. She loved being encompassed by Ethan's height and width. As they glided across the dance floor, she felt graceful. A fairy princess. A prom queen. The object of attention.

All things she wasn't.

How would it be tomorrow, with a roomful of guests scrutinizing her? They wouldn't think she was beautiful enough for a man like Ethan! Everyone would know that she wasn't pedigreed and educated. They'd wonder why a Benton had settled for someone as ordinary as her.

Although she would be wearing the magnificent sky-blue gown covered in crystals. That gown alone would convince leaders and kings that she was one of them. Her hair and makeup would be professionally done. The smoke and mirrors tricks would be believable.

She'd hobnobbed with the New York elite last night and no one had guessed that she was not of their social standing. They hadn't known that she'd grown up in a trailer park with an unmarried mother who'd been too drunk to get out of bed half of the time.

Of course at the gala Ethan's fiancée would be under closer examination.

She tilted her head back to study her hand on Ethan's shoulder. Just as she had last night, she actually missed wearing the gargantuan diamond ring that labeled her Ethan's intended. She thought back to the paper ring he had used to propose to her. When he had bent down on one knee with a ring made from a beer bottle label.

And then she flashed back to the shopping spree on Fifth Avenue. To the blue topaz ring she had loved. But

Ethan was right, of course. The ring he'd chosen was one befitting the future Mrs. Benton.

Leaning back further, to look up into Ethan's handsome face, she asked him, "Being in the spotlight doesn't faze you in the least?"

"I suppose I have always been visible to the shareholders. They watched me grow up."

"You came to the galas as a child?"

His muscles twitched. "When I was younger I was kept upstairs in a suite with my mother, who hated these evenings. We would come down and make an appearance."

Holly had noticed that Ethan's voice became squeezed every time his mother came up in conversation. Hints of rage had come spitting out when he'd explained how they had edited her out of all the photos in the slideshow.

"Wasn't your mother obligated to attend?" Holly persisted.

"She would call the kitchen to find out exactly what time dinner was being served. A half-hour before she would trot me down here in a tuxedo. We would do our annual mother-and-son spin around this dance floor. Then she would tug me to the exit, offering excuses that it was my bedtime or that she had a migraine."

"What about your dad?"

"He was not much the tuxedo-and-martini type, but he would soldier through alone. My mother was not gracious, like Aunt Louise. She would not mingle and exchange pleasantries with the guests. Not even to support my father. He knew that she was not an asset to the company."

"Was it awful for you, being paraded around?"

"Not really. I understood at an early age that my mother was not good for business but that I was. Whether it had been a profitable year or a struggle, seeing that there was a next generation of leadership instilled confidence in the shareholders. I have always been proud to represent our company."

"Is your mother still alive?"

"I have no idea," he bit out. "Nor do I care in the least. I have always assumed the shareholders believe that she went into seclusion and retired from public life after my father died."

With that, he tightened his hold around Holly's waist, bolted her against him and guided her with an absolute command that started at the top of his head and ended at the tip of his toes.

Holly molded herself to him and allowed his confident lead. Knowing that talk of his mother had unleashed the beast that he had now locked back into the cage inside him.

As they circled the music got louder, then softer. The low bass tones became more pronounced and then were corrected. Lights were adjusted as well, becoming hotter, then diffused and milky.

"Just one minute more, Mr. Benton!" the technician announced.

The music changed to a swinging standard.

Ethan relaxed his grip and backed Holly away to arm's distance ready for a quickstep. He twirled her once under his arm. She stumbled and they chuckled into each other's eyes.

His head tilted to the side. They leaned in toward each other's smiles. Drawn to each other.

Out of the corner of her eye Holly saw Aunt Louise's husband, Fernando, enter the ballroom and scurry toward them.

When they had come to the apartment for dinner she had noticed the way Fernando walked with small, mincing steps. She hadn't liked how he had snooped at the things on Ethan's desk and taken a fax from the machine. And she had overheard him telling Ethan that he didn't want to spend his life in Barbados when Louise retired.

But at this moment it was important for them to unify for the sake of Louise. Since the older woman wasn't well today, Ethan and Fernando had taken charge of the final details for the gala. Ethan had to be grateful for whatever help Fernando was offering. Perhaps he had a report on the status of the menu…

"I've been trying to call you!" Fernando approached and yapped at Ethan.

Ethan glanced over to one of the empty tables, where he had left his phone while he was on stage at the podium and while he and Holly had danced. "Is everything in order?" he asked.

"No, it's not. Louise has taken a bad fall. I've called the paramedics."

# CHAPTER TEN

ETHAN LED THE charge out of the ballroom and toward the hotel elevators, with Fernando and Holly racing behind him to keep up. When they reached the bronze elevator bank Ethan rapped the call button incessantly until one set of doors opened. Pressing for the twenty-sixth floor as soon as he'd stepped in, he backed against the gilded and mirrored wall of the elevator car.

His neck muscles pulsed. As the elevator ascended he kept his eyes peeled on the digital read-out of the floor numbers.

*One, two, seven, twelve...*

"What happened?" He forced the question out of a tight throat.

"Louise had been resting on the sofa in the suite's living room," Fernando reported. "She stood up and said she was going to make a phone call. Then, as she started to walk, she tripped on the coffee table and fell face-forward."

"Why did you not help her get up from the sofa in the first place?" Ethan seethed.

"She didn't tell me she was going to stand up. She just did it. I rushed to her, but it was too late."

Ethan's jaw ground as he fought to keep himself together. This incompetent idiot should have never been allowed to care for Aunt Louise. She was going to need full-time nurses. He'd arrange that immediately.

The read-out reached twenty-three, twenty-four...

On the twenty-sixth floor, Ethan pushed through the elevator doors before they had fully opened. Holly and Fernando followed. At the room's door, he snatched the key card from Fernando's hand.

Ethan rushed into the suite. "Aunt Louise?"

Louise sat on the floor with her back against the sofa. Angry scrapes had left red stripes across her right cheek and her knees. She massaged her wrist.

"I'm all right, dear," she assured him in a fairly steady voice. "Don't embarrass me any more than I've already embarrassed myself."

"There is no reason to be embarrassed," Ethan said, trying to soothe her. These incidences must be so humiliating for her. She'd always been such an able woman.

"Falls happen," Fernando chimed in. "We've been here before, Louise. You'll be fine."

Ethan fired a piercing glower at Fernando. He didn't need to try to make light of the situation.

"Oh, goodness. Holly!" Louise spotted Holly standing back from them. She managed a dry smile. "Somehow I've become an old woman."

"Thank goodness you weren't hurt worse." Holly nodded her respect.

"At this point we do not know if or how much she is injured," Ethan snapped, angry with everyone. "She needs to be examined."

Right on cue, there was a soft knock on the door. Ethan let in the hotel manager, who confirmed that they were expecting paramedics. Two emergency medical technicians filed in.

One checked Louise's vital signs, such as her blood pressure and heart-rate. He shone a small light into her eyes. Another technician asked questions about her medical history and what had happened.

While that was going on Ethan noticed Fernando pouring himself a cocktail. Holly had noticed too.

He and Holly raised eyebrows at each other. This was hardly a time for drinks.

Ethan clenched his fists and mashed his lips tightly. He stood silently.

Fernando had accused Ethan at dinner the other night of finding himself a wife just so that Louise would retire. Fernando had said he had no intention of spending his life on boring Barbados, as he characterized it, with Louise.

So, following that logic, Fernando should be doing everything he could to try to keep Louise as healthy as possible. Yet he obviously didn't bother with trivial matters, such as protecting her from falling. And now—with paramedics in the room, no less—he clearly thought it was cocktail hour.

"There don't appear to be any broken bones," one of the technicians informed them. "But, given her overall medical condition, we're going to transport her to the hospital for a more complete evaluation."

Ethan brought a hand over his mouth, overcome with worry. This woman had shown him so much love—had gone above and beyond the call of duty for him his entire life. Maybe his caring so much for his aunt was a sign. That he was capable of loyalty. Of devotion.

He refused his inclination to look over to Holly.

The technician issued instructions into his phone.

Fernando walked over to pat Louise gently on the shoulder in between sips of his drink.

"Can we take her down in a private elevator?" Ethan asked the manager, who waited quietly beside the door. "And out through a private garage? Many of our shareholders are staying here at the hotel, and we would like to keep this matter to ourselves."

"Of course, Mr. Benton."

Fernando settled himself closer to where Ethan was standing. "Clever..." he said under his breath. "Always thinking about image. I've got a little surprise for you with regards to that."

Ethan whipped his head to look into Fernando's eyes. "What on earth are you talking about at a time like this?" he demanded.

Two more paramedics came through the door with a stretcher.

Louise protested, "Oh, please, gentlemen—a wheel-chair would do."

"It's for your protection, ma'am."

"I will ride in the ambulance with Louise," Ethan declared.

"No. *I* will," Fernando countered.

"Family only, please," one of the technicians said over his shoulder as he secured Louise onto the stretcher.

"I'm her husband."

"I am coming as well," Ethan insisted.

To the outside eye they must look like an odd sort of family. Elderly Aunt Louise. Nephew Ethan, who was probably being mistaken for her son, and Holly for his wife. Then Fernando, with his tanning salon skin and over-styled hair, who looked exactly the part of a cougar's husband.

The hotel manager headed the pack as the technicians began wheeling the stretcher out of the suite. Fernando and Ethan followed closely behind.

Ethan turned his head back to Holly. "You go home to the apartment."

"I'd like to come to the hospital, too."

Irritated at even having to discuss this further, Ethan

repeated his order. "There is no need for you to be at the hospital. Go back to the apartment."

The hotel manager led them to a private elevator and swiped her access card.

Ethan dashed a text into his phone.

"I could take a taxi and meet you there," Holly pleaded. "I want to be there for you and—"

He cut her off. "I have just instructed Leonard to pick you up in front of the hotel."

This was a private matter that Holly had no place in, despite appearances. While he had certainly become accustomed to having her around, she was still only an employee, and Louise's health was a personal thing. Ethan did not want Holly to overhear any discussions with doctors, or any information regarding a prognosis for his aunt. What Holly had just witnessed in the suite was beyond what his fiancée-for-hire should be privy to.

Ethan feared that he was starting to lose his better judgment around Holly. It was becoming so easy, so natural to let her into his life. If he allowed himself to, he might long for her support at the hospital. He knew it would be hours of waiting and worrying while Aunt Louise was examined.

He had nothing to say to Fernando. Wouldn't sitting with Holly in the waiting area, sharing a paper cup full of coffee, huddled together, be a comfort?

*No!* Once again, he reminded himself of Holly's place in this dynamic. Despite how they might appear, to the paramedics or anyone else, Holly was not part of this family.

Not. Family.

He pointed down the hall toward the public elevator they had ridden up to the suite. "Holly, please return to ground floor and retrieve my things from the ballroom. Thank you."

Louise was wheeled into the private elevator, and everyone but Holly got in.

Just as the doors were closing Ethan saw in Holly's eyes that he'd upset her by not allowing her to come along. But this was no time to focus on her. She should know and respect that.

"I will phone you as soon as I hear anything, all right?" He didn't wait for an answer.

So much for being part of the family.

Holly made it through the car ride home from the hotel, and it wasn't until she opened the door to the dark, empty apartment that tears spilled down her face.

Louise's condition was heartbreaking, and Holly hoped that she wasn't seriously injured after the tumble she'd taken. That she would be able to make it to the gala tomorrow night.

Ethan and Louise had such a finely tuned strategy to keep the extent of her illness hidden from the public. Holly admired their efforts. And thankfully the paramedics were only taking Louise to the hospital as a precaution.

She flipped on the lights. Slung her jacket on the coat rack. Kicked off her boots. And then she allowed in some self-pity. If she ever needed a reminder that this engagement was all a front, she had her proof. She was not, and nor would she ever be, a member of this clan.

Once they'd arrived at Louise's hotel suite Ethan had barely acknowledged her presence. Not that she would have expected him to pay lots of attention to her, but she had to admit she was surprised at how completely he had shut her out.

Holly had offered to go along to the hospital to be there for Louise *and* for Ethan—as a friend who rallied round when maybe a hand to hold would be welcome. But Ethan would have none of it, and hadn't been able to get her out of the picture swiftly enough.

Everything had moved so fast this week. How had she

got here? To feeling sorry for herself because she was left behind? How had she come to care so much for these people so quickly? She'd become so involved in Ethan's life she could hardly remember a time when she hadn't been. Had she forgotten who she was?

Holly Motta was an artist who had spent four long years married to the wrong man.

Ricky hadn't made it easy for her to leave. Even after she'd moved out of the last place they'd been living he'd shown up at her work and insisted on talking to her. Or he'd followed her car and confronted her at a supermarket or in a bank parking lot. It had got to the point that she'd had to change her phone number. Month after month he had refused to sign the legal documents divorcing them, leaving her hanging in limbo. Finally he'd given up and cut her loose.

It had taken her two years to feel truly unshackled from the demanding and possessive hold Ricky had on her. Now she was determined to move forward with her life. This prospect with Ethan had presented itself and she'd snatched it. The job, this apartment, the clothes…the promise of a glamorous escapade with an exciting man.

Nothing wrong with any of that. Life was throwing her a bone, for once. And she was taking it. Life on life's terms.

The problem was the illusion was so convincing that she was starting to buy it.

Twenty-nine years of hurt overtook her. She wasn't tough, like New York. She couldn't endure another defeat. Withstand another wound. Her heart functioned in broken pieces that were only taped together and could collapse at any minute. Maybe this masquerade was too dangerous. She didn't think she had it in her to bounce back from anguish yet again.

Restless, she went to the kitchen. Drank a full glass of water in one gulp. It had been hours since she'd eaten. A few slices of cheese and bread went down easily as she munched them standing up.

She hoped Ethan would get a bite to eat at the hospital. He'd be hungry, too. *Ugh!* She needed to stop caring about things like whether or not he had eaten. Had to break her habit of always looking after people.

She paced back to the living room. Judged the paintings she had been working on in the little studio area she had created by the window. They were a good start to the ideas she had in her head. A drawing pad perched on the easel. She mindlessly picked up a stick of charcoal and began to put it to paper.

After a few minutes she cranked up some funky music and swung her hips from left to right to the beat. A little sketching, a little boogie-woogie—that was always how she got through everything in her life.

Curved lines on the page. A man's jaw. Not square and chiseled like Ethan's. That buzz-cut hair. The thick swash of eyelashes.

A smile crossed her lips.

Small ears. The rounded shoulders. The only person she could count on. Her brother.

Yet she hadn't been honest with Vince about the events of the past few days. She had called him the first night she was here, when the mix-up with the apartment had started everything that had come since. She'd hinted that something had come her way. Vince had reminded her that it was *her* time now. That she should take hold of any prospect life threw at her.

They'd had so little in the way of support as kids. They'd always had to be each other's cheering section.

*Straight up or fall down...* Holly mouthed their childhood chant.

They had been texting every day, as they always did. She'd told him that New York was amazing. That it was mostly raining. But she hadn't told him about this weird arrangement she'd agreed to. Which had become a wild rollercoaster of feeling so right and then, in the next moment, feeling so wrong.

She hadn't even told Vince about meeting Ethan. And she hadn't told Ethan about her rat ex-husband, Ricky. It wasn't like her to keep secrets. But she didn't know where anything stood anymore. She didn't want to make things more complicated than they already were. Even if nothing were to work out for her here in New York, Holly needed to make sure that Ethan kept his word about helping Vince.

Her brother was a good man. She was so proud of him. Every day she hoped and prayed for a bright future for him. That separately, yet bound in spirit, they'd rise up like phoenixes from the ashes of their childhood.

She thumbed her phone.

"Holz?" Vince used his nickname for his sister.

"Vinz!" Holly sandwiched the phone between her ear and her shoulder as she finished drawing her brother's arm. Their builds were so different... It was only in the eyes of their mother where the resemblance was undeniable.

"How's New York treating you?"

"Oh... I kinda got involved in something I thought was one thing but now it seems like it's another."

As in tonight. Which had been reinforcement of the fact that Ethan would never regard her as anything more than a hired hand. That the feelings she'd started to have for him could only lead to misfortune.

"What are you talking about?"

"I don't know... I met a man."

"Well, sis, it's about time you met a man. You haven't dated anyone since you left the Rat."

"I know. But this might not be the right thing."

Somehow she couldn't bring herself to tell him that the man she was talking about was Ethan Benton. The billionaire vice president, soon to be CEO, of the company Vince worked for.

"So you'll move on to something else. We've done that enough times in our life, haven't we?"

"That we have, bro."

How often had their mother made promises? Then broken them.

"Straight up or fall down!" they recited in unison.

"Get some sleep, Holz. You sound tired."

Holly continued sketching after the call. Line after line, listening to song after song. More glasses of water downed in one go.

Finally she sprawled across the sofa and pondered the painting of Ethan on the wall. His mouth... That urgent mouth that had covered hers a few midnights ago atop the Empire State Building. He had kissed her lips. Along her throat. Behind her ear. Her eyelids.

They fluttered with the memory.

The phone woke her up.

"Hello?" Her voice was gravelly.

"Ethan, here."

"How's Louise?"

"Stable. She was not badly injured by the fall."

"Thank heavens."

Holly's eyes didn't want to open fully. The sound of his voice caressed her, but didn't erase the sting of him banning her from the hospital yesterday. Despite wishing he'd make mention of it, she knew he wouldn't.

She had to carry on forward. "What time is it?"

"Eight in the morning."

Tonight was the gala. Her end of the bargain was due.

"Are you still at the hospital?"

"No, I came back to one of the hotel suites to get some sleep. I did not want to wake you by coming in during the middle of the night."

Holly stroked the leather of the sofa where Ethan had been sleeping the past few nights. If he had come home he'd have found her conked out on it after she simply hadn't been able to stand at the easel any longer.

She'd done eight different renderings of Vince. Must have been some sort of homesickness, she mused to herself now, in the gray haze of the cloudy morning.

She stretched her neck. "What happens now?"

"Aunt Louise will be discharged in a couple of hours. Then I will send Leonard to pick you up. He will help you manage my tuxedo and your gown and whatever else you need. We can get dressed in this suite. I have ordered food. And a makeup artist and hairstylist are coming."

"Okay."

Ethan had everything so organized it made her head spin. How did he keep himself together? She needed a shower and coffee.

"Be prepared for a busy day and night," he continued. "I hope you are ready, my fiancée. Because it is showtime."

When the makeup and hair people departed the hotel suite, Holly and Ethan were finally alone for the first time all afternoon.

The last few hours had flown by. People from Benton Worldwide and from their public relations firm had come and gone from the lavish suite that had a bedroom, living room and dining table in addition to the spacious dressing area where they were now.

All of the suite's Zen-like furnishings and décor were made from precious woods and fine fabrics, while floor-to-ceiling windows provided panoramic views of the Manhattan skyline, where the gloomy and rain-drenched day had turned to dusk.

It had been a whirlwind of introductions as Ethan had presented Holly, although of course he hadn't yet revealed their engagement. Members of the shareholders' board of directors had been in to confer with Ethan. And Holly had finally met Ethan's trusted assistant, Nathan—a young man wielding four electronic devices in his two hands.

A sandwich buffet and barista bar had kept everyone fortified. Then the glam squad had arrived to give Ethan a haircut and work their magic on Holly, before filing out just now to do the same for Louise.

In the first quiet moment since she had arrived, Holly inspected herself in the mirror. She wore a white satin robe, but had already put on her jewelry and heels.

Shimmery eye makeup and soft pink lipstick gave her skin a luminous glow. The style wizards had managed to remove every speck of paint from her cuticles, so that a pearly pink manicure could complement the gown. Her hair was magically doubled in volume, thanks to the expert blow-dry she'd just received.

They had experimented with hairstyles, but gave Ethan veto power. Every time she'd asked his opinion of one of the looks they'd tried he had taken a long gander at her. He'd stopped to scratch his chin, or shot her a wink or half a smile. The way he'd studied every inch of her had been almost obscenely exciting.

And seemingly had had little to do with her hairstyle. Because each time he had decreed that he liked her hair better down.

Now she observed Ethan's reflection behind her in the mirror. He was perched on a stool in the dressing area, reading over some papers, already in tuxedo pants and dress shoes. His stiff white shirt was on, but had not yet been buttoned. She imagined her fingers tracing down the center of his bare, lean chest.

This was really happening. She was in this castle of a hotel, about to be crowned as princess and then ride off on a majestic horse with this regal prince.

Of course in real life at the end of the night they'd shake hands on a con well played. But what the heck? She might as well enjoy it.

"Louise was okay when you talked to her a little while ago?"

"Under the circumstances." Ethan didn't look up from his work.

"I have an idea for tonight that might make it easier on her," Holly said as she tightened one of her earrings in front of the mirror.

"Oh?"

"You were telling me that when it's time for her to give her CEO speech you'll escort her from the table up the stairs to the stage?"

"Yes."

"I was thinking it may be difficult for her to walk up the stairs after her fall. And it won't help to have a thousand people staring at her."

"What is the alternative?"

"I noticed that there is a side entrance to the stage from the waiters' station. While the video montage is playing, and it's dark in the ballroom, we could help Louise get away from the table and up to the stage that way. With no one watching her. Then, when she's introduced, all she has to do is come out from the side of the stage and go to the podium."

Holly followed Ethan's reflection in the mirror as he walked toward her. He came up behind her and circled his arms around her shoulders. He hugged her so authentically, so affectionately, she melted.

"Thank you for thinking of that," he said softly into her ear. "Thank you for thinking about it at all. My, my.... You have already gone far beyond what I expected of you. Please accept my gratitude."

She wanted to tell him how horribly it had hurt when

he hadn't let her go to the hospital yesterday. How much she'd wanted to be part of his family, and not just what her obligations required. How she longed to be there for him in good times and in bad.

She still had so much of her heart left to share. Nothing in her past had squelched that out of her.

But she'd never get to give that heart to him.

Even though she was now positive that he was the only man to whom she ever could.

Fearing she might cry, and tarnish her stellar makeup job, she flicked an internal switch and squirmed away from him.

"Can you help me into my gown? It weighs about ten pounds!"

Ethan went to back to the stool he had been sitting on and patted his tablet for music. A smooth male voice sang a romantic song.

Not taking his eyes off her, he drank a sip from his water bottle and then recapped it. "I would love to help you into your dress."

She raced over and punched into his tablet the upbeat music that she favored.

Ethan's grin swept across his lips.

Holly couldn't resist sashaying her hips to the rhythm as she turned and headed to the closet where her gown hung. She was sure she heard him gasp when she let her robe fall to the floor to reveal the skimpy undergarments underneath.

And so the pretend soon-to-be-married couple helped each other get dressed for the gala.

"Careful with the base of the zipper—it's delicate."

"Blast! Do this right cufflink for me. I am no good at all with my left hand."

"I hope this eye makeup doesn't look too dark in the photos."

"I do not know how women can dance in those heels. I am booking you a foot massage for tomorrow."

"Is my hair perfect?"

"Shoulders back."

"How do I look?"

"How do *I* look?"

The supposed future Mr. and Mrs. Ethan Benton exited the suite preened, perfumed and polished to perfection.

Just as they reached the entrance to the ballroom Ethan remembered he had the engagement ring in his pocket. He skimmed it onto Holly's finger.

Yet again.

They entered the gala to a cacophony of guests, cameras and lights befitting a royal wedding.

# CHAPTER ELEVEN

THE BALLROOM VIBRATED with the din of a thousand people. Holly's heart thundered in her chest as Ethan maneuvered them from table to table for introductions. He charmed all the women and the men regarded him with great respect.

"Ethan, how has another year passed already?"

"Lovely to see you, Mrs. Thorpe. Good evening, Mr. Thorpe." Ethan pecked the older lady's cheek and shook the hand of her white-haired husband. "I would like to introduce you to Holly Motta."

Mrs. Thorpe's crinkly eyes lit up. "Well, now, Ethan, are we to believe that you have given up the single life at last?"

"Only because *you* are already spoken for," Ethan said, flattering her.

Holly was dumbstruck and could only squeak out, "Nice to meet you."

She felt horribly out of place. The giddy fun of getting dressed was gone now, and in this moment she felt like a young child in a Halloween princess costume. It was one thing to imagine being the fiancée of a respected and victorious billionaire. But it was another thing entirely actually to be presented as such.

"You look exquisite," Ethan whispered in her ear, as if he sensed her discomfort.

It offered no reassurance.

This wasn't going at all the way she'd thought it would. She hadn't felt this kind of pressure on the yacht the other evening, when Ethan had made small talk with casual acquaintances. The people here tonight knew him well, and she felt as if everyone—but *everyone*—was inspecting her. Panic pricked at her skin like needles, even while her brain told her she must not let Ethan down.

Taking short and fast breaths, she shook hands with a plastered-on smile.

"Henri!" Ethan clasped the shoulder of a mustached man. *"Cela fait longtemps."*

*"Ça va?"*

"Marie. *Magnifique, comme toujours.*" Ethan kissed the man's wife on both cheeks. *"Je vous présente Holly Motta."*

French. Naturally Ethan spoke perfect French. As men who take showers on private planes were likely to do.

As they walked away he told her, "Mr. and Mrs. Arnaud made a substantial personal donation to a low-income housing project we did outside of Paris."

*"Merci!"* Holly threw over her shoulder.

Ethan's eyes always took on a special shine when he mentioned those charity projects that were so important to him.

They approached a stone-faced man whose huge muscles were all but bursting out of a tuxedo that was a size too small. He stood ramrod-straight, with his arms folded across his chest. Holly saw that he wore a discreet earpiece with a barely noticeable wire.

"Holly Motta, this is Chip Foley, our head of security," Ethan introduced her.

Chip bent toward Ethan's ear. "I take it you received that fax with the information you requested, sir?"

Ethan looked confused. "No, I did not."

A Japanese couple were coming toward them.

"Ethan. *Ogenki desu ka?*"

The woman wore an elaborate kimono.

*"Hai, genki desu,"* he answered back.

French wasn't intimidating enough. He had to speak Japanese, too.

The evening was starting off like a freezing cold shower.

Holly had imagined it was going to be easier. And more fun. What girl wouldn't want to be at the ball with the dashing prince she was madly in love with?

Madly. In. Love. With.

The four words echoed through her as if someone had yelled them into her ear. Especially the third word. Because there was no denying its truth.

She was in love with this sophisticated, handsome, brilliant man beside her.

Had it happened the very night she'd arrived in New York, when she'd opened the door to the apartment and found him reading his newspaper with that one curl of hair hanging in front of his eyes?

Had it been when he'd bought her all the painting supplies she'd been able to point to, because took her seriously as an artist in a way that no one else ever had?

Maybe it had been atop the Empire State Building, when those earth-shattering kisses had quaked through her like nothing she'd known before?

Or had it been on the yacht, under the tender shadow of the Statue of Liberty, when they'd danced together as one, late into the night?

It didn't matter.

Because she was in love with Ethan Benton.

And that was about the worst thing that had ever happened to her.

"We should make our way to the table now," Ethan said, after finishing his small talk in Japanese.

He took her hand and led them toward the head table, where Aunt Louise and Fernando were already sitting.

Awareness of his touch was a painful reminder that Holly would never have a bona fide seat at this family table. There would be no keeping the glass slippers. The Ethan Bentons of this world didn't marry the Holly Mottas. She was a commoner, hired to do a job—hardly any different from either a scullery maid or an office assistant in his corporation.

Ethan's world was a tightly coiled mechanism of wheels. She was but one small cog. Loving him was going to be *her* problem, not his.

She willed herself not to fall apart now. Overall, Ethan had been kind and generous to her. She had to hold her end up. That much she owed him. Despite the fact that she was crumbling inside.

Love was awful.

"Louise, you look wonderful tonight." Holly greeted the older woman with a kiss on the cheek.

The style magicians had worked wonders. None of the scrapes and bruises from her fall were visible. No one would guess she wore a wig that was thicker and more lustrous than her own thinning hair. Shiny baubles complemented her black gown.

Holly nodded hello to Fernando who, in return, lifted his nose and looked away.

Fernando sat on one side of Louise and Ethan the other. Holly sat next to Ethan. Rounding out their table were company VIPs whom she'd been introduced to earlier today but couldn't remember their names.

As the ballroom's lights were slightly dimmed a spotlight was aimed on Louise, and a waiter brought her a microphone. Louise stood, subtly using the table for leverage and balance. Holly saw a grimace pass quickly across her face.

"Good evening, Benton Worldwide extended family," Louise greeted the guests. "It's been another profitable and productive year for us, which you'll hear about in my report later. As you know my late husband, Melvin Benton, and his brother, Joseph Benton, began this company with the purchase of a one-bedroom apartment in South Boston. And look where we are today."

The ballroom filled with the sound of applause.

"Together we have made this happen. Melvin taught me many things. The most important of which is that money in our wallets means nothing without love in our hearts."

Louise smiled at Ethan and Holly.

"And so," she continued, "if you'll indulge an old woman before we get on to pie charts and growth projections, I'd like to share something personal with you."

A hush swept the room.

"Many of you have watched my nephew Ethan grow up over the decades. I hope you share in my pride at the man he's become. He's a leader who drives himself hard, a savvy negotiator who insists on fairness, and a shrewd businessman with a philanthropic spirit."

The guests applauded again.

Ethan bowed his head, clearly embarrassed by the accolades. Holly touched his arm. He turned his head slightly toward her.

"Yet there's been one thing missing. It has always been my greatest wish for Ethan that he would find a partner to share his life with. To rejoice with in triumph and to weep with in sorrow. To have a home. To have children. To know a love like Mel and I had. And it's with great joy tonight that I announce that Ethan has found that soul mate. And, although it's asking a lot of her to meet her extended family of one thousand all in one evening, I'd like to introduce you to Ethan's fiancée: Miss Holly Motta."

Ethan and Holly looked at each other, both knowing this was their moment. They rose from their chairs in unison and turned to face the crowd. Holly's chest crackled at the irony of the moment.

Applause and good wishes flooded the room.

"Bravo!"

"Bravo!"

"It's about time!"

"Holly!"

"Ethan!"

They smiled and waved on cue—as if they were a royal couple on a palace balcony. Guests began tapping their knives against their water glasses in a signal for a couple to kiss.

Without hesitation, Ethan leaned in to Holly's lips. Thankfully not with a passionate kiss that would have thrown her off balance. But it wasn't a quick peck either. Perhaps he was incapable of a kiss that didn't stir her up inside.

She felt herself blushing. When she giggled a little the guests cheered.

As planned, the chandeliers were dimmed further and the dance floor became bathed in a golden light. Ethan took Holly's hand and brought her to the center of the dance floor, this time as two thousand eyes fixed on them.

The love song from their practice session boomed out of the sound system.

Holly lifted one hand to Ethan's shoulder. One of his fastened around her waist. Their other hands met palm to palm.

They floated across the dance floor, bodies locked, legs in sync. The moment was so perfect Holly wanted to cry.

It was a moment she would never forget. Yet, in time she must learn to forget, if she was ever to love someone who could return her love.

With the gleam of lights beaming down on the dance floor and the rest of the ballroom darker, it was hard to see. Yet Holly's eyes landed on the table where they had been seated. Ethan turned her as they danced, but she kept craning her neck to focus on a strange sight.

Louise was chatting with a couple who had come over to the table. Meanwhile Fernando finished his drink and stood up. He reached into his tuxedo jacket's pocket and pulled out two pieces of paper. He placed one on the chair where Holly was sitting and the other on Ethan's seat. Then he smirked with a satisfied nod.

Holly was so spectacularly beautiful Ethan couldn't help glancing down at her as they danced. She was really just as fetching—if not more so—casual and barefoot in a tee shirt and jeans, having breakfast at the apartment. But tonight… The dance floor lights cast an incandescent glow on her face. The baby pink of her lipstick emphasized the sensual plumpness of her mouth.

It made him want to brand her with kiss after kiss, until he had to hold her up to keep her from falling to the ground. His body reacted—in fact overreacted—to the intimate feel of her breasts, belly and hips pressed to him as he held her close.

Every now and then the sobering fact that Holly wasn't really his fiancée would flit across his mind. There wasn't ever going to be the wedding, home and children that Aunt Louise had spoken of during her toast. He batted away the reality of those thoughts every time they came near. If only for tonight, he actually did want to believe the masquerade was real.

He could risk that much.

Yet a voice in his gut pleaded with him to stop. Told him that he knew better. That his mission had been to guard and defend. That dangerous fantasies would confuse his intentions and lead to irrevocably bad decisions.

Opposing forces argued within him. So his rational

mind welcomed the distraction when he followed Holly's eyes to the table where they'd been sitting. He watched with curiosity as Fernando placed a piece of paper on his and Holly's chairs.

As soon as the dance was over Ethan nodded politely at the applauding guests to the left and to the right. When the next song began he gestured for others to join in the dancing. Couples stood and approached. Once the rhythm was underway, and the dance floor was well populated, he gestured to Holly to return to their table.

Ethan slipped the piece of paper on his chair into his jacket pocket and sat down, trying not to draw any attention to the action. When everyone was occupied with their first-course salads and dinner conversation, he'd discreetly look at it.

Holly held her piece of paper in her lap. She looked downward to read it.

Her face changed instantly. The rosy blush of her cheeks turned ashen white. The blue in her eyes darkened to a flat gray. She blinked back tears.

Trancelike, she slowly stood.

Her murmur was barely audible, and directed to no one in particular. "Excuse me…"

Fortunately, with the dance floor in full swing and one of the video presentations playing on several screens throughout the room, Holly's exit from the table didn't appear too dramatic.

Ethan watched her cross the ballroom as if she was headed to the ladies' lounge.

Instead she opened a sliver of one of the French doors that led to the ballroom's terrace. She slipped through and closed it behind her.

At the table, Ethan caught Fernando's eye. He grinned at Ethan like a Cheshire cat. Ethan's blood began to boil.

But he kept his cool as he rose. He moved slowly toward the terrace. And slid out through the same door Holly had.

The frigid and windy evening slapped across his face and straight under the fabric of his tuxedo. Holly stood across the large plaza of the terrace with her back to him. He figured she must be chilled to the bone.

What was it that had upset her so much that she'd had to leave the ballroom and retreat to this empty space that was not in use during the winter months?

With dread in his heart, Ethan pulled the paper from his pocket.

His temples pulsated louder with each word he read.

*Fax to Ethan Benton from Chip Foley, Head of Security, Benton Worldwide Properties.*

*Regarding Holly Motta.*

*Per your request, I have gathered the following intelligence.*

*Holly Motta, age twenty-nine, last known residence Fort Pierce, Florida.*

*Internet and social media presence significant only as it relates to her occupation as an artist.*

*No criminal record.*

*Sometimes known as Holly Dowd.*

*Married until two years ago to a Ricky Dowd, age twenty-eight, also of Fort Pierce.*

Married and divorced.

"Holly!" he spat.

Her shoulders arched at the sound of his voice.

She spun around and they marched toward each other. Meeting in the middle of the grand stone terrace.

"You had me *investigated*?" she accused, rather than questioned.

"You were *married*?" he fired back.

"Without telling me?"

"Without telling me?"

"That must simply be business as usual for you, Mr. Benton. Background checks on the hired help and all that."

"As a matter of fact, it is. My family has spent two generations building our empire. We had better damn well protect it with every tool we have."

"You might have let me know."

The hammering at Ethan's temples threatened to crack open his skull as he read the fax aloud.

"'Ricky Dowd, also known as Rick Dowd and Riff Dowd, indicted for armed robbery at age nineteen. Served twenty-two months in prison, released early due to penitentiary overcrowding. Indicted six months ago, again for armed robbery. Currently serving a sentence at Hansen Correctional Facility in central Florida.'"

Ethan broke away from the page to glare at Holly.

"Twice indicted for armed robbery?"

He felt heat rise through his body in a fury that, for once, he might not be able to contain.

Holly's face was lifeless. Her eyes downcast. She didn't even seem to be breathing.

Finally she muttered softly, "I didn't know Ricky was in prison again."

"But you knew who you married." Ethan's jaw locked.

"The first robbery was before we were married. This new incident happened after our divorce. I haven't seen or talked to him in two years."

"Yet you married a convicted criminal? And deliberately withheld that from me? How will that look to my shareholders? Do you not understand the importance of an impeccable reputation?"

Ethan was approaching cruelty. Rubbing salt into her wounds. But he couldn't stop himself.

Women were never who they seemed! Once again a fe-

male had betrayed him. Had not been honest. The same as
every other woman he had known. The same as his mother.

This was exactly what he'd been warning himself of,
despite his growing attachment to Holly. Why would she
turn out to be any different from the others? How dense
was he still not to have learned his lesson?

They'd spent so much time together this week. Yet all
along she'd withheld the information that not only had she
been married, but to someone convicted of serious crimes.
She obviously didn't understand how, if that information
was to be revealed publicly, it would become an integral
part of people's perception of her. Of them.

What else was she hiding? Omission was its own form
of lying. And he'd always known that if this engagement
façade was to work, they'd have to be straightforward with
each other. He'd told her about his future plans for Benton
Worldwide. She knew about his aunt's health problems.
He'd even let her witness Louise being wheeled out on a
stretcher by the paramedics. Without measuring the risks
of his actions, he had, in fact, trusted Holly.

*Trust.* Every year, at every shareholders' gala at this
hotel, Ethan got a reminder that *trust* was a dirty word.
One that he should never factor into an equation. After all,
a boy whose father had just died should have been able to
trust that his mother had his best interests at heart.

To read this background information about Holly, to
confirm that he didn't know her at all, was an unbearable
confusion. Just like the one he'd suffered as a boy, never
really knowing his mother, or what could make a woman
betray her only child.

A familiar fist pummeled his gut more viciously than
ever. He wanted to scream. For the nine-year-old boy who'd
lost both his parents within a few months of each other.
One in a horrifying car accident.

To complicate matters even more, he was also seething

with jealousy that Holly had given her hand in marriage to another man. *Any* other man! Irrationally, he wanted her only for himself.

Ethan clenched his teeth and read on while Holly clutched her own copy of the fax.

> *Brother Vincent Motta, age twenty-six.*
> *Well-regarded employee at Benton Miami office.*
> *Mother Sally Motta, age forty-eight.*
> *Dozens of jobs, ranging from waitress to telemar-keter to factory employee. No position held longer than six months. Never married. Motta appears to be maiden name.*
> *Father of Holly Motta—unknown.*
> *Father of Vincent Motta—unknown.*
> *Unknown whether Holly and Vincent have the same father.*

It was hard to say whose story was sadder—his or Holly's.

Her lower lip trembled uncontrollably until a sob erupted from her throat. "So now you know everything, Mr. Benton!" she cried. "Do you want to share my humiliating past with everyone in the ballroom?"

As tears rolled down her face she shivered in the cold and used both hands to rub at her bare arms.

"I do not know *what* I want to do!" Ethan shouted—uncharacteristically.

He yanked off his tuxedo jacket and wrapped it around her shoulders. "If you had given me all this information at the outset I could have discussed it with my team."

*"Discussed it with your team?"* She pulled the jacket closer around her. "What would you have done? Created a new identity for me? Erased the past? You masters of the world think of everything, don't you?"

"That is exactly what we have been doing, is it not? We have dressed you up and presented you as a suitable bride for me. Which is what we agreed upon in the beginning."

"Yes. Playing dress-up. Pretending someone like me could be *suitable* for someone like you. My mistake, Ethan. I thought we had become more than our contract. I thought we had..." She eyed the ground again. "I thought we had become friends."

He blamed himself for this predicament. It had been insanity to hire someone he'd only just met for this charade. In fact the whole ruse had been preposterous. Paying someone to pose as his fiancée in order to get Aunt Louise to retire. His heart had been in the right place, but he'd had a temporary lapse in judgment.

In fact he'd been deceitful to Aunt Louise. The one and only woman in his life who had always been truthful with him. Although he knew that no matter how big a mess he'd made of everything his aunt would still love him. That he could depend on.

For one of the only times in his life Ethan didn't know what to do. Didn't know how to reckon with all the events of the past few days. Just as he didn't know where to put the decades of shame that had mixed with the years of phenomenal successes.

And he surely didn't know how to make sense of his feelings for Holly. For once he was out of his league.

After a stare-down with her that had them both turning blue with cold, logic set in.

He wondered aloud, "How did Fernando get this fax from Chip Foley?"

Holly explained how she had seen Fernando take a fax from the machine when they'd had him and Louise over for dinner. Because Fernando used the apartment during his trips to New York, she hadn't thought it unusual that he'd receive a fax there.

"That weasel…" Ethan scowled with disgust.

All along Fernando had been conjuring up ways to ruin Ethan's engagement because he didn't want to move to Barbados with Aunt Louise. He no doubt planned to use Holly's history as a way to prove her an unbefitting bride.

"I will deal with him later. We will sort *all* this out later. For now, we will go back inside and finish the evening as planned."

"Okay," Holly whispered, but it wasn't convincing. She looked utterly shell-shocked with his jacket grasped tightly around her. The rims of her eyes were red and her makeup had smeared.

"I will slip back into the ballroom. You will go up to the suite and pull yourself together. I will meet you back at the table."

"Yes," she consented.

Ethan only hoped she'd be able to get through the rest of the night.

Once inside, Holly handed him his jacket and ducked toward the exit. Ethan soon got roped into a conversation with a Swedish architect. He returned to the table just as the wait staff cleared the salad plates. His and Holly's were untouched.

Ethan made small talk with his tablemates as the main course was served. Over and over again the information in the fax repeated itself in his brain. And he kept glancing in the direction Holly should be returning from. It seemed to be taking her an inordinate amount of time.

Guests were enjoying their surf-and-turf entrées of lobster and filet mignon. A pleasant buzz filled the ballroom.

Still no Holly.

Maybe she'd fallen and hurt herself.

Maybe she'd been taken ill.

Maybe she'd been so upset by the fax that she was crying her eyes out.

Ethan had to go find her. But just as he was about to get up the president of the board of shareholders, Denny Wheton, stood from his seat at the next table. A spotlight landed on him. A waiter gave him a microphone.

"Ladies and gentlemen..." Denny began.

Ethan scanned the whole ballroom for Holly, his insides filling with fear that Denny was going to make a toast to them.

"On behalf of the shareholders' board," Denny continued, confirming Ethan's worry, "I want to express our delight at the news of Ethan's engagement. As Louise said earlier, we've watched Ethan become the driving force of Benton Worldwide. His father and uncle would be proud. As to his bride...we haven't had a chance to get to know her yet, but we're sure Ethan has chosen her with the same diligence and discernment he puts into all his endeavors. To Holly and Ethan! Congratulations!"

Guests at the other tables lifted their glasses.

"Congratulations!"

Voices came from every corner of the room.

Ethan froze as a second spotlight beamed onto him. Hadn't Denny stopped to notice that Holly was not in her seat? He'd probably had too much to drink.

"Holly?" Denny called into his microphone.

The congratulations ceased. The room became silent.

"Holly?"

A microphone was handed to Ethan.

Who had to think fast.

"Thank you for your good wishes," Ethan stated robotically.

He'd kill himself if something bad had happened to her.

"I apologize that Holly is not present for this toast. She is feeling a bit under the weather."

"Under the weather?" Denny boomed into his microphone. *"Under the weather? Will Benton Worldwide be introducing the next generation's CEO nine months from now?"*

The ballroom exploded with applause and cheers.

# CHAPTER TWELVE

HOLLY HAD NEVER been so relieved to be home in her entire life. She toed the apartment door closed and leaned back against it. With a deep sigh she dropped the couple of bags she had retrieved from the hotel suite before catching a taxi.

She closed her eyes for a few breaths, hoping to shut out all that had happened.

When she opened them again everything was still the same.

Only she had made matters worse by running away from Ethan and the gala.

En route to the bedroom, she heard her crystal gown swish audibly in the quiet of the apartment. A sound that hadn't been heard under all the activity at the gala. The sky-high heels were killing her, so they were quickly nudged off.

It was a struggle to reach the zipper of her dress. Much nicer earlier tonight, when Ethan had zipped her in. Eventually she was carefully able to wriggle out of the dress. Her impulse was to leave it pooled on the floor, but the adult in her at least managed to put it on the bed.

This gown wasn't her life.

Her jeans and tee shirt were familiar friends.

This wasn't her home.

It was time to go.

Time to cut her losses.

Holly had too much experience with that. Her marriage. Her mother. False hopes and grand promises that hadn't panned out. This was simply another.

With her tail between her legs, it was time to take two steps backward and keep striving for that next step ahead.

Sure, memories of New York would sting. Memories of Ethan would slice deeper than any wounds she'd ever endured before. But she was no stranger to pain.

Besides, she was supposed to be working on herself. Not getting mixed up in someone else's priorities. Not falling in love. This was the wrong road. Time to change direction.

Packing her clothes took less time than she'd thought it would. It was still the middle of the night. With plans to leave in the morning, she paced the apartment.

In the living room, the paper ring Ethan had made from his beer bottle label still sat on the coffee table. The one he'd used to propose to her with. When he had asked her to embark on a business venture that was *not* to become a matter of the heart. For the moment she still wore the enormous diamond that had been on and off her finger all week.

Holly rolled the ring round and round on her finger. She thought about the symbolism of rings—how the circle could never be broken. It had no beginning and it had no end. Continuous. Lasting. Eternal.

Undying love was *not* her and Ethan's story.

Their tale was of two people who had crossed paths in a New York City apartment. Now they both needed to continue on their separate journeys. Ethan built skyscrapers, but was determined not to build love. Holly had a past she could never escape.

His investigation into her hadn't even uncovered all her dirty laundry. He hadn't found out that she wasn't sure if the man who'd shown up every few years while she was growing up was really her father. Despite her mother's insistence that he was.

Wayne had been nice enough to her and Vince when he'd pass through town. He'd take them to get some cheap clothes that he'd pay for with a short fold of twenty-dollar bills he'd pull from his front pants pocket. Then they'd be shuffled off to a neighbor's house so that he could spend time alone with their mother.

Neither Holly nor Vince looked like him. But nor did they look like each other. It wasn't something they talked about much. They couldn't be any closer than they already were. What difference did it make? They could have DNA testing, but it wouldn't matter.

So she had never known whether she and her brother were half or full siblings. Or who their father—or fathers—were. They shared the same eyes as their mother. That was all Holly could be sure of.

Sally's blue eyes had been cloudy and bloodshot the last time Holly had seen her, five years ago.

*Vince!* Sorrow rained down on her. Her actions— lashing out at Ethan about the investigation and then abruptly leaving the gala without a word to him or to Louise— would cast an unprofessional shadow on Vince.

Her knees buckled and she sank down to the edge of a chair, vowing never to forgive herself if she had ruined her brother's chances at the promotion he'd worked so hard for.

Head in hands, she began to cry for all she and Vince had lacked when they were children. Not just material things, but adults to provide the care that every child needed. As much as they had looked out for each other, they'd always have holes in their hearts.

She wept for this week—for this failed chance to catapult her career to a potential high. For this lost opportunity to turn her goals into reality.

And she sobbed because she'd unexpectedly found a love in Ethan truer than any she could have imagined.

A love that the crux of her knew she would never have again. But she wasn't able to claim it.

Numbly, she picked up her phone. "Vinz...?"

"What's wrong?"

Only her brother would know after one syllable that she was shattered.

With the back of her hand she wiped the tears from her face. "I guess New York is not how I thought it would be."

"You wouldn't be the first person to say that."

"The thing is, I sort of think I've let you down."

Holly stopped herself there. She didn't have to explain everything right now. Maybe Ethan wouldn't hold all this against Vince. At this point she didn't have any control over the situation. All she had was regrets.

"Why would you have let me down? Because you took a shot and it didn't pan out? At least you did it."

"I'm just licking my wounds. I want to come home."

Where was home? She'd given up her dingy apartment in Fort Pierce to pin everything on her future. Neither she nor Vince had any current information on their mother's whereabouts.

"Fly here to Miami. My garage is yours to paint in. And my sofa bed has your name on it. I'll pick you up at the airport."

After the call, Holly took inventory of the mini art studio she'd set up by the window. Methodically she cleaned brushes. Tucked sketches into portfolios. She organized neatly, remembering the open tube of paint that had started this magical ride in New York. Cobalt Two Eleven all over her face.

Her gaze darted to the blue-painted sketch of Ethan on the wall. She was so proud of that piece—felt that she had caught his spirit in each line. Power and gravity and sensuality, with demons fighting behind his eyes.

As a matter of fact she would take the painting with her. It would either be a testament to the legacy Ethan would hold in her heart forever. Or it would be a torment that would haunt her for the rest of her days. Either way, it was hers and she wanted it.

With a small knife she found in the kitchen she carefully removed the staples attaching the canvas to its frame. She'd roll up the painting and buy a tube to transport it in before she left town.

There was nothing more to do.

She wasn't interested in sleeping. Didn't want to give up even one last minute of this magical city and its hex that made people believe dreams could come true. These moments were all she had, and she'd treasure them for a lifetime.

She stared out the window. A million stories were unfolding in the city. Hers would end here.

Inching off the diamond engagement ring, she placed it next to the paper ring on the coffee table. Beside each other they were as odd a couple as she and Ethan.

As usual, not knowing what else to do with her feelings, Holly said goodbye to her fancy manicure and reached for her charcoals.

Ethan closed the door on the hotel room where he'd managed a few hours of tortured sleep in a chair. He walked down the hall to Aunt Louise's suite. Still in his tuxedo pants, although his tie was off and the first two buttons of his shirt were undone, he scratched his beard stubble. He'd been unable to face a shower just yet, and had promised his aunt they'd reconvene their discussion during breakfast.

"Come in, Ethan," Louise called out as soon as she heard the keycard click to unlock the door.

"I have not had coffee!" Ethan managed a trace of a smile for his beloved aunt.

"I'll pour you a cup." Louise wore a dressing gown and slippers. She sat at the dining table in her luxury suite, heavy drapes open to the city.

Ethan took the seat across from her.

"Does anything look different to you in the light of morning?" She tipped her eyebrow to him in a familiar way.

When he was a teenager, living with her and Uncle Mel, if he'd been grappling with a dilemma or regretting a bad choice, Aunt Louise would always tell him to sleep on it and see if a new day brought any fresh insight.

The insistence in her arched brow today told him that she had decided what realization he should have come to. His intuition told him what her conclusion was. He peered into his coffee cup to try to shut the thought down.

Something like a tribal drum pounded inside him, urging him to lift his eyes and embrace the truth.

"Where is Fernando?" Ethan tried to change the subject—at least for a moment.

But on and on the internal drum sounded.

"Gone. Good riddance," Louise clipped. "Before dawn this morning I called Bob Parcell to draw up a non-disclosure agreement."

Ethan snorted. "Lawyers work around the clock."

"Ours do. I signed a generous check, contingent on the fact that Fernando never speaks a word about our family, our company or anything to do with us. If he does, our people will make sure the rest of his life is spent behind bars."

"Well done."

Louise took a sip of her coffee, then smacked the cup loudly back onto the saucer. "And *that*, my dear nephew, is the end of my foray into having a younger companion."

After Holly had disappeared last night he and Louise

had held their heads high until the last guest had left the gala. Then they'd sat up together until the wee hours. He'd confessed about the engagement ploy and his motivation behind it. Begged for her forgiveness. Told her about the fax and Fernando's part in it.

Now Ethan lifted his aunt's hand and gently kissed the back of it. "I am so sorry you fell prey to him"

"Don't you think I knew what he was doing?" she retorted. "His trips down here to New York while I stayed in Boston. The restaurant bills that were surely more expensive than dinner for one. Charges to women's clothing shops although I never received any gifts. Fernando was clearly taking advantage of me from the beginning."

"You never told me."

"The vanity of a rich old woman… Perhaps I thought I could simply buy myself something to replace the emptiness left by your Uncle Mel's death. But even with all the money in the world you can't purchase or declare love. You can't arrange it. It's love that rearranges *you*."

Ethan knew what she was telling him. The drum beat louder in his ears. Yet he couldn't. Mustn't. Wouldn't.

"I know that you're torn inside…" Louise continued.

For all her health problems, when Louise Benton was clearheaded she was a shrewd and intelligent woman.

"It's what I feared for you. That after so much loss you wouldn't be able to love. When your mother went—"

"You were the only mother I ever had," Ethan interrupted, taking her hand again. "Everything I have achieved is because of you."

Louise's eyes welled. "I must have done something right. You're a rare man to go through all this trouble to get me to retire. When I said I wanted you to be married and settled before you took over, I never imagined you'd concoct such an elaborate scheme just because I've been too hardheaded to see that my time has come. And I had no idea I'd raised such a skilled imposter!"

She snickered, forcing a crack through Ethan's tight lips.

"We Bentons do what we have to, do we not?" he joked in a hushed voice.

"My guess is that your playacting became real and you've fallen in love with Holly. Am I right, Ethan?"

He wanted to cover his ears, like a young child who didn't want to hear what was being said. *Love* her? Those drumbeats inside him sped up like a jungle warrior charging toward his most threatening battle.

Yes, he loved Holly. He loved her completely—like nothing he'd ever loved before. He wanted to give her everything she'd never had. Wanted to have children with her. Wanted to spend every minute of his life with her. Wanted to hold her forever as both his wife and his best friend.

That invisible opponent marched toward him and pushed him back behind the battle lines.

He lashed out without thinking. "Holly deceived me about her past. She lied to me. Look at what she came from."

"Oh, hogwash!" Louise dismissed. "How about what *you* came from? What *I* came from? Your father and Uncle Mel were brought up on the tough streets of South Boston without a dime or a university degree between them. I was a poor Southie girl whose father skinned fish for a living. It's not shame about Holly's past that you're concerned with. The time has come for you to let go of shame about your own."

Of course he wore shame—like a suit of armor. Who wouldn't be ashamed that his own mother didn't want him?

He studied his aunt's face. Hard-earned wrinkles told the story of a life embraced. Could he let go of his pain and open up to the fullness the world had to offer?

Could he gamble again on trust?

Gamble on Holly?

On himself?

In an instant he knew that if he didn't now, he never would.

He sprang to his feet. Leaned down to Louise and kissed both her cheeks. Moved to the office desk in the well-appointed suite. Wrote a quick note and then sent it through the fax machine.

"Wish me luck," he said as he flew out the door, too impatient to wait for a response.

In his hotel room, he shaved and showered. Called Leonard to bring the car around. He placed a second call to George Alvarez, manager of the Miami office.

"What are your thoughts about the site supervisor position?" Ethan asked him.

Liz Washington, the previous supervisor, had transferred to the Houston office.

"I've had a young guy apprenticing with Liz for a couple of years now. Done a terrific job," George pitched. "He's ready for the step up. Name of Vince Motta."

"Yes, Vince Motta," Ethan approved with relief.

He valued George, and wouldn't want to go against his expertise. But he knew that if he was able to help Vince it would mean a lot to Holly. That was the kind of sister she was. The kind of woman she was.

The kind of woman he was going to make his.

He raced down the hotel corridor to the elevators, and then out through the front entrance of the hotel. Because once Ethan Benton had made up his mind about something, it couldn't happen fast enough.

"To the apartment," he instructed Leonard as he got into the car.

After Holly had vanished from the gala last night Ethan had checked the hotel suites. She had been nowhere to be found. Even though there had been no answer on her cell phone, or at the apartment, that was where he figured she'd gone. A midnight phone call to the building's doorman had confirmed that Holly had indeed arrived by taxi.

Yes, he had called the doorman to investigate her whereabouts! How could she blame him for an action like that? He oversaw a corporation with thousands of employees all over the world. He couldn't possibly command that without being on top of all available knowledge. Information was power. Artistic Holly Motta might not understand that, but he relied on it. She'd have to get used to the way he thought.

Just as he'd have to get used to her freewheeling ways. How she slammed doors closed with one foot. Ordered pizza with everything but the kitchen sink on it. Said whatever came into her mind. Needed to devote hours of scrubbing to getting her hands clean of paint. Ethan thought he wouldn't mind spending a lifetime looking at and holding those graceful fingers that brought art and beauty into the world. Seeing the ring on her finger that proclaimed her lo—

"Leonard! I need to make a stop first. Take me to Fifth and Fifty-Seventh."

Holly winced when she heard the key in the door. If only she'd stuck to her original plan and left at the crack of dawn after her sleepless night. She'd known that Ethan would make his way back here to the apartment. It would have been easier to slink away than to say goodbye in person. What was it that had kept her from going?

Her heart dropped in freefall to the floor as he strode through the door. She wanted to run to him. To put her arms around him. To kiss him until all the problems of the world faded away and there was just the two of them.

"Why did you leave last night?"

His eyes looked weary. His cheeks were flushed.

That one perfect curl of hair that always fell forward on his forehead was dotted with snowflakes. So was his coat.

Holly shifted her gaze out the window to see that it had started to snow. The whole week she'd been in New York it had rained and been cold and dreary. But it hadn't snowed.

She'd fantasized about walking the city streets during a snowfall. Seeing the soft powder billowing down as she crossed busy intersections and marveled at architectural landmarks that stood proudly dusted with white.

Instead she'd be returning to the sunny Florida winter. Snow—*ha!* That was what fantasy was. By definition not real.

"Answer my question," he insisted.

Holly's voice came out hoarse. "I'm truly embarrassed by my behavior. I know it was completely unprofessional."

She cut her eyes toward the floor.

"Look at me. How about the fact that I was worried about you?"

"What do *you* care? Let's be honest."

He stepped in and took her chin in his hand, lifting her face to meet his. "Certainly you leaving the gala without a word was not good business…" he began.

"I'm so sorry."

"But this is not business anymore, and if you want to be honest you know that."

"Know what?"

He moved his hand to caress her cheek tenderly, sending warmth across her skin.

"I love you, Holly. I *love* you. And I suspect you love me, too."

Tears pooled somewhere far behind her eyes. She fought them before saying what she needed to. "Now that you know the truth about me from your investigation, you've found out that I'm not who you want. I'm not a match for you. I'm damaged goods."

"You think you are the only one?"

"What do you mean?"

He let the hand that was touching her face fall to his side. His mouth set in a straight line.

"After my father died…" he started, but then let the words dangle in the air for a minute.

Holly anxiously awaited what he was so hesitant to say.

"Within a few months of my father dying, my mother—who was not much of a mother to begin with—met a man. And together they came up with an idea."

Bare pain burned in Ethan's eyes. Holly knew he was going to tell her something he had to dig out from the rock bottom of his core, where he kept it submerged.

"My mother told Uncle Mel and Aunt Louise that she and this man were going to take me away. That they would never see or hear from me again unless…"

He swallowed hard, his breath rasping and broken.

He regained his voice, "Unless *they* wanted to keep me instead. Which she would allow them to do in exchange for five hundred thousand dollars. In cash. She specified cash."

Agony poured from every cell in Holly's body. Grief for the little boy Ethan. And for herself. For her brother, Vince. For all the children unlucky enough to be born to parents who didn't give them the devotion they deserved.

"So, you see, my mother sold me to my aunt and uncle. I believe that means that you are not the only package of damaged goods around here."

The spoken words swirled around the room.

Again Holly wanted to hug the man she loved.

And again she didn't.

It was time for her to go.

He thought he loved her. He'd fallen for the drama they were starring in.

She'd have to have the cooler head. If she let him believe he loved her, one day he'd wake up and realize that he didn't want something this raw. That instead he could stuff his hurt right back down and act in a different play, with another kind of woman. With someone who'd never have to know about the betrayed and discarded child. About the gashes that still bled, the sores that would never heal. In his next pantomime he could be with a woman who knew only the functional and successful adult he'd managed to become.

She averted her eyes to the diamond ring on the table. To the beer wrapper ring beside it. She bent down for them and handed both to Ethan.

"I am glad you've returned these rings," he said. "They do not belong on your finger."

His words confirmed what she already knew. That it was time to leave.

He reached in his pocket and pulled out a small turquoise box. Holly's breath quickened.

He knelt down on one knee and held it out to her in the palm of his hand.

"Because an ordinary diamond ring does not fit the uniqueness of you. Like this, you are one of a kind."

He opened the box. Inside was the blue topaz ring she had admired from the private gemstone collection they'd seen that day they had gone shopping.

Uncontainable tears rolled down Holly's cheeks.

"I love you, Holly. I have loved you since you bounced through the door with that ridiculous blue paint on your face. I have never met anyone like you. Pretending to be engaged to you has shown me something I never thought I could see."

"What?" Holly asked, her spirits soaring.

"That our pain does not have to define us. That a past and a future can coexist. That there is beauty to be had every day. I want to share those miracles with you. To walk through life together. Please. *Please.* Will you marry me? This time the ring will never leave your finger."

She had to take the chance if he was willing to. To trust their authentic selves—scars and all. Together.

"I will." She nodded as he fitted the ring onto her finger.

Ethan stood. Holly reached her arms up around his neck and drew him into a kiss that couldn't wait a second longer.

Many minutes later he whispered, "Did you check the fax machine?"

"No." She'd heard the sounds and beeps of the machine before he arrived, but she hadn't looked to see what had come. She'd had quite enough of faxes already.

"Go," he prodded.

The piece of paper contained a two-word question.

*Will you?*

Had she read it earlier, she'd have known he was coming to propose.

She flirted with her fiancé. "Will I...?"

The smile kicked at the corner of his mouth. "Will you teach me how to draw?"

"It's a deal." Her grin joined his.

They pressed their lips to each other's in an ironclad merger, valid for eternity.

\* \* \* \* \*

# Kiss me.

The stray thought caught her off guard and she jerked away from temptation, stumbling like a klutz over a box. Brandon grabbed her before she fell. The warmth from his hands sent heat coursing through her body. This was so not good.

"Thanks," Arden said breathlessly.

Brandon raised an eyebrow and stared at her as if he knew what she'd been thinking. "Don't you want to know what he said?"

"Who?"

"John." She must have looked as blank as she felt because he spoke the next words very slowly. "The guy who's fixing your car."

"Oh, yeah. Right. What did he say?"

"He towed it in, but he needs the keys. Once we get this stuff inside, I'll drop you off at the garage."

The thought of sitting shoulder to shoulder again in the cab of his truck, his masculine scent swirling around her, tempted her to forget she wasn't interested in getting involved with another man. "You don't have to do that."

"It's not a problem," Brandon replied as he hoisted a box onto his right shoulder.

Then he glanced at the woman before him and wondered, not for the first time, what the heck he was doing.

\* \* \*

**Sweet Briar Sweethearts:**
There's something about Sweet Briar…

# THE WAITRESS'S SECRET

BY
KATHY DOUGLASS

First Published in Great Britain 2017
By Mills & Boon, an imprint of HarperCollins*Publishers*
1 London Bridge Street, London, SE1 9GF

© 2017 Kathleen Gregory

ISBN: 978-0-263-92329-2

23-0917

Our policy is to use papers that are natural, renewable and recyclable products and made from wood grown in sustainable forests. The logging and manufacturing processes conform to the legal environmental regulations of the country of origin.

Printed and bound in Spain
by CPI, Barcelona

**Kathy Douglass** came by her love of reading naturally—both of her parents were readers. She would finish one book and pick up another. Then she attended law school and traded romances for legal opinions.

After the birth of her two children, her love of reading turned into a love of writing. Kathy now spends her days writing the small-town contemporary novels she enjoys reading.

This book is dedicated with love and appreciation
to the following people:

To my best friend, Joya, who has been a true friend
since the day we met. Thanks for reminding me
that I wanted to be a writer.

To Ehryck, Teri and Sandra, who celebrated
with me when I signed my first contract.

To Lauren Canan, the best critique partner
on the planet.

To my editor, Charles Griemsman, who helps
make my books better than even I could imagine.

To my mother-in-law and father-in-law, who raised my
husband to be the most wonderful man in the world.

To my siblings, for a lifetime of love and support.
A special mention to Marc, who actually did refer
to his daughters' playpen as Attica.

To my parents, who loved and supported
me in everything I did.

And last, but certainly not least, to my husband
and sons, who fill my life with love and happiness.
I love all of you more than you can ever imagine.

# Chapter One

Arden Wexford pounded on the steering wheel, then turned the ignition key one more time. Still dead. Funny how that worked. Apparently the nineteenth time wasn't the charm. Sighing heavily, she got out of her car and slammed the door, releasing a bit of frustration. She looked under the hood even though she didn't have the foggiest idea what she was searching for.

Her great big adventure, as she had been sarcastically referring to it since her beloved Beetle had broken down, wasn't turning out the way she'd planned. If things had gone the way she'd intended, she would be closer to her parents' house in Florida by now. Instead, she was stranded in Nowhere, North Carolina. She wished she'd driven the Mercedes sedan her parents had given her when she'd graduated from college two years ago. But her candy-red Bug felt like a big hug from her brothers. Driving it always made her happy. After the disaster with Michael-the-jerk, she needed cheering.

Now, though, she wished she had driven the old-lady car. She'd be that much farther away from Baltimore and men willing to stoop to the lowest depths to turn her money into theirs. She was done with greedy men. She was going to hole up in her parents' winter home and enjoy life away from the vipers.

If she ever got out of North Carolina.

She kicked the tire of the offending vehicle even though it wasn't to blame for her predicament. It was properly inflated and ready to roll. All it needed was the car to start.

Arden considered turning the key for the twentieth time, but decided against it. Twenty wasn't going to be any luckier than nineteen. And if she didn't want to spend the night on the side of the road hoping that 2,019 was the charm, she needed to start walking.

She locked the car, then dug through her purse and grabbed her cell phone. She glanced at the screen one more time, hoping that service bars would magically appear. None did.

She'd passed a road sign a couple of miles back indicating she was six miles from some town she'd never heard of. Small Briar or something like that. It couldn't be more than four or so miles away. She ran that far most mornings at her health club. Of course the walk would be easier if she wasn't wearing her cute-to-look-at-but-not-good-for-much-else high-heeled sandals. They were perfect for the airplane flight she'd originally planned. But then her brother commandeered the family jet at the last minute to fly to Monte Carlo for a meeting at one of the Wexford luxury hotels. He'd invited her to come along to relax while he worked, but she'd declined. Her brothers might not mind having their pictures appear in gossip rags catering to people enamored of the rich and famous, but she did. So, she'd decided to drive.

Traffic on the highway was light, with cars passing only occasionally. None of the drivers so much as slowed down. Weren't people in the South supposed to be friendly? Not that she blamed them. She'd never pick up a stranger. And, truthfully, she wasn't sure she'd take a ride even if one was offered.

The day had started out warm and breezy with a clear blue sky. Her T-shirt and color-coordinated skirt had been perfect then, but in the past twenty or so minutes, the temperature had plunged. The cool wind made her long for a sweater. Dark clouds were gathering and the sky was growing threatening. The smell of rain filled the air. She remembered hearing something about a storm in the weather forecast, but since she hadn't expected to still be in the area, she hadn't paid close attention.

Arden picked up her pace, hoping to get to shelter before the clouds burst and she got drenched. After walking about a mile, she checked her cell phone for service again. Still none. Amazing. Her car, which couldn't make it from Baltimore to Tampa, had somehow managed time travel, propelling her into the Dark Ages.

Well, there was no use crying over it. She'd just have to keep walking. She eased a foot from her sandal and shook out yet another pebble. Rubbing her right foot on top of her left, she wondered if shoes that cost nearly a thousand dollars shouldn't be as comfortable as they were beautiful.

Arden slid her foot back into her sandal and, after promising herself a good foot massage as soon as she reached civilization, continued her trek to town. She'd taken a handful of steps when a late-model silver pickup pulled to a stop several yards ahead of her. The driver's door opened and a giant of a man got out. He closed the door and walked around to the back of the truck.

He had thick dreadlocks that were pulled back into a ponytail that hung to the middle of his back. His shoulders were so wide that she imagined he took up more than his share of an airline seat. His broad shoulders only emphasized his flat stomach and trim hips.

He was truly handsome, with dark chocolate skin, a jaw that could only be described as rugged and black eyes that quickly scanned her from head to toe before returning to meet her gaze. A shiver that had nothing to do with the temperature danced down her spine.

Although he had not done anything remotely intimidating, every warning her parents and older brothers had drilled into her since birth about stranger danger raced through her mind. Weren't rich kids always at risk of being kidnapped and held for ransom? Arden looked around. There wasn't another car in sight. She was alone on a deserted highway with a huge man. And no cell service. She stumbled back, cursing her high-heeled shoes.

As if sensing her trepidation, the man backed up until he bumped into his truck, his hands raised, palms out. "I'm not going to hurt you. I want to help you. I passed your car a couple miles back. That is, if you're driving a red Beetle."

His voice was deep, and she noted that he spoke in a calm manner as if soothing a child. She nodded.

"You've walked a long way. You still have about two miles to go until you reach Sweet Briar." He looked up at the darkening sky. "There's a severe thunderstorm warning in effect. Hop in and I'll drop you off in town."

Although he seemed harmless, her family's lessons were too deeply ingrained to cast off simply because a guy had a smooth disc-jockey voice.

Arden shook her head. "Thanks. That's really nice of you to offer, but I'll walk. A little rain never hurt anybody. Besides, it's not raining yet. Maybe it won't."

On cue, lightning streaked across the sky, followed by a loud clap of thunder. And then it started to rain.

"I really don't mind giving you a lift."

Arden tilted her head as she stared at him. Something was off. Although the words were correct and his posture nonthreatening, he didn't appear at all pleased to offer her the ride. He was grimacing and seemed to be forcing the words out of his mouth as if he really didn't want to say them. He reminded her of a reluctant twelve-year-old whose mother kept poking him in the back, prodding him to ask a girl to dance. That reluctance certainly didn't engender confidence.

"No, thanks. I'll take my chances with the rain." It was becoming more of a steady downfall by the second but, still, wet was better than dead or whatever else he might have in mind.

Brandon stared at the woman, wondering if she'd lost her mind. Her hair was plastered to her head and water streamed down her face. Her T-shirt, a pale gray with some sort of orange-and-pink design, now clung to her breasts and tiny waist. He had a feeling she had not as yet realized that her top was fast becoming transparent, revealing the lacy white bra she wore beneath it. She was getting soaked to the bone and she wanted to walk?

Of course she did. That was the cherry on top of a perfectly terrible day. He'd wasted hours in a bank being shuffled from person to person as he unsuccessfully tried to straighten out a mess with the restaurant's account. Now he was wasting even more time standing in the pouring rain trying to convince a stubborn woman to accept his help.

He was tired and irritated and ready to put this day behind him, but he couldn't in good conscience leave her to hoof it to town. It was out of the question. His parents and grandparents had raised him too well to leave her stranded. He could practically hear his father reminding him that a gentleman never left a woman in distress while his mother stood in the background, nodding and murmuring in agreement.

He rubbed a hand across his neck.

The woman lifted her cute little chin in hardheaded resolve.

"Look, I can't just leave you here. I have a sister, and I hope someone would stop and offer assistance if her car broke down. I also hope she'd have sense enough to take the ride."

"Even with a man she's never seen before in her life?"

Brandon huffed out a breath. She had him there. "My name is Brandon Danielson. I own a restaurant in Sweet Briar."

He reached into the back pocket of his jeans, removed his driver's license from his wallet and held it up for her to see although he doubted she could read it from the distance that separated them. "This is me. You can keep it if it makes you feel better. Hell, you can drive if that's what it takes for you to feel safe."

She nodded but still looked unsure. "Okay," she finally agreed. "Thanks."

"Thank me after we get out of this storm."

Slipping and sliding on the unpaved shoulder, the woman reached the passenger door. She stepped on the running board of the truck, then grabbed at the hanging strap to pull herself up the rest of the way. Suddenly her foot slid out from under her. Instinctively, he reached out to help her, grabbing her around her impossibly small waist.

The feel of her soft body sent a jolt of awareness surging through him. He set her away as quickly as he could and frowned at the reaction of his body. He was a Good Samaritan, not some player picking up women on the side of the road.

"I'm going to help you into the truck." Before she could respond, he lifted her into his arms and settled her into the passenger seat. Even soaking wet, she couldn't have weighed more than a hundred and fifteen or twenty pounds. Closing her door, he lost no time getting to the other side and slipping behind the wheel. As soon as he started the truck and the air began to circulate, he got a whiff of her scent. Man, she smelled good. Like rain and shampoo—which was expected—but also like sunshine and flowers. Like happiness. Where had that come from? He shook his head slightly in the hope the foolishness would rattle out his ears, then glanced at his passenger.

Even with most of her makeup washed off, she was

incredibly beautiful. She had remarkably clear caramel-colored skin and light brown eyes. With high cheek-bones and a perfectly shaped nose and lips, she could have been a model. Of course, he would have appreciated her beauty more if he didn't need to start building an ark. And, like any beautiful work of art, she was best viewed from a distance. He would do well to keep that in mind.

She returned his glance with wide eyes. Her teeth were chattering, whether from nerves or because she was drenched and cold, he didn't know. Maybe a little of both. He flipped on the heater and edged back onto the road. The wipers were on the fastest setting, yet they could barely keep up with the downfall.

"The truck has heated seats. And there's a jacket in the back you can use."

She moved her hand off the door handle and pressed the button he indicated. "I don't need your jacket. I'm fine. Besides, you're just as wet as I am."

"Maybe." He reached behind the seat and grabbed his denim jacket. "But perhaps you should look at your shirt. You might reconsider."

She looked down and squeaked. "I look like a refugee from a wet T-shirt contest."

He couldn't help chuckling as she took the jacket and draped it over her torso. Although her breasts weren't nearly the size of the women's who entered such contests, they were still appealing. Not that he was looking. Much.

"What's your name?"

The question really wasn't that difficult, yet she hesitated as if trying to find the right answer. "It's Arden… Arden W…West."

"So, Arden, what brings you to North Carolina?"

She raised a suspicious eyebrow and leaned closer to her door. "How do you know I'm not from here?"

"No accent. You don't have that Southern way of speaking."

She nodded. "True."

"And I saw your car, remember? Maryland plates."

"Oh." She heaved out a breath. A bit of remorse fell over her fine features and the stiffness left her spine.

"So, what brings you to our neck of the woods?"

"My car broke down here." Arden had an impish smile on her face, which hit him in the center of his chest with unexpected force, momentarily making breathing hard.

"Sweet Briar is a small town. There's a magnetic field that captures new people and won't let them leave. Sort of like the Hotel California."

"Where you can check out but never leave?"

Brandon nodded, pleased that she understood his reference to the classic Eagles song.

"Are you from here?"

"No."

When he didn't say anything more, she looked at him, her eyebrows raised in question.

"Chicago. I moved here three years ago." A man who preferred to keep things on the surface, he didn't normally volunteer information about himself. But being open seemed to put her at ease. So, as long as they kept to generalities, it was all good.

She tilted her head and looked him over, a mischievous expression on her face. "Did the magnet catch you or did you stay by choice?"

"Choice." He hadn't been able to leave Chicago and

that lying Sylvia fast enough. When a friend mentioned his cousins loved living in Sweet Briar, Brandon had been on the first plane to North Carolina.

Arden nodded, then turned to look out the window. Lightning flashed, followed by loud, booming thunder. The rain was coming down too fast for the drainage system to keep up. At the rate water was beginning to flood the road, he wouldn't be surprised if several streets in town were already closed.

After several frustrating minutes of inching down the highway and ten minutes spent sitting under an overpass when the downpour made driving too hazardous, they finally saw the sign welcoming them to Sweet Briar, population 1,976. He heard his passenger's sigh of relief and wondered if maybe she was more nervous than she let on.

"Is there a hotel where you can drop me? Or, better yet, a garage where I can arrange a tow?"

"No hotel. We only have a couple of bed-and-breakfasts." He wiped the condensation off the windshield and leaned forward for a better look. Just as he thought. There was close to three inches of water on the roads and the level was rising. "We have a garage, but I'm sure John has closed up for the night."

She checked her watch, then glanced over at him, disbelief on her lovely face. "It's only five o'clock."

"He generally closes around four thirty or five. You know, small town."

"I guess." She agreed but still looked doubtful. "Is there another mechanic in town?"

"Nope. Just John. And, to be honest, the way the streets are flooding, he probably wouldn't tow you now anyway."

Arden considered a minute. "Okay. Then I guess you can just drop me at the B and B."

"No problem. The Sunrise B and B is just a couple of blocks away. Call John in the morning. Let him know you're in a hurry and he'll have you back on the road in no time."

"Thanks."

"Kristina will be able to give you John's number. She owns the B and B, by the way."

"Speaking of calling." Arden pulled out her phone and checked it. Grinning, she held it up to him. "Bars. I have bars. I'm out of the seventies."

Brandon blinked. "What?"

She laughed. "I couldn't get service where the car died."

He nodded his understanding. "Ah. Gotcha. Cell service is spotty in this area. It takes some getting used to. But you shouldn't have trouble in town."

"That's good to know."

He pulled in front of an old Victorian mansion that Kristina Harrison had converted into a thriving business.

Arden peered out the window. At that moment, lightning streaked across the sky and thunder rolled. "You called this the *Sunrise* B and B?"

"Yeah."

"It looks more like a haunted house." She glanced at the building and then back at him. "You sure Herman and Lily don't live here?"

He barked out a surprised laugh. So she liked the old sixties television show *The Munsters*. So did he. "I'm positive. Although the name of the street is Mockingbird Lane."

"Are you kidding me? The Munsters lived at 1313 Mockingbird Lane."

"Yeah. I'm kidding. This is Rose Street."

She shook her small fist at him. "That's so not funny."

Brandon resisted the urge to laugh but couldn't suppress a smile. "Yeah, it was."

She grinned with him. "Okay, it was."

"I know this place looks spooky in this storm, but it's actually a well-kept building. And the inside is great. You'll be comfortable."

"Have you ever stayed here?"

"Well, no. I have a house in town. But trust me. Kristina Harrison has great taste. And she's a nice person. You'll be fine."

"Okay."

"Stay here. I'll help you." He was halfway around the front of the truck when the passenger door opened and Arden hopped out. A splash was followed by a squeal.

"I know. I know. Don't say it." She laughed as she stepped onto the curb. "I just thought I could get out and save you the trouble."

He shook his head. How much trouble could it be to help her out of his truck and carry her across a few puddles? Apparently, she'd rather do that crazy hop-tiptoe step through several inches of cold water than wait for his assistance. He understood the need to be independent since he liked to do things for himself as well, so he resisted the urge to sweep her into his arms and carry her to the stairs, even though it meant getting drenched again. He did stay close by, ready to catch her if she stumbled.

She finally slip-slid her way to the stairs and grabbed

a railing. Letting out a breath, he climbed the steps beside her, eager to reach the porch and get them both out of the driving rain. He rang the doorbell and in less than a minute the glass door swung open.

"Goodness. Get in here before you catch pneumonia," Kristina said, motioning for them to enter.

"Thanks." Brandon stepped aside to let Arden go before him.

Arden didn't need to be told twice. She stepped inside the door held open by a pretty woman who looked to be in her midtwenties. Brandon closed the door behind them and made the introductions.

"I'll grab some towels so you can dry off," Kristina said. Arden hated the idea of tracking water across the gleaming marble floors, but when the woman gave her a gentle nudge, she moved toward the sitting room. Two comfy-looking sofas flanked a fireplace that Arden wished was lit. Kristina bustled out of the room.

"Brandon, what brings you and your friend out on such a horrible night?" she said as she hurried back, carrying two fluffy towels. She handed one to Arden, who blotted her face, then began drying her arms.

Brandon took the other towel and smiled at Kristina. For a split second illogical possessiveness and jealousy battled for dominance inside Arden, which didn't make sense. Why should she care who Brandon smiled at? She'd only just met the man. Besides, men were snakes. Just because she hadn't heard him rattle didn't mean he didn't bite. Arden definitely wasn't interested in being bitten again.

As they dried themselves off, Brandon explained about Arden's car breaking down on the highway.

"Oh, you poor thing. How awful," Kristina said, shaking her head.

Brandon rubbed the towel over his face, his enormous chest muscles flexing. A jolt of awareness shot through her, and Arden suddenly went from chilled to overheated. She rubbed the towel over her hair, reminding herself that a beautiful body didn't necessarily translate to a good heart. Though, to be fair, he had been more than kind so far. And he didn't even know she was rich.

"I gave her a lift and brought her here. She needs a place to stay the night."

"Oh, no. I'm booked. Carmen and Trent's wedding is this weekend. People started arriving this afternoon."

"So early? It's only Monday."

"Apparently, some of the guests are turning this trip into a vacation. Sweet Briar has become a popular destination in the past couple years. In fact, I'm filled for most of the summer." Kristina turned to Arden to include her in the conversation. "Trent is our chief of police and a great guy. His first wife was killed in a car accident a few years back. How long ago was it, Brandon?"

He shrugged his massive shoulders. "It was before my time."

Kristina turned back to Arden. "Anyway, Carmen was born here but moved to New York years ago. She came back for her mother's funeral, God rest her soul. Anyhow, they fell in love and are getting married. Don't you just love a happy ending?"

Kristina sighed. Arden sneezed.

"Bless you. I'm so sorry I don't have a place for you to stay. I would suggest the Come On Inn, even though

Reginald Thomas annoys me enough to make me swear, but they're booked, too. Of course we were filled days before they were. They only got our overflow."

Arden nodded and rubbed the towel over her legs. She really needed to get out of these wet clothes.

"So, what are you going to do?" Kristina asked. It was clear to Arden that the other woman was sincerely concerned, which surprised her, given that they were complete strangers.

"The only thing we can do. I'm taking her home with me."

## Chapter Two

"You're taking me home with you?" Arden asked the minute they were alone in his truck. "There has to be somewhere else I can stay the night."

Brandon glanced over at Arden. She was watching him almost as closely as she had when he'd picked her up on the highway. He could understand her unease although she had nothing to be afraid of. "You heard Kristina. Both bed-and-breakfasts are filled. There's not another place in town. There are a couple of chain hotels twenty or so miles down the highway, but I'm not sure all the roads are passable. And, even if we make it, there's no guarantee they'll have rooms available."

She nodded, but she didn't appear pleased by his answer. Still, she couldn't argue the facts. The rain showed no sign of letting up anytime soon. Truth be told, he wished there was somewhere else she could spend the night. He'd rather be done with the whole thing, too, but he had picked her up and now bore some responsibility for her welfare. He couldn't just dump her on the side of the road in the middle of a storm and bid her adieu. He'd arrange for her to get her car towed to town first thing in the morning so she could go on her merry way. Surely that would be enough chivalry to satisfy even his parents.

He started the truck and drove down the street, passing the town's lone gas station. The lights over the pumps were dim, casting odd shadows on the street. Not a soul was around. "You'll be perfectly safe. My sister, Joni, lives with me."

"And she'll be there?"

He nodded and stopped at the corner. He grabbed his cell phone, punched in his home number and put the phone on speaker. Joni answered on the third ring.

"Hey, Brandon."

"Joni, I'll be home in a couple of minutes. I'm bringing someone with me."

Joni laughed. "I know. I just got off the phone with Kristina."

"That woman is in the wrong business. She should be a reporter."

Joni laughed again. "Can your friend hear me?"

"Yeah."

Brandon looked at Arden, who smiled tentatively.

"Don't worry. My brother is perfectly harmless. And I know you're soaked to the skin. I have dry clothes ready for you to change into."

"Thanks. I really appreciate it."

"Not a problem."

Brandon ended the call and looked at Arden. "Better?"

She smiled and for a second the sun seemed to break through the clouds. He felt a stirring where his heart used to be and immediately quashed it.

"Much better. Thanks for calling her."

"Sure. I can't have you worried about your safety like some woman in a horror story."

Arden glanced at the dark street. The wind was blowing the trees every which way, casting shadows that shifted so much they looked like arms reaching out to grab something. "It does look kind of creepy out here. Like some chainsaw-wielding maniac could jump from a dark corner and attack us. Well, me anyway. You're kind of big for someone to mess with."

Brandon continued driving. "Don't worry. There's no one hiding in the shadows or anywhere else. And if someone did try to hurt you, I'd protect you."

The grateful look she sent him made his chest grow tight and warmed the cold bitterness in his soul. He rubbed his hand across the raised scar near his heart as a reminder to keep his emotional distance. The last time he'd gotten close to a woman he'd ended up in intensive care. It was okay to be friendly—Arden needed that to be at ease. But genial chatter was one thing; an emotional connection was something entirely different.

"My brothers always said I have a vivid imagination. Which is why I never watch scary movies."

"Never?"

"Not ever. Afterward, I'd be so busy checking under my bed and jumping at every bump in the night that I'd never get any sleep."

He nodded. "That's our house right there. Third one on the left."

Arden leaned back in her seat and sighed. "It looks normal from here."

"We keep the dragon in the basement."

"That's good to know." She leaned forward and peered out the window at the rising water. "What I really want to know is where you keep the rowboat."

"Not interested in wading through the water again?"

"No." She looked down at her ruined sandals. "Once was enough for me. I think I can cross that off my bucket list."

"Walking through rainwater up to your ankles was on your bucket list?"

She lifted the corner of her mouth in a mischievous grin. "I want to have a wide range of experiences."

"I'm glad we could oblige," he said, pulling into the driveway.

Less than a minute later they were running through the large backyard and racing up a flight of stairs. A woman Arden assumed was Brandon's sister opened the door and stepped back to let them inside. She had friendly eyes and introduced herself with a bright smile.

"It's really coming down out there," Joni said, closing the door against the wind. Arden slipped off her damp and muddy sandals and placed them beside the door so she wouldn't track mud through the house. Joni led the way through the utility room and into the kitchen. The room was huge, with restaurant-quality appliances. There were miles of glistening marble countertops. A solid wood farmhouse table sat near an unlit stone fireplace. Wonderful aromas floated in the air and Arden's stomach growled.

"Sorry." Cheeks burning, Arden placed a hand over her stomach, trying to muffle the sound.

Joni waved away Arden's apology. "Don't be. You're not only soaked to the bone, you're also hungry. If I were you I'd be grabbing food from the pots with my bare hands."

Arden laughed, her embarrassment dissipating. She liked Joni.

"I've got some dry clothes for you that will fit better than my brother's jacket. Come on, you can take a quick shower and get warm. You'll feel a lot better. It'll be a few minutes before dinner's ready."

Warm water and dry clothes sounded wonderful. "Are you sure you don't mind? I don't want to put you out."

"Nonsense. It's no bother."

"Thanks."

"The stairs are this way."

Joni put her arm around Arden in a sisterly way and led her farther into the house. Although Arden had run as fast as she dared through the slippery yard, she'd still gotten drenched again. She hated dripping onto the beautiful hardwood floor, but she couldn't strip in the kitchen.

Joni didn't seem to mind about the mess, and seconds later they were climbing a flight of stairs. Brandon followed them in silence.

"You can use this room," Joni said, opening a door to a bedroom and stepping through to the en suite. "Brandon had some renovations done to the house when we moved here. He turned a couple of tiny rooms into bathrooms. I didn't agree with his decision at first, but I totally love it now."

As she talked, Joni bustled about the room, pulling plush towels out of a linen closet, then stacking them on the marble counter. She grabbed bottles of shampoo and conditioner and several different types of body wash from a cabinet beside the sink. "I'll be right back."

Arden nodded, grateful when the other woman returned with a stack of dry clothes.

After Joni left, Arden took one look in the mirror and groaned. Her makeup was completely washed off, but her face was far from clean. Somehow mud had gotten spattered on her cheeks, with one long smear down the side of her face. Her wet hair was wind whipped and going in every direction. She ran her hand through it and discovered a leaf-covered twig had gotten tangled in her mane, completing the puppy-playing-in-a-mud-puddle look. She stripped and stepped into the shower.

A moan of pure pleasure escaped her lips as the hot water began to warm her, slowing the chatter of her teeth. No shower had ever felt this good. If it wasn't for the fact that her hosts were waiting for her, she'd spend the next hour letting the warm water pound every ache out of her body. As a guest, an unexpected one at that, it would be rude to linger.

She hurriedly poured shampoo into her hands and quickly lathered her hair. Joni used the same brand she did and the familiar scent soothed the last of Arden's nerves. Her remaining tension disappeared down the drain with the bubbles.

She gathered her wet clothes and placed them on the counter. She would ask Joni where she could launder them later. Joni had left an assortment of clothes and she sorted through them before selecting a long-sleeved cotton top and denim pants. The jeans were a little long, so she rolled them up before pulling on socks and heading downstairs.

When she'd entered the house, she'd been too cold and uncomfortable to give more than a cursory glance at her surroundings. Now, though, she looked carefully. The house was a wonderful blend of old charm and modern convenience. The rooms had wide baseboards and crown molding around the high ceilings. Painted white, they were a nice accent to the darker-colored walls.

The furniture in the living room, while stylish, had clearly been chosen for comfort. With randomly placed pillows and a throw tossed over a leather ottoman, this room was used for living and not just for show.

Arden heard voices coming from the back of the house and followed them to the kitchen. The aromas wafting through the air reminded her that it had been hours since she'd eaten lunch. If scarfing down a hot dog and bag of chips in her car qualified as eating lunch.

"Come sit down. Dinner is just about ready." Joni pointed to a seat at the table. A small vase of wildflowers was in the center. The curtains were closed so Arden couldn't see the storm. She could hear it, though. The rain pounded on the windows like it was trying to get in, and the wind howled like an injured animal. This was definitely not a night to be outside. And if it wasn't for Brandon, she'd be out in this wicked weather.

Arden glanced at Brandon. He'd changed into a gray polo shirt that pulled tight across his barrel chest and loose-fitting jeans that couldn't disguise his muscular thighs. The man put all the statues she'd studied in her art-history class to shame.

She shook her head. What was wrong with her? She'd seen plenty of handsome men in her life, yet she didn't gawk at them like some teenager with no home training. "I can't thank you enough for your hospitality and the clothes, Joni. I'll return them as soon as possible."

Joni smiled. "Don't worry about it. I have way more clothes than I need." She then fixed her brother with a mock glare. "Don't say a word."

"I didn't open my mouth."

"Good."

"But if I had said anything, it would be that you have more clothes than any three people need." Joni tossed a linen napkin at him. He caught it with ease and dropped it onto the counter. Then he pulled open the oven door for a quick look and nodded with apparent satisfaction.

Arden watched them banter back and forth with a smile on her face. It was clear to her they not only loved each other, they genuinely liked each other. They were friends.

She sighed wistfully. She wished she could say the same of her relationship with her brothers. She knew they loved her. They'd do anything for her. But Blake and Jax were stuck in protective-big-brother mode. To them, she was still the child who got into jams and waited for them to bail her out, which they'd done without fail. She'd grown up, but they hadn't noticed. Because they didn't view her as an adult, their relationship hadn't evolved to the point of friendship.

And the near disaster with Michael-the-sneak wouldn't help them see her as an equal. Which was why she had told them only that she'd ended the relationship, keeping the disgusting details to herself.

Brandon stirred, then began ladling soup out of a

pot into large bowls while Joni placed warm bread on the table.

"Is there anything I can do to help?" Arden asked, shoving aside the depressing thoughts.

"Not a thing," Joni said, taking the bowls from her brother and setting one before Arden. "Just relax."

Brandon joined them. As he scooted his chair closer to the table, the scent of soap teased her nostrils and her heart began to beat double time. He looked at her expectantly, waiting for her to sample her food before he ate.

Arden picked up a spoon and sipped her soup. Incredible flavors exploded in her mouth. She'd eaten at some of the best restaurants in the world, but nothing compared to this Italian sausage soup. Before she could stop it, a moan of unadulterated pleasure slipped from between her lips.

Brandon stared at her, his dark eyes unreadable. For a moment their gazes locked and time stood still. Her breath caught in her throat. Trapped like a fly in a web, Arden couldn't look away to save her life.

"My, my," Joni said with a laugh, looking from Brandon to Arden.

Joni's voice broke the spell, freeing Arden from Brandon's hypnotic gaze.

"Sorry." She looked down at the bowl to hide her embarrassment. *What is wrong with me?* She looked at Joni. "This soup is the best thing I've ever tasted in my life. You're a great cook."

Joni shook her head. "Not me. I can't toast bread without burning it. Brandon is the chef."

Arden risked a glance at him, warning herself not to get caught in those dark, amazing eyes again. "You made this? Wow. It's wonderful."

"Thanks." His voice sounded strained and low. He'd been charming in the car, but now he seemed more reserved with her. It was as if he regretted their earlier camaraderie.

"Brandon is chef and owner of the most popular restaurant in the state. Heaven on Earth."

"The name fits," Arden added, wishing her bowl was larger. She'd just hit bottom when Brandon removed her empty dish. A couple moments later he returned with three plates.

"Be careful," Brandon said, setting the dishes on the table. "It's hot."

"This looks wonderful. What is it?"

"Oven-roasted sea bass with oranges, tomatoes and olives."

Arden stared at him in amazement. "You made all of this while I was in the shower?"

"No. I prepared it earlier today. Joni put it in the oven when we got home."

She took a bite and this time managed to stifle the sound of pleasure that threatened to escape. The perfect combination of flavors was unlike anything she had ever experienced, even during the summer after high school she'd spent in France and Italy.

Joni sipped her drink, then looked at Arden. "Where were you headed when your car broke down?"

"Don't be so nosy," Brandon said, shaking his head.

Joni waved away his comment like she would a pesky gnat, then looked at Arden expectantly. Ordinarily Arden would be annoyed by such a personal question from a complete stranger. But Joni didn't feel like a stranger, she felt like a friend. "I'm on my way to Florida."

"For vacation? A new job?"

Arden shook her head. "Neither. I just need to get away for a while."

"From what?" Brandon asked, apparently forgetting the no-prying rule.

"I thought we weren't going to be nosy," Joni pointed out.

Brandon glared playfully at his sister, then smiled at Arden. "Sorry. Forget I said anything."

"No, it's okay. A relationship I was in ended badly. I just needed some space to get my head together. I'm a middle school science teacher, so I'm off for the summer. Since there was nothing holding me in town, I decided to get out while the getting was good."

"So…what are your plans when you get to Florida?" Joni asked.

Brandon shook his head at his sister but did appear interested in Arden's answer.

"I don't really have plans," Arden confessed. Suddenly, sitting alone in her parents' home hiding from the world and licking her wounds lost its appeal. It actually sounded pretty pathetic. Was she so fragile that she needed weeks in seclusion because her boyfriend had turned out to be a jerk? Heck, no. Double heck, no. She was stronger than that.

"And now you're stuck in Sweet Briar." Brandon finished his meal and pushed his plate into the center of the table. She did the same. "John's good. He'll have you back on the road in no time."

He stood and began clearing the table. Before she or Joni could move, he'd rinsed the plates and bowls and loaded them into the dishwasher. When that task was complete, he excused himself and left the kitchen.

Arden watched him leave, noting once again what a

fine specimen of a man he was. He was the definition of masculinity. She might not be in the market for a man, but she wasn't opposed to window-shopping. Realizing she was gawking at Brandon in front of his sister, she pulled her gaze away and reached for her coffee cup. She stifled her attraction before it could turn into interest or something more. She might not know much, but she knew better than to let her emotions get the upper hand on her common sense. No way. She wasn't going to open herself up even for a minute and end up getting hurt again.

Thankfully, she wasn't going to be around long enough to put that theory to the test. As soon as her car was fixed she was out of Sweet Briar.

# Chapter Three

Arden woke to the sound of birds chirping and a dog barking in the distance. Stretching languidly, she smiled and opened her eyes. Momentarily startled by the unfamiliar surroundings, she jerked upright to a sitting position. A heartbeat later she remembered everything: her car breaking down, Brandon rescuing her and bringing her to his home.

Slipping from the bed, Arden crossed the room to the en suite. Not a morning person by nature, she felt unusually refreshed. She credited her vigor to the early hour she'd gone to bed and the fact that she'd slept like the proverbial baby.

She brushed her teeth, washed up and applied some lip gloss. After dressing in the clothes she'd washed last night, she tidied the bathroom and made her bed. When she stepped into the hallway she heard voices, so she knew Brandon and Joni were awake. Following the sound, Arden arrived at the kitchen.

"Good morning," Joni said from her seat at the table. "Help yourself to some coffee."

"Thanks." Arden grabbed a mug from beside the coffeemaker, filled it, and added sugar and amaretto cream.

"Brandon and I were just talking about you."

"Were you?"

"Yes," Brandon replied.

Until he spoke, Arden had avoided looking at him. Now, though, she forced her gaze to where he leaned near the window. She'd thought he was to-die-for gorgeous yesterday, but it was nothing compared to the way he looked this morning. His jaw was scraped clean of all stubble and appeared baby-bottom smooth. She curled her hand into a fist to resist the urge to caress his face and find out. His dreadlocks were hanging loose around his shoulders. Dressed in a simple white T-shirt, his denim-clad legs crossed at the ankle, he looked perfectly relaxed.

Although her heart thumped wildly in her chest at the sight of him, she managed to speak normally. "Do I want to know what you were saying, or should I go back upstairs?"

He smiled. "We were discussing your situation."

His smile momentarily stopped her brain from functioning. "What situation?"

"Your car."

"Right." She took a swallow of her coffee, hoping a jolt of caffeine would help her follow a simple conversation.

"I talked to John. He'll tow it to his garage this morning and get to work on it as soon as he can. I didn't know your cell phone number, so I told him to call me when he knows what the problem is and has an estimate. Does that work for you?"

She nodded. He'd handled everything with one phone call, saving her the hassle and the stress. She knew she should be grateful, and she was. If only he didn't remind her of her brothers rushing in to save the day. "That works great. Thanks."

"Sure." He glanced at his watch, then pushed away from the wall. "I need to get to the restaurant. I'll catch up with you two later."

Arden managed to keep her eyes from following him as he left.

"How about breakfast?" Joni asked. From the twinkle in her eyes, she hadn't missed Arden's struggle to not watch Brandon leave.

"Breakfast sounds great. But you told me you're not much of a cook and, to be honest, neither am I. The best cook just left the house."

Joni laughed. "I didn't mean here. Brandon would lose his mind if I touched his precious stove without his written permission and step-by-step instructions. There's a great diner in town where everyone goes for breakfast. Even Brandon, and he doesn't make a practice of eating other people's cooking."

"Okay. I'm in."

Ten minutes later Arden and Joni entered Mabel's Diner. The place looked exactly like Arden imagined a small-town diner should. Red vinyl booths lined the walls. Square tables with chrome chairs with red vinyl cushions filled the middle of the room. Framed pictures of movie stars hung on the walls at odd intervals. An old-fashioned jukebox played an ancient doo-wop song. It was positively charming.

Several people called hello to Joni, who returned their greetings. Every booth was filled, so Joni led the way to one of the tables. Arden grabbed a laminated menu from between an old-fashioned sugar bowl and the salt-and-pepper shakers. There was so much to choose from. Omelets, waffles, pancakes, bacon, sausage, even pork chops and fish.

After looking over the selections, she glanced up at Joni, whose menu remained untouched. "You already know what you want?" Arden didn't know how she was going to decide what to eat. She loved food and considered eating her hobby. Fortunately, she had a high metabolism or she'd be the size of a sumo wrestler.

Joni nodded. "The special on Tuesday is excellent. Grits, breakfast potatoes, two sausage links, two strips of bacon, two pancakes and two eggs cooked any way you want as long as you want them fried."

"All for two dollars?" Arden quipped.

Joni didn't laugh or even smile. Instead, she placed her hand on Arden's and gave a squeeze. "Don't worry about the cost. Breakfast is on me."

Arden had opened her mouth to correct Joni's misconception about her finances when the waitress stepped up to their table, pad in hand and ready to take their orders.

"Hi, I'm Lynn and I'll be your server. Are you ready?"

Joni nodded at the perky teenager. "I know what I want. What about you, Arden?"

"I think I'll try the special."

"Good choice," Joni said. "Two specials."

"Okay." The waitress scribbled down their orders and promised to return right away with their orange juice.

"You don't have to buy me breakfast. I have money."

"And a broken-down car. My mother is a teacher and I know they don't make much money. Especially new ones."

"I know how this must look, but—"

"No buts. Just accept breakfast with the same good grace you accepted our hospitality last night. Simply smile and say thanks."

Having someone offer to pay for anything was a new experience for Arden. Usually it was the other way around. People sat on their hands waiting for Arden to whip out her wallet and pay for their meals. And if someone did treat her, it was only because they wanted something in return. Joni didn't know she was a Wexford, so she obviously didn't have an ulterior motive. Joni was being nice because she was a nice person.

Still, she didn't feel right leaving Joni with the wrong impression. It felt like lying by omission. And she hated liars. But Joni was adamant about buying breakfast and Arden didn't want to insult her by refusing her offer. She'd let Joni buy her breakfast now and she'd treat Joni later.

Arden smiled. "Thanks. I really appreciate it."

"You're welcome," Joni replied.

Their waitress returned with their food, setting the plates before them. Arden picked up her fork, breathing in the delicious aromas. As they ate, Joni told Arden about life in Sweet Briar. She mentioned little tidbits about the different residents, but none of it was mean-spirited or gossipy. From what Arden heard and saw, Sweet Briar was almost too good to be believed.

When they finished eating, Joni took several bills from her wallet and dropped them on the table.

"I should at least leave the tip," Arden offered, rummaging through her purse.

"Not a chance. But if you want, you can help out at the youth center. I need to get some things together before the kids arrive."

"Sure. Whatever you need."

"Great."

After a short drive Joni pulled into a paved parking lot in front of a three-story building. Arden had come to think of Sweet Briar as a quaint town, so the dynamic mural with graffiti art wrapping around the outside of the building came as a pleasant surprise.

Joni looked with pride at the building. "The youth center was built by the city, but the tax dollars we receive only go so far. Donations and grants keep us afloat. At least most of the time. We're popular with the kids, though, and we're filling a need. That's what matters."

Joni popped open the trunk and grabbed a couple of boxes. Arden did the same and followed her inside. The trunk was loaded with bags and boxes so she knew several trips would be necessary. Joni turned off the alarm and flipped on the lights. "Just drop everything on the front counter for now."

Arden set down her load and looked around. The most fabulous mural drew her attention and she crossed the room to get a better look.

"What do you think?" Joni asked, walking up behind her.

"It's great. Very dynamic." And that was putting it mildly. It was one of the best pieces of art she'd ever seen. Not that she was an expert by any stretch of the imagination. But she had been dragged to art galleries more times than she cared to remember and had been exposed to top-tier art. This was definitely of that quality. It was not something she expected to see in a small-town youth center.

"Isn't it? The artist is Carmen Taylor. She grew up here and moved to New York some years ago, where she did quite well. From what I understand, she's very famous in the art world. She donated this mural and designed the one outside. Volunteers painted that one, but she did this one herself. She's getting married Saturday."

"To the chief of police. Trent somebody."

Joni arched her eyebrows. "My, my. You haven't been in town twenty-four hours and already you're in the know."

"Not really. Kristina Harrison mentioned the wedding yesterday. The bed-and-breakfast is full of wedding guests, which is why I couldn't stay there."

"Brandon is catering the rehearsal dinner and the reception. It's quite the coup. A few bigwigs from New York are coming. This could really help Brandon out."

"I thought his restaurant was doing well."

"It is. But he always says that if you aren't growing and moving up, you're stagnating and on your way down."

Arden nodded. She'd heard her father and brothers make similar statements over the years. Even though Wexford Industries was a huge corporation, the principle still applied.

"Come on, let's grab the rest."

When they stepped outside, Arden saw Brandon reaching into Joni's trunk, two boxes near his feet while he hefted out another. His shirt was taut across the muscles of his back as they flexed with his movement. Arden's mouth watered at the sight, but she managed to keep from drooling.

"What are you doing here?" Joni asked, leaning against the bumper.

"John called. I forgot to get Arden's number and, as usual, your phone is turned off."

"Oops." Joni didn't sound even the tiniest bit sorry. She shrugged, picked up a couple of bags and carried them inside.

Arden grabbed a box, eager to get away from the gorgeous man before she did something ridiculous like flirt or bat her eyelashes. The weight inside shifted and the box began to slip. Brandon reached out to help her steady the load. His hand brushed against her arm and her knees actually went weak. Her eyes flew to his and time seemed to stop. She found herself swaying closer to him.

*Kiss me.* The stray thought caught her off guard and she jerked away from temptation, stumbling like a klutz over a box beside him. He grabbed her before she fell. The warmth from his hands sent heat coursing through her body. This was so not good.

"Thanks," Arden said breathlessly, and took a step toward the youth center, hoping to get away and gather herself.

Brandon raised an eyebrow and stared at her as if he knew what she'd been thinking. "Don't you want to know what he said?"

"Who?"

"John." She must have looked as blank as she felt because he spoke the next words very slowly. "The guy who's fixing your car."

"Oh, yeah. Right. What did he say?"

"He towed it in, but he needs the keys. Once we get this stuff inside, I'll drop you off at the garage."

The thought of their sitting shoulder to shoulder again in the cab of Brandon's truck, his masculine scent swirling around her, tempted her to forget she was not interested in getting involved with another man. "You don't have to do that. I've caused you enough trouble as it is."

"It's not a problem," Brandon replied as he hoisted a box onto his right shoulder and grabbed another under his left arm. "John's place is on the way to my restaurant."

Brandon glanced at the woman beside him and wondered, not for the first time, what the heck he was doing. Although he'd previously had no problem keeping women at arm's distance, he was being drawn into Arden's orbit. Worse, he was doing nothing to resist her pull. He knew Joni would have dropped Arden off at John's garage, but instead he heard himself offering her a ride. What was it about her that had his mouth running miles ahead of his brain and leading his body in the totally wrong direction?

Sure, she was pretty and liked some of the same things he did. Before Sylvia's treachery, that would have been a good thing and he would have pursued her. Now... If he knew what was good for him he would stay away from her before she drew him in and made him feel things he didn't want to feel ever again.

The morning was warm with the promise of becoming a scorcher as the day wore on. The sun was shining in the cloudless sky so he pulled down the visor. Still, the sun was no match for the brilliance of Arden's smile.

It was almost hot enough to melt the ice encasing his heart. Almost. Lucky for him she was leaving soon or he might be in danger of letting her get too close.

She peered out the window. "Sweet Briar has got to be the cutest place I've ever seen."

He bit back a sigh of relief. Talking about impersonal things was safe and easy. Figuring out his attraction to her and how to get control of it was not. "Our town is making a better impression on you today than last night?"

"Oh, yeah. I can't believe the difference a little sunlight makes. It looks like a picture postcard, advertising the perfect little town. The shops are so pretty with their striped awnings and old-fashioned signs. Best of all there's not a chain restaurant in sight to ruin the effect. There's not a stray branch or leaf in sight, either. If I hadn't lived through it, I wouldn't believe a storm blew through here only hours ago. It's like elves or fairies cleaned up everything overnight."

"Fairies and elves?"

"Okay. Shop owners." Understanding lit her eyes. "That's what you were doing this morning. Clearing the street and walkways around your restaurant."

"Guilty as charged."

He drove past Wilson's Hardware and waved at Hank, grandson of the founder. Two doors down, Carlo and Mario Marconi were setting red-and-white-checkered tablecloths, vinyl place mats and napkin-wrapped silverware on the tables in front of their family-owned pizza parlor.

"Ooh."

"What?"

"Do you see that?" Arden's reverent whisper made

her sound like a kid looking at a pile of presents under the Christmas tree.

"See what?"

"The chocolate fountain in the window of Louanne's Homemade Candy Shoppe. It was surrounded by strawberries and pretzels and a whole bunch of other goodies. I'm definitely going to visit that store before I leave."

"You and every other woman in this town." He glanced at the popular shop and drove another block.

Arden laughed suddenly and pointed out her window. "Fit To Be Dyed Beauty Shop. Is that where little old ladies go to get their hair tinted Easter-egg blue?"

Brandon huffed out a laugh. He couldn't help it. Her quirky sense of humor appealed to him. He was almost sorry to reach their destination. Howard and Son's Garage was across the street from the salon. He parked, turned off the engine and opened his door.

Arden placed her hand on his arm and stopped him from getting out. Her skin was warm and soft and awakened feelings in him he'd rather remained dormant. He'd never responded that way to such an innocent touch. "You don't need to go in with me. You must have a hundred things to do."

That was true, yet he wanted to insist on accompanying her. But why should he? John was totally trustworthy. Joni had already volunteered to pick her up when she was finished. Not only that, Arden wasn't his responsibility. He wasn't going to fall back into the habit of rescuing women. Hadn't he just been thinking he needed to maintain his distance? Becoming more involved in her life and her problems was the total opposite of that.

He nodded and restarted the truck, forcing himself to drive off the minute she stepped onto the sidewalk. He needed to get a grip, and fast.

Arden stepped into the building and looked around. A black leather couch that had seen better days was pushed against a windowless wall, a glass coffee table covered with magazines inches in front of it. The smell of oil and brake fluid filled the air. Clanging sounds mingled with Bruce Springsteen, and a howling noise that almost sounded like singing came from the back of the shop.

She crossed the empty waiting room to the laminate counter that divided it from the work area. There was a small silver bell on the counter and she gave it a good ring. A few moments later the noise stopped and the volume on the Springsteen song was lowered.

"Hi. How can I help you?"

She glanced up into smiling brown eyes in a round tan face. "Are you John?"

"In the flesh." He wiped his hands on a stained rag, then shoved the cloth into the pocket of his blue-striped coveralls. He leaned against the counter and swiped a yellow sucker from a bowl. "My wife insisted I give up smoking when she was pregnant with our first child. Now I'm hooked on these."

Arden laughed. "Brandon sent me."

"Ah, so you're Arden."

She nodded and looked longingly at the candy.

He slid the bowl across the counter. "Help yourself. I buy them by the gross. I haven't had a chance to get to your car yet. Emma Johnson's daughter had her baby a month early, so she needs to get to Tennessee as soon as possible to help out. There's no way I could let her hit the road without checking her car first. It's a good thing I did. She needed new brakes and a tune-up. I have a couple more cars to get to, so I might not get to yours for a bit."

"Okay." Arden was astonished by how easily he spilled another person's business. She hoped he wouldn't be as free with her information as he was with this Emma person's.

"Is my car in the back?"

"Yep." He chewed his sucker, then tossed the stick into a trash can.

"I need to get some things out."

"Sure. I need the keys from you anyway."

He grabbed a couple more suckers before leading her to her car. They passed a small office. A pink dollhouse and large cardboard building blocks were squeezed beside a cluttered desk. "Every once in a while I have to bring my kids with me. Toys keep them out of trouble. If not, there's always Attica."

"Attica? Like the prison?"

He nodded toward a folded playpen. "They hate that thing. Can't much say I blame them."

Arden grinned and followed him through the work area and out a steel door. Her Beetle was parked in a small paved lot between a late-model Cadillac and a classic Mustang. After retrieving her overnight bag, she dropped the keys into the mechanic's hand.

"Don't worry. I'll take good care of her."

"Thanks." She left the garage and paused outside, not sure where to go. Her cell phone rang and she set down her suitcase. Arden glanced at the screen and groaned. Jax. No doubt she was on speakerphone. She knew Jax would do all the talking, but Blake would be listening. Her brothers meant well, but they were smothering her and driving her crazy by being so overprotective.

"Hello." She sounded calm and mentally patted herself on the back.

"Where are you? You were supposed to call last night. The hotel in Virginia said you checked out yesterday morning."

"I'm fine, Jackson. There's no need for you to worry."

"Of course there is. You finally broke up with that no-good bum. Instead of turning to Blake or me, you go halfway across the country."

She pulled her suitcase over to a black iron bench and sat. This could take a while, so she might as well be comfortable. "Florida is on the same side of the country."

"You know what I mean."

She did. He wanted her to stay in Baltimore where they could wrap her up in cotton balls to keep her from getting hurt. If they could, they'd keep her from having problems, which in essence was keeping her from having a life. Barring that, they wanted to jump in and solve them for her. That was part of the reason she needed to get away. It would be too easy for her to fall back into her old ways and lean on them instead of standing on her own two feet. She'd never gain their respect if she continued to let them bail her out. She was willing to admit she had played a part in their relationship becoming unequal. If it was to change, she knew she had to do things differently.

"Since you haven't made it to Florida yet, why don't you just turn around and come home?"

And run the risk of seeing Michael-the-pig? Not for a lifetime supply of chocolate-covered pecans. "No."

There was a long pause and she could just envision them whispering furiously as they plotted their next move. Heaven help her from meddling brothers. A bird flew down from its perch in the tree and landed on the edge of a flowerpot overflowing with purple, orange, red and yellow blooms. The wind blew and the scent of the flowers filled her nostrils and she sighed. The bird turned at the sound, then hopped into the flower bed where it began digging in the dirt, perhaps looking for a worm.

"We want to help."

Her brother's voice pulled her attention away from the bird and back to her situation. "I know you do. And I love you both for it. I just need space."

"We understand that. But we need to know you're okay."

She blew out a breath. Just because she was ready to cut the apron strings didn't mean they were. But she was willing to take baby steps to help them along. At least for now. "I'll call you every Sunday."

"And Wednesday."

"No way. Once a week is enough." She had to draw a line somewhere.

There was another long silence, until Jax finally said, "Okay. But you'll call if you need anything—"

This was becoming ridiculous. "Yeah. Sure. Bye."

"Bye. We love you, Arden."

She ended the call and returned her phone to her purse. All things considered, that had gone better than expected. She was finally making strides, no matter how small, in getting her brothers to see her as an adult.

Standing, Arden wheeled the suitcase behind her, curious to see more of the town in the light of day. She'd gone only one block when she came upon Brandon's restaurant. A redbrick building with large windows and purple-and-yellow flowers in pots on either side of the gold-trimmed glass door, Heaven on Earth had a welcoming look. For a moment Arden hesitated, then tried the knob. It turned under her hand. She didn't need to check in with Brandon, but she owed him the courtesy of keeping him abreast of the status of her car. After all, she was a guest in his home.

The dining area was empty, but she figured he must be around. Leaving her suitcase inside the main entrance, she walked through the maze of tables until she stood outside his office. Hearing his voice, she realized he was not alone and had turned to go when a woman's voice stopped her.

"I hate to leave you shorthanded with the rehearsal dinner and reception coming up. I know how important they are to you, Brandon. But I have to go home. My great-aunt raised me and there's nobody else to care for her after her stroke."

"Of course you do. Family is important. Don't worry about work. I'll handle it."

"But you're already short two waitresses. You'll really be in a mess."

"We'll be fine. Is there anything I can do to help?"

"No. I'm set. I didn't have much to pack."

Arden heard paper rustling. "Here's your last check. I've also included a reference letter."

"Thanks. I've been so worried, I didn't even think of that."

"I want you to know, if you decide to return to Sweet Briar, you'll always have a job here."

"I can't even think that far ahead. I'll never forget you. Would you please tell everyone bye for me and that I'll be in touch when I can?"

"Absolutely. And if you need anything, just call."

"Thanks."

The young woman left the office and brushed past Arden, wiping tears as she hurried through the restaurant. Arden hesitantly knocked on Brandon's open door. He was sitting at his desk filling out a form. Pen in hand, he looked up. When he saw her he smiled and leaned back in his chair. Her pulse began to race. What was it about this man that rang her chimes? If she wasn't careful she'd forget she wasn't interested in men anymore.

"I hope I'm not interrupting."

He shook his head and waved her in. "Have a seat."

"Thanks. I met with John. He's not sure he'll be able to get to my car today. I hate to impose on you and Joni another night, so maybe I should get a room at one of the hotels you mentioned."

"That's not necessary. You're not an imposition. You're welcome to stay as long as you need."

"I appreciate that. I couldn't help but overhear your conversation a minute ago."

"With Nora?"

"The waitress?" At his nod she continued. "I know you have a couple of important jobs coming up. I'd love to help if I can."

"You wouldn't by any chance have experience as a waitress, would you?" He sounded as if he was half-joking.

"Actually, I do. I worked as a waitress in a four-

star restaurant my last two years of college." Although
her family was wealthy, her parents wanted Arden and
her brothers to know the value of work. They'd seen
too many rich kids living off their trust funds, burning
through money they hadn't earned. *A perfect waste of a
strong back* was how her father referred to them. Determined that his kids weren't going to become spoiled and
lazy, Winston Wexford insisted that his children have
summer jobs while in high school. They'd also been
required to work part-time while in college. He paid
tuition, room and board, and other necessities. Arden
and her brothers had paid for any extras they wanted.

Although they each had a sizable trust fund, her father controlled the funds until their thirtieth birthdays,
when he expected them to have learned how to be con-
tributing members of society. They received regular
generous payments, but, like her brothers, Arden prided
herself on making her own way.

"Really?"

She nodded. "Yes. So if you need help I'm willing."

"I appreciate it. Joni usually fills in when I need a
waitress, but she's a member of the wedding party. How
about you come in tonight and work a shift so you can
get a feel for things? I'll pay you, of course."

"You don't need to pay me. I am staying in your
house after all."

"Doesn't matter. You'll be paid. If you have a couple of minutes now, we can go over a few things to get
you oriented."

Arden followed Brandon out of the office, watching as he moved confidently through the kitchen. He
showed her around the spotless room, his pride evident
in his every word, before leading her to the dining room.

Although she tried to focus, she was distracted by the play of his muscles under his shirt. His shoulders were broad, his chest well-sculpted, but it was his back that was most interesting to her. The muscles there were strong and flexed as he moved a chair out of the way.

When the tour was over, they returned to his office. He smiled and butterflies began fluttering in her stomach. He might not know it, but his grin was a lethal weapon.

"So, you still interested?"

"Absolutely."

"Good. Let's take care of the paperwork."

"Paperwork?"

"Yes. I want to be able to pay you properly."

She couldn't fill out anything. He'd need a copy of her driver's license. And then he'd know her last name. She hated to think that he would change once he knew who she was, but she'd seen it too many times to believe differently. Money changed people. But she still wanted to help him. Joni had told her this reception was a big opportunity for him, and she didn't want him to look bad simply because he needed more waitresses. She blew out a breath and inspiration hit her. "Do you pay Joni?"

"No. She's pretty hardheaded and won't let me. She does keep her tips, though."

"Then I'll take the same deal Joni has. No salary and I'll keep my tips." She didn't need the money, after all. And he did need the help.

"That's ridiculous. You can't work without pay."

"Why not? You aren't charging me rent. If you insist on paying me, I'll have to pay rent. Either that or I'll move out. Since the bed-and-breakfasts are full, and my car is in the shop and I have no way of getting to one of the hotels you mentioned, I'll probably end up sleeping on a park bench." She was playing dirty, but she wanted to help. She hadn't been raised to be a taker. She needed to pull her own weight.

He opened his mouth and she knew he was going to continue to argue. She cut him off. "That's the deal. Take it or leave it."

He frowned with displeasure and ran a frustrated hand down his face. "I guess I'll take it."

## Chapter Four

Brandon plated the seared sesame tuna, and expertly added the side dishes, dipping sauce and wasabi paste, thus finishing the order for table seven. He gestured to the waitress, who grabbed the tray and hustled into the dining area of the restaurant.

The crowd was unexpectedly large for a Tuesday night. He knew part of the reason was all the visitors in town for the wedding. Ordinarily he would be thrilled with the turnout, but tonight he was concerned because of his newest waitress. He didn't want poor service to result in a less-than-spectacular dining experience for his guests, new and regular alike. Great food was only a portion of what Heaven on Earth offered.

True, Arden had experience, but every restaurant had a different way of operating. Although he'd given her a quick orientation, he didn't expect her to remem-

ber everything the first night. It generally took at least
a week before the waitstaff met his expectations. Of
course he had no idea how long she intended to stay
in Sweet Briar or if she was interested in working for
him on a long-term basis. He'd just be grateful if she
stayed through the reception and didn't do any harm to
his restaurant's reputation in the process.

Brandon turned his attention back to work. The next
hour flew as he prepared dinners quickly yet carefully,
ensuring each one was cooked perfectly and attractively
presented. Once things slowed down, he went into his
office, stripped off his stained whites and put on a navy
suit jacket. He removed his hairnet and adjusted the
leather strap holding his dreadlocks in place.

He visited the dining room at least once each night.
As owner, Brandon wanted his patrons to know he valued them and appreciated their business. More than that,
he wanted their feedback. If there was a problem with
the food or the service, he wanted them to tell him, not
their Facebook friends or Yelp.

He stood at the entrance to the dining room for a
moment soaking in the sight and the sounds of his restaurant. The pale gray walls and bluish gray floor-to-
ceiling curtains provided the perfect backdrop to the
snow-white tablecloths and napkins. The silver-and-
crystal chandeliers gave off just the right amount of
light to be flattering and cozy at the same time. The soft
background music added ambience, but didn't interfere
with the quiet conversations his patrons were having.

Satisfied that all was well, Brandon stepped into the
dining area. His eyes immediately found Arden. Several
diners were scooted to one side of a table and she was
taking their picture. She saw him and her face lit up.

His pulse leaped and his blood pounded in his veins. He cursed under his breath. No way was he getting caught under her spell. He brushed a hand over the scars his jacket covered. His days of trusting women were in the past. The last time he'd put his faith in a woman he'd barely escaped with his life. A woman could pass a lie-detector test and he still wouldn't believe a word she said. Not anymore.

"You're in luck," Arden told the patrons, still holding his gaze captive. "The chef is in the dining room. Perhaps he'll pose for a picture with you."

As one, the group of eight people turned and looked at him expectantly. Even though taking pictures did not come close to the top hundred things he wanted to do each day, he'd long since accepted it as part of the job. For a reason that still escaped his comprehension, his guests loved being photographed with him. Apparently, it made the dining experience even more special.

Holding back a sigh, he took his place among the men who were standing behind their seated dates. After Arden snapped a few photos—which she showed to the women, who cooed appreciatively—he shook hands and chatted briefly with them. Each person raved about their meal and the service, promising to return soon and to tell their friends about their experience.

As he crossed the room to greet other diners, he caught another glimpse of Arden. She was the one who should have been photographed. Even in the waitress uniform of a white blouse and straight black skirt, she was absolutely stunning.

Her haircut wasn't traditional, but the short waves were extremely sensual. He'd always liked long hair, believing it was more feminine. Of course, since he now wore his hair long, perhaps he should change his way of thinking. On Arden, he loved the way her hairstyle allowed him to see her face. And what a face it was.

Her brown eyes were warm, revealing an inner kindness. Having seen her face washed clear of makeup he knew her light brown skin was truly flawless and not the result of artfully applied makeup. But it was her quick smile and general openness that appealed to him most, drawing him in even as he did his best to resist.

He dragged his eyes from Arden and continued to work his way around the room. Leah, one of his veteran waitresses, grabbed his arm and steered him to a nearby table where a couple in their forties sat, holding hands and gazing into each other's eyes. "This is Chuck and Valerie Harris. They're celebrating their twentieth anniversary."

Brandon shook the man's hand and smiled at the woman. "Congratulations. I'm honored that you chose to celebrate here."

"My wife and I heard so many things about your restaurant we just had to try it."

"I hope we lived up to your expectations."

"Our meals were perfect and the service was outstanding. Now we know why everyone was raving about this place."

Brandon smiled again. "I never get tired of hearing that. Have you ordered dessert?"

"Not yet," Mrs. Harris said. "I've narrowed it down to three choices, but I can't make up my mind."

"Get them all. Eat one now and take the other two for later as an anniversary gift from us to you."

"Are you sure?" Mrs. Harris asked, beaming.

"Positive." He glanced back and forth between the two. "Again, have a happy anniversary."

He spoke with a few more customers, posed for one more picture, then returned to the kitchen, his favorite place in the world. The next hours sped by as he prepared a variety of perfect meals.

Finally the night ended and the last patrons left, happy sighs trailing them out the door. The waitstaff punched their time cards and then left, calling goodbye as they went.

He'd offered Arden a ride home, which she'd eagerly accepted. He told himself it only made sense as she was currently sleeping in his guest room and not because he wanted to spend time alone with her. She watched him now with a quizzical expression.

"You can wait in my office if you like. Matt has to clean in here and I need to sanitize the kitchen. It won't take long, okay?"

Arden's gaze went to Matt, Brandon's young dishwasher and custodian, who was busy clearing tables. The teen was placing the centerpieces on a serving tray, tossing stray silverware in a bin, then bundling the tablecloths and napkins together. He moved quickly and efficiently.

"I'll help Matt."

"You don't have to do that."

"I know, but there's no sense in sitting around when there's work to be done."

She saw surprise and approval in Brandon's eyes before he turned and left the dining room. Ordering herself not to stare after him, Arden approached the young man. "Want some help?"

"Waitresses don't clean up."

"I won't tell if you don't."

"Sure. As long as you don't mess up. It'll take twice as long if I have to go behind you to fix your mistakes."

He was so serious Arden had to swallow a smile. "Tell me what you want me to do. And how."

He gave such elaborate instructions it was clear he believed his job cleaning the dining room was more important than Brandon's job of preparing the food. The teen watched her clear a table of four, hovering like a mother hen and ready to pounce at the first sign of a mistake. When she finished he nodded, satisfied she wouldn't mess it up too badly. "You can put the tablecloths and napkins on the bench in the entry so Brandon can take them to be laundered."

"Okay."

Matt grabbed a vacuum cleaner and set to work on the floor, laboring over each square inch as if *dirt* was another word for *sin*. Well, cleanliness was next to godliness. She laughed at her own wit, then got back to work. They had just finished when Brandon returned, his stained chef's jacket draped over his arm. He bundled it along with the linens into a laundry bag.

"It looks great in here." He clapped Matt on the shoulder. "Good man."

"Arden helped," Matt mumbled, shuffling his feet, yet standing a bit taller. Obviously Brandon's praise meant a lot.

"I hardly did anything. Besides, you showed me what to do."

Matt flashed a grin that disappeared quickly and he pulled on a gray hoodie. "I'd better get going. Mom has to get up early for work, but she won't go to bed until I'm home." Brandon grabbed the bag of laundry and set the alarm. The three of them stepped outside and Matt headed for a bicycle leaning against the side of the building. A moment later he was pedaling down the moonlit street.

The wind blew and the silver chimes dangling in the trees tinkled. Although the day had been warm, the ocean breeze cooled the town at night. Arden wished she had thought to bring a sweater. She folded her arms across her chest in a futile attempt to ward off the chilly air.

"Cold?" Brandon asked. He was so near she felt his warm breath on her cheek. Her stomach imitated a carnival ride and looped the loop.

"Not really." The wind gusted again, harder this time, and she shivered. "Well, maybe a little."

He slipped off his suit jacket and draped it over her shoulders.

She closed her eyes briefly, indulging in the comfort of that simple gesture. His jacket was still warm from his body and when she inhaled, his clean, musky scent surrounded her and she sighed.

Her eyes popped open. Was she crazy? Back in Baltimore, she'd just been misled and betrayed by a man who on the outside appeared to be a perfect gentleman. But her experience with Michael-the-weasel had turned out to be worse than finding gunk on the bottom of her favorite shoes. She wasn't going to be so gullible again. Just because Brandon was gorgeous and smelled so good didn't mean she had to go and do something stupid like fall for him. She was on a man-free diet.

Brandon dropped the bag of linen into the back of his truck, then opened the passenger door for her. Despite reminding herself of the need to embrace the single lifestyle, her heart beat a mean pitter-patter at his nearness. Trying not to flutter her eyelashes, she smiled graciously and climbed into the truck, then used the seconds it took him to circle the car and get in to mentally shake some sense into herself.

As he pulled out of the parking lot and into the street, her mind searched for something to distract her from the man beside her. Perhaps conversation would help tamp down her attraction. "Tell me about Matt."

Brandon glanced over at her and smiled. "Matt was my first employee."

"Really? But I thought your restaurant was three years old. No way is that kid a day over seventeen."

"Sixteen. Matt started hanging around a few days after Justin and I started building the restaurant."

"Who's Justin?"

"He and I were partners. I bought him out a couple of months ago. Anyway, Matt was thirteen at the time and begged me for a job. I brushed him off and told him to come back when he was sixteen."

Brandon shook his head at a memory he clearly found amusing. "He showed up the next day saying he was ready for work. He'd come equipped with a broom that was more stick than straw and started sweeping the walk in front of the building. I shooed him away and told him to come back in three years. The next morning I got to work shortly after dawn. Believe it or not, the kid was already there. He was washing the pane window with Windex and a ratty T-shirt."

"Impressive."

"I thought so. I couldn't hire him to work in the restaurant, but I told him he could run errands for me with a parent's permission. He returned the next day with his mother. She thanked me profusely for hiring her son. Apparently, her husband had run out four years earlier, leaving her to raise Matt and his two younger siblings on her own. While Matt grabbed a broom and kicked up a cloud of dust, his mother confided that the family was barely staying afloat. Matt had been picking up odd jobs, giving his mother all of his earnings."

"And you hired him to do jobs you could have done on your own."

Brandon shrugged. "It was nothing."

Maybe not to him. She was sure it was a big deal to Matt and his family who needed the cash. And Brandon had taken Arden into his home without a second thought. True, she had the money to take care of herself, but money wouldn't put a roof over her head when there was no room in the inn. He'd just stepped in and helped. If she wasn't careful she would start thinking of Brandon as a real-live hero.

"When he turned sixteen I hired him to work in the restaurant. He's probably the best employee I've ever had." He looked at her and winked. "Well, besides you, that is."

She laughed. "Of course."

Brandon pulled the car into the driveway. It felt so natural to walk by his side at the end of the day. Was it only yesterday that her car had broken down and he'd rescued her, welcoming her into his home? She felt so close to him, so comfortable with him, they could have known each other all of their lives. And now, she couldn't imagine her life without him.

Arden peered into the restaurant's dining room. Over the past couple of days she'd worked the lunch shift once and the dinner shift three times. At first she worried that Brandon was giving the opportunity to work to her instead of someone who might actually need the money. She was relieved to discover that wasn't the case. Apparently, he had a hard time keeping waitresses and actually needed her help. That made her feel better about accepting his continuing hospitality. This was a fair trade with each giving something the other needed.

Tonight the restaurant was closed for Carmen and Trent's wedding rehearsal dinner. The bride had chosen purple and teal as her wedding colors and the dining room was decorated accordingly. The usual white napkins had been replaced with blue-green ones. The beautiful centerpieces were comprised of flowers ranging from the palest lilac to the deepest violet. Light flickering from the numerous candles around the room bounced off the softly lit crystal chandeliers. She had never seen a more romantic setting.

She sighed.

"Do I even want to know what that sigh means?" Brandon asked, startling her. He moved incredibly silently for such a large man.

Telling herself her heart was racing because she'd been surprised and not because of the gorgeous specimen standing an arm's length away, Arden brushed a hand over her black skirt, removing imaginary lint. "Sometimes a sigh is nothing more than a sigh. Like the song 'As Time Goes By' says."

He met her gaze, mischief dancing in his dark eyes. *"Casablanca."*

"I know. I love Bogart."

"Do you? The Movie Box Theater in Willow Creek is having a Bogart film festival on Sunday."

"I know. I saw the ad in the newspaper. It sounds like great fun." She tried to control the yearning in her voice, but she heard it.

"It's the day after the wedding. If you're still in town you should go."

"I'll still be here. Unfortunately, my car still won't be fixed. John is still waiting on a part." She grinned. "You weren't kidding about this place being like the Hotel California."

"You itching to leave?"

"Not really," she said, and amazingly it was the truth. There was something about Sweet Briar that appealed to her. The town was beautiful, the citizens friendly and, best of all, no one knew she was a Wexford.

Brandon nodded and rubbed his hand over his chest. He seemed to be debating something and she let him take the time he needed. Finally he spoke. "I'm going to the festival. If you want, you can hitch a ride with me."

"Are you sure?" Arden asked, noticing that Brandon looked as surprised as she felt and guessed he'd shove the words back into his mouth and swallow them if he could. Although he continued to be cordial and friendly, he was maintaining a distance that he hadn't when she first arrived. She couldn't quite put a finger on exactly why he was different, though. Perhaps his reticence was because she was his occasional employee and he wanted to be sure not to cross a line. Whatever the reason, he seemed to be fighting to not be the warm, charming man he was the day they'd met.

"Yep. It's not a big deal."

"In that case, it's a date." Her eyes flew to his and she sputtered. "I don't mean a *date* date."

"I know what you mean," he assured her, stepping

back and once more raising a wall between them. "Now let's get to work."

She watched him walk away, looking for all the world like he regretted asking her. She considered letting him off the hook, but her heart sank to her toes at the thought. Although he might not really want her around, going out with a man who didn't know who she was held an appeal too good to let go.

*Chapter Five*

The next day, Arden paused by the front window, watching the arrival of the bridal party. The wedding guests had arrived about forty-five minutes earlier and had been dining on finger food and sipping wine while they awaited the bride and groom. There was an excited buzz that had started as a low hum but increased in volume and intensity with each passing moment. The couple's imminent arrival filled the room with anticipation. Disposable cameras had been placed on the tables, and Arden had taken several photographs of the guests as they laughed and posed in small groups, capturing moments the official photographers would have missed.

A white limousine pulled up to the curb in front of the restaurant and someone called out that the bride and groom had arrived. A hush settled over the room as people grabbed their phones and cameras to get good shots of the newly wedded couple as they entered the dining room.

The excitement was contagious. Arden peered out the window again as she hurried to get more bottles of champagne. The chauffeur opened the door and the tuxedoed groom emerged, then reached inside to assist his bride. Dressed in a long white gown covered with beads and lace, Carmen looked like a princess. As she gazed up at her new husband, she smiled and seemed to glow. Arden had never believed love was a visible thing, but in that moment she realized she'd been wrong. She could practically see the love between them. It was as if a sparkly, glistening cord joined the two of them together.

She'd once believed she was in love, but it had been nothing like what she saw between the couple posing for pictures outside the restaurant. Michael-the-creep had never looked at her with the love that was lighting Trent's eyes as he gazed at Carmen. Truth be told, the only time Michael-the-louse had looked that happy was when he was discussing the house he wanted to buy for them, with her money. Or the car… Or any other thing he thought she might like. Of course it would all be purchased with her money. He had been quite clear that he didn't expect her to live off the salary he made as a middle school principal. He'd always said he wanted her to live the life she had been accustomed to. Now she knew the truth. He'd wanted to grow accustomed to that life, as well.

What she hadn't expected was the depths to which he would sink in order to get his hands on her money. That he was willing to make a secret sex tape to try to blackmail her with was bad enough. Worse was finding out that her so-called best friend was in cahoots with him. All her life her parents and brothers had warned her to be careful when choosing friends. She'd really messed up this time. The only saving grace was that she'd found out his plan and left town before he could put it into motion.

The pitiful thing was that she thought she'd learned her lesson about people with her sophomore year roommate in college. Eva had pretended to like Arden and had even insisted on paying her own way when they went to movies and concerts. Arden had thought she'd found a bosom buddy. Overhearing Eva say she'd befriended Arden as part of a plan to land one of Arden's older brothers had really hurt. Even more painful was hearing Eva say it didn't matter whether it was Jax or Blake she ended up with since they were equally capable of buying her everything she wanted.

Thank goodness no one in Sweet Briar knew she had money. She could trust the friendship she'd found with Joni, Brandon and several of her coworkers. As long as no one knew she was an heiress, she would be able to continue to enjoy the relationships she was building.

Arden joined the rest of the staff as a man with a fabulous voice announced the members of the wedding party. She was swept up in the beauty and romance of the moment and her eyes filled with unexpected tears. The joy and love that filled the room was almost too much to take. Blinking fast, she wiped away the tears.

As the bride and groom were finally announced and made their entrance, Arden joined in the applause. She was happy for them, yet a part of her wondered if she would ever find her happily-ever-after.

Arden studied her reflection in the mirror, swirled from side to side and smiled. She'd planned on engaging in some serious retail therapy in Florida, so she'd packed only a couple changes of clothes. The limited wardrobe had worked because most days she was either volunteering at the youth center, helping Brandon at the restaurant or exploring the town. She wanted something more for today's movie festival and had found the perfect outfit in a small boutique across from the diner.

The floral-patterned coral halter dress was perfect for a day at the movies. Fitted at the waist, the skirt flared and hit several inches above her knees. She added three-inch silver sandals and hoop earrings, and the look was complete. Checking her light makeup, Arden glanced in the mirror once more, then scooped her purse from the bed.

There was a knock on her bedroom door. "Ready?"

"Yes," she called. Her heart beat a rapid pitter-patter as she opened the door. Brandon stood in front of her with a sexy grin on his face, looking so good she nearly forgot her name. Both of them. Dressed in faded jeans that hugged his muscular thighs and a lightweight beige top that showed off his incredible upper body, he was the epitome of good-looking male. Definitely Mother Nature had been showing off when she created him. How was a girl supposed to remember she'd sworn off men with Brandon Danielson close enough to touch and smelling like something out of a dream?

"Do you know which movies they're showing today?" Arden asked as they walked to his truck. She mentally patted herself on the back for managing to look at him without her tongue hanging out her mouth.

"I think they're showing *The Maltese Falcon*, *The Big Sleep*, *To Have and Have Not* and my favorite, *The Treasure of the Sierra Madre*. There may be one or two others, but I don't recall the titles," Brandon said as he pulled out of the driveway.

"Oh, I hope they show *Sabrina*. I love that movie."

Brandon tsked. "That is such a chick flick."

"It's a romance."

"Only made bearable by the greatness of Bogart."

"I take it you're not a fan of romantic comedy."

"Nope."

She shook her head and feigned sorrow. "That is so sad. I can see you starring in one. You could totally be the hero and win the girl in the end."

"The last thing I'm interested in is being somebody's hero." He rubbed a hand against his chest. She noticed he did that quite often and wondered if he was even aware he was doing it.

"Too bad. You'd be a great one."

He gave a bitter laugh. "Trust me, it's not all it's cracked up to be."

"You sound like you have experience."

"Nope. Turns out I was just a fool."

"And you'd rather not talk about it."

He glanced at her briefly before returning his attention to the road. "You, Arden West, are both gorgeous and smart."

His casual compliment warmed her even as she felt a twinge of guilt for misleading him. Clearly someone— no doubt a woman—had hurt him. Although curious, Arden didn't press for more information. She'd never deliberately make him uncomfortable. "Flattery will earn you a change in subject."

"Thanks."

They drove along for a while in companionable silence. Leafy trees and wildflowers lined the country road. In the distance a small herd of cows grazed lazily and a few horses raced in an open field. The scenery was so peaceful Arden sighed. "It's so beautiful here."

"That it is."

"But, still, you must miss Chicago." Sweet Briar was a nice time-out from her regular life and she was amazed by how much she was enjoying her stay. The people were so welcoming and she fit in so easily it was as if she'd known many of them for much longer than a week. Still, she couldn't imagine living here year-round. She would miss her parents. And as much as they aggravated her, she would miss Jax and Blake, too.

Brandon laughed. "It's not like I've been banished. I go back to visit my family and friends regularly."

"That's not what I mean."

"I know. And, yes, there are things I miss. I miss the energy of the city. I loved all of the little neighborhood theaters showcasing plays by local artists. And there were so many jazz clubs and piano bars. And don't even mention the symphony. No matter what your interests, there's always something to do." He grinned. "Believe it or not, I really miss public transportation. I liked being able to catch the bus or jump on the 'L' to get where I wanted to go without the hassle of driving."

He pulled into the parking lot of the movie theater. It was nearly full so he had to park in the last row. "But still," he continued as he removed the key from the ignition, "there's something to be said about small-town living. Everyone knows everyone else. There are no secrets or hidden agendas. What you see is what you get. People are truly who they seem to be."

Except her. Guilt filled her when she thought of how she hadn't been truthful about her identity. But her secret wasn't harmful to anyone. No one's life would change if they knew her real last name and net worth. The only thing guaranteed to change was how people treated her, which was something she wanted to avoid as long as possible. The oasis she'd found in Sweet Briar would vanish once people knew she was a Wexford.

"Come on." Brandon opened his door. "We don't want to miss anything. And we need popcorn."

"With extra butter."

"Is there any other way?" he asked, holding out his hand to her. She took it.

"I can't remember the last time I had this much fun."

They were sitting at an old-fashioned ice-cream parlor on the outskirts of Willow Creek Brandon thought she would enjoy. Arden dragged her tongue over her orange sherbet, dabbing at a drip on her cone. His stomach clenched in response. Eating his chocolate ice cream didn't give him nearly as much pleasure as watching her eat her dessert.

"You're only saying that because they showed your chick flick."

She gave a delectable little giggle as she took another taste. "I like happy endings. There aren't enough of those in life."

"Are you looking for yours?"

"Not anymore. I'm through with men. My life is more of a horror story than a romance."

"You're young. This is only the beginning. You don't know what's going to happen in the middle or how your story is going to end."

"The credits don't have to roll for me to know what kind of movie I'm in. It's definitely not a romance." She finished her cone, wiped her mouth with a napkin and tossed it into the garbage, flashing him a smile. "Maybe my life is a mystery."

"That's better than horror, I suppose."

"Or slapstick. I would hate to get a pie in the face. I don't think that would be much fun."

"Trust me, it's not."

"Are you speaking from experience?"

"Unfortunately."

She leaned her chin into her hand. "This sounds interesting."

He tossed his napkin into the trash and dusted his hands on his jeans. He looked around the parlor. They were the only customers left and the waiter was leaning against the bar, alternately looking at the giant clock on the wall and throwing dirty looks in their direction. "We should leave so he can close."

She stood and followed him. "No way you're getting out of telling me what happened."

He waited until they were on the road home before telling her the story. "It wasn't exactly pie in the face. It was crème brûlée tossed on my chef whites by an irate waitress."

"Wow. I wouldn't have had the nerve. What did you do?"

"What could I do? I wiped off my clothes and kept cooking. After I fired her."

She tossed him a mischievous grin. "No. I mean what did you do to make her throw dessert at you?"

"Nothing. I just expected her to do her job. She preferred to go on a hot date with a lawyer."

"Ah, romance."

"For him it was probably more like a big-budget disaster movie."

She laughed, her eyes dancing with humor. If he wasn't careful, he could fall for her. That was a sobering thought and the smile died on his lips. He wasn't going to open his heart again no matter how appealing Arden was. Not in this lifetime.

"Thanks again for taking me," she said, pulling him out of his reverie.

"No problem. I enjoyed the company."

"You know, I've been thinking," Arden said as they walked into the house. "You and Joni have been great to let me stay with you, but I should probably move out. John says the part for my car won't arrive until Tuesday, so I'll be in Sweet Briar a couple more days. The last of the wedding guests left town this morning, so I can check into the bed-and-breakfast tomorrow."

He tried to meet her gaze, but she was looking everywhere but at him. Without thinking, he tilted her chin so their eyes met. He saw the surprise and immediately dropped his hand, shoving it into the pocket of his jeans, trying to downplay the electric spark that he'd felt when he touched her face. "Don't you remember? Kristina said she was booked for the summer."

"Right." She frowned and two lines appeared between her eyebrows. A second later they disappeared and a slight smile lifted her full lips. "But she mentioned that other place."

"The Come On Inn?"

She nodded. "I can try to get a room there."

"You can try. Call them in the morning to see what is available if that's what you want to do." His heart pinched at the thought of her leaving, which was ridiculous—and proof that he really did need for her to leave his home, if not Sweet Briar. How could he possibly be attached to her? He barely knew her. Sure she was sweet and funny, not to mention beautiful. But so were a lot of women. He had no problem hanging around them when the urge struck him. Nor did he have any difficulty walking away when the time came.

So what made Arden different? Why was the thought of her leaving his home so difficult if not painful? It wasn't, he decided. She was no different from any other woman. He wouldn't allow her to be.

"That's what I'll do."

She smiled at him and the two of them stood as if frozen, which was odd since he was suddenly over-heated. The air between them crackled with electricity and her heady scent swirled around him, enticing him to move closer. The urge to take her into his arms very nearly overcame him. He inhaled and forced himself to remember the danger that came from getting emotion-ally involved with a woman. Normally he was able to separate the physical and the emotional, but he knew he would not be able to do that with Arden. At least not easily. So he muttered good-night and walked away be-fore he did something stupid.

Arden hung up the phone and sighed. There was no room at the Come On Inn. For good measure, she'd con-tacted Kristina at the Sunrise and been told the same thing. Kristina had enthused about having every room booked for the next two months then rambled on in what could only be called free association, talking about ev-erything from the flowers lining the street to spinach

salad. She had promised to let Arden know if she had
any cancellations.

Not having a room to rent wasn't the worst thing
in the world. Far from it. In fact it wasn't the worst
news she'd had that day. That news had been delivered
bright and early by John. Apparently, there was labor
strife at the parts factory and he didn't know when he
would receive the part he needed for her Beetle. He'd
tried calling around to other suppliers but hadn't been
able to get his hands on it. He had no idea when her car
would be ready.

At this point, Arden had a decision to make. She
could hire a tow truck and return to Baltimore. That
thought roiled her stomach. She was not ready to return
home and face the situation with Michael-the-peanut-
brain. She also wasn't ready to deal with her smothering brothers. Especially not since she was finally able
to breathe freely. She needed the distance, which was
why she'd been going to Florida in the first place. Going
back home wasn't an option.

Hopping a flight and going to her parents' winter
home in Florida had also lost its appeal. She no longer wanted to spend her days alone in that big house
while her parents traveled through Europe. She no longer craved the solitude.

She could remain in Sweet Briar. Brandon had
said she could stay with him and Joni until her car
was ready. Of course at the time they'd all believed it
would be only a day or two, three at the most. Surely
he wouldn't have made such a generous offer had he
known it would be open-ended. She didn't want to become the houseguest who wouldn't leave.

She could always go somewhere else, but Sweet Briar

was growing on her. It had taken only a couple of days to discover why this place had become a tourist destination. There were so many cute shops to explore, fun places to visit and, of course, the beach. This was a wonderful place for a vacation.

More than that, the people were warm and welcoming, making her want to stay. Unlike the Hotel California, she didn't want to check out. She definitely wasn't ready to leave. She could envision spending a few more weeks here. But she had to find another place to stay.

She didn't feel right staying in Brandon's home. There was something very intimate about that. And the more she was around him, the more attracted she became. He was unlike any man she'd ever met. Sure, he was strong and hardworking. But, more than that, he gave his best in everything and expected others to do the same. His high standards and belief in others inspired them to give their all.

How could she help but admire him? She couldn't. Which was why she needed to put some physical distance between them so she could maintain her emotional distance.

Joni seemed to know everyone and she had her finger on the pulse of this town. If anyone had a place for rent, she would know.

Slipping her phone into her pocket, Arden headed for the youth center. Over the past few days she had spent many hours volunteering there. She was quite impressed with Joni and what she managed to do on a shoestring budget. The place was filled with kids of all ages engaged in a variety of activities. A group of young teenage girls walked slowly by two older boys. One of the boys smiled and the other said hello. The girls burst into giggles and hurried away.

Arden shook her head and bit back a smile.

"Ah, young love."

Arden turned at the sound of Brandon's voice. "What are you doing here?"

He held up a round tray with a clear plastic cover. "One of the kids is having a birthday today and Joni needed cupcakes."

She looked closer at the treats. "You baked them?"

"Perish the thought. I stopped at Polly Wants A Cookie and picked them up for her. What are you doing here?"

"Looking for Joni. I was hoping she knew of a place I can rent for a couple of weeks."

"Oh."

She couldn't tell what that one word meant, but a crazy part of her hoped it was disappointment that she wouldn't be staying in his guest room any longer. That thought only proved that she was losing her mind and that she needed to put distance between them.

"Yes. There's some sort of labor dispute at the place where the part for my car is being manufactured. Long story short, John doesn't know when he'll be able to fix my car so I need to find a place to stay. Joni knows everyone so…" Arden's voice trailed off as she realized that Brandon was staring mutely as she babbled. She clamped her jaw shut, refusing to let another word escape.

"Did I hear you say you were looking for a place to stay?" Joni asked from behind Arden, making her jump. She'd been so entranced by Brandon that she hadn't heard the other woman approach.

"Yes." She quickly summarized her conversation

with the mechanic. "Since you know everyone, I figured you might have a lead on a room I can rent."

"You know you can stay in the house."

"Three days for fish and houseguests. Any longer and they start to smell. I've been in your house for a week. I don't want you to hold your nose when you see me."

Joni laughed. "I get your point although I don't agree. But I can do better than a room. Brandon and I have a garage apartment. It's renovated and just sitting empty. You're welcome to stay there as long as you need. Isn't that right, Brandon?"

Arden's eyes flew to his. His poker face was firmly in place but he nodded. After a long moment he replied, "Sure."

"I don't want to impose."

"You're not imposing," Joni replied before he had a chance.

"If you're sure." Arden glanced at Brandon again.

He nodded, but a part of her wondered if he really was envisioning strangling his sister. "Stay as long as you need."

"Thanks."

He handed the tray of cupcakes to his sister. "I need to get going. I'll catch up with you two later."

Brandon was gone so fast Arden didn't have a chance to thank him for his continued hospitality. "Are you sure it's okay? Brandon seems kind of reluctant."

"Positive." Joni juggled the tray of pink-iced cupcakes. "Do you have time to hang out for a while? I need to set up a party for one of our little girls, then I'll be available to show you the apartment in about an hour."

"Sure. If you need an extra hand, I have two."

"I always need help."

Arden helped Joni decorate a room for the party. They draped streamers from the ceiling and taped some on the walls. Next they blew up blue and green balloons and bundled them into centerpieces they placed on the paper tablecloths covering the long table. They blew up pink balloons and tied them to the back of the gray folding chairs. Finally they hung up a colorful banner, then stood back to admire the festive room.

"Impressive, if I do say so myself," Joni said, folding the step stool and carrying it to the closet.

"I agree, but not only about the room. I mean you. I didn't know youth centers hosted birthday parties." Arden would have smiled, but blowing up balloons was hard on the jaws. They needed a helium tank something fierce.

Joni closed the door and leaned against it. "We're an all-purpose center. Sweet Briar is prospering, but there are still some families that are struggling. We try to help out when we can. Like the party for this girl. Her mother has cancer and is fighting to live. The father is not in the picture."

"Hence the party."

"Yes."

Arden followed Joni from the room, her mind busy. She wanted to make a donation to the youth center to help them continue their good work. Because she wanted to maintain her anonymity, she wouldn't be able to make the gift until she returned home. But she didn't want to wait. They could do even more good if they had the funds. She would contact her brothers and convince them to give, as well. They were always supporting worthy causes and she couldn't think of one more deserving than the youth center.

Arden and Joni chatted nonstop on the ride to the apartment. Joni ran into the house for the keys, then met Arden outside the garage. Arden followed Joni up the flight of stairs, holding her breath until she opened the door.

"It's beautiful," Arden said as she stepped inside and looked around.

"Do you think you'll be comfortable here?"

"Definitely." Arden ran her hand across the black granite breakfast bar that separated the kitchen from the living room, then straightened one of the three stools with black-and-white-striped cushions that comprised the dining area. The living room was quaint with a cream love seat and matching chair with gray, black and red decorative throw pillows. A small bookcase overflowed with a variety of paperbacks.

"Okay. It's yours for as long as you want."

"Thanks. Now about rent."

"Arden."

"Joni."

"You're my friend."

"Exactly. Friends don't take advantage of friends."

Joni sighed and named an absurdly low figure. Arden raised her eyebrow and Joni doubled the number.

Arden smiled. "Agreed."

"You drive a hard bargain."

"I just want to do what's fair."

Shaking her head, Joni handed over the key and left. Arden walked through the apartment again, her home for the foreseeable future. Of course, if there was one thing life had taught her, it was that nothing about the future could be foreseen.

# Chapter Six

Brandon leaned against the back door and stared across the dark yard. A ribbon of light filtered through the window of the garage apartment. He wondered what Arden was doing. He hadn't seen her since this morning at the youth center when he'd run away like his pants were on fire.

Despite the fact that she'd stayed with them for only a week, he missed her presence. He'd grown accustomed to her easy laughter and quick if somewhat offbeat wit. Her wicked and quirky sense of humor matched his and he found himself relaxing around her. In fact, he felt more at ease with her than he did with anyone besides Joni. The feeling of rightness that filled him whenever they were together caught him off guard and he wasn't sure how to handle it. Thus, the race away from her this morning.

After Sylvia, he'd sworn off relationships, choosing

instead to focus on his restaurant. Sure, he had dated in the past three years, but he was always careful to let the woman know the rules. No hearts were involved under any circumstances. He didn't do love. But dating an endless stream of women, no matter how beautiful or charming they were, had become tiresome and left him empty. Being alone had become preferable.

No woman had attracted his interest until Arden stumbled into his life. She'd already found a way into his mind and was consuming his thoughts. He wasn't ready for anything serious or emotional. What he needed was to reinforce the barrier around his heart before she tunneled her way in there, too.

And now he stood here in his kitchen like some teenager, lurking in the shadows hoping to get a glimpse of the object of his affection. This was pathetic. *He* was pathetic. He needed to get a grip.

"I'm all packed and ready to go," Joni said, sauntering into the room. He spun around, but not fast enough to fool her. She smirked. "My brother, the Peeping Tom."

"I don't know what you're talking about." Could he sound any guiltier?

"Uh-huh. Sure. I can spell it out if you need me to."

"Leave it alone."

She wrapped her arms around him and gave him a tight hug. "Not all women are like Sonya."

"Sylvia. Her name was Sylvia."

"Right. Not that it makes a difference. My point is the same. Not every woman is a liar."

"I never said they were."

"You don't need to. Your actions speak loud and

clear. You never let a woman get close enough to find out what her character is."

"I don't have time for that. I'm concentrating on my restaurant."

"Hiding behind it is more like it."

He pulled out of her embrace and sat at the table. The garage apartment was still visible from his chair and he forced his eyes to look anywhere but there. He should have sat somewhere else. It was too late to switch seats with Joni watching and interpreting his every move. "That's not what I'm doing. I need to work hard so I can succeed."

"You have more than succeeded and you know it."

He shrugged. "Maybe, but you know how tough the restaurant business can be. I have to work hard to keep from growing stale and losing ground. If I want to grow my reputation in the industry, I have to continue to create and innovate. That takes time and energy."

He'd taken out a loan in order to buy out Justin. He was making his payments, but a decline in business would make that difficult. He needed to stay focused on what was important, and that wasn't the woman currently occupying his garage apartment.

"Even if you need to work, you still need to make time for love."

"Love? I finally got the folks off my back and you want to start in? I'll tell you what I told them. I'm not interested in love anymore." He stood to his full height. He always needed every advantage when debating with Joni. "And speaking of love, I don't exactly see you marching down the aisle."

"Touché. Consider the topic closed."

Now that he'd won the argument, he smiled at his sister. "You need a ride to the airport?"

"No. Lex is going to drop me."

"Ah."

"Ah, nothing." Joni hopped to her feet, proving that a good offense was the best defense. "I'd better get some sleep. I have an early flight. But before I go, I need you to do something for me."

"What's that?"

"Look after Arden."

"Joni."

She raised a hand. "I'm just asking you to spend a bit of time with her. She's alone in town with no transportation or friends. I'm going to introduce her around when I get back, but in the meantime, you're all she has. Remember, she just broke off with her boyfriend. Don't let her spend all her time alone in that apartment. Be nice to her. Please."

"Joni. I don't need you matchmaking."

"I'm not. I'm just imagining how I would feel in her shoes."

He shook his head. Joni drew people to her without trying. She would always have friends, new to town or not. But Arden was more reticent than Joni. She didn't seem to make friends as easily as his sister. Knowing he'd been played but unable to fight back, he huffed out a breath and nodded. "I won't leave her alone."

"You'll hang out with her?"

"Didn't I just say that?"

"You're the world's best brother." Joni kissed his cheek then bade him good-night.

When he had the kitchen to himself once more, Brandon wondered why he had agreed. He hoped it was be-

cause he shared Joni's compassion. Somehow he didn't
think that was the entire reason. Still it was the best he
could come up with on short notice.

Brandon sniffed the soup, spooned a bit of it into his
mouth, let it settle on his tongue for a few seconds and
then swallowed. Frowning, he set the spoon beside the
bowl and leaned against the kitchen counter. Something
was missing from the new bouillabaisse recipe he was
creating, but he couldn't put his finger on it.

One of the things he really enjoyed was putting a
new spin on old favorites. Anyone could follow a recipe
and make a good meal. It took a special gift to create a
dish that people made reservations weeks in advance
in order to try. He had that gift.

He took another taste. He wished Joni was around
so he could ask her opinion, but she was in Chicago
visiting their parents and no doubt getting grilled like
a good steak. They wanted grandchildren and none of
their three children were cooperating. As the oldest,
Russell should have been their target. A career military
officer, he was currently stationed outside the United
States and safely out of nagging range. After the mess
with Sylvia, Brandon's parents were giving him a re-
prieve. Thankfully, they'd stopped trying to introduce
him to the unmarried daughters of their friends. That
left Joni the sole focus of their attention. She always
took their pressure with a smile in her good-natured
way. No doubt she was enjoying her visit and catching
up with her friends, coming up with creative ways to
avoid countless blind dates with men, each of whom
their parents were sure was *the one*.

Still, he wished she was here so she could serve as his taste tester.

A movement outside the window caught his eye. Arden. Dressed in a short denim skirt that showcased her world-class legs and a white T-shirt with a gray design that fit perfectly over her perky breasts, she was skipping down the steps like a young girl. His window was open and he could hear her singing a song he always turned off whenever it came on the radio. His music preferences ranged from jazz and blues to his preferred classical but didn't include pop.

Brandon remembered his promise to Joni. He'd said he wouldn't leave Arden to her own devices until Joni returned. And he did need someone to taste his soup. Before he could change his mind, he called out to her. "Do you have a few minutes?"

She paused, one foot on the bottom step, met his eyes through the screen, then nodded. Even from this distance, he could see the brilliant smile on her face and his body responded. There was just something about Arden that appealed to him on a basic level. Despite knowing it would be better if he kept her at arm's length, part of him longed to draw her closer. And not just physically. Sexual attraction could be easily understood and dismissed. But more than wanting her body, he wanted to know her. He wanted to discover what made her laugh and what upset her. He wanted to hear about her dreams and share his with her. Given the fact that he didn't want to open his heart to anyone, the last thing he should have done was give her a place to stay.

Though she claimed to have sworn off relationships, he knew that vow wouldn't last. She had too much love inside to keep it to herself. Eventually she'd want to share that love with a man and, later, children. She'd want the white picket fence and all the trimmings. Before Sylvia, he'd wanted forever as well, and Arden would have fit into his life perfectly. But he didn't believe in happily-ever-after. Not anymore.

Arden stepped inside the kitchen, bringing with her the happiness and sunshine that followed her around even on the gloomiest day. "Did you need me?"

"Yes." He grabbed a spoon and dipped it into the pot. "Taste this." He held the spoon up to her. Her eyes widened and she hesitated before opening her mouth and then closing her lips over the spoon. She swallowed but didn't say anything.

"Well?"

"Bouillabaisse."

"And?"

She tilted her head. "And what?"

"What do you think?"

"It tastes different somehow. Better."

"I'm trying to create a new recipe but can't figure out what's missing."

"Nothing's missing. It's good."

"But not great."

She laughed and her eyes lit as she looked longingly at the pot. "I think it's great. It's the best I've ever had."

He filled a bowl, offered it to her, then pulled out a chair for her. "Sit down and eat."

"Thanks. I thought you'd never ask." She ate another spoonful of soup, then looked up with her ever-present smile. "So do you do this a lot?"

"Work on new recipes? Every Tuesday. I want to offer the best food to my customers and create new twists on old favorites. That requires work." He rubbed his chin. "Well, not exactly work, but concentration and time."

"It sounds like fun."

"It is."

The spoon disappeared between her perfect lips and she moaned softly. He struggled to keep his imagination under control. She swallowed and he forced himself to refocus his attention on the missing ingredient and not the way her pink tongue flicked against her plump bottom lip.

"How old were you when you decided you wanted to be a chef?"

"Nine."

"Really? I thought boys that age wanted to be athletes or police officers or firefighters."

"Not me. I always knew I wanted to own my own restaurant. My grandfather had a soul-food restaurant. I started hanging out with him when I was about eight. Just a couple of hours a day in the summer and on Saturdays during the school year. I had my own stool in the kitchen where I watched him cook." Brandon folded his arms against his chest, seeing the past so clearly it could have happened only yesterday. "He was something. A genuine artist. His food was phenomenal. Granddad made macaroni and cheese that was so good it made you want to slap your mama."

Arden's laugh was a sweet sound that battered his flagging resistance. She was getting to him.

"And his greens? Please. People came from all over the Midwest for a forkful. He didn't play music in the restaurant because people loved his food so much they sang while they ate. The top choir directors used to get their best inspiration just from eating there."

"You're making that up."

"Exaggerating maybe. But only a little."

"Well, if his food was anywhere near as good as yours, then it had to be great."

"Thanks."

"Did you study cooking in school, too?"

"Yeah. I was the only dude in high school who took home ec. All the other guys were taking wood shop and auto mechanics. I might not be able to rebuild a car engine, but I can make a soufflé that can bring tears to your eyes."

"And bouillabaisse that is so good one bowl isn't enough."

Taking her less-than-subtle hint, he refilled her bowl. "After high school I studied at the CIA."

"You're a spy, too?" she asked, her spoon frozen inches away from her mouth.

He chuckled. She really was cute. "No. The Culinary Institute of America. From there I went to France and later to Italy and Spain to learn."

"Then you came to Sweet Briar to open your restaurant," she said, finishing the story for him.

"Not quite." His cell phone rang and he looked down at the screen. Sylvia. Again. Think of the devil and she'll show up. She'd called him out of the blue three days ago. He'd been shocked to hear her voice after all this time. Before his lungs had filled with his next breath, an all-consuming rage had filled him and he'd told her never to call him again. Clearly she'd chosen to ignore that request. No surprise there. She didn't believe rules applied to her.

She'd cost him his dream and nearly his life, and yet she still had the nerve to track him down. Nothing she could say would ever be of the slightest interest to him. He'd been fooled once, but it wouldn't happen again.

Memories of his time working at a famous Chicago restaurant flashed through his mind, flushing his previous good mood. He'd been close to accomplishing his dream of becoming a nationally known chef when she'd entered his life with her treachery and all but destroyed him. In the end nothing remained of the life he'd mapped out for himself, so he'd moved to Sweet Briar and begun building a new life. A life that didn't include love.

The sudden glacial look in Brandon's eyes puzzled Arden. One moment they were laughing and talking, and then his phone rang. He'd frowned as he looked at the screen but hadn't taken the call. Now the look on his face was cold enough to give her frostbite. A part of Arden told her to leave, but she ignored it. She wanted to know what had made him morph from a charming man into a living, breathing Popsicle. And why pain had flashed in his eyes before he masked it.

"Oh. That's right. You moved from Chicago three years ago. I remember you telling me that. Why did you move here?" She didn't know if the phone call was responsible for the change in his attitude or if talking about his reason for moving to Sweet Briar was the cause, but she was curious about the rest of his story. Maybe hearing it would help her understand why his mood had shifted so radically. And she wanted to understand. "Why move from Chicago, which has some of the best and most famous restaurants in the country, to a small town? You could get way more recognition there. And you deserve it. With your talent you could have your own cooking show and publish bestselling cookbooks."

"I had my reasons."

That answer should have been enough of a hint. Clearly he didn't want to talk about it. A wiser woman would have let it go. She would have, too, if she hadn't seen the pain behind the wall he'd erected and recognized that pain as one she'd experienced herself.

It was the pain of betrayal. Although thinking of Michael-the-turd annoyed her, she didn't hurt with the same intensity as she had when she'd discovered that he was only using her. But she knew now she hadn't been in love. Not really.

Whatever had happened to Brandon must have been truly devastating for him to still feel the ache. And it was clear he was hurting. Not only that, he'd uprooted himself, moving from Chicago, where his career knew no limits, to Sweet Briar. No matter how much praise he received from his customers, his career would never reach the zenith it once could have.

It occurred to her that he was hiding from his life. Something she knew about all too well. Sure, he'd opened a restaurant and continued to create dishes, but his potential was severely limited. Maybe if she pressed, he would talk about it. And maybe, please God, maybe, he would get over the pain. She took a breath and let it out. "I'm sure you do have your reasons. But you have a great gift. An incredible gift. And you're hiding your light under a bushel. Did you really study all those years just to open a restaurant in a town of less than two thousand people?"

He placed both hands on the table and inhaled deeply. When he looked up, she met his eyes and knew she'd made a mistake. He'd been angry before. Now he was furious. "I don't have to explain myself to you."

"I'm not asking for an explanation. It's just that I care. I don't think your grandfather would be happy to see you're not living up to your potential."

Brandon held up his hand, indicating she should stop. "You don't know anything about me, so stop. Now."

"You're right. I'm sorry. I'll leave." Guilt and sorrow filled her. She had wanted to make things better but, instead, had made them worse. Jumping up, she headed for the back door. Blinded by guilty tears, she missed a step and tumbled down two stairs before she was able to grab on to the railing.

"Arden." Brandon materialized, reaching out to her.

She swatted his hand away, ashamed that she'd overstepped. Didn't she hate it when her brothers tried to tell her what to do, like they thought they knew better than she did what was best for her life? And she had done the same to Brandon. "I don't need your help. Thanks. I can make it down the stairs on my own."

"Obviously," he said drily, and moved out of the way.

Straightening, she put weight on her right foot and nearly crumpled. She must have made a sound of pain because he was there in an instant, sweeping her off her feet. Holding her in his arms, he hesitated a moment as if trying to decide what to do with her now that he had her. He shook his head and then climbed the stairs. He strode through the kitchen and down a hall, nudging open a partially closed door to what she guessed was his home office. After shoving books and papers onto the floor, he set her on a butter-soft leather couch.

The room was bright although nothing to write home about. There were piles of cookbooks and magazines on a brown leather chair, the oak table and the floor. In fact, the only surface that wasn't piled with books and papers was the enormous, gleaming desk. It held a phone, a desk calendar and a computer, all of which appeared to be perfectly centered. Interesting. It was as if two people inhabited this one space—one neat and the other incredibly disorganized. Sort of like the evil genius meets his anal twin.

"Let me look at your ankle."

"I'm fine." She tried to pull her leg away, but he grasped her calf firmly. Hot fire shot through her body. She wanted to believe the pain from her ankle caused the reaction, but that would have been the biggest lie ever told. His callused and knife-nicked hands gently holding her foot was responsible for the tingles that wiggled up and down her spine.

"You're not fine. Now hold still. I'm not going to hurt you."

"I know. But I feel like I hurt you. I'm just so embarrassed. I shouldn't have overstepped. I know we've only known each other for a short time, but I feel close to you. Like I know you. But, still, I shouldn't have said what I did. Please, please, please forgive me."

His intense eyes bored into her as if trying to see clear to her soul. She looked away and forced herself to continue, her voice much softer. "I don't have a lot of friends and I thought you could be one. Believe it or not, I was trying to be a friend to you. But I forgot, friends don't step over the line. Especially one so clearly drawn."

"I see."

Arden let the silence go on as long as she could stand.

Was he her friend or not? Did he accept her apology? "Well?"

"I don't think your ankle is broken or even sprained. You just twisted it. I'll get some ice." He placed a couple of throw pillows under her ankle before leaving her alone, his actions speaking more eloquently than any words could. He wasn't interested in being her friend. Her eyes welled and she blinked back tears, determined not to let him see just how deeply his rejection cut.

"This should help," he said as he returned. She turned her head away and swiped at the tear that had escaped, then turned back to him. He squatted beside her and gently placed the towel-wrapped ice on her swelling ankle before meeting her eyes. "And I accept your apology."

That was it? Well, what did she expect? She'd insulted him. Now she had to accept the fallout. She'd ruined something good. She blinked furiously, but another tear escaped and trickled down her face.

"Don't cry."

The kindness in Brandon's voice was her undoing and the tears came faster. It would have been easier to maintain her control if he'd acted like a jerk the way she deserved. But his understanding broke the dam holding back the flood of emotions and sobs she'd refused to shed when she'd learned the truth about her so-called friends back in Baltimore.

He sat on the couch and pulled her into his arms, his masculine scent surrounding her. She didn't resist, but went gratefully, thankful for the comfort.

He brushed his lips across her hair. His hands caressed her back gently. Gradually her tears slowed and the mood in the room shifted. It wasn't a slow shift, but rather a dramatic one. One minute the feel was comforting. The next the room crackled with sexual tension.

She'd found him attractive almost from the first second she'd laid eyes on him. What woman wouldn't? With his handsome face, intelligent eyes and muscular physique, he was sex appeal personified. As she'd gotten to know him, she had discovered that a kind man lived within that gorgeous body.

With her head against his chest, she felt his heartbeat change from slow and steady, the rate increasing until it matched the rapid beat of her own. She lifted her head and searched his eyes. They were so dark that the pupil and iris were nearly the same color. He lifted one corner of his mouth and huffed out what almost passed as a laugh, then lowered his head until his lips almost touched hers. "This is such a bad idea."

"I know." But when he touched her lips with his own she didn't think about turning away.

Kissing her temporary boss and landlord might not be among her brightest decisions, but it was definitely one of the most pleasurable.

## *Chapter Seven*

Brandon heard Arden sigh as she leaned closer. Her soft breasts pressed against his chest, igniting a fire within him. Kissing her broke at least two of his rules, but when she put her arms around his neck and settled more comfortably on his lap, he couldn't remember what they were. He angled his head and deepened the kiss. She tasted of the savory bouillabaisse she'd been eating and her own natural sweetness. The combination was heady and delicious, and his body responded as his desire grew.

The telephone rang, bringing with it his sanity. He didn't look at the screen, letting the call go to voice mail. It was enough to cool him off and help him regain control. He shouldn't be doing this. Arden worked for him, even if only sporadically and despite the fact that she refused to accept payment beyond her tips. In his mind she was his employee, which put any type of physical relationship off-limits. Not only that, she was vulnerable. She might not be mourning the breakup with the jerk, but she'd been hurt recently. The pain was bad enough for her to go chasing across the country for some time away. Only deep hurt could cause such a re-action. He ought to know. With the two violated rules now clear in his mind, he reluctantly set her on the sofa beside him and leaned his forehead against hers.

"I know I should apologize, but to be honest I'm not sorry." Far from it. He wanted to kiss her until she didn't know her own name.

"Why should you be? I was a willing participant." She scrunched up her nose, looking sexier than she should. "Do you apologize to all the women you kiss? I mean, I could see saying you're sorry if you were a rotten kisser, but you're not."

His chest puffed out with pride, which was ridicu-lous. He'd been kissing girls since he was thirteen. With fifteen years of practice he should be good. He brushed a finger across her flushed cheek, then across her lips, which were damp and a bit swollen. "That's not why I'm apologizing. You were upset. I should have considered your state of mind and exercised more self-control."

She shrugged away his concern, then nibbled her bottom lip. "I'm sorry for what I said. I do admire you. But I have no right to try to run your life. I know what that feels like."

He considered her words and admitted to himself that she hadn't been entirely wrong. He had been running from his life when he'd first come to town. He'd been both physically and mentally scarred. But he liked the life he was creating here. "I know. And I believe you spoke from concern and friendship."

"I did. I don't want to be a judgmental know-it-all."

"You're not." He cut her off, knowing she would apologize ceaselessly if he didn't. Anyone could make a mistake. Certainly he had made his share. He rubbed the back of his neck. "Arden, this can't happen again."

"The kiss, you mean?"

"Yes. I shouldn't have done that. I won't do it again."

"What if I kiss you first?"

"Still no."

"Oh, phooey."

He laughed. She was such a determined little thing. But he had rules. He might have considered overlooking the employer/employee rule since she was only temporary, but he wasn't willing to break the most important rule of all: never become involved with a woman with whom he could fall in love. And Arden most assuredly fit into that category. Heck, the category might as well have been made for her. Even now he had to fight the urge to sweep her into his arms and pick up where they'd left off. But he wouldn't want to stop there. And it wasn't just because he desired her physically. He cared for her.

"Can we still be friends?" Her voice sounded small and tentative, almost as if she expected him to say no.

"Yes. We can absolutely still be friends." He just needed to make sure his body understood the meaning of the word and that kissing was not included.

She tilted her head to the side and smiled. "Good. Because outside of my family I don't have very many people in my life I can trust."

He could understand her lack of faith. He could

count on one hand and still have fingers left the number of people he truly trusted who weren't related to him. Somehow she was easing her way into that small circle. As much as he enjoyed holding her and despite how perfectly she fit in his arms or, perhaps, because of it, he needed to establish the necessary distance between them before he did something foolish like let her into his heart.

He rose and shifted the pile of papers and books from a chair to the floor in order to give his hands something to do.

"I should leave so you can get back to what you were doing."

Arden swung her legs around slowly as if trying to avoid bumping her ankle into anything. Brandon knew the sensible thing—the right thing—was to offer her his arm and help her walk out of his house. So naturally he bent and scooped her into his arms.

He expected her to make at least a token protest, but she didn't. Instead, she wrapped her arms around his neck and leaned her head against his shoulder. The warmth from her soft body heated him and he was instantly aroused. Her sweet scent was too delicate to have come from a bottle of perfume. It could have been her shampoo or lotion or any number of things, but he knew it was just Arden. That unique scent that turned him on so much could never be duplicated.

He carried her through the kitchen, down his back stairs, across the lawn and up the stairs to her garage apartment, wishing the distance was farther. She felt so right in his arms. With every step he tried to extinguish his growing desire. It wasn't just physical. That he could handle. What worried him was the part of him that wanted more from Arden. The part that forgot the agony of being burned by a woman's lies. Of being shot and nearly killed because of her deceit. The part that wanted a future.

The rational part of him reasserted itself and he mentally withdrew to a safe distance. He would never make himself vulnerable again. Even with Arden.

Arden stretched, straightened her legs, then immediately winced and sucked in her breath as pain shot through her ankle. Most of the swelling had gone down, but an ache remained.

After Brandon had settled her on the couch, she'd insisted that she would be fine once she'd taken a pain pill. Her ankle was hurting so badly she'd ignored the fact that she was a real lightweight when it came to any type of medicine. One little pill was all it took to knock her out for the afternoon.

She looked at the clock and jerked upright. It was nearly six thirty. After limping to the bathroom she hopped to the kitchen, using the wall and any pieces of furniture she could get her hands on for balance. Although small, the kitchen had all the modern conveniences she needed. Too bad she didn't have food.

She'd been on her way to buy groceries when Brandon had interrupted her. The two bowls of bouillabaisse she'd eaten were a distant memory. Her stomach growled and she grabbed the telephone and the takeout menus she had acquired, deciding on Italian. Pizza Palace made great pizza, with plenty of melted cheese. Best of all, they delivered.

She was about to call in her order when there was a knock on her door.

"Coming," she called, hobbling to the door.

"Take your time."

At Brandon's voice she stumbled and grabbed on to the arm of the couch. Great. She nearly injured her *other* ankle. She reached the door without further incident and quickly undid the locks he'd insisted she set after he left.

He looked far too tempting holding a tray filled with several covered dishes. Dressed in the relaxed jeans he favored and a plain white T-shirt, he gave her an easy grin that had her wobbling.

"I knew you wouldn't be able to cook with that ankle, so I whipped up a little something for you."

"You didn't have to do that. I could have ordered pizza."

He shuddered and headed for the kitchen. "Pizza? When you're injured, you need comfort food. It helps with the healing process and lifts the spirits. Sit. I'll be right back."

She ignored his command and slowly followed him to the kitchen, careful to keep weight off her foot. "I'm practically healed. My ankle isn't as swollen anymore."

"You don't follow orders very well."

"Not anymore." Once she'd been the proverbial good girl, doing what her parents said. She'd trusted in their love and wisdom and followed where they led. She'd consulted them when selecting a college, relying on their input. She knew they had her best interests at heart. But for all their good intentions, they'd ended up crippling her. She'd always had them to lean on so she hadn't developed the skills necessary to recognize the wolves disguising themselves as sheep among her so-called friends.

"That can be good under certain circumstances. In others, not so much."

"Don't worry. I'll follow orders while I'm on the clock. But since we're in my apartment, it's okay to ignore you."

He laughed and pulled a stool from the breakfast bar and helped her climb on. Her skin tingled from his simple touch, something she wouldn't mind experiencing over and over again. She forced herself to ignore the sensations and make conversation. "So what did you bring?"

"Exactly what you need to ease the pain. Macaroni and cheese, my famous fried pork chops, mixed greens and, for dessert, chocolate cake."

"Will you stay and eat with me?"

He hesitated for a minute, then nodded. "I think I have enough for two."

"It looks like you have enough for four."

He set a plate in front of her, then sat down beside her. The heat from his body warmed the cold places in her heart and she yearned to move closer.

He watched her, waiting for her to eat before he did. She dipped her fork into the cheesy pasta. She closed her eyes and moaned in appreciation. "This is wonderful."

He smiled, his perfect white teeth gleaming in his brown face. The skin beside his eyes crinkled and, incredibly, he looked even more handsome than before, something she didn't believe possible. "Thanks. It's my grandfather's recipe."

She took another satisfying bite. "You should serve this in the restaurant. It would be a big hit."

"So I've been told. But it doesn't fit with the rest of the menu. I only make this for my friends."

Her heart leaped. He did consider her a friend. For a minute she'd worried that he'd brought the meal out of some misplaced sense of guilt. He'd told her they were friends, but part of her was unsure he'd meant it. She'd been used so often she'd lost her ability to trust. But, then again, Brandon had no reason to lie. He had no clue who she was, so he couldn't have an ulterior motive. At least not one that involved money. If he was after her body…well, she was after his, too.

"What's so funny?"

She didn't realize she'd laughed out loud. "I was just thinking."

"Care to share the joke?"

*Not for my weight in chocolate-covered strawberries.* "No joke. Your food is just as powerful as your grandfather's. Both of you bring joy. And since I can't sing I just laughed." That didn't make sense to her, but fortunately he didn't act like he thought the comment was nuts.

"The power of good food. I guarantee pizza would not have had the same result."

They ate in comfortable silence for a few minutes, enjoying the food. Finally Brandon looked at her. "Tell me about yourself."

"What do you want to know?"

He swallowed a forkful of greens before answering. "Whatever you want to share. Tell me your goals. Your dreams. Tell me about your childhood or about your family. Anything."

"Wow. There's not that much to tell. At least nothing interesting," she said, setting her fork on the edge of her plate while pondering his request. He already knew the basics of her breakup. She didn't feel the need to tell him about catching Michael-the-toad hiding cameras in his bedroom so he could make a sex video that would be his "ride to easy street." A revelation like that was definitely not in the getting-to-know-you category Brandon had in mind.

"I'm the youngest of three kids. I'm the only girl."

"How much younger?"

"I'm twenty-three. My brothers are thirty and thirty-two."

"Are you close?"

"Yes and no. They love me and I love them, but we don't hang out together. Well, they hang out but I'm generally not included." She would have loved to attend baseball games and other sporting events with them. If only they would invite her. "Our relationship is slightly better than when I was a teenager. Then they bossed me around so much it was like having two extra dads. Now they aren't as bad although they could step back some and let me live my life."

"They're protecting you."

"Spoken like a big brother."

"It's part of the unwritten code."

Arden just laughed. Somehow she knew he would see it that way.

"I can't believe they let you stay here on your own."

She punched his arm. She'd seen him in short sleeves on numerous occasions, but she was still surprised by how rock hard his muscles were. "They didn't *let* me do anything."

He raised an eyebrow. "How often do you have to call them?"

*How did he know?* "Every Sunday."

"That sounds about right. Still, I would expect them to pop up just to assure themselves that you're okay."

Jax and Blake in Sweet Briar? That thought chilled

her to the bone. The last thing she needed was for her brothers to show up in town. As the face of the corporation, Blake was easily recognizable. Although Jax was less visible as general counsel, he was regularly named by magazines as one of the country's most eligible bachelors. One mention that she was their sister and her vacation from real life would be over.

"Let's just change the subject."

"Sure." He topped off her lemonade. "Tell me about your dreams for the future. My grandfather always used to talk about a five-year plan. Do you have one?"

"I'm a middle school science teacher. Last year was my first year teaching."

"How'd it go?"

"Well, the kids were great."

"That's always good. I hear a *but* in there, though."

"I made the mistake of getting involved with the principal. Now I'm not sure about returning to that school in the fall. I've got some feelers out, but it might be too late to change schools next year. I might have to tough it out, which is not a pleasant thought."

"Is he the jerk you just broke up with?"

She nodded, her face growing hot with embarrassment. She couldn't believe she had been so stupid as to become involved with her boss. How clichéd.

"Do you think he'll harass you or make your life miserable? Will he make it hard for you to do your job?" Brandon's eyes were flinty as all warmth had vanished from his voice.

"No." Of that she was certain. If he tried, her brothers would grind him into dust. Even a worm like him was bright enough to know that. People might go out of their way to become friends with the Wexfords, but no one made the extra effort to become an enemy. At least not without some sort of leverage, and Michael had none. Thank goodness she'd discovered his plot before he'd had a chance to act on it.

"If he does, that would be illegal. I have a lawyer who handles restaurant business. I can contact him and see if he can refer anyone to you if you need legal assistance. It might be good to talk to someone so you can be prepared."

Arden was touched but not surprised by Brandon's offer. He was a protector by nature. Despite his claim to the contrary, he was a hero.

She put her hand atop his. A tingle danced up her fingertips and down her spine, hitting every place in between. "You know, you really are a nice guy."

"Thanks. I think."

"Why don't guys like being thought of as nice?"

"It's the way we're wired."

"It's insane."

"You're probably right." He shrugged and looked at his watch. "I had better get going." He began clearing the remains of dinner. "I'll leave the leftovers in case you get hungry later."

"Thanks." She was so full she couldn't imagine eating again, but a woman never knew when chocolate cake would call her name. She started to rise to help him, but he stopped her with a hand on her shoulder.

"You stay sitting. I'll have this clean in no time."

She knew that was true. She'd seen him clean and sanitize the much-larger kitchen at the restaurant. He had a system and worked steadily yet quickly. Sure enough, he had her kitchen in order in less time than it would take her to stack the dishwasher.

"Do you need anything before I go?" he asked as he walked to the front door. She hopped along beside him, using his arm for balance. A bunch of naughty images flitted through her mind, but she tamped them down. After he made it plain he would not kiss her again, she didn't think necking on the couch was what he meant.

"No. I'll probably just read for a while and then go to bed."

He nodded but didn't say anything more. He didn't move to open the door, and she got the feeling he wasn't any more anxious to leave than she was for him to go. The awareness that had been simmering just below the surface bubbled and boiled over. His clean masculine scent swirled around her, bringing with it memories of how good it had felt to be kissed by him.

She met his eyes and the desire in his gaze ignited a fire in her that had her skin yearning for his touch. She swayed toward him and he placed his hand on her shoulder, stilling her before she could get closer.

He heaved out a breath. "This is such a bad idea."

"Is it?"

He groaned. "Help me out, Arden."

"I can't," she whispered. "I don't have the strength."

"Hell," he muttered, pulling her close to him. He hesitated half a second as if giving her a chance to change her mind, and then lowered his mouth and kissed her. The kiss in the den had been gentle and tentative. This kiss was hot and demanding, shooting fierce need through every part of her body.

She tried to step closer to him, but he held her at a distance, not letting her get too close. Then he wrenched his mouth away from hers. "We shouldn't be doing this."

"Why? And please don't say because I work for you

occasionally." Her voice sounded breathless in her ears. Although how she heard it over the thundering of the blood racing through her veins was a mystery.

"Okay. I won't, but that won't change the fact that you do." With a finger to her lips, he once more stifled any protest she might have had. When he realized what he had done, he quickly removed his finger and shoved his hands into his pockets.

"That's not the only reason we need to keep things from getting out of control. You're coming off a bad breakup. You're vulnerable. And I'm not looking to get involved. Not now. Maybe not ever. And you may be hurt now, but I can't picture you turning your back on love forever. Let's face it, you want kids and a house. The whole nine yards. Maybe not now, but one day. I don't. There's no use starting something when we want different things."

She hated to admit it, but he was right. There was no future for them. And there never could be as long as she was keeping her identity a secret. But since he didn't want her long term, there was no reason for her to reveal who she was and ruin the paradise she'd found in Sweet Briar.

## Chapter Eight

Arden awoke the next morning, bright and early. In fact, it was so early the sun had only begun to make its appearance. There was something to be said for taking an insanely long nap and then going to bed early. She had planned to read, but nothing seemed to hold her attention. After attempting to become interested in three different books, she realized she was too unsettled to focus. If she could have, she would have gone for a run. But her ankle still pained her, so she'd stayed in, taken a long bubble bath and then called Blake.

He'd been surprised to hear from her and they'd had a good conversation. Until she'd asked for money for the youth center. Then he had immediately begun to interrogate her. Where was she? How long had she been there? How could she trust these people so easily? Didn't she know people would always mention their need for money when the Wexfords were around? Hadn't she learned anything from her experiences?

She'd tried to explain that she had learned. To his credit he'd listened, something that surprised the heck out of her. But then he had always been more level-headed than Jax, which was why she'd called him. In the end Blake had agreed to keep an open mind about the Wexford Foundation making a sizable donation and he hadn't criticized her desire to make a personal one. She promised to get more information for him, which the foundation would need to make such a donation, although she had no idea how she would do that without arousing suspicion.

After that, they chatted for a few more minutes before ending the call. Perhaps it was the remnants of painkillers floating through her bloodstream, or maybe it was the good feelings from having a decent conversation with her brother, but, whatever the reason, she had slept long and deep.

Now she pointed her toes, testing her ankle. No pain. She turned her ankles in circles and didn't experience even the slightest twinge. The swelling had gone down. Standing, she walked across the room, first gingerly then with more confidence. A sigh escaped her lips. She was fine. Good, because she was hungry and the cupboard was bare. Although the diner wasn't open yet, it would be soon.

She skipped down the stairs and noticed Brandon coming across the driveway. She waved and smiled. After a hesitation so slight she wondered if she had imagined it, he lifted his hand in return.

"You're up early," she said when he was within hearing distance.

"No earlier than usual. I'm surprised to see you awake."

"No more surprised than I am. I love sleeping in, but I don't have another wink left in me. Where are you going?"

"The fish and produce markets."

"Do you want company or is this something you prefer to do on your own?"

He seemed to debate that internally. "You're more than welcome to come with me, but I have to warn you there's a lot of walking involved."

She lifted her leg and showed him her ankle. "No swelling or pain, so I'm good to go. Am I dressed okay or should I put on jeans like you?"

He looked at her and as his eyes swept over her legs, she felt the heat of his stare all the way to her bones. She knew she was blushing, but when their gazes met she didn't look away.

"Your shorts are fine. We need to get moving before all the good stuff is gone."

His voice sounded gruff, but Arden didn't let it offend her. She knew how seriously Brandon took everything that had to do with Heaven on Earth. It was his pride and joy and she was glad he was allowing her to accompany him. She found the restaurant business interesting and wanted to learn more about every facet.

Twenty-five minutes later they were walking along a pier with several small stores selling fresh fish. Trucks lined the street and the drivers raced about unloading boxes and barrels of fish and seafood. The place was jumping and Arden was immediately caught up in the energy.

"Do you come here every day?"

"Most days."

Arden rubbed her hands together. "So what exactly do you do?"

"I buy the fish and seafood that look best on a particular day and offer specials if what I buy isn't on the regular menu. It's a great way to try out new recipes and see how they go over."

"It also keeps people coming in to see what's new."

"True. Some places like the diner thrive because patrons know exactly what to expect. Their menu hasn't changed in the three years I've been here. And that works fine for them. I like having fixed menu items for people who come in for a specific dish, but I also like to create new food for the more adventurous customers. That way everyone is happy."

Arden nodded. There was a lot more to running his restaurant than met the eye. He was a shrewd businessman. Her father and brothers would be impressed. Not that they would ever meet him. She'd be back in Baltimore soon and Brandon would remain in Sweet Briar.

That thought cast shadows on her heart and dimmed the joy of the moment. But she needed to remember their relationship was only temporary and keep her heart out of it.

"Is something wrong?" Brandon's brow was drawn in concern.

"No. I'm fine."

"Are you sure? You seem a little sad."

"I'm just taking it all in. The sights. The sounds. The fresh air. Well, it's not exactly fresh, but the fish smell kind of makes me think of the ocean, which is fresh. If that makes any sense."

"It makes perfect sense. That's one of the reasons I

like coming here. Well, that and it reminds me of my grandfather."

For a moment Arden envied Brandon. He'd shared such a close relationship with his grandfather. And he had Joni and his parents and they all supported him in his endeavor. Her parents and brothers loved her, of course, but she yearned for them to see her as an adult instead of a big girl. She wanted to be respected like another adult and welcomed as a friend, not as a child to be overprotected. She knew her past behavior hadn't helped her cause, but she had changed. She just needed to show them how much.

Brandon clasped her hand and they entered one of the shops. She tightened her fingers around his, determined to enjoy the moment.

They went into several different stores where Brandon checked out the offerings. He made notes to himself on a little pad of paper he kept in his shirt pocket. By the time they were done, he'd bought an assortment of fresh fish. The shopkeepers promised to have the orders ready in two hours.

Next they drove a couple of miles to the produce market. The process was similar, with Brandon going to several stores and making notes of what he liked. He purchased a variety of fresh vegetables and fruit. Unlike the fish markets, they didn't have to wait for their purchases.

Once they'd made it through all the stalls, Brandon stacked two crates of raspberries and headed for his pickup. Arden grabbed a crate of strawberries and followed.

He turned. "Just what do you think you're doing?"

"I'm helping you. Why, what does it look like?"

"It looks like you're about to get into trouble. Now put down that heavy box."

"You're nuts," she said, placing her load in the truck beside his.

"I didn't bring you here to work."

"Then why did you bring me?"

Brandon stared into Arden's lovely eyes, temporarily lost as he tried to formulate an answer. "I brought you here to share the experience. I wanted you to enjoy it."

"I am. I'm having a great time." She wiped a hand across her forehead, leaving a red smear behind.

Before he could stop himself, he was gently brushing off the remains of the crushed fruit. Instead of removing his hand, he allowed his fingers to travel over her delicate cheekbones, down her soft cheek, finally coming to rest on her sweet lips. Pink and perfectly shaped, they called to him even without uttering a word.

"Oh, Arden," he murmured, catching her chin as he leaned forward. A small rational part of him warned that he was getting in way too deep. The bigger part of him didn't care.

He hesitated only a moment before touching his lips to hers. If she'd given even the slightest indication she didn't want him to kiss her, he would have backed off. What he saw settled it for him. In her eyes he saw a want that matched his own.

That's all he needed. He immediately closed the distance between them and captured her lips with his own. He'd planned for the kiss to be brief and gentle. But once his lips made contact with hers, he was consumed by an intense fire and all of his best intentions went up in smoke.

She stepped even closer. He inhaled her sweet scent, which added fuel to his already raging desire, and he wrapped her in his arms, holding her tight. She opened her mouth and he angled his head, deepening the kiss. He felt her heart beating against his chest, the rhythm matching the pounding of his own.

"Excuse me."

Brandon and Arden sprang apart at the sound of the amused voice. He kept his hand on her waist, though, as he looked into the grinning face of his older friend from the produce market.

"Sorry to interrupt, son. It took you so long to come back, I was afraid you forgot your blueberries and collard greens. I would hate for you to have to come all the way back here to get them." The man gestured to two smirking teens, who loaded the remaining crates into the cargo hold of Brandon's truck and then raced away.

"Thanks."

"No problem." The older man smiled as he glanced at Arden, clearly waiting for an introduction. He knew a little about Brandon's past and had been encouraging him to date. Brandon had never brought a woman with him to the markets so his friend probably assumed more than he should. Of course, he'd caught them in a serious clench, so he couldn't introduce her as his occasional employee. Well, he could, but that would embarrass and hurt Arden, something she didn't deserve.

"Ronnie, this is Arden West. Arden, this is Ronnie Leonard, owner of Leonard's Produce."

The older man extended his hand. "The freshest produce north of the equator. Come to think of it, we've got the best produce south of the equator, too."

Arden smiled and shook his hand. "It's very nice to meet you, Mr. Leonard."

"Pleasure's all mine. And it's Ronnie to all the pretty ladies."

"All right, Ronnie."

Was he flirting? Brandon frowned a little and stepped closer to Arden. Ronnie raised his eyebrows in obvious amusement.

"It's nice meeting you, Ms. West. Come see me again. I'll fix you up a box of our freshest fruit. A gift, you know."

Arden smiled at Ronnie. "I'd enjoy that. Next time I come this way I'll stop in."

"Good enough. Well, I'd better get back to the store before those kids mess up everything and I have to fire them."

Brandon laughed as the other man hurried away. But then he faced Arden, all humor gone. "We've got to stop doing this."

Arden breathed out a sigh. "I know."

"We're just friends," he said, hoping he sounded more convincing to her ears than he did to his own.

"Just friends," she repeated in a voice so soft he barely heard it. She looked over his shoulder so he couldn't read the emotions in her eyes. For some reason that bothered him more than it should have.

He was doing this as much for her as for himself. There was no sense in starting something they wouldn't be able to finish. Arden was just passing through. Neither of them was open to a relationship. She was still hurt from her last one and he wasn't willing to trust another woman.

It didn't matter that she fit so perfectly in his arms—

heck, into his life—she might have been made for him. He no longer believed such nonsense. He'd once believed that of Sylvia. What a fool he'd been. He hadn't even known her real name.

"That was fun," Arden said, finally breaking the silence as Brandon steered his truck onto the road leading to Sweet Briar.

"I'm glad you enjoyed yourself." He had to admit that he had enjoyed himself more today than he had any other time shopping at the markets. Arden had been so enthusiastic and curious, asking questions and making insightful comments so that he experienced everything anew through her eyes.

"I did." Her stomach growled loudly and she blushed prettily. "Sorry. I didn't eat yet. Do you think you could drop me off at the diner? I'll get breakfast there."

He looked at the clock. "They'll be packed right about now. How about I make something for you after we leave the stuff at the restaurant?"

"Are you sure you don't mind?"

"I haven't eaten, either. I generally eat when I get back. It's just as easy to make breakfast for two as it is for one."

"In that case, yes." She wiped at a smear on her thigh. There was another stain on her T-shirt. She pulled her shirt away from her chest and grimaced. "Do I have time to change? I won't be but a minute."

He forced his eyes away from the smooth skin of her legs and tried not to imagine what wonders were hidden under the soiled shirt. "Sure."

They dropped off the purchases at the restaurant, where his assistant chef took care of putting them into the cooler. Then Brandon drove the short distance home and parked. She hopped out, waited until he was beside her and then looked up at him. "What are we having?"

"I thought I'd throw together some crepes with fresh strawberries, a side of crispy bacon and scrambled eggs."

"You know how to make crepes?" She slapped a hand across her forehead. "Of course you know how to make crepes. Forget I said that." She aimed a thumb over her shoulder. "I'll go get changed."

He watched her go, trying not to notice the perfect curve of her hips in her denim cutoffs. Turning away from the delectable sight, he got his wayward libido under control and kept his feet moving toward the back stairs of his house and to the kitchen. As he gathered the breakfast ingredients, images of her stripping out of her clothes filled his mind. He reminded himself that they were only friends, and friends didn't see each other naked.

"How can I help?" Arden asked as she stepped into the room. She'd changed into a pair of red linen shorts and a white cotton shirt that wrapped around her tiny waist and tied beneath her perfect breasts. She'd also washed away the remnants of the strawberry from her face. She hadn't put on a bit of makeup, but she looked cover-girl beautiful. He wanted to pull her into his arms and kiss her, which despite being crazy somehow seemed right.

He yanked out a chair at the table, instead. "I've got it under control. All you have to do is have a seat and keep me company."

"Why won't you let me help? Are you afraid I'll steal your secret recipes?" Her eyes sparkled and he found himself grinning at her goofiness. She snapped her fingers. "That's it, isn't it? You're afraid I'll steal your recipe and open a crepe restaurant."

She was beautiful. Her bright smile reached the darkness in his soul, illuminating it with its warmth. Yes, her teeth were perfectly straight and incredibly white, but it was the sincerity in her expression that touched him. Too often people smiled to be polite or to cover their real emotions. He'd been guilty of that a time or two. Arden didn't do that. When she smiled it was because she truly felt joy.

"I'm not worried about you stealing my recipe. Especially since I've got it locked in here." He pointed to his head with one hand and cracked eggs into a bowl with the other. He noticed the impressed look on her face and wondered why he was showing off. He hadn't shown off for a woman in years. Not since—

He jerked his thoughts back from where they threatened to stray. He refused to let thoughts of Sylvia ruin this perfect morning. Her sudden calls out of the blue were stirring up memories he'd thought long forgotten. Clearly he couldn't keep her from calling him, but he wasn't going to let her ruin this day.

"Honestly, there's no chance anyway. I can't cook to save my life. But I make a mean microwave dinner. And toast. My toast is always the perfect shade of brown on both sides."

He laughed. "I'm not sure tossing bread into a toaster qualifies as cooking. And I know a microwave dinner doesn't come anywhere near qualifying as food."

She grinned. "You're a food snob."

"Not really. I just want my food to taste good, and

I don't want it full of chemical ingredients some mad scientist cooked up in his lab."

Despite his saying he didn't need her help, she filled the coffeepot with water and grabbed a bag of beans from the freezer. "I don't know about mad scientists, but I do admit the nuked food leaves something to be desired in the taste department."

"My point exactly." She began to set the table. Her movements were graceful, and he paused momentarily to enjoy the view before speaking again. "Food should be enjoyed. It should nourish the soul, as well as the body."

"So you believe cooking is an art."

"It's more than that. It's a labor of love. My grandfather taught me that."

She smiled at him. "Your grandfather sounds like a wonderful man."

"The best. Not a day goes by that I don't miss him. The world lost a great man when he died."

"I'm sure. But you keep him alive with everything you do. No wonder you're so particular. It's your homage to him."

Brandon nodded. She understood him in a way no one else ever had.

He whipped the first crepe onto a plate, placed it in the oven to keep warm and then quickly made another. A few minutes later, he plated the food and set it on the table. Arden poured the coffee and they sat down to breakfast.

He'd been a chef for years, and claiming he was one of the best wasn't bragging. It was the truth. He didn't indulge in false modesty. Even though he knew he'd prepared the food perfectly, he was a bit nervous as Arden lifted a bit of crepe to her mouth.

"Oh, my goodness. This is incredible." She took another bite and chewed slowly, then closed her eyes. "If people knew how good these tasted, they'd be pounding on your door demanding that you open your restaurant for breakfast."

"Then this will have to be our secret." He scooped eggs onto a fork, trying to ignore the moans that she was making.

She closed an imaginary lock on her lips. "Your secret is safe with me."

"I knew I could trust you." The words he'd spoken so easily in jest gave him pause. Did he mean them? Could he trust Arden? And if he did, did that change the kind of relationship they could have?

## Chapter Nine

"Arden? This is John. I have good news for you. The part arrived last night and your car is fixed. You can pick it up anytime."

"Thanks," Arden managed to stutter before ending the call and sagging onto her bed. Her car was ready. She could leave Sweet Briar whenever she wanted. But she didn't want to leave. She was enjoying her time here, especially the time she spent with Brandon. She'd long since decided she didn't want to go to Florida, but hadn't told Brandon or Joni. After all, her car was broken down so there had been no reason to mention it. Now that it was fixed, she was going to have to tell them. Hopefully, they would let her continue to rent the garage apartment.

She was descending the stairs when Brandon pulled into the driveway. Was he coming back from the fish and vegetable markets? It was around the time they'd gotten back yesterday, so it was possible. Quashing the disappointment at not being invited to tag along and reminding herself that visiting the markets was part of his job and not a field trip, she waited until he was near enough to speak. "We've got to stop meeting this way."

He smiled, but she saw the worry in his eyes, then noticed he had his cell phone to his ear. He frowned and pushed a button, ending the call.

"Is something wrong?"

"I'm trying to reach one of my friends. He isn't answering his house or cell phones."

"Maybe he's out of town."

"No." The worry in Brandon's eyes spread to the rest of his face and his brow wrinkled. After a long moment of silence, she started to walk away. He didn't need her around while he tried to work through his problem.

She'd only taken a step when she felt his hand on her arm. The warmth of his touch sent tingles all the way to her toes in less time than it took her to exhale. This wasn't good. Brandon had been perfectly clear that he only wanted to be her friend. And given the whopper of a secret she was keeping, it was for the best. Throw in the fact that she was returning home to Baltimore, and the physical attraction was not something she needed. But how in the world could she control something that had her longing to toss away her good sense and see where another kiss would lead?

"Are you busy now?"

"Not really. Why?"

"My friend Jericho's wife died five months ago. I've been trying to get in touch with him for a couple of days. The last time I went to check on him, he said he was doing fine, but I suspect he was lying. He practically threw me off his property the minute I got there. I was thinking about taking a trip to his ranch this afternoon. Would you go with me? We can pack a lunch and ride horses. I can leave the leftovers for him."

"Are you sure about this? If he doesn't want you to visit, he definitely won't want a stranger hanging around."

"I'm sure. He may get angry with me, but he'll be polite to you. I'd get Joni to go, but she's still visiting the folks. This way I can get a look at him and leave some food so I know he'll have something to eat for the next couple of days. He won't accept the food if I just bring it to him. But if I ask to borrow some horses, he'll consider it an even trade. I know it doesn't make sense, but nothing about Jericho makes sense now."

She nodded. "You can count me in."

"Great. I'll whip up some food. We can leave in a couple of hours."

"Okay."

As Arden watched him stride away, she tried to control her pounding heart and racing imagination. She was going on a picnic with Brandon. True, she was only going because Joni wasn't around, but she'd take it. Spending time with a man who cared so deeply about his friends was a win no matter how it came about.

Brandon sealed the lid on the plastic container and set it into the wicker basket. He added ceramic plates and wineglasses, cloth napkins and silver before closing the top. Even as he worked, his mind flitted between worry about Jericho Jones and his own growing attraction to Arden. Jericho was one of the first people Brandon met when he'd moved to Sweet Briar. Jericho and his wife had been regulars at the restaurant. Brandon knew Jericho was in serious pain. Jeanette had been more than his wife. She'd been the driving force behind everything he'd done. He had turned a small ranch into a successful horse operation. Since Jeanette's untimely death, he'd lost all interest in the horses. From what Brandon could see on the rare occasions Jericho allowed him to visit, he was no longer trying to improve his business; rather, he worked sunup to sundown doing the most physical labor he could find. It was as if he wanted to work himself to death.

Brandon didn't claim to know what Jericho was going through, but Brandon knew it wasn't good for him to continue to isolate himself from his friends. From the world. Jericho had ignored Brandon's many invitations to dinner or to drop by the house or restaurant whenever he was in town. And now Jericho wasn't answering his phone. Brandon knew from personal experience that if someone didn't intervene, Jericho could spiral into serious depression. Joni and his parents had been there for him at his lowest point. He wanted to be there for Jericho.

A date with Arden provided a good excuse to drop in.

He wiped down the counters, rinsed the sponge and tossed it into the sink. After glancing around to be sure the kitchen was clean, he grabbed the basket and blanket and headed out the door. He had just placed everything in the back of his truck when Arden called out to him. Apparently, she must have been looking out her window. He smiled despite himself. Clearly she was as eager to spend time with him as he was with her.

Dressed in jeans and gym shoes and a pink-and-gray-striped shirt, she looked fresh yet sexy. Her eyes sparkled with excitement.

"I was watching for you," she said, confirming his earlier assumption. "I'm so excited to be going to the ranch. I love horses, although I haven't ridden in quite a while."

"Then let's not waste another minute." He helped her into the truck and set off down the road.

"How far away is this ranch?" Arden was peering out the window like a young girl, eagerness on her face. She turned to look at him when he didn't answer right away.

He was struck again by just how beautiful she was. Her caramel skin was perfectly clear, her eyes so open, hiding nothing. She should never play poker because her every emotion was reflected on her face. There was no way she could keep her cards a secret.

"The ranch is about ninety miles inland so it'll take us an hour or so to get there. Do you think you can contain your enthusiasm that long?"

She ran a hand over her hair. It was about an inch longer than it had been when she arrived, but it was still short and emphasized her delicate features. The style was growing on him. "If I have to. It won't be easy. My brothers always make fun of the way I get impatient. They still tease me about the time I got out of the bed in the middle of the night and slept in the car when we were going to Disney World. My parents were frantic when they woke up and I was gone. I don't think I'll ever live that down."

He caught the wistfulness in her voice. She rarely mentioned her family. Suddenly he wanted to know more about her life before she came to Sweet Briar.

"You don't talk much about your family. Why is that? Aren't you close to them?"

She shrugged and seemed to consider her response before answering. Finally she nodded. "Not in the same way that you're close with Joni. What the two of you have is pretty special."

"I know. We have another brother who we don't see as much because he's in the military. We all love each other, but I can't say that he's as good a friend as Joni."

"That's how it is with us. My brothers are close friends. They're both older than I am and still treat me like their baby sister. And to be honest, I wasn't the most mature of teens, so I might deserve it. On the plus side, I know I can always depend on them when I need them."

Brandon nodded. The van in front of them was driving too slowly, so he signaled and passed it. "Do I need to worry about your brothers coming to see me in the near future?"

She laughed and squeezed his bicep. "Don't worry. I think you can take them."

"I wasn't worried about that." He glanced over at her. "You didn't answer. Do you expect them to come and check up on you?"

"No. Why would they? I'm on a vacation."

"That's what you're calling this? A vacation?"

"Yes. It may not be what I planned, but it is definitely turning out great."

"Having your car break down and being stranded in a small town is vacation? I think I need to see your bucket list. It might need a few adjustments."

Arden laughed. "John called me today. My car is finally fixed. I'm no longer stranded, as you call it."

"So does that mean you'll be moving on?" He spoke

as casually as he could, hoping to mask the anxiety that suddenly grew inside him at the thought of her leaving so soon.

She bit her bottom lip. "Actually, I wanted to talk to you about that. I'm really enjoying my time here. Do you mind if I stay for another week or so?"

His heart thumped in his chest. She'd be in town for a while longer. He shouldn't like that as much as he did, but he couldn't help himself. He knew the relationship or whatever it was between them had an expiration date. He just wanted to enjoy her company a bit longer. At least that was the story he was telling himself. "Sure. You're welcome to stay."

"Thanks." She flashed him a blinding smile that had him doubting the wisdom of letting her remain longer. But it was too late to turn back now. And, right or wrong, part of him was glad.

"This place is beautiful," Arden exclaimed, trying to find the right words to describe the Double J ranch. So far she'd exhausted every superlative the teachers at the exclusive girls school she'd attended had drilled into her. She'd nearly run out of words and yet there was so much more to describe.

Jericho Jones, the thirtyish owner, flashed a devilish grin. The expression on his face had been grim when Brandon pulled onto his property, but he had turned on the charm when Arden hopped out of the truck. Brandon had been right about his friend's reaction. He was all smiles for her. Too bad the smile never reached his eyes, which could only be described as bleak. Her heart ached at his obvious pain. "Thanks. I'm kind of partial to this piece of land myself."

Brandon stepped closer to Arden and placed his arm around her waist, making her heart skip a beat. His hand was warm and she felt the heat through the fabric of her shirt. She immediately pictured them alone, his fingers caressing her bare skin, and a moan nearly escaped her lips.

"I was hoping we could borrow some horses," Brandon said. "Arden loves to ride. I'll show her all of the best spots. We'll be back in a couple of hours if that's okay with you."

"Sure. Take your time." Jericho's smile broadened slowly. He led the way across the brick patio, past the in-ground pool, to the stable. Arden heard horses neighing and saw a few more in the corral. "I'll saddle Buttercup for you, Arden. She's a sweet mare who'll give you a gentle ride."

Arden rubbed the sorrel's nose and was rewarded with soft nuzzling on her shoulder. "She's a pretty girl."

"That she is." Jericho moved to a large black horse. "Of course it's Diablo for you, Brandon."

"Thanks. We'll take good care of them."

"I know you will." The rancher nodded and walked away.

"You're right. He is sad," Arden said when Jericho was out of hearing range.

"Most people wouldn't pick up on it because of the way he was laughing and making jokes."

"It's so awful to see how hard he was trying to cover his pain." That was something she was familiar with. She hadn't been quite as obvious. At least she hoped not. But maybe others could see the sorrow she tried so hard to keep hidden.

"He's barely hanging on since Jeanette died in childbirth five months ago. The baby died the next day. I know that's not a long time, but I don't think he is making progress in his healing. But then, I could be wrong. The grieving process is different for everyone. I just can't help worrying."

"You're a good friend and an even better man," Arden said, meaning every word. Too bad he only wanted to be her friend. Her foolish heart wanted him to be so much more. Apparently, she didn't need as much time to recover from Michael-the-dirtbag as she thought.

Brandon seemed embarrassed by her compliment. He quickly helped her settle on her horse, then swung onto his mount with surprising ease. For someone from Chicago, a place not exactly known for its open spaces and horses, he was incredibly competent on horseback.

He led her away from the house and across a meadow. They walked until she became comfortable on her mount.

"Let's go a little faster," Arden said, increasing to a canter.

"Sure." Brandon's horse sped up eagerly. Clearly Diablo preferred a faster speed. In a few minutes they began to gallop.

"This is so much fun," Arden said, her spirits soaring. It had been quite a while since she'd felt so carefree.

Brandon nodded.

After a while, they arrived at a small lake surrounded by tall trees. Brandon dismounted and then helped Arden from her horse. She spread out her arms and turned in circles, lifting her face to the sun. The sky was perfectly blue and there wasn't a cloud for miles and miles. A gentle breeze blew, rustling the leaves in the trees, cooling her skin.

When she opened her eyes, she found Brandon staring at her, an odd expression on his face. She couldn't quite name it, but it almost looked like longing. Wistfulness. That was it. He looked wistful. Then he blinked and the expression vanished.

"I hope you're hungry," he said.

"Starved. Which is funny when you think about it. I had a huge breakfast, which would normally tide me over until lunch. But I'm really hungry when I haven't been doing much of anything. It's crazy."

"Not really. You were riding a horse."

"The horse did all the moving. All I did was sit."

"People underestimate just how much work is involved in horseback riding. You worked. You just enjoyed it."

Arden spread the blanket while Brandon unloaded the basket. He'd filled it with the most delicious-smelling food and now placed generous portions on the plates. She opened a bottle of sparkling water and poured it into two glasses, keeping one for herself and handing the other to Brandon, then accepted the plate he handed to her.

"This all looks so good."

He grinned. "Nothing but the best for you."

She lifted a small quiche to her mouth. "You're totally spoiling me."

"I'm loving every minute of it."

"Me, too." No man had ever gone to so much trouble to please her. Although this was a spur-of-the-moment date, he had taken care of every detail.

"So what do you plan to do now that your car is working?"

She sipped her sparkling water. "I'm not sure. Do you have any suggestions?"

He leaned back on his elbows, the movement drawing her attention to his muscular chest. She took another swallow in an attempt to cool down.

"Have you been to the beach yet? It's beautiful at sundown."

It probably was. And more than a little romantic. "Sounds nice. Maybe you would like to go with me some night."

He inhaled and then blew out his breath slowly. "I don't think that's a good idea."

"Why not? Don't you like beaches or sundown?"

He straightened, then reached out and touched her cheek. "You know why not. I don't want to lead you on. I'm not interested in a relationship. Not now. Not ever. I feel like we're walking a fine line now."

They were. And she was losing her balance. If she wasn't careful she would fall over the line and end up in love with him. No matter what they did, she knew it was going to hurt like heck when she left.

But she wouldn't worry about leaving now. Instead, she took another sip of her drink, determined to enjoy the wonderful meal and Brandon's company.

## Chapter Ten

"So, what's going on with you and my brother?"

Arden jumped and nearly dropped the basket of folded clothes in her arms. Although the garage apartment was great, it lacked a washer and dryer. Joni had offered to let Arden use the ones in the house, but she'd refused. She didn't want to blur the lines further between tenant and landlord. Of course she'd blurred so many other lines she was beginning to think there weren't any left. Still, she felt she was doing her part to maintain order by using the machines at the Laundromat a couple of blocks away.

"You scared me."

"Sorry. I thought you saw me." Joni had just returned from her weeklong visit with her family and was wasting no time before she pounced. "Well, what's the scoop? Inquiring minds want to know."

"Inquiring minds?" Arden closed the trunk of her car and grabbed the basket off the ground. "Or is it just one mind and that would be yours?"

Joni laughed and followed Arden up the stairs and into the cozy apartment Arden had come to think of as home. "You can change things if you want. Make it your own."

"I like it just the way it is."

"I used to live here."

"You did?" Arden hung a couple of shirts on hangers and laid them across the back of a chair.

"When I first came to town. I moved here a few months after Brandon. I needed a space of my own, so he renovated it for me."

"Do you miss being on your own?"

"Nah. I like living with my brother. It's not like he tries to tell me what to do or interferes in my life. We're roommates. And we've become really good friends. Plus, he's a better cook than I'll ever be."

"That must be nice. Being friends with your brother, I mean." Arden heard the yearning in her voice.

Joni leaned forward in the chair, pouncing on that comment like a dog on a T-bone steak. "You and your brother don't get along?"

"Brothers. I have two. And it's not that. They're best friends and I'm sorta out there."

"Don't give up hope. Brandon and I weren't always close." Joni twirled her hair around her fingers. "But the real question is, how close are you and my brother?"

"Back to that, are we?"

"Yes. Notice how smoothly I transitioned."

Arden laughed.

"So come on, friend, spill."

Such a simple word. *Friend*. And yet it meant so

much. A friend was someone to share good times and bad. Someone to laugh with about a guy she liked. And knowing that Joni included her in that category was great.

"There's nothing to spill. We're friends." The word didn't make her as happy when she thought about it in relation to Brandon. But he'd emphasized that they were just friends after they'd shared kisses so hot her lips were singed. Message received.

"Really? What about him carrying you up the stairs? That sounds like something serious and totally out of character for Brandon."

"Who told you that? Certainly not Brandon."

"Girl, please. Getting information out of him is harder than prying open clams with your fingernails."

That was a relief. After having a so-called boyfriend who was going to share the most intimate details of her life with the entire internet if she hadn't caught him first, it was nice to know that Brandon respected her privacy.

"Then how did you know? You weren't even in town that day. And how was Chicago, by the way?"

"Chicago was just as I'd left it. As to your other question, I have my ways."

Arden put her hands on her hips and waited.

"Okay. Kristina Harrison saw you. You remember, the owner of the Sunrise."

Arden nodded.

"She stopped by to talk to Brandon and saw him carrying you up the stairs. According to her, it was quite romantic."

It had been. But Arden would never admit that, even to herself. Especially to herself. She had walls around her heart for a reason. Brandon was chopping away at them even if he didn't know it. "I twisted my ankle and he helped me inside. That's all."

"Rats. That's just what he said."

"Sorry to disappoint you."

"So there was no kissing."

Arden's face heated and she didn't answer. She didn't want to lie, but she didn't think Brandon would appreciate her discussing the specifics of their relationship with his sister.

"So you did. I knew it."

"Surely you don't want details."

"About my brother? No way. That's just icky. Of course, it would be good to have something to taunt him with. You know, as payback for all those times he teased me when we were kids. But, seriously, I'm just happy that he's finally moving on."

"He's not moving on. At least not with me. It was just a friendly kiss between pals." A kiss so hot her lips were still sizzling. But that was a result of chemistry. Even she knew better than to confuse physical attraction with something deeper.

Joni didn't look convinced, but thankfully she let the subject drop. "What are you doing for dinner tonight? I know you're not helping Brandon since he has hired a couple of new waitresses and you're not covering as many shifts."

"I actually haven't thought about it."

"Come to girls' night out with me."

"What's involved?"

"It's nothing formal. My friends and I get together whenever we can. Sometimes we go to a movie or dinner. Tonight we're meeting at Kayla's house. She's married to John, the mechanic who fixed your car. He's grilling and the rest of us are bringing sides."

"I thought you said it was girls' night," Arden said.

"John's not hanging around. He's going out with the guys from the choir."

"He sings?" Arden choked out. John sounded like a foghorn, but maybe the church was desperate. Small towns would have a smaller talent pool.

"Goodness, no. He's terrible. He plays the drums. Anyway, we're going to have a great time. We'll eat, then just hang around and talk. It's a lot of fun and a great chance for you to meet more people."

"You sure they won't mind?"

"Positive. In case you haven't noticed, we're a welcoming bunch in Sweet Briar."

She had noticed that everyone smiled and said hello when they passed her on the street. The other people at the Laundromat talked to her while they washed their clothes. She'd had conversations with the waitresses at the restaurant. Everyone had been nice. But Joni was taking it a step further by including Arden in her intimate group of friends.

"In that case, I'd love to come. Should I bring anything?"

"That's not necessary. You're my guest."

Arden grinned. "I can hardly wait."

At six o'clock Arden jumped into Joni's car and they were off. After a short and scenic drive through town, Joni parked in front of a redbrick house with a well-groomed yard. Instead of heading for the front porch, Joni and Arden followed the sound of feminine laughter around the side of the house and to the backyard.

Several women lounged in chairs grouped around the patio while John manned the grill.

Dressed in jeans and a Carolina Panthers jersey, he looked like he was having the time of his life. He took foil packets off the grill and set them on a platter. "These vegetables and chicken are nice, but are you sure you don't want some meat? I have some great steak that will put a little meat on your bones."

"Our bones are happy with the meat they have," one of the women said, tossing a napkin at him.

He shrugged and flashed a grin. "Don't say I didn't offer." Done with the grill, he went to a petite woman and kissed her long and deep before waving goodbye.

"Everyone, this is Arden," Joni said, sweeping her into the middle of the women. "She's staying with Brandon and me for a while."

"Hi," she said, suddenly ridiculously nervous.

"I'm Kayla. We haven't officially met yet although I've seen you around. Welcome to my home. That was my husband who just left." She pointed to each of the women, introducing them by name. "That's Liz, and Hannah, and Katrina, and Veronica." They each waved back in turn. "Help yourself to a drink and come sit down. We want to know all about you."

Arden grabbed a can of soda and joined the group. "I'm afraid you'll be bored to tears."

"Kayla, a little bird told me you had news," Joni said.

"Yeah. There are no secrets in this town. I'm pregnant again."

"That's wonderful," Liz said, hugging their hostess. Arden added her congratulations to those being offered by the other women.

"I'm happy, although I could strangle my husband. I seem to get pregnant whenever he looks at me."

"You must not have paid enough attention in biology. It's not the looks that get you into trouble. It's what happens afterward," Joni quipped.

Everyone laughed, including Kayla. When everyone quieted, she turned to look at Arden. "So how do you like our town?"

Arden looked at the eager faces of the women. They actually seemed interested in her answer. Maybe they were just being polite, but she didn't get that vibe. If they were Joni's friends, they were probably as nice as she was. That thought set her at ease and she knew she could enjoy herself. "I like it. Sweet Briar is beautiful. The people are great."

"And the men are so good-looking," Veronica added. "Especially a certain chef of a fabulous restaurant."

Joni made the time-out sign with her hands. "No talking about my brother. That's just too weird."

"Okay. Then I won't mention his cute butt," Hannah added.

"Or that muscled chest," Liz put in, fanning her face with a napkin.

"Ignore them. They just do this because it bugs me." Joni shook her unopened can of cola and aimed it at the other women.

"Okay. We give. Let's talk about you and the mayor."

Joni rolled her eyes. "I told you, move along. There's nothing to see there. Lex and I are just friends."

"I don't understand you," Hannah said, a sudden frown marring her face. She wagged a manicured finger in Joni's direction. "That man is hot."

"Seriously hot," Veronica added. "Ice cubes melt the minute he walks into a room."

Arden did agree that the mayor was attractive in a pretty-boy way. She just didn't feel the same pull she felt with Brandon. Brandon may not have been as classically handsome as Lex, but something about him lit her fire.

"I'm not disputing his hotness," Joni said. "I do have eyes in my head. I'm just not interested in a romance with him or anyone else right now."

"Are you crazy?" Hannah gaped, then shook her head again. She began to list his good qualities, using her fingers to count. "He's hot. He's nice. He treats you well. You know he went out on a limb to convince the city council to give the youth center that funding."

"And don't forget the best quality of all," Liz said.

"What's that?" Arden asked, getting into the spirit. Listening to the other women, she wondered if Joni should consider having a relationship with the mayor. She'd seen them together and sparks did fly. The pull between them was so strong you could practically see it. Evidently, he had even more good qualities than she knew.

"He's rich."

Arden nearly choked on her drink. "What?"

"He's loaded. His entire family is."

"That doesn't matter to me," Joni said.

"Really? My mama always said it's just as easy to love a rich man as it is to love a poor one." Liz laughed.

"Easier," Hannah chimed in. "You don't have the financial worries that other couples do."

Arden knew they were joking, but jokes often contained insights into a person's true feelings. Maybe these women did believe wealth was a good enough reason to become involved with someone. But then they laughed. And they had listed many of Lex's other qualities first. Maybe she was overreacting. She was still raw from having been involved with someone who actually lived by those words. Of course Michael-the-worm hadn't loved her, but he'd certainly been willing to fake it in order to get his hands on her trust fund. She forced that thought away. She refused to let thoughts of him ruin another of her days. That fool was in the past and that was where he was going to stay.

The evening passed quickly and plans were made to get together again the following week at Hannah's house. If the weather was good, they'd swim in her pool. Arden exchanged numbers and even made lunch plans with Veronica for the following week.

"Did you have a good time?" Joni asked after they said goodbye to everyone and headed to the car.

"The best. Everyone was great." Arden fastened her seat belt and leaned back, the pleasure of the evening still bubbling inside her. Aside from the one little hiccup when the subject of marrying for money had come up, everything had been wonderful. "Thanks for including me. I feel like I've just made a bunch of really great friends."

Joni pulled away from the curb and blew the horn, tossing a final wave to Kayla, who stood on her front lawn. "That's because you did make a bunch of really great friends. Before you know it, you won't be able to remember living anywhere but here. You'll put down roots so deep and so fast your head will spin."

Joni's words struck a chord. She could easily see the picture Joni painted. And, boy, did she like it. But she knew she would never be able to remain here. The day was rapidly approaching when she'd have to give up the identity of Arden West, waitress, and return to her life as Arden Wexford, heiress.

## Chapter Eleven

Arden and Joni were blocks away from Heaven on Earth when Joni's phone rang. She put it on hands-free and answered.

"Is this my favorite sister in the world?"

Arden's heart sped up as Brandon's voice filled the car. It was as if he'd suddenly materialized beside her. She smiled and glanced at Joni, who looked back at her with a raised eyebrow. Arden tried to hide her expression, but when Joni smirked she knew it was too late.

"Nope. She's home in bed because she has to be at the youth center early tomorrow."

"Come on, Joni. I wouldn't call you unless it was an emergency. Lydia went home sick. I only need you for a couple of hours."

Arden looked at her tired friend and spoke up. "I can come. We're not far away."

She heard him expel his breath. What was that about? Finally he replied. "Thanks. I owe you."

"I'm not keeping score."

Joni disconnected the call and turned to Arden. "I'm not going to ask what's going on between you two. That's none of my business. But I will ask you to be careful with my brother's heart. He's been hurt. It changed him. He was the most playful and charming guy. Now he tries to protect himself."

"As are you."

"I'm his sister."

"I would never hurt Brandon. At least not on purpose."

"Good enough." Joni smiled and pulled to the curb. "Thanks for helping my brother."

"I'm just returning one of many favors."

"I thought you weren't keeping score."

Arden laughed and ran inside the building. Ten minutes later she was dressed in the uniform Joni kept at the restaurant for emergencies. Every seat in the dining room was filled. After she found out which tables she would be serving, she went to each one, introduced herself and asked what the patrons needed. She delivered the requested items with a smile, easing into the familiar routine.

The night flew quickly and before long the last customers—a party of eight—left amid boisterous laughter. The waitresses followed soon after, followed by the kitchen staff. As had been her practice whenever she worked, Arden helped Matt clean. When the dining room was straightened, she let him out, locked the door and then joined Brandon in the kitchen.

He looked up from a counter he was wiping. "Thanks. You really saved me tonight."

"No worries." She looked around the sparkling kitchen. It looked clean, but you never knew. Brandon was a stickler, and what looked perfect to her might not be perfect to him. "You need any help?"

He shook his head. "I'm finished." He disposed of the cloth and then gestured for her to proceed out the kitchen. He flipped off the lights, then followed her. He grabbed the linens, turned on the alarm, then led her to his truck.

"How was girls' night out?" he asked as they drove down the silent streets. The night was dark and peaceful. Sweet air blew through the open windows. It was as if they were the only two people in the world.

"It was fun. Everybody was so nice."

"Why do you sound surprised?"

She couldn't explain about her past experiences without going into detail about who she was. But maybe it was time for her to do just that. She'd been around Brandon long enough to know he wasn't the type to let a large bank account change his behavior. His character was solid. He wasn't greedy and there wasn't a deceitful bone in his body. She was ashamed that she'd ever thought he could be. Her only excuse was that past hurts had made her cautious and suspicious.

"I've had some pretty bad experiences that have made me more jaded than the average person my age."

He nodded as he pulled to the curb, but his attention was clearly not on what she was saying. She followed his gaze to his front porch. The light was on, illuminating a woman sitting on the front steps. Joni was standing beside her with her arms crossed. Even from this distance, it was clear from Joni's rigid posture that she was fuming.

"Son of a…" Brandon slammed the brakes and

jumped from the vehicle, leaving the keys dangling in the ignition. Arden felt uncertainty battling with a willingness to help, as well as plain old curiosity. She removed the keys, locked the doors and slowly walked to the porch.

"I tried to get her to leave, but she refuses. I'm tempted to call the police. Really, I'd like to drag her off by her hair."

"It's okay, Joni. Go inside. I'll take care of her once and for all." He never took his eyes off the other woman.

"What about Arden?"

Brandon blinked and looked around. He'd been so focused on the other woman that he had forgotten all about her. "Thanks for your help. I'll talk to you later."

She nodded, clearly dismissed. She handed him his car keys. "Sure. I was glad to help." She started around to the side of the house toward the garage, questions bombarding her from every direction. Who was that woman? What did she have to do with Brandon? It was obvious he was angry with her, but was that anger simply love turned inside out? Was she the woman who had hurt Brandon?

If so, did she want him back?

Would he take her back?

Brandon inhaled deeply, trying to gain control of his emotions as he stared at the woman he'd hoped never to see again. Sylvia. He couldn't believe she was here. He'd been clear that he didn't want her in his life. He'd told her as much. And then he had not answered another of her calls. Even she should have figured out that the last thing he wanted was for her to show up at his front door.

Did she think she would have an advantage if she

blindsided him? Not a chance. Maybe if he was still in love with her, but those tender feelings had died the night he almost did.

He looked around. Although Arden had left, Joni still stood on the porch, her body shaking with barely contained fury. Sylvia must have sensed the danger, because her eyes kept darting to Joni. Sylvia looked ready to take flight at any moment.

"I've got this, Joni. Go on to bed." He looked over at Sylvia and didn't try to mask his distaste. Joni still didn't move so he repeated himself. "I'll handle this and be inside in a minute."

"Okay." His sister glared at Sylvia, then stalked inside.

When the door was firmly closed behind Joni, Brandon turned his attention to Sylvia. "What part of leave me the hell alone is too difficult for you to understand?"

He expected her to become defensive or, worse yet, to turn on the sex appeal. She'd had that act down in spades. Tall and curvy, she'd known how to dress to accentuate her attributes and attract a man. He'd fallen into her trap even as she was using him to get close to Jason Smith, the silent partner in the restaurant where Brandon had worked in Chicago. Nothing about her had revealed that she was a rogue FBI agent seeking revenge on the man she'd blamed for her brother's death even if it had meant pretending to be in love with Brandon and endangering his life.

He stared at her. He'd never seen her look anything other than well put together. Even when she was pulling a gun and shooting at drug lords, she'd been wearing designer clothes. The porch light wasn't as good as daylight, but he could see her clearly. Her previously long, thick hair looked thin and dull, her clothes cheap. She had definitely come down in the world.

She dug short, unpolished nails into the palms of her hands. "I understand. I don't want to make trouble. I just needed to see you."

"Well, now you've seen me. You can go."

He started to walk around her and she grabbed his forearm. He wanted to shove her away, but a lifetime of being taught never to hurt a woman wouldn't let him. He settled for lifting her hand away and stepping back.

"Please. Just listen to me. I promise to never bother you again."

"I can accomplish the same thing with a restraining order."

"Please, Brandon. For old times' sake."

That was the wrong thing to say. "You are mistaken if you think bringing up the past is a way to win points with me."

"I'm sorry. You're right. But please…" She looked more uneasy than he'd ever seen her.

He paused, still glaring at her.

She took a deep breath. "I'm here to make amends."

"What?"

"I want to make amends."

"You have got to be kidding me. What sort of angle are you working now? Don't tell me—you're investigating someone in town and need me as part of your new cover."

She flinched but didn't argue back. "No angle. You are one of the people I hurt. I want to apologize to you and try to make it right."

He looked at her again. *Really* looked. Her appearance wasn't the only thing that had changed. Her demeanor was different. Less confident. Humble. Unsure. He leaned his head back and looked at the sky and then blew out a long breath. She might actually be sincere. And even if she wasn't, she was determined to speak her piece. He was willing to give her a chance if that meant he'd be rid of her for good. "You have five minutes."

She nodded and rubbed her hands against her slacks, then hesitated as if she didn't know where to start.

He didn't say a word. He certainly wasn't going to help her get started. She'd been bugging him for weeks. She should have scribbled notes on cards. Leaning against the porch post, he crossed his arms and waited. She only had five minutes. Whether she talked or not was up to her. But when her time was up, he was gone.

"I loved my brother. Evan was the cutest baby and the best kid in the world. When he turned thirteen he changed. My parents adored him and didn't see the change until it was too late."

She stared into the distance, then looked at Brandon. He didn't want to get sucked into her story and start to feel compassion for her, so he tapped a finger on his watch.

"Right. Well, Evan started getting into trouble with the police when he was sixteen. I'd already begun working for the FBI. I thought it would help if he came to stay with me in Chicago for the summer so I could keep an eye on him. I even had a job lined up for him." She shook her head slowly. Sorrowfully. "Bringing Evan to Chicago was a mistake. Within a week he'd found a group of messed-up kids to hang around. I didn't know it, but he had started selling drugs. He got on the wrong side of Jason Smith, a major dealer who just happened to be a silent partner in the restaurant where you worked. He had Evan killed.

"My parents blamed me. They said their son would still be alive if I hadn't convinced them to let him come to Chicago. Maybe they were right." Her voice broke and she wiped a tear from beneath her eye. "I was blinded by pain. That's no excuse, I know, but I couldn't let Smith get away with murdering my brother. I needed a way to get close to him and you were it. I'm sorry."

Despite his intent to keep his heart hard toward her, a part of Brandon understood. He would lose it if something happened to Joni. "Are things better with your family?"

She shook her head. "I convinced myself that if I got justice—really revenge—for Evan's death they would forgive me. I was wrong. I went to see them after...after. They told me I wasn't welcome at their home anymore. As far as they were concerned, I died to them the same day Evan did."

"Oh. Wow." He couldn't imagine parents being so cold to their own child. Families were supposed to pull together in times of tragedy, not turn on their own.

"I was already in trouble at work and their rejection tipped me over the edge. I went off the rails. I stopped caring about myself and started drinking. I hit rock bottom about a year ago and stayed down there for a while. I lost my job. My condo. The few friends I had left. Anyway, about a month ago I started a program. Got a job. Started to make amends to the people I hurt.

"I know you want me out of your life, and I'll stay away. I just wanted to explain what happened and to apologize. I am so sorry you got hurt. I did care about you. I just cared about revenge more."

He nodded. Who was to say he wouldn't have acted the same way in her situation? Blind pain could bring out the worst in even the best person. "I forgive you."

Her eyes met his and something akin to hope flashed there. "Thank you. You have no idea how much that means to me."

He extended a hand. He hadn't known what had motivated her to act as she had. Now that he did, he could understand. "I wish you the best in the future."

"Thanks. I hope the same for you."

Brandon watched her drive away. Miraculously, he felt lighter than he had in years. Forgiving Sylvia had lifted the distrust he'd held inside for so long. He didn't need the walls around his heart any longer. He was finally free to love again.

## Chapter Twelve

Arden heard the knock on her door. She'd been anticipating it since she'd walked away from Brandon an hour ago. While she'd waited, she'd showered and changed into a tank and shorts, then polished her toenails a cheery red.

"Coming," she called as she removed the last cotton ball from between her toes. She scooped up the others and shoved them into her pocket. She'd dispose of them later.

"I'm glad you're still up," Brandon said, walking into the room. "I imagine you have quite a few questions."

"I know your private life is none of my business, but…" She shrugged and her words faded out as she didn't quite know how to continue. She had felt those full warm lips on hers on several occasions. Been wrapped in his strong arms. She and Brandon had been spending a lot of time together. Nothing official had been said, but their relationship was evolving into something more than friendship. At least it felt that way to her. She wanted to know more about the mystery woman and her relationship with Brandon.

"Can we sit down?"

Arden nodded and joined him on the small love seat. She had been around him for a while, but it still amazed her how completely he overwhelmed a room. The space suddenly felt a lot smaller. More intimate. And, darn it, despite the fact that there was a lot to be straightened out between them, when the heat from his body reached her, her stomach did a little topsy-turvy thing and she longed to lean into him and let his warmth envelop her. She settled for leaning against the armrest and facing him.

"Sylvia is my ex-fiancée."

The warmth vanished and was immediately replaced by a chill. "Fiancée?"

"*Ex*-fiancée. Sort of."

"You're not making sense." At least she didn't think he was. It was hard to be sure when the word *fiancée* kept reverberating in her mind, crashing into the other words he was saying.

"I told you that I used to work in a restaurant in Chicago." He glanced at her. She managed to nod. "I didn't know it at the time, but one of the partners was actually a drug dealer. I'm talking big-time. He didn't have any input in the daily operation of the business, so we didn't have any interactions to speak of.

"One day, Sylvia came to the restaurant. I was making the rounds, talking with some customers. She introduced herself. I thought she was attractive, but that was about it. A few days later she returned and later became a regular. We struck up a friendship and eventually started dating. It wasn't unusual for her to stop in after work and then hang out until closing time." He shook his head and Arden wondered what he was thinking. Was he remembering the good times he'd shared with this other woman? His face certainly didn't give anything away.

"Anyhow, eventually I proposed and she said yes."

A lump formed in Arden's stomach. She wanted to know more, but at the same time she wanted to cover her ears and hum show tunes loudly. He must not have noticed her inner turmoil because he kept right on talking.

"A few months later we were at the restaurant. It had just closed for the day. We were walking to her car when all hell broke loose. One minute the night was quiet and the next bullets were flying. Sylvia was right in the middle of it. A guy was shooting at her. I knocked her down to protect her. The next thing I knew I was waking up in the hospital. I'd been shot three times."

"What?" Arden thought she was prepared for anything, but hearing about a gun battle when she expected to hear about an unfaithful fiancée was something no one could prepare for.

"It turns out Sylvia was an FBI agent. Her brother had been murdered by a drug dealer and she wanted revenge. The restaurant's silent partner was that drug dealer. She'd been hanging around so she could find out how he operated. A takedown had been planned for that night, but a police officer was on Smith's payroll and alerted him to the plan before it went down."

"Wow. Just...wow."

"That's one way of putting it, although I've used more colorful words myself."

"I bet. When did this happen? And why is she here now? Don't tell me she wants to get back together with

you." *Please, no.* But then Arden would soon be returning to Baltimore, so what did it matter? Still, it felt like
someone had shoved a knife into her stomach and started
twisting it.

"Just over three years ago. I moved to Sweet Briar when
I was well enough. Sylvia said she came here to make
amends."

"Did she even love you?" What would be the worse
answer? Hearing that she did and sacrificed that love,
or hearing that she didn't and had only been using him?

"Who knows. She said she did, but how can I ever
be sure? She lied about everything else, including her
name. One part of me understands why she did that. She
was undercover, after all. But, still, she created a whole
different identity. I don't think I ever knew who she
was inside. At this point, I don't think it even matters."

"Brandon, I'm sorry that happened to you." Arden's
voice was reduced to a whisper. She tried to swallow
but her mouth had gone dry.

"Hell, it's in the past, but I know you have an active imagination and I didn't want to leave you in here
imagining the worst. I wanted you to know the truth."
He stood and stretched. "I'm beat and I guess you probably are, too. I'd better let you get some sleep."

She nodded and tried to stay calm as fear gripped
her heart. Why hadn't she told him the truth sooner? He
might not be willing to listen to her explanation about
why she'd used an alias all this time. And didn't that stink.

Maybe she should just leave town without telling
him who she really was. Her car was running and she
could leave anytime. Would she? That was the question
she couldn't answer.

\* \* \*

After a restless night of tossing and turning, Arden hadn't reached a decision on whether to leave or stay. She did know that she was going to come clean with Brandon and Joni. She didn't feel comfortable continuing to keep her identity a secret when she knew the hurt Brandon had experienced at the hands of another woman who'd deceived him. Actually, she had begun to feel uncomfortable before then. She wished she had acted sooner.

Oddly enough, unless someone referred to her as Arden West, she hadn't thought about the name she was using. She simply thought of herself as Arden. Now that she knew the type of person Brandon was, she knew he would have treated her with the same kindness whether or not he'd known her real last name. Of course, hindsight was twenty-twenty.

She did know one thing for sure: she was through running from difficult situations. She was going to face her problems head-on. That was what she should have done with Michael-the-pond-scum. When she'd overheard him plotting to secretly make a sex tape so he could blackmail her, she should have confronted him. Instead, she'd tucked her tail between her legs and left town like she'd been the weasel. She'd run when she should have stood and fought. After all, she had recorded him plotting on her cell phone. She didn't have everything he'd said, but she had enough to prove what he had been planning. Her brothers wouldn't have acted like cowards. They would have let that jerk know he'd made the mistake of his life when he decided to take on a Wexford. They would have fought as hard and dirty as necessary. And they would have won.

Maybe part of her problem was that she had relied on Jax and Blake to fight her battles for her. Standing on her own two feet meant doing it herself instead of running away. Depending on herself actually meant being dependable. She would start today. Now. She had to act no matter how afraid she was of losing Brandon.

That decided, she dressed quickly, combed her hair and headed down the stairs. She'd expected Brandon's truck to be gone, but still felt a twinge of disappointment that he wasn't around now when she was feeling strong. Who knew if she would be this ready to confess her wrongdoing in an hour or two?

"Hey, Joni," Arden said, crossing the back lawn to where her friend stood hanging laundry to dry in the sun and fresh air. She was tempted to confide the truth about her identity to Joni as sort of a practice run, but didn't. She had to tell Brandon first. Sure, she was close to Joni, but she had begun to feel a different type of closeness with Brandon since the first time he'd pressed his tantalizing lips to hers. As she'd listened to him describe his relationship with his former fiancée—man, she hated the sound of that—she could tell he still carried the pain of betrayal. And if she didn't do something immediately, she would be the one hurting him. Her stomach churned at the thought.

"You're up mighty early."

"I know. It's becoming a habit. I haven't decided whether it's good or bad. You're up pretty early yourself."

"I have so much to do I have to get up at this ungodly hour just to keep my head above water. The summer days are really hectic at the youth center. It's as if kids save up all of their energy throughout the school year and explode over the summer. We have so many fun things to do and they're determined to do them all at least once." Joni reached into a clothes basket and grabbed a wet pillowcase, draped it on the clothesline and pinned it in place. "I'm going to be working like a madwoman these next few days, so I want to reward myself by sleeping on sun-dried sheets when I finally get to fall into bed."

"Need help?"

"With the laundry or the youth center?"

"Either. Both." Being busy might help her settle her nerves and hold on to her resolve to come clean with Brandon.

"Yes to both."

Arden pulled out another pillowcase and secured it to the line. "I love the smell of clothes dried by the sun."

"Me, too. I try to dry my laundry this way as often as possible, but normally I'm so busy I just toss everything in the dryer."

"What kind of help do you need at the youth center?"

"We're about to have our summer bash."

"What's that?"

Joni rolled her eyes. "Organized insanity."

Arden laughed and helped Joni hang a queen-size sheet. She wondered idly if it belonged to Brandon and imagined lying on his bed with him before forcing herself to pay attention to what Joni was saying.

"Seriously, it's a weekend-long festival. The whole town is involved." Joni hung the last bit of laundry on the line and dropped a couple of unused clothespins into the basket. "The summer bash is like the rest of the summer on steroids. We have activities day and night and a giant sleepover. We start Saturday at noon with a parade through town. We don't have many floats, but kids ride their bikes or pull wagons. The high school marching band comes. We even have a fire engine, which delights the younger set. Fingers crossed the weather is great because we'll be at the beach a lot of the weekend. We end things with fireworks. Then I'll come home and collapse."

"Sounds hectic and wonderful. What can I do to help? And when?"

"I could use you any time you can help out."

"Done."

"Would you be interested in judging a talent show Saturday after dinner?"

"You mean with singing and dancing? Sure. Sounds fun."

"It is. The hardest part is finding unbiased judges. Most everyone in this town is related to one of the contestants. I had one mother who didn't believe anyone was more talented than her little Tommy who fell off his pogo stick every other hop. She and another judge whose daughters perform synchronized hula-hooping nearly came to blows. True story. Made me think we should add mud-wrestling moms. Of course, if you would rather participate in the show, you can do that, too."

"Adults participate?"

"Yep. It's a hoot although they can't win any of the prizes. You wouldn't believe some of the talent we have in this town."

"I think I'll stick to judging. I wouldn't want to embarrass myself."

"Good enough. If you can be at the center around noon today we can get set up. The weekend will be here before you know it and there's a lot of work to be done before then."

"Okay." Arden wandered away, wondering why she was getting more involved with the community instead of distancing herself before the truth about her identity came out. Of course, helping at the youth center gave her one more reason to stay in town longer. Truthfully, she saw the value in the work Joni did and she wanted to be an active participant. Anybody could donate money—and she still planned to do that—but Joni needed willing workers. She was making a difference in the lives of so many people. By helping, Arden was making a difference, too.

And there was always the hope that Brandon would understand why she had lied and forgive her. If that happened, everything would be good. Somehow she didn't think it was going to be that easy. She didn't have to be a fortune-teller to predict that messy days were in her near future. But she would wait until after the festival was over before telling Brandon the truth. She wanted to help at the center and didn't want to risk bad feelings on his or Joni's part. What difference would a couple of days make?

"I've never been so happy to see the end of the night," Arden said, slipping her feet from her gym shoes without bothering to untie them, dropping onto a plush sofa in Joni's office and stretching out. Brandon raised his eyebrows at the way she had appropriated the entire couch, but she didn't move. It was three o'clock in the morning and she was beat, so it was every man for himself. "I could sleep standing up."

The summer bash was even more insane than Joni

had warned her. Kids must have come from all over the state to participate. Arden was glad that she was around to volunteer. Joni had definitely needed her help. And she was equally as glad that another volunteer had relieved her minutes ago.

"Don't tell me a few kids wore you out," Brandon said as he closed the door behind them. The scent of chlorine from the center's swimming pool clung to his hair. He pulled the chair from behind the desk, then sat across from her. The tweens and teens were scattered throughout the center participating in various activities while the little ones were sleeping off a sugar high. At least they were supposed to be sleeping.

"They aren't kids. Kids don't move that much." She ran a hand through her damp curls. She wouldn't be surprised to discover strands of gray throughout the black in the morning. "They're motion machines. They're like that carnival game."

"Which one?"

"You know. The one where the furry little animal sticks his head out of a hole. You try to hit him, but it's too late. He's popping out another hole. You can never catch him."

"Whac-A-Mole."

"Exactly. As soon as I got one kid settled down another kid popped up. It's some kind of plot, I tell you. Kids against the adults. They're trying to run us ragged so they can take over the world. Or at least Sweet Briar."

Brandon leaned back and stretched his long legs in front of him, looking completely relaxed. How could he look like he could go on a three-mile run right now when Arden couldn't move a muscle to save her life? But, he wasn't weighed down by a guilty secret that was beginning to make breathing difficult. Her conscience was becoming like Whac-A-Mole. Every time she felt justified in keeping her secret, guilt popped free and stared her in the face.

Brandon's deep laughter had her pushing that guilt down with even more determination. She was going to tell him the truth. So why not enjoy the moment? Besides, she didn't think she'd ever seen him this carefree and lighthearted. Telling him the truth now might ease her sense of guilt, but it would ruin his pleasure. After everything he'd endured, he deserved some plain old fun.

"Arden, don't take this personally, but you're nuts."

"Don't laugh. I saw the mayor here earlier. He was helping Joni with a bunch of kids. I haven't seen him since then. They've probably tied him up somewhere and gagged him so he can't call for help. Something sinister is definitely happening here."

Brandon finally stopped laughing enough to speak. "I don't think it's a plot by kids to take over the world. It's the abundance of sugar. I warned Joni that she should insist on fruit and vegetables as snacks, but she wouldn't listen. She let parents bring all kinds of cookies and candy. Now the kids are overdosing on sugar and you're paying for it."

Arden covered a yawn. Who would have thought spending the day supervising a handful of seven- and eight-year-olds would be more tiring than working a busy shift at the Heaven on Earth? "How were things at the restaurant tonight?"

"Good. We were full all night."

No surprise there. The dining room was usually filled to capacity and Brandon had mentioned expanding into the building next door if the numbers worked. "How did your new special go over?"

Brandon smiled and heat bloomed in her stomach, pushing aside guilt in a way that her mind hadn't been able to. Arden couldn't help being attracted to him. He was so handsome, although his looks were only a small part of his appeal. He had such a kind heart. After working in the restaurant, he had come to the youth center to help his sister with the kids. He had to be exhausted, but that hadn't stopped him from hopping into the pool and playing water volleyball with some of the high school kids. She'd been hustling the younger kids out of the shallow end after their swim, but she'd managed to sneak an occasional peek at his bare torso. The water dripping from his hair and trickling down his muscular chest had warmed her despite the fact that she'd been waist deep in cold water.

"I'm pleased to say it was a hit."

"I'm not surprised. I loved it."

"Thanks. Your support means a lot to me."

He sounded so sincere Arden felt herself blushing.

He rose, lifted her feet from the sofa, sat down and placed her feet on his lap. Before she could guess his intentions, he began to massage her right foot. A satisfied moan slipped from her lips. No man had ever treated her with such care.

"I take it you like that?" His voice was deeper than ever and it sent shivers down her spine. His hands were gentle yet firm as they soothed the ache in that foot, then switched to her left.

She sighed and closed her eyes. "More than words can express."

"Then don't try to use words." His hands worked

their magic as he increased the pressure on the balls of her feet, drawing murmurs of satisfaction from her lips. Surely it couldn't be wrong to enjoy this moment. And maybe a few more.

The silence of the room surrounded them, wrapping them in an intimate cocoon. It was as if they were the only people in the world. A single lamp offered soft illumination while a line of moonlight filtered through an opening in the otherwise closed curtains. Brandon leaned closer and Arden's senses were filled with the scent of clean male with that hint of chlorine. His fingers moved over her feet, traveling to her ankles and calves. His hands moved gently over her legs, leaving tingling heat with each touch.

Brandon made an agonized sound and stopped caressing her. "I know I should keep my distance, but I just can't keep from wanting to touch you."

Arden opened her eyes and took in Brandon's tortured expression. Sitting up, she reached a hand to his cheek. "What if I want you to touch me?"

"Arden." His voice issued a warning she chose to ignore. "I know you've been hurt. I don't want to add to that. I'm still working out some things."

Which just proved how nice a guy he was. And since he was so nice, so caring, he would understand why she'd lied. Wouldn't he? But if she actually believed that, why did she keep putting off telling him the truth? What had happened to all the bravery she'd felt a couple of days ago? She knew. A couple of days ago she had only liked him. Now she realized she was falling in love with him and didn't want to lose him. Maybe with time he would fall in love with her. Then he would understand and be more likely to forgive her.

"I'm not hurting any longer. I haven't been for a long time." She sat up and scooted closer to him. She didn't want him to have any doubts about what she wanted. "And maybe I can help you work things out. Just let me."

She brushed her lips against his, then moved back and smiled at him. She really did want to help him move forward.

They could move forward together.

Brandon pulled Arden toward him until she was sitting in his lap and placed his lips on hers. Even as their lips met he knew he was making a mistake by giving in to his desires. She wasn't the kind of woman who gave her body without her heart coming along for the ride. He knew her feelings for him were growing. That was bad enough. Worse was admitting to himself that his feelings for her were stronger now, too. Despite his attempts to keep her at a distance, he was constantly drawn closer in a way he'd never been with another woman.

And it scared him silly.

But still. The feel of her lips beneath his was too good to resist. She tasted like the chocolate icing he'd caught her licking off a cupcake earlier. The sight of her tongue sliding across the treat had been so arousing he'd known he had to get away from her before his desire overcame his common sense. He'd rounded up a group of kids for an impromptu game of water volleyball. The cold water had cooled his body but done nothing to the fire that was still raging inside at this moment. The inferno had been burning too long for him to even try to extinguish. He slanted his head and deepened the kiss.

The sound of someone loudly clearing her throat

forced them apart. "Well, well. Maybe I need to get a chaperone for the chaperones."

Brandon shook his head. "Joni, did anyone ever tell you your timing was rotten?"

"No one I ever listen to."

"Then I won't waste my breath."

Arden slid off his lap and he immediately missed her slight weight. In that moment he knew that he wanted her with him forever. Despite his best efforts not to, he'd fallen in love with her. She'd managed to work her way inside his heart. He loved her. More than that, he trusted her. The walls he'd built around his heart after the debacle with Sylvia had fallen and crumbled into dust. Even thinking of Sylvia was no longer painful. It was as if the entire relationship had happened in another life. Or to another person. The healing he'd heard about but didn't believe in had occurred. And the reason was clear. Arden.

Sweet Arden had healed his broken heart with her caring and innocent manner. He was ready to love again. To trust again. To open himself up to a relationship.

He needed some time to think about things and be absolutely sure of his feelings. He didn't want to act in haste and hurt Arden by accident. Or, worse, scare her off.

"I'll get to my post supervising the boys." Unable to stop himself, he reached out and caressed Arden's soft cheek. "Will you have dinner with me tomorrow night?"

She nodded and he left the room, happier and more optimistic than he'd been in years.

## *Chapter Thirteen*

Arden removed the envelope from her door, then stepped inside her apartment. She pulled out the folded note.

I'll be by to pick you up at seven. Wear something casual and as beautiful as you are. Until tonight. B.

Her heart skipped a beat as she read the words again. A second later it plummeted to her toes. These weren't the words of a man who only wanted to be friends. Was Brandon interested in pursuing a relationship? Was she? Sure, her feelings for him had changed and grown as she'd gotten to know him better. But was she ready for something real? Now that it was looking like a distinct possibility she had a few doubts. Just how would a relationship work? They lived and worked in two different states.

No matter what else did or didn't happen, she had to tell him the truth. She couldn't expect to start a relationship with him as long as there was deception between them.

Oh, why had she let this go on for so long? Why had she lied in the first place? Okay, she remembered why. Still, she wished she had thought things through before giving Brandon a false name. Hadn't she always gotten into trouble by being impetuous?

Well, she couldn't change the past. And she might be jumping to conclusions. She could be reading more into this date than he intended. The only way to know for sure would be to let the night unfold. Then she would know for sure.

It couldn't hurt anything to look and smell her best. If she hurried, she would have enough time for a bubble bath. Flipping through her closet, she pulled out a pair of peach capris she'd bought at the boutique on an impromptu shopping trip. The pants were well made and fit her like a glove. Best of all, they matched a top she'd brought with her from Baltimore. She'd pair them with low-heeled sandals and knock Brandon's socks off.

Brandon inhaled and knocked on Arden's door. He held a bouquet of pink and cream roses in his right hand and a box of Louanne's chocolate-covered almonds in his left. He'd promised himself he would never put himself out there again where his heart could be trampled, and yet amazingly here he stood, ready to begin a relationship with a woman he'd known only a few weeks. A woman planning to leave town soon. Unless he found a way to convince her to stay. He must be crazy to take this kind of risk again, yet here he was.

The door swung open and she stood there looking as lovely as anyone he'd ever seen. For a moment he was struck dumb. Her eyes lit up when she saw him and his heart leaped in response.

"Hi." She sounded breathless and excited as she noticed the flowers and candy. "Are those for me?"

"Only you."

"Thank you. They're beautiful. And you know I love chocolate." She stepped aside. "Come on in."

The roses were already in a vase so all she needed to do was set them on the breakfast bar. She looked longingly at the candy before setting it beside the flowers. She turned to face him and suddenly seemed a bit shy. "I hope I'm dressed all right."

She looked delicious in her cropped peach pants and fitted print top. "You're dressed just fine."

"So where are we going?"

"It's a surprise."

"Will you give me a hint?"

"Nope."

"What if I guess?"

"Still no."

She giggled and grabbed her bag. "Well, then, let's get going. The sooner we get there, the sooner my suspense will end."

"In that case, maybe I'll take the scenic route."

"Do that and I'll sing that song you hate."

"Direct route coming right up."


"Is this my surprise?" Arden asked breathlessly. She had never seen anything so romantic.

Brandon nodded. "Yeah. I hope you like it."

A canopy had been erected on a secluded section of the beach. The starry sky provided the perfect backdrop. Inside there was a table draped with a pink cloth and two chairs. Candlelight flickered in a globe, softly illuminating the area. Glass vases filled with pink and yellow roses lined the path to the entrance. The wind blew the perfumed air, teasing Arden's senses. The sound of waves lapping against the shore filled the silent night. She sighed with pleasure. "It's beautiful. How did you do this?"

"A friend of mine owns one of the new beachfront homes. He's out of town for the night and let me use his place." Brandon led her to the table and pulled out a chair. Still overwhelmed by the absolute beauty and romance of it all, she sat.

He gestured to a person she hadn't noticed before as he took the seat across from her. A young man dressed in a black shirt and pants appeared seemingly out of nowhere carrying a bottle of wine, which he handed to Brandon. Arden recognized Tim as a waiter who worked at Heaven on Earth. She smiled at him.

Tim grinned, nodded and disappeared as quietly and quickly as he had arrived. Brandon expertly opened the bottle and filled their glasses. He raised his in a toast. "To a wonderful evening."

Arden smiled and sipped her wine. "This is delicious."

"It's from my private collection."

The young waiter returned carrying a tray of appetizers that he placed in front of them before once more vanishing.

"I heard you once say that you loved crab cakes so

I worked up a new recipe just for you." Brandon gestured toward her plate. "Try one and let me know what you think."

If the tantalizing aroma was any indication, they were going to be beyond delicious. She took a bite and flavor burst through her mouth. "Oh, this is great. Better than great. I could be happy eating crab cakes for the main course."

"You only say that because you don't know the rest of the menu. I've tried to create a meal that includes all of your favorites."

Arden's heart nearly exploded with happiness. He was definitely spoiling her. No one had ever put so much effort into making her happy.

As she ate course after magnificent course her joy grew so that she was nearly overwhelmed. By the end of the meal, as she dug into her chocolate brownie, the sound of violins filled the air.

"Boy, this dessert is better than I thought. I'm hearing music."

Brandon chuckled. "I can't take credit for that. I brought a CD of my favorite music and asked Tim to play it when he brought out dessert. I thought it would be a nice touch."

"It's perfect. This has been the most perfect night."

Brandon reached out and gently wiped a few crumbs from the corner of her bottom lip. His hand lingered and caressed her cheek. In his eyes she saw a flicker of desire that matched the longing growing inside her. "The night isn't over yet."

Her heart leaped, then stuttered before returning to beat at its normal pace. Brandon put his napkin on his empty dessert plate and she followed suit. He reached out a hand and she took it, following him to the edge of the water. Waves lapped against the shore, leaving damp sand in their wake. They removed their shoes and walked in the warm water. She smiled as she remembered the night they'd met. She'd waded in cold water then and was chilled to the bone. Nothing about her was chilled now. If anything she was overheated.

Brandon clasped Arden's hand, her small palm pressed against his. Her hand felt even softer against his calluses. Nothing had ever felt this right. He'd been involved with women many times in his life, but he had to admit he'd never experienced the connection with any of them that he shared with Arden. Even the feelings he'd had for Sylvia, someone he'd proposed to, paled in comparison. Nothing in his past prepared him for the depth of emotion Arden awakened in him. Those emotions were growing rapidly and showed no signs of slowing down or diminishing.

He'd been fighting his feelings from the beginning, trying to convince himself he was infatuated and that it would all blow over. His life would return to normal and Arden would fade into the background. His restaurant would once more be the entire focus of his life. Instead, she continued to occupy his thoughts. He wanted to spend more time with her. Despite his intention to hold her at a distance, he repeatedly found himself drawn to her. Like any wise man, he knew when he was beaten. So he stopped fighting. No longer worried about defending his heart, he decided to try to win hers.

The old saying about food and a man's heart also applied to women. As a chef he had that nailed. One of the first things he'd noticed about Arden was her love of food. Too many women came close to starving themselves in order to attain a Photoshop size that didn't exist in the real world. At least not among healthy adult females. Arden enjoyed eating and didn't care who knew. Nothing appealed to a chef more than someone who delighted in his food. So he'd prepared a lavish feast for her and she'd clearly enjoyed it.

Arden squeezed his hand, and he looked down and returned her smile. They walked in easy silence, the only sound the slap the steady waves made as they softly crashed against the sand before the foam caressed their bare feet. The moonlight shone brightly, spotlighting her delicate features. A gentle breeze blew against his skin and Arden's tempting scent filled the air.

An unusually strong wave crashed against their legs, causing Arden to stumble against him.

"Sorry," she murmured.

"What, getting knocked down by a rogue wave isn't on your bucket list?"

"Believe it or not, very few things on that list involve water." She scooped a handful of water and tossed him a mischievous look before letting the water drain through her fingers. Smiling, she splashed and scampered across the beach.

He followed more slowly, enjoying the sway of her hips in her tight pants. She found a place that appealed to her and sat down, stretching out her legs. He sat beside her on the sand. He could feel the warmth of her smaller body, heating him in a way the sun never could. She turned toward him, still laughing. There were a few grains of sand clinging to her cheek and, without thinking, he lifted his finger to her cheek and brushed them away. No matter how often he touched her skin, he was always amazed by just how soft it was. "Please tell me kissing on a moonlit beach made the cut and is on the list."

She leaned into his hand. "It is as of now."

He needed to feel her in his arms, to taste her lips and hear her whisper his name on a sigh. His body was hard with need, his passion held back by a single thread. Despite the intense longing surging through his body, Brandon slowly lowered his head until his lips barely brushed hers, keeping the pressure light.

He could do this. He could allow them some pleasure without crossing the line making return impossible. Although Arden wasn't as vulnerable as she had been when they'd met, her heart had still been battered. She shouldn't be rushed. He needed to be patient and give her time to fall in love with him.

She moved closer and increased the pressure with her own lips, opening to him. Her hands gripped his shirt, pulling him to her, and the thread snapped. His control gone, he wrapped her in his arms and kissed her with all the longing that had been building for weeks, allowing himself this brief moment of heaven.

Beneath the flavor of the chocolate dessert was a sweetness that Arden alone could claim. One sample simply wasn't enough. It was as if he'd been stranded on a deserted island, slowly starving, and now was being gifted with pure nectar of the gods.

Arden's sigh beneath his lips was nearly his undoing. He called upon a discipline he'd never had to use before and reluctantly ended the kiss. Breathing hard, he brushed a trembling finger against her kiss-swollen lower lip and leaned his forehead against hers.

"Wow," she breathed, her breath a sexy whisper against his face.

He exhaled. "Yeah, wow."

"So now what?"

*Good question.* "Now I take you home and we say good-night." Even though everything in him screamed in protest, he forced himself to stand, then reached a hand to her.

She was silent for a long moment. "Must we?"

The reluctance in her voice matched his. He didn't want to end the night. At least not this way. But he was determined to stick to the vow he'd made earlier and not take the chance of making their relationship awkward by pushing her to make love. His resolve was weakening when every breath he took was filled with her totally distracting scent. There was no way he could concentrate when her very sexy body was within arm's reach. "It's late. Tomorrow will be here before you know it. I have to go to the markets in the morning."

She took his hand and he pulled her to her feet. Her soft breasts pressed into his arm and he nearly groaned aloud. Sometimes being a gentleman sucked.

She dusted the sand from the seat of her pants. "Do you mind if I go with you again?"

"Sure. That would be great." Brandon wasn't ready to say he'd fallen in love with her, but he definitely liked the idea of the two of them being together. Perhaps for the rest of their lives.

## Chapter Fourteen

Arden blinked as the alarm clock blared from across the dark room. She'd learned the hard way the consequences of having the clock close enough for her to hit the snooze button repeatedly. Covering her head with her pillow, she tried to block out the persistent noise, but couldn't. Finally she sighed and sat up, then rose and stumbled across the room to stop the irritating sound.

She'd barely slept at all, so she was sleepier than normal. Then she remembered last night with Brandon and the reason she'd set the alarm and all sleepiness fled, leaving behind a blur of emotions. She wrapped her arms around her middle as she relived Brandon staring deep into her eyes before he lowered his head ever so slowly to kiss her. And what a kiss. Even now her toes curled at the memory. The sensation of his lips was like nothing she'd ever felt before and something she couldn't wait to experience again.

Although Brandon had told her he wasn't looking for a relationship, she believed his feelings had changed. Even though he hadn't said a word, his actions spoke for him. He cared for her. He often reached for her hand as they walked, holding it tight as if he didn't want to let her get too far from him. When she helped at the restaurant, she felt his eyes searching her out as soon as he entered the dining room. And when their eyes met, he always nodded and smiled, his eyes communicating more eloquently than any words could.

True, none of these things meant that he was falling in love with her. Still, a girl could hope. Especially since she was head over heels in love with him and her love for him grew each day. She still wasn't sure how it had happened, but her broken heart had healed and was functioning quite nicely. Now she knew she'd never been in love with Michael-the-twerp. It was only her pride that had been hurt. She hated how easily he'd duped her, but none of that mattered now. The only thing that did was Brandon. She hoped that he loved her as much as she loved him. If he wasn't there yet, that was okay. She'd give him as much time as he needed. But would any feelings he had survive when she revealed her secret?

She bit her lip. She needed to tell him the truth. Today. She had already let so many opportunities to come clean slip through her hands, each one another nail in her coffin. She knew how much Brandon valued honesty. He deserved to know her real name and identity. And he deserved to know why she'd kept it a secret. Having been on the receiving end of deception, she knew how much it hurt to be betrayed. It was worse when the person doing the deceiving claimed to love you.

She should have come clean when he'd told her about Sylvia's deception. That would have been the perfect time. Before then she hadn't known her using a fake name would echo a painful incident in his past. After he'd told her about Sylvia, every day that passed only made her look as if she didn't intend to tell him the truth.

Her stomach churned and she muttered an unlady-like swear word. She didn't look forward to the conversation they were about to have.

If only she'd been honest in the beginning, she wouldn't be in this pickle. Then again, if he'd known her last name he might not have taken the time to get to know her. And she might have been suspicious of his kindness, believing he'd had an ulterior motive. It didn't matter now. The past was over and done. She had to deal with now. She was helping at Heaven on Earth tonight. She'd tell him the truth after the restaurant closed.

Arden forced a smile and smothered the urge to yell at the young customer to make up her mind and choose something. Generally, indecisive diners didn't bother her; she'd patiently try to help them choose a meal they would enjoy. Tonight she didn't have the inclination to do that. The conversation she needed to have with Brandon weighed heavily on her mind. Her head ached with fear and anticipation.

She remembered how furious he'd been with Sylvia. True, he'd been physically injured because of the other woman's lies. She'd be just as angry with any person who put her life in danger like that. She was certain Brandon would see the difference in what she had done and what Sylvia had done. Wouldn't he? Man, she hoped so.

"Have you made up your mind?" Arden asked.

The conflicted twentysomething had been sure she wanted seafood-stuffed crepes when she'd first ordered. She'd changed her selection as each of her three companions ordered, mirroring their choice. Now she was opening her menu again.

"I don't know."

"How about I give you a few more minutes to decide what you want?"

Her three friends groaned. Arden knew how they felt.

"What do you think I should get?" the woman asked Arden.

"Everything you've selected tastes wonderful. If I were you, though, I'd go with the crepes. That is what you initially wanted."

The young woman bit her lower lip. "Okay," she said in a rush.

Arden scribbled the order while the other three clapped.

"Hurry before she changes her mind," said the young man sitting next to the woman.

"You'd better hope I don't change my mind about you," she teased. She smiled at Arden and lifted her left hand. An enormous emerald that matched the woman's eyes perfectly glistened on her ring finger. "We got engaged last night."

"Congratulations." Arden smiled and felt a sudden longing for a ring of her own with all the love it represented. An image of Brandon offering her one on bended knee flashed in her mind. She quickly banished it.

As if she'd conjured him up, Brandon emerged from the kitchen to make his customary visit to the dining room, starting in the back and moving toward the front.

Dressed impeccably in a tailored gray suit that emphasized his broad shoulders, he shook hands with a gray-haired gentleman, then chatted briefly with the woman seated across from him. Whatever he said must have been amusing because they all laughed.

The front door opened, letting in more patrons. Suddenly an unusual hush filled the dining room. Conversation quieted and then stopped abruptly. There wasn't even the sound of silverware connecting with plates. Then a slow buzz grew as people began to talk excitedly. Arden shivered and the hair on the back of her neck stood up as a sense of dread filled her. She heard his voice and her stomach plummeted to her toes.

*Jax.*

Slowly she turned and saw her brothers. Her mind was filled with horror. What were they doing here?

Her eyes returned to Brandon. He had ended his conversation with the older couple and was now weaving his way to the front of the restaurant to discover the source of the unusual mood that had settled on the room. Any second he'd encounter her brothers and the jig would be up.

*No.* Brandon couldn't find out this way. He'd never believe she'd meant to tell him the truth if he found out her identity from someone else. She had to get her brothers out of there before they ruined everything. Dropping her pad, she brushed past two young women who were being seated, mumbling an apology. Several heads turned, including Brandon's, as she began a mad dash to the front of the restaurant. It was as if she was running through sludge. No matter how fast she pumped her legs, she didn't seem to move.

She heard Margo, the hostess, asking if they had

reservations, followed by her brother's response in the negative. A tall man on crutches blocked her path and she could only watch as her world began to crumble around her.

"There are no openings for tonight, Mr. Wexford," Margo said apologetically. Neither of her brothers shunned the spotlight the way Arden did, so they were frequently the subject of celebrity gossip that passed as entertainment. There was no chance celebrity follower Margo wouldn't recognize them. Margo smiled her brightest and Arden knew she'd been correct. "Maybe I can check with the chef if you want to wait, Mr. Wexford. He is also the owner."

Before either of her brothers could respond, she signaled to Brandon, who joined them

"These are Blake and Jackson Wexford," Margo said, giving special emphasis to the last name. "You know, of Wexford Industries. The hotel people. They don't have reservations, but I was hoping you could work out something for them."

"Thank you for the offer, but we aren't here to eat," Jax said. "We're here to see our sister. We were told she works here."

"Nobody with that last name works here," Brandon said. "You must have been misinformed."

Arden's heart pounded in her chest, her dread growing as she watched the events unfold. She'd waited too long to tell the truth. The man in her path finally made it to his seat and she was able to cross the remaining distance to the hostess station.

"No, we weren't. I'm looking right at her."

"Who?" Brandon's voice sounded puzzled and his head swiveled to encompass the dining room.

"Arden. Arden Wexford."

"Arden *Wexford*?" Brandon's quiet voice ripped through her as if her name had been shouted. He turned to her, confusion in his eyes, quickly followed by accusation and hurt. Then he blinked and the only expression that remained was red-hot fury. He swung an arm toward Blake and Jax. "Your brothers?" he asked, as if he needed to hear her confirm Jax's words.

A lump the size of a mountain appeared in her throat and all she could do was nod.

"I see." He turned his back to her and faced her brothers. "I guess I was wrong about her."

She flinched. He'd spoken to Blake and Jax, but the words were directed to her. But he hadn't been wrong to trust her. He wasn't wrong about the type of person she was. And he certainly wasn't wrong about her feelings for him. She was the one who had been wrong. She'd been wrong to continue to hide her identity from him once she'd discovered what a good man he was. She'd been wrong to not tell him of her growing feelings for him.

He started to walk away and she grabbed his arm. If he left this way he might never listen. And she had to tell him the truth. "Please let me explain."

He stiffened, then shook off her hand as if he found her touch distasteful. "Now you want to explain. You had your chance. Many chances. And to think…" He clenched his jaw and looked back at her brothers. "We don't have any open tables so you'll have to leave. And Arden, you can clock out. That way you can go with them."

"Brandon, please." She was begging, but she didn't care. Her pride would mean nothing if she didn't have Brandon.

"Actually, we'd like to talk to you, too," Blake said.

"Me?" Brandon narrowed his eyes.

"Why?" Arden asked suspiciously. How did they even know about Brandon? For that matter, how did they know she'd been working here? She hadn't mentioned it. They must have hired a private investigator to keep tabs on her. Apparently, they were only pretending to believe she could run her own life. And given the mistake she had just made with Brandon, they might be right.

But that was different. She hadn't become involved with the wrong man again. Her mistake had been taking too long to realize he was just as good as he seemed.

"I don't have time for this. I have a restaurant to run." Brandon turned on his heel and strode to the kitchen and away from her.

Jax took a step after him, but Arden stopped him with a hand on his arm. "He's working. We need to leave."

She looked around the dining room. People were beginning to eat and to pick up the strands of their conversation. She caught the eyes of several of the other waitstaff. Their expressions ranged from curious to confused to downright angry. Nobody liked being deceived and made to feel like a fool. No doubt about it. She'd lost more than her anonymity tonight. She'd lost friends.

Worse, she'd lost Brandon.

She lifted her chin and walked out of the restaurant with as much dignity as she could muster. When she felt the cool night air, she rounded on her brothers, her sadness morphing into fury. "What are you doing here?"

"Trying to keep you from making another stupid mistake," Jax replied.

Arden gasped and drew her hands to her chest as if to protect her heart.

"He didn't mean it the way it sounded," Blake interjected with a sharp look at Jax.

"Oh, I think he did. You two don't respect me. You never have. You treat me like a child. I've grown up but you refuse to see that." Her voice was a croak, as the hurt she'd tried for years to hide was revealed.

"If you're so grown-up, then why are you playing make-believe?" Jax demanded. "Adults don't pretend to be someone that they aren't. Or are you going to tell me that Danielson forgot your name?"

"You don't understand. And it isn't any of your business!"

"You're right. I don't understand. Don't tell me you're in that waitress getup because of your low salary as a teacher. You do get regular payments from your trust fund."

"He needed help."

"And you just volunteered. Next he's going to need money. Are you going to volunteer that, too? Blake already told me you plan on giving money to his sister."

"Jax. That's enough." Blake stepped in between Arden and Jax. "Come on, Arden. It's time to leave."

"I'm not getting into a car with him." She glared at Jax, wishing she had the power to vaporize him. Or that she could at least knock that smug look off his face. "I'll walk."

"You don't need to walk. I'll leave Jax here and drop you off. A little fresh air will do him some good."

"Fine." Arden let Blake lead her to a late-model luxury sedan and snatched open the door before he could. She stared straight ahead, her feelings a jumbled mess. She was angry and disappointed. And hurt. She wouldn't let herself feel the pain of losing Brandon now or she would cry. Instead, she let out her sense of betrayal. "I trusted you, Blake."

"I didn't do anything wrong. You wanted money for this community center. I don't usually make site visits, but I figured I could check it out and see you at the same time. I didn't know you were pretending to be someone else." He gave her a pointed look.

Arden huffed out a breath. As much as she wanted to blame her brothers for this mess, she knew the fault was hers. She was the one who'd lied over and over. When her friendship with Brandon had developed into a more romantic relationship, she should have come clean. She'd had plenty of opportunities and, like a coward, had let them pass by.

Heck, she should have been honest before then. She'd known almost from the time they'd met that Brandon was nothing like Michael-the-pit-stain. Brandon was as honorable a man as they came. He was a real live hero.

And because she hadn't given him enough credit— hadn't given him the trust he had earned—she'd lost him.

She couldn't imagine what he must be thinking. That was a lie. She knew exactly the painful thoughts that were circling his mind. He thought she was just like Sylvia, a woman who had lied to him about her identity. True, Arden had lied, too. But she hadn't played with his heart with no care as to whether or not she broke it. She cared very much. But nothing in her actions would tell him that.

If only he knew how much she loved him. If only he'd give her a second chance. This time she'd take the utmost care with his heart.

* * *

Brandon held his anger and hurt in check as he prepared meal after perfect meal. Ordinarily cooking soothed him in a way nothing else could. Tonight it didn't. He was more unsettled than he had ever been and had to rely on his training. It took all of his focus just to keep the orders straight.

The urge to smash something—anything—nearly consumed him, but he resisted the impulse. His grandfather would never have tolerated such behavior in anyone, much less his own grandson, and Brandon respected his memory too much to act that way. Besides, his employees were present and he wouldn't create a scene in their presence. They were already sneaking glances at him and murmuring about Arden. Apparently, news of her true identity had already made the rounds.

He stole a glance at the clock. What was taking the night so long to pass? The one time he needed to lose himself in the work, he couldn't. His usual pleasure in the kitchen was missing and all he wanted to do was leave. He needed to be alone where he could yell out his pain.

His mind kept replaying the scene in the dining room. He could see Arden's shocked and guilty face as she was caught in her lie. Would she ever have told him the truth? He doubted it. To her, the entire thing had been a lark. She'd been a bored heiress wanting to see how the other half lived. Fool that he was, he'd fallen for her act, believing every word she'd uttered while she'd laughed at him. He'd been falling in love while she'd been playing a game.

Frowning, he checked the finished meals on a tray and then nodded to the waitress. She touched his arm before she took it, and he saw the sympathy in her eyes.

Great. He'd become an object of pity among his employees. A moment later Joni rushed into the kitchen. Good news sure traveled fast.

"If you came to check on me, you shouldn't have bothered. I'm fine."

Joni glanced around the kitchen before speaking. Everyone was busy working, but she stepped closer and kept her voice down anyway. "You don't have to pretend with me. I know you're hurt by Arden's betrayal. I'm pretty furious with her myself."

He exhaled slowly. "She lied."

"I know."

He gritted his teeth at what a fool he'd been. Again. "You might believe every woman is not a liar, but you can't prove it by me. I should have kept my distance."

"At least give her a chance to explain."

"I don't need to hear an explanation or some lame excuse. All I want is for her to leave and never come back."

"Brandon."

"I can't take any more hits. Every time I open myself up, I end up on the losing end. I'm done, Joni. I'm done." He turned back to the stove, determined to put Arden out of his heart and mind.

Arden was sitting on the bottom step of her apartment when Brandon's truck swung into the driveway, headlights illuminating the rows of flowers lining the yard. Nerves set butterflies free in her stomach, and she circled her arms around her waist in a futile attempt to still the churning inside. Her body went suddenly weak and she wondered if her legs would hold her.

Brandon parked beside her car and slammed the

door. She heard him swear as he stalked angrily across the lawn. He stopped abruptly when he saw her. Nibbling on her bottom lip, Arden stood shakily and wiped her suddenly moist hands on her skirt.

"What are you doing here?" he asked.

"I wanted to talk."

"I'm not interested in what you want." He headed for his house, cutting through the grass. She ran to catch up, grabbing his arm. The look he shot her chilled her very soul. She had expected anger and disappointment, but this was something more. This was rage. Controlled rage, but rage, nonetheless. For the first time that night, she worried that he might not give her a chance to explain. And if he didn't understand, he'd never forgive her.

"Please, Brandon, just listen to me. Then if you still want me to go, I'll leave and stay out of your life. I promise." She'd already piled her belongings into the back of the Beetle and booked a room at the Come On Inn just in case.

He pulled away from her grasp and folded his arms across his chest. Those arms had once wrapped around her, providing protection and comfort. Now they created an impenetrable barrier between her heart and his. "You seem to believe you have a say in this. You don't. This is my home. My property. I let you stay in my apartment because I believed you needed a place to live. But you don't. So you can get out of my apartment and out of my life."

"I can explain everything if you would just listen."

"I don't want to hear your explanation. There is nothing you can say that will justify lying to me. If you wouldn't even tell me your real name, what else are you hiding?"

He climbed the back stairs to his house and she ran

to keep up with him. This was her one and only opportunity to talk to him. If he made it inside, the chance would be lost. "I love you," she yelled.

He stopped and spun around. "What?"

She exhaled and said more softly. "I love you."

"Don't even try it," he snarled. "You don't love me. You don't know what love is."

His words cut her to the bone and she staggered back from the impact. "It may look like that to you, but you're wrong. I love you with everything inside me."

"You've got a funny way of showing it. I may not be an expert on the methods of expressing love, but I know lies and deceit aren't among them. You might want to remember that the next time you decide you *love* someone. He might not appreciate being involved with a liar any more than I do."

Arden sucked in a painful breath. When she spoke her voice trembled with emotion. "There won't be anyone else. I won't love anyone else because my heart belongs to you."

"I don't want your heart, Arden. Feel free to give it to another sucker. Then you can play all the games you want with his heart."

"It wasn't a game, Brandon. I just wanted you to like me for me."

He climbed the stairs and disappeared into his house. A moment later the door closed firmly and the lock clicked into place. She sank to the ground and cried. It was over.

Standing inside the kitchen, Brandon steeled his heart against the sound of Arden's heartrending sobs. No doubt she wanted him to hear, run to her like a fool and say all was forgiven. She probably was only crying crocodile tears. She was nothing if not a world-class actress. She'd certainly had him fooled. He'd believed she was as honest as they came. Instead, she was no different than Sylvia. In fact, she was worse.

At least Sylvia had a justifiable reason for her lie. She was trying to bring down the drug dealer who'd killed her brother. Arden had just been looking to amuse herself, pretending to be a regular person when she was from one of the wealthiest families in the country. How she must have laughed at him. No doubt she and her worthless friends would have a good chuckle at the expense of the country bumpkins she'd met in Sweet Briar. She could entertain for hours on end with details of their less-than-sophisticated ways.

He turned out the light and walked to his bedroom, refusing to turn his head when he passed the guest room. She hadn't stayed there in weeks, yet the scent of her perfume lingered in the air as if taunting him.

His mistake had been getting seriously involved with Arden. He'd foolishly opened his heart to her and basically let her move in. He thought he'd learned his lesson with Sylvia. Somehow he'd let Arden convince him to take a risk again. What an idiot. That was a mistake he was never going to make again. He let himself feel the pain, searing it into his memory so that he'd never forget this agony. No woman was ever getting close to his heart again. In the future he would limit his involvement with women to brief and unemotional encounters.

The old gullible Brandon Danielson was gone for good.

## Chapter Fifteen

Brandon frowned at the first rays of sunlight streaming through his window. He'd barely slept, but he needed to get to the markets. His assistant manager, Marcus, had offered to go, but Brandon refused to allow Arden to control his actions. She may have made a fool of him with her lies, but he would not allow her to diminish him in the eyes of his employees. He'd recovered from a woman's treachery before and he could do it again. He would carry on as he always had.

Twenty minutes later he pulled into the parking lot at the fish market. He was nearing the store when he heard his name being called. He recognized the voice and spun around, fury and joy battling for dominance inside him.

Arden stepped away from her car and tentatively crossed the lot until she stood directly in front of him. Despite his anger at her, he couldn't help but notice how lovely she looked in white denim shorts that hit midthigh and a purple floral top that clung to her breasts. The wind ruffled her short curls and she lifted a delicate hand and pushed the locks out of her eyes. Although she clearly hadn't gotten any more sleep last night than he had, she still was more beautiful than any woman he'd ever seen. She nibbled her full bottom lip, something she always did when she was nervous.

Irritated with himself for remembering that habit of hers, he stepped around her without speaking and headed toward a small fish store.

"Brandon, wait. Please."

He heard the anguish in her voice but suppressed his concern for her. There was no way he was going to feel compassion for someone who didn't care a bit about him. He stopped but didn't turn around. "What are you doing here?"

She stepped around him until they were face-to-face. Her familiar scent teased his nostrils. "You wouldn't listen to me last night."

"So you took that to mean I'd listen to you today?"

"I hoped you had time to cool off." When he didn't respond she rushed on, her words running into each other. "I know you think the worst of me, but I wish you'd just listen. Please."

Brandon told himself to ignore the begging in her voice and the sorrow on her face. He might have succeeded in doing that, but he couldn't ignore the tears that glistened in her eyes no matter how badly he wanted to. "Fine. You've got five minutes."

He grabbed her elbow and led her to a secluded area away from the stores where they wouldn't be disturbed. Leaning against a light pole, he folded his arms against

his chest so he wouldn't give in to the traitorous desire to touch her. He remembered all too well how soft
she felt and longed to experience that sensation just
one more time before she was out of his life forever.
"Well, talk."

Arden seemed to shrink at his words and she looked
at him with hurt in her eyes. "I was going to tell you
my real name last night."

"Of course you were."

"I'm telling the truth."

He raised an eyebrow and steeled his heart. He'd been
down this road before. Luckily, this time bullets weren't
involved so there was no risk of being killed. Too bad
the pain in his heart was just as bad if not worse.

She huffed out a breath and rubbed her hands against
her shorts, another sign of just how nervous she was.
"Let me start at the beginning."

He shrugged. "This is your show. Use your time however you want. But in five minutes, I'm gone."

"My name is Arden Isabella Wexford. I'm the
youngest child of Winston and Lorelei Wexford. The
Wexford name is well-known in Baltimore. Heck, it's
well-known all over America. People treat me differently because of my family name."

"Poor little rich girl."

"You said *I* had five minutes to talk."

He waved a hand at her. "I'm just letting you know
I don't understand why you decided it would be fun
to use a fake name and create a whole new persona."

"It wasn't like that. At least not at first. I had been involved with someone who was only with me because he
wanted to get his hands on my money. Can you maybe
understand how much that hurt? I was through with

guys like that. I was through with guys, period. That experience made me cautious. I didn't trust my judgment anymore."

"And you thought I would do the same? I don't want your money, Arden. I never did." It was amazing how deeply it hurt to realize how little she thought of him.

"I know that now. But at the time I didn't know anything about you. And I wasn't planning on staying in Sweet Briar any longer than it took to get my car fixed. But then everything changed. You needed a waitress. You'd helped me and I wanted the opportunity to return the favor.

"I started making friends and became a part of this wonderful close-knit community. I have never felt such a sense of belonging in all my life. It felt so good I just didn't want to give it up. Then I fell in love with you and knew I had to tell the truth. I just hadn't figured out how."

Although part of him wanted to believe her, he couldn't take that leap. His trust had been battered too badly to take her at her word. He knew how skillfully she lied. She'd had him believing every word she said and none of it had been true. He'd fallen for a deceitful woman twice now. That was two times too many. "Is that the whole story? Because if you're telling me you lied because you didn't want people to know you were rich, that doesn't change my mind about you."

Her head dipped and she didn't respond. Apparently, she had nothing more to say.

Disappointment flooded him. He'd hoped to hear an explanation that would somehow warrant forgiveness for her lies. Instead, she'd revealed how she'd questioned his character. He pushed away from the post. "Time's up. Have a nice life."

She jumped in front of him and grabbed his arm. "Remember I told you a relationship I was in ended badly? What I didn't tell you was that I caught my boyfriend and my supposed best friend hiding cameras around his bedroom. He was planning on making a secret sex tape. Once he had the tape he planned to blackmail me. He was going to post it on the internet if I didn't give him a million dollars. He didn't care about me. He only wanted my money."

Brandon sucked in a breath. He'd run into some low-lifes in his time, but this guy took the cake. He could only imagine how deeply Arden had been hurt. Yet, that didn't give her the right to turn around and play games with him. *He* hadn't been after her money. "That's low. And I hope he gets what is coming to him. But that didn't give you the right to deceive me."

She sagged as if all the fight had gone out of her. "I just want you to understand where my head was when I arrived. I had planned to seclude myself in my parents' Florida home so I could lick my wounds in private. But then I met you and Joni. I liked you both so much. You became my friends."

"Why lie?"

She shrugged. "I liked being a regular person. You called me a poor little rich girl, and to you my problems might seem petty. But you have no idea what it feels like to never be sure who your friends are. People have tried to use me all of my life. It felt good to know you liked me for who I am and not what I have. Then we got closer and I knew I had to tell you the truth. So many times I opened my mouth to tell you."

"But you didn't." And that was the crux of the matter. Her voice dropped. "No. I didn't."

"I can understand keeping your identity a secret when you arrived. You didn't know anything about me. But once we were close, continuing to deceive me is beyond comprehension. And after I told you about Sylvia, continuing to deceive me is unforgivable."

"I know that now. But then…"

"So…what? This was a test? I had to prove myself worthy of knowing the truth? Worthy of being in a relationship with you?"

"That's not what I meant. I had been wrong before and didn't trust myself to be right about another man."

"Well, regardless of what you meant to do, that's what you did. I opened myself up to you. I shared my thoughts and feelings with you in a way I hadn't with anyone else before. And you were lying to me the entire time. I can't forgive that. Now, if there's nothing else, I need to get going before all the freshest seafood is gone. I still have a restaurant to run."

She shook her head, blinking rapidly. "Doesn't anything I say make a difference?"

"No." He turned around and left, forcing himself not to look back.

He had to consign Arden to a past he wouldn't revisit.

"What are you doing here?" Brandon sneered as he got out of his truck in the restaurant parking lot. The last people in the world he wanted to see were Arden's brothers. Wasn't dealing with one Wexford enough for today? He huffed out an impatient breath, then slammed his truck door.

"We want to talk." Blake Wexford was the elder and

had the reputation of being the more controlled of the two. And wasn't Brandon annoyed with himself for knowing that and anything else about the Wexfords? He'd berated himself most of the night for not recognizing Arden. It didn't matter that no one else had known who she was, either. Unable to sleep, he'd spent hours last night searching the internet for information about her. Impossible as it might seem, there wasn't a single picture of her anywhere. There was barely a mention of her name. That must have cost big bucks. When you were as wealthy as the Wexfords anything was possible, but there had been plenty of information about her brothers and he'd read it all.

"I've spoken to my quota of Wexfords for the day."

"You talked to Arden?" Jax, the more annoying one, butted in. Brandon hadn't needed to read an article about Jax to know that. He'd reached that conclusion at the restaurant last night. And since that question didn't warrant an answer, Brandon didn't give him one.

"We only want a minute of your time," Blake said.

"I'm working." He pushed past them and opened the tailgate of his truck. They followed.

Jax looked at the crates of fresh food with undisguised disdain and then back at him. "This won't take long. Then you can get back to whatever you were doing."

That pissed him off. Did this guy ever utter a word that wasn't condescending? Brandon might not be the CEO of a major corporation, but no one disrespected him. He closed the hatch and leaned against the bumper, arms crossed over his chest. "I'll tell you what. How about I barge into your office at Wexford Industries sometime when it's convenient for *me* and you stop whatever you're doing. Then we'll talk."

"You might have enough time on your hands to do that sooner than you think," Jax said.

Brandon pushed off the bumper and closed the distance between himself and the other man. He wasn't violent by nature, but he was angry enough to make an exception. "Just what are you saying?"

"I'm saying stay away from my sister or you'll wish you had."

He already wished he had, but there was no way he would admit it to this arrogant jerk. "Who I see or don't see is my business."

"And Arden is ours. She's always had guys trying to use her for her money. She doesn't need another one."

"I know it must be hard for you to believe, but I don't want Arden's money. I never did. Maybe if you actually took the time to get to know your sister, you'd see that she is enough of a prize on her own. She doesn't need money to get or hold on to a man."

The brothers exchanged a look Brandon couldn't decipher. "I've got to go. If you want more of my time, make an appointment."

Jax blocked his path. "You expect me to believe her trust fund doesn't matter. You would be the first."

"You don't have to believe it. I don't care. The truth is, I no longer want Arden." Brandon grabbed a crate of fruit and pushed past Arden's brothers.

But as Brandon walked away, he realized what he'd just said was as far away from the truth as he could get.

## Chapter Sixteen

Arden pulled into the circular drive in front of her parents' Baltimore home. Her Beetle drove like new since John's repairs, but she couldn't drive it without thinking of Brandon and Sweet Briar, so she drove the Mercedes that usually sat in her garage.

The past week without Brandon had been so lonely. Even now her heart ached as she thought of the last time she'd seen him at the fish market. That morning she'd managed to keep her tears from falling until he was no longer in sight. How could something so wonderful have turned into heartbreak so fast?

Maybe they weren't meant to be. Given his past, it might not have mattered to Brandon when she told the truth. Once she'd given a false name, she had poisoned their relationship and made it easy for him to say goodbye. She should have known him well enough to understand that he wouldn't change his mind about her.

There had been no point in her staying in Sweet
Briar, so she'd driven straight from the markets and
out of town that very day, not stopping to say goodbye
to anyone. The friends she'd made had been friends
of Brandon and Joni, so they probably didn't care that
she'd left.

Now that she was home she had to try to put the
pieces of her life back together. She wasn't the same
person who'd run away all those weeks ago. She never
would be again.

She couldn't think about how she'd run away from
Michael-the-hairball without feeling ashamed. What
had she been thinking? He had been the one in the
wrong. And she was not going to let him get away with
it. There was no way he should be in a position of power
over anyone, but especially not innocent children. She
intended to let the school board know just what kind of
person they had running one of their middle schools.

She hated to admit it, but her brothers had been right.
Adults not only didn't play make-believe, they didn't
pretend they were ostriches, burying their heads in the
sand in the hope that their problems would vanish. It
was time for her to act like the adult she was.

Her decision to report Michael to the school board
would impact more than just her. It would affect her
family, as well. The meeting before the board would
be private, but because of the nature of her allega-
tions, it might attract the attention of the local papers.
It wouldn't make a ripple in the national press if her
name really was Arden West. But as a Wexford, anything she did that was even slightly newsworthy would
be a field day for the media. She'd always tried to live
under the radar and go about her business like most

people. She wouldn't be able to maintain her low public profile once this story broke. And that was okay. Some things were worth the sacrifice.

She turned off the car and quickly mounted the stone stairs leading to the family mansion. Despite the fact that the house had twenty rooms and was situated on seven acres, it had always felt homey to her. She gave her parents credit for that. They may have been wealthy, but she and her brothers had been raised with middle-class values. Winston and Lorelei had never been overly concerned with maintaining a certain type of public image. She had no doubt her parents would support her, but she did feel they deserved advance notice so they wouldn't be blindsided.

"Welcome home," her mother said, pulling her into a warm, perfumed embrace the moment Arden stepped inside.

"I should be saying that to you," Arden replied with a laugh. "You're the one who just got back from vacation last night."

"True. But I understand you had a bit of an adventure yourself."

"I take it you spoke to one of my brothers."

"Both. You know they can't hold water."

No. She was the one gifted with the ability to keep a secret. Now it seemed like a curse.

"Come on. Everyone is in the family room."

Arden walked beside her mother around the central staircase to the room where her family usually gathered. She heard the murmur of jovial conversation as she and her mother stepped inside the room.

"Well, little girl, are you going to just stand there, or are you going to give your old dad a hug?"

Arden pretended to ponder the question for a moment, then rushed into her father's arms. "I feel like it has been forever since I've seen you."

"The feeling is mutual." He tightened the embrace and held her for a moment longer. Arden inhaled the familiar scent of butterscotch candy. Winston Wexford had a sweet tooth he had passed down to her. She closed her eyes and recalled their many trips to the candy store after her Thursday-night dance lessons when she'd been in grade school. She hadn't enjoyed ballet a bit, but she had loved the secret candy runs they had made on the way home. Her three-year dancing career had lasted two years longer than it would have but for those trips.

"So, what's this I hear about you getting involved with a chef?"

Arden glanced at her brothers. Blake shrugged and Jax smirked. She was past caring. "I met a guy, but that's over. I need to talk to all of you about something else altogether."

"It sounds serious."

"It is." Arden looked around the room. Her family settled into comfortable chairs, then waited for her to start talking. "I don't know where to start."

"The beginning always worked for me," her father said. He turned an affectionate glance toward her mother. "But your mother always preferred to start with the most shocking part and then move backward. Whatever works best for you. We've got all day, right, boys?"

Blake and Jax nodded, but Arden knew they would prefer the CliffsNotes version, which was good because she didn't feel inclined to go into the dirty details.

"I'm going to the school board to try to get Michael Wallace removed from his position as principal at my school." She waited for the explosion of questions but none came.

Her father simply nodded once. "I'm sure you have your reasons."

"Yes." No one spoke and she knew they wouldn't. It was her story to tell at her pace. "He's a jerk but, more, he can't be trusted. Especially around kids. I'm telling you this because when the press finds out it might get ugly.

"I caught him hiding cameras in his bedroom so he could make a secret sex tape. With me. He thought he could blackmail me with it." She felt her cheeks warming and suddenly found a spot on the wall incredibly interesting and stared at it.

Jax leaped to his feet. "I'm going to kill him."

"I'm going to help," Blake added, hurrying behind his brother.

"Stop right there."

Blake and Jax froze at their father's quiet voice.

"Come back and sit down." He waited until they had returned to their chairs before continuing. "Since when do we use violence to solve our problems?"

"Since some jerk decided to hurt our sister," Jax replied angrily. "You can't mean to let him get away with this."

"No one is saying he is getting away with anything. Let's listen to Arden."

"All she wants to do is have him fired," Jax scoffed. "That's not enough."

"You're not the injured party, Jackson, so the decision isn't yours."

Jax breathed loudly through his nose, reminding Arden of a bull. It touched her to see her brothers so ready to defend her. Thankfully, she was strong enough to defend herself now. "I appreciate that you guys want to take care of me. I'm strong enough now to handle it myself."

"Is that the reason you ran away?"

Arden didn't shy away from Blake's words. She had run away rather than fight, so there was no reason to pretend she hadn't. She lifted her chin. "Yes. I didn't know what to do and I was too ashamed and embarrassed to come to any of you."

"Why?" His tone was a mixture of confusion and what sounded like hurt.

"I knew nobody liked Michael. I'd made a bad choice."

"You're not alone there," her father added. "We've all made mistakes."

"I know that now." She cleared her throat. "Anyway, I just want to take away Michael's power as much as I can. I have evidence I recorded on my phone of him telling someone his plans. It's all in the audio file. The school board can take it from there. If the police need a statement I'll give them one. What happens after that won't matter a bit to me. I am sorry if it makes the news, though." She looked at Jax, who was still seething, his breathing loud.

"Is that really all you want?" Jax demanded. Clearly he didn't agree with her decision, but he respected their father's authority and wouldn't go against him. And maybe her brother trusted that she knew what was best for her.

"It is."

"Fine. If that makes you happy."

"It will." Or at least as happy as she could be, given her broken heart.

"We're here if you need us," her mother said, and her father nodded. "And we're proud of you."

"Thank you."

After that, her father and brothers began to discuss business, and Arden and her mother left them to it. Lorelei wrapped her arm around Arden's shoulder. "Tell me more about the man you met."

"Oh, Mom. I messed up. I love him and I hurt him so badly."

"How?"

Arden explained about Brandon's past with his former fiancée. "And then I did the exact same thing she did."

"So what are you going to do now? I understand why you felt the need to come home to straighten out things with the school board, but how are you going to make things right with Brandon?"

If only she could. "He's done with me. He doesn't love me anymore. I'm going to respect his feelings and stay out of his life."

"If his love died that easily, it wasn't real."

"It was real, Mom," Arden replied instantly. She knew that for sure.

"Then fight for it. Love is too precious to let slip through your fingers."

"But what if he can't forgive me?"

"Then you'll know that you gave it all that you had. Don't run away just because you're afraid of getting hurt. The worst thing in the world would be to wake up next year and wonder what if. Do all that you can to set things right. Keep fighting for a second chance. If he loves you, it will work out in the end."

"You're right," Arden said, giving her mother a big hug. "You're absolutely right." And for the first time since she'd returned home, Arden could breathe without the constant pain in her heart. She wasn't happy, but if she could work things out with Brandon she would be. Somehow, some way, she was going to win him back. When the situation with the school board was settled, she was going to do some more running, this time toward something instead of away.

## Chapter Seventeen

Brandon sampled the new shrimp appetizer he was creating, then dropped the fork on the counter with a loud clatter. Even though all the ingredients were mixed properly, the taste was off. In fact, nothing he had cooked the past two weeks tasted right. There was a bitter aftertaste that lingered even after the meal had been eaten. No one else noticed. People continued to rave over their food. The problem was with him. His heart wasn't in it. He'd never thought he'd see the day when he didn't enjoy cooking, but that day had arrived when he'd found out the truth about Arden. He couldn't believe he'd been such a fool again.

He'd always looked forward to Tuesdays so he could let his creative juices flow. That wasn't happening today. He dumped the food into a plastic container and snapped the lid closed. There was enough for Joni to take for lunch and share with her friends.

"I thought I'd find you in here."

He groaned. He loved his sister, but he couldn't handle another dose of her sympathy or her subtle defense of Arden. Joni really liked Arden and had been willing to give her friend the benefit of the doubt. Joni hadn't done anything overt to get him to change his mind, but she had let him know when Arden sent an enormous personal check for the youth center. Despite himself, he recalled how much fun he'd had with Arden volunteering at the center. The kids had really loved her enthusiasm. They had loved *her*.

He wiped a sponge across the counter and tossed it into the sink. "Actually, I'm on my way out."

"Why are you running away from me?"

That question froze him. "I'm not. I have to get to the restaurant."

"Sure."

He pulled his sister into a quick hug. "I'm fine, Joni. You don't need to worry about me."

"I hate that you're angry at me."

He reeled back in surprise. "Angry at you? Why would I be angry at you?"

"I encouraged you to date Arden and did everything I could to throw the two of you together. I even left town so you'd have some time alone. I'm sorry. I just thought she was a good person who could make you happy again. I was wrong and you got hurt. If I'd minded my own business you never would have gotten involved with her."

"None of this is your fault. I was attracted to Arden from the beginning. I spent time with her because I wanted to. And I'm not angry at you. Okay? Now I do need to get going. I have a bunch of paperwork waiting for me." He dropped a kiss on his sister's forehead, then headed out the door.

The restaurant was quiet when he arrived and headed to his office. The walls were a bright white, and framed photos of the restaurant in various stages of construction were hung in such a way that he could see them from his desk. They normally filled him with a sense of pride at what he'd accomplished. Today he felt nothing.

He raised the window to allow in fresh air, as well as sunlight. He'd wasted enough time stumbling around in the dark having his own personal pity party. His kind-hearted sister blamed herself for his poor judgment. That was unacceptable.

He rubbed his hand across his chest. Arden was out of his life. She'd gotten that message. Now he had to find a way to get her out of his mind. And then maybe he'd figure out a way to get her out of his heart.

He turned on his computer and opened the shift schedule. Before he could make changes based upon the number of advance reservations, his desk phone rang, its shrill sound shattering the silence. He idly checked the caller ID. What did Joni want now? Surely she wasn't checking on him again. Enough was enough. He let the call go to voice mail. A few seconds later there was a knock on his open office door. Looking up, he saw Marcus standing there. "What's up?"

"Sorry to disturb you, but Joni called and said to check your email. She sent you something she wants you to see right now."

"I'll get to it later." Brandon said, continuing to work.

Marcus stood there. Clearly Joni had told him not to leave until Brandon had done what she asked.

"Fine," Brandon huffed, then pulled up his email, opening the one from Joni. She hadn't written anything but had sent a link to an article. Curious, he clicked on it. It was a short video. He waited until it started. It was Arden. She was descending stairs of what looked like a government building surrounded by her family, a woman dressed in a suit by her side. Reporters called out questions to her and the cameras tightened to a close-up. She nibbled her bottom lip.

Despite the fact that he was still angry with her for not being honest, his heart clenched at the sight of her discomfort. A part of him he couldn't ignore wished he was there to stand between her and anything that hurt her.

His eyes hungered for her. It had been so long. She was as beautiful as he remembered, if slightly thinner. Her hair curled softly around her face and her eyes seemed to reach out and stare directly at him. In a moment, she got into a black sedan and sped out of sight.

The camera then turned to a reporter holding a microphone. "And there you have it. Arden Wexford, daughter of Winston Wexford, owner of Wexford Industries, leaving a meeting of the Baltimore school board where she testified against her former principal."

The reporter droned on for a minute, repeating information Arden had already shared with Brandon. He knew how hard having this information go public had to be for Arden. She guarded her privacy fiercely. And she had just put the most embarrassing moment in her life out there for people to discuss and decide if she was telling the truth. All because she believed secrets were dangerous. She hadn't known that before coming to Sweet Briar, so obviously she had grown. Good for her.

But what did that have to do with him? Did he care? Did she even care about him anymore?

Suddenly filled with energy, Brandon headed for the kitchen. He did some of his best thinking while cooking. And he had a lot of thinking to do. For the first time since Arden had left, he believed he could do some of his best creating.

One cutting-edge recipe for salmon later, Brandon had thought enough to realize he'd been wrong. Arden wasn't a self-centered rich girl looking for fun at his expense. She was a kind, loving woman who'd done what she thought best to protect herself. He was willing to admit that his past with Sylvia had affected the way he viewed all women, including Arden. If he felt justified in doing that, then surely she was justified in looking at men through the same lens as she'd seen her ex-boyfriend. Certainly she wouldn't be wrong in putting the lessons she'd learned in the past to use.

He was able to admit that one of the lessons she'd learned was that some people would sink to the lowest levels if they thought they could profit from it. Most people were honest, but there were enough greedy ones out there to make a wealthy woman wary. She'd be foolish not to be cognizant of that and to act accordingly. He didn't trust anyone blindly, so why should he expect her to? Arden was a product of her past, the same as he was.

As hard as it was to admit, her decision to use a fake name didn't have anything to do with him. She hadn't even known him, so it was a bit ridiculous to expect her to know his character.

Maybe it was time for them both to break away from their pasts and take a leap of faith. His parents might have the right idea, after all. Although he wasn't interested in dating any of the women they shoved in his path, they were right to urge him to get on with his life. It was time. Now he had to convince Arden to give him another chance.

Brandon stifled the urge to barge into Blake Wexford's office, waiting instead for the secretary to announce him. Once he'd reached the conclusion that Arden hadn't committed an unforgivable act, he'd wanted to get to her as soon as possible so they could start over. He first spoke to Joni, who'd been relieved that he was willing to give love a chance. She'd confessed that she missed her new friend horribly and urged him to do whatever was necessary to win Arden's heart again.

After assuring himself that Marcus could handle the restaurant for a couple of days, Brandon had tossed a change of clothes in a bag and hopped on the first plane to Baltimore. On the flight he'd prepared what he hoped was a speech that would convince Arden to forgive him and give them another shot. He hadn't quite worked out the details of how a relationship between them would work, given the fact that they lived in two different cities. He just knew that if she was willing, he would try.

"Mr. Wexford will see you now."

Rising, Brandon followed the woman through the quiet hallway to an open door. She stepped aside and gestured for him to enter. He thanked her and went in. He was surprised to see Arden's other brother, as well as her father. Obviously, this was going to be a family meeting. Good. That would save him some time. If they thought to intimidate him by their greater number, they were sadly mistaken.

"Thanks for seeing me," he said, extending his hand.

"My curiosity got the best of me," Blake said as he shook Brandon's hand. "You remember my brother, Jax. And this is our father, Winston Wexford."

Brandon shook each of the other men's hands. Blake offered drinks, but they all refused.

"So, what brings you to our fair city?" Winston asked once they were all seated.

"I'm here about Arden."

"Really? The last I heard you didn't want anything more to do with her," Jax said. "You not only let us know that loud and clear, you were blunt about that to her, too."

Brandon remembered the unshed tears glistening in Arden's eyes the last time he saw her, and his stomach knotted. "I regret the way I talked to Arden. That's not one of my proudest moments."

"Blake. Jax. Give us some privacy, would you?" Winston said.

"You're kicking me out of my office?" Blake asked in apparent disbelief.

Winston smiled. "Think of it as a chance for you to take a break."

Blake sighed and followed his brother out of the office. Brandon watched them go, wondering just what the elder Wexford was about to say that he didn't want his sons there.

"What do you mean you're here about Arden?"

Brandon rubbed a hand over his chin. Winston didn't strike him as the kind of man who would appreciate someone beating around the bush, so he decided to cut to the chase. "I hurt her badly. I want to set things right."

"What do you mean by right?"

"I love her. Setting things right would involve making sure she knows that."

Mr. Wexford's eyebrows shot up and he nodded. "Is that so?"

"Yes." Was that a hint of a smile on the older man's face? "You don't know me, but I'm prepared to tell you anything you need to know."

"I already know everything I need to about you. Arden and I had many talks. And then there are my sons. They've told me plenty. But to be honest, you showing up here tells me more about your character than anything else."

"So that's it?"

"I trust my instincts. They haven't led me astray very often. And my sons are very protective of their sister. They wouldn't have left this room if they thought you were up to no good."

"That other guy fooled them." And he had hurt Arden in the process.

"No, he didn't."

Brandon couldn't believe it was this easy. He'd come prepared to do battle for the right to be with Arden. "So you aren't going to threaten me with a fate worse than death?"

"Is there one?"

"Yes." He looked directly into Mr. Wexford's eyes. "Living without Arden."

That answer seemed to satisfy Arden's father.

"So what's your plan?"

"I'm still working on the details, but I know it will involve begging."

Winston laughed. "Throw in some chocolate and you just might have a chance."

Arden rode the elevator to the top floor that housed her father's office, silently rehearsing her speech. Packing had taken longer than she'd anticipated, so it was already nearly three. She wouldn't be able to leave until tomorrow, but since she wanted to start out early, she'd say her goodbyes now.

The conversation with her mother had gone better than she'd expected. Then again, Lorelei was a romantic at heart. Not that she wouldn't have let Arden know if she disagreed with her decision to return to Sweet Briar. Lorelei had seen how unhappy Arden had been with the way things ended with Brandon.

She could still hear her mother's words. *Give it everything you have. If it doesn't work, then at least you'll know you tried. Only then will you be able to go forward, even if your heart hurts for a while.* She just hoped her father agreed.

When she stepped from the elevator, she saw Jax and Blake huddled together in a corner. Odd, considering they each had their own office.

"What are you guys doing?"

"What does it look like?" Jax asked.

"Like you're loitering in the hall, waiting to pounce on some unsuspecting passerby."

Blake muttered something that sounded like, "Close." Was he pouting?

"What are you doing here?" Jax countered.

"Actually, I'm here to see you guys and Dad. Can we go to his office?"

"We can, but he's not there." Blake folded his arms over his chest.

"How do you know?"

"Because he just kicked me out of mine."

Goodness. He was pouting. Arden barely kept herself from laughing. The men in her family tended to be territorial about the craziest things. "Okay. Then let's go there."

"Why? What's so important?"

Arden sighed. She could practice on her brothers. "I'm going back to Sweet Briar."

"Why?" Jax straightened.

"The short answer is because that's where Brandon is."

"What's the longer answer?"

"I ran. I should have stayed and fought for us, but I didn't."

"So, you're going to just go back there unannounced?" Jax asked, his eyes narrowed.

"Yes. And I'm going to make him listen no matter how long it takes."

Blake looked over her shoulder. "I have a feeling it's not going to take all that long."

Arden turned and gasped. "Brandon." Her voice was reduced to a whisper. "What are you doing here?"

"I've come for you."

Her heart leaped at his words, yet she couldn't give it free rein. Not yet. "For me? But I thought… I thought you didn't want me."

He stepped closer and held out his hand. She automatically took it and let him lead her to the reception area and away from her family's eyes. "I want you,

Arden. You have no idea how much. I just needed to work through my own issues. I accused you of not trusting me, when I didn't trust you as much as I proclaimed. I'm sorry for that. I hope you can forgive me."

"I didn't know about your past when we met. But I am sorry for not telling you my real name sooner."

"A rose by any other name would smell as sweet. I believe Arden Wexford is just as perfect as Arden West."

"I'm not perfect. I'll make mistakes."

"So will I. But if we forgive as easily as we want forgiveness, everything will be okay."

Arden nodded. "I can."

"You obviously came here to see your family. I can wait while you talk to them."

"I was only going to tell them goodbye. I was on my way to Sweet Briar in the morning to convince you to give us another chance."

He smiled and it was as if a weight had been lifted from her shoulders. "How long were you planning on staying?"

"As long as it took to make you love me."

Brandon leaned in closer, his fingers gently cupping her face, his thumb teasing her lower lip, making her want to fall into his arms. "What's your plan?"

"I didn't think that far." Her voice was a mere whisper.

"Good thing I did. We can go with my plan."

"Which is?"

"First I make sure you know I love you. Then I convince you to stay forever."

Forever. It had a certain ring to it. "Sounds like a perfect plan to me."

His lips curved into a sexy smile before they covered hers. Forever might not be long enough, but it was a perfect start.

\* \* \* \* \*

*If you loved this story,*
*don't miss the first book in the*
SWEET BRIAR SWEETHEARTS,
*by Kathy Douglass*

*HOW TO STEAL THE LAWMAN'S HEART*

*Available from Mills & Boon Cherish Edition.*

# MILLS & BOON®

## EXCLUSIVE EXTRACT

Crown Prince Frederick of Lycander needs a wife
and an heir, and discovering he has a secret son with
beautiful supermodel Sunita makes him determined
to claim both!

*Read on for a sneak preview of*
**CLAIMING HIS SECRET HEIR**

'You have a baby?'

Frederick's hazel eyes widened in puzzlement, a small
frown creasing his brow as he took another step into her
sanctum. His gaze rested on each and every item of Amil's.

'Yes.' The word was a whisper, all Sunita could
manage as her tummy hollowed and she grasped the
door jamb with lifeless fingers.

'How old?' Each syllable was ice cold, edged with
glass and she nearly flinched. No, she would not be
intimidated. Not here. Not now. What was done was
done, and, rightly or wrongly, she knew if she could
turn back time she would make the same decision.

'Girl or boy?'

'Boy.' Each question, each answer brought them
closer and closer to the inevitable and her brain wouldn't
function. Instead, all she could focus on was his face,
the dawn of emotion – wonder, anger, fear and surely
hope too? That last was so unexpected that it jolted her
into further words. 'His name is Amil.'

'Amil,' he repeated. He took another step forward and instinctively she moved as well, as if to protect the life she had built, putting herself between him and her home. 'Is he mine?'

For an instant it was if the world went out of focus. She could almost see a line being drawn in the sands of time – this was the instant that separated before and after. For one brief instant she nearly took the coward's route, wondered if he would swallow the lie that Amil was Sam's. Then realised she could not, would not do that. 'Yes. He is yours. Amil is your son.'

Now she understood the origins of a deafening silence. This one trolled the room, echoed in her ears until she wanted to shout. Instead she waited, saw his body freeze, saw the gamut of emotion cross his face, watched as it settled into an anger so ice cold a shiver rippled her skin. Panic twisted her insides – the die had been cast and she knew now that whatever happened, life would never be the same.

*Don't miss*
**CLAIMING HIS SECRET HEIR**
by Nina Milne

Available October 2017
www.millsandboon.co.uk

# MILLS & BOON®

# Join Britain's BIGGEST Romance Book Club

**50% OFF** your first parcel

- **EXCLUSIVE offers** every month

- **FREE delivery direct to your door**

- **NEVER MISS a title**

- **EARN Bonus Book points**

Call Customer Services
**0844 844 1358***

or visit
**nillsandboon.co.uk/subscriptions**

\* This call will cost you 7 pence per minute plus your phone company's price per minute access charge.